D1527949

To Mary
Thank you –
With Love
In Joy
Laurie

1.

DEDICATION

This book is dedicated to my husband, Jon. Thank you for your unconditional love, support, and patience.
Thank you to my mom, stepson, and aunts for offering honest feedback.
Thank you, also, to my Tai Chi instructor. This book is in part due to your dedication and love of the art.

CONTENTS

1
Looking Out

Judy Tanner gazed out of her picture window. She loved the scene from the window. She had put up three bird feeders when she first moved in and found it very relaxing, no even more than relaxing, it was meditative to watch the birds.

She particularly loved observing the interactions between the doves and the cardinals, the woodpeckers and the sparrows. Everyone gathered, sharing space, chatting, communing. Then the blue jays would appear and scare off the rest of the birds.

The police of the sky, Judy said out loud to no one in particular. She was slightly disturbed by their aggression.

Hey, she'd yell through the glass. Don't pick on that cute little Chickadee you big blue bully.

But I guess that's how they're able to survive, she thought. We all have unique personalities. Why should birds be any different? Survival is survival no matter who or what we are.

At certain times of the year, the crows would come. They had an entire culture all their own. They seemed particularly loyal and communicative with one another.

By watching the birds Judy felt present, focused, and connected to nature. She often gained insights and perspective. Being a passive observer was actively therapeutic.

But she realized she couldn't stare out the window all day. She had to get herself together and get on with it.

Judy had moved to New England one year ago. She had always been a city/suburban girl, and she particularly loved the anonymity of being an urban dweller but decided she needed to change it up, to turn her life upside down. So, just after she turned twenty-five, she packed what she could fit in her Prius and gave the rest of her stuff to the Salvation Army. This provided a sense of cleansing.

She was starting a new life, putting her past behind her.

This is a good move. I'm not sure what's ahead, but it feels right.

Judy found an affordable little cottage in the woods and moved in.

There wasn't much to it-one bedroom, one bathroom, a kitchen, and a living area with a grand fireplace, but it had a lot of character and personality: hand carved beams, stone walls, stained glass windows, and a thatched roof. Her furnishings were sparse – a small café table with two chairs for the kitchen space, an overstuffed reading chair, a comfortably worn in couch, a bed, a night stand, and a couple of lamps. Judy acquired things from second hand shops in the area and was determined to make her new home comfortable and simple. It reminded her of the cottage in *Snow White and the Seven Dwarfs.*

She was surrounded by woods on three sides with a small clearing in the back and approached the cottage by turning off a main road and driving about a quarter mile down a small dirt road, a path really, to the house. It suited her. She was content exploring the woods, watching the wildlife, meditating, and writing.

She didn't need much; she had saved some money and had received some inheritance over the years, so as long as she lived simply, she would be okay for a while.

Now however, two years later, she felt as if she'd just awoken from a strange dream. Something had changed.
Judy couldn't put her finger on it, but she sensed a reality shift. Who is she? Is there a reason, a purpose to her life? She was frustrated. She told herself to stop seeking answers but was driven to know and understand. She wanted to make sense of things, to be open to possibilities.

But as an introvert, she didn't know how to fit in.
Her whole life, she felt like the outsider looking in at a world she couldn't relate to. She was always fascinated by people and their behaviors and mostly gave them permission, in her mind, to act the way they did, but never gave herself permission to be or feel. She learned at a very young age to repress desires and emotions, making expressing herself very difficult.

Judy did always relate to animals, though. Animals had been her saving grace. Their presence and mystery were fascinating. She could spend hours with any creature, big or small, and was thrilled when she was given the opportunity to rescue a pure Maine Coon named Chloe. Together, she and Chloe spent hours-Judy talking and Chloe "listening", purring, and generally being a very supportive cat.

2
Chloe

Chloe was born on a farm way up in northern Maine where cats, for the most part, were used as barn cats to take care of the mouse and rat problem. Chloe was one of four in the litter, and from the get go really had no interest in killing anything. She was extremely large, even by Maine Coon standards, and so required way more food than her rat killing siblings. By the age of two, it was clear to the farmer that he couldn't keep Chloe. She was free loading, and he had enough trouble keeping all of the working mouths fed.

He wasn't a cruel man; he believed every living creature should have a chance at a decent life, so he took Chloe to the nearest animal shelter. He hoped she would find a home with a family that could afford to feed her.

Soon after Chloe got to the shelter, the place closed down. They had been having some financial difficulties and felt it was time to throw in the towel. Fortunately, the management saw the end coming and so held a few big adoption drives to start re-homing as many cats and dogs as they could.

Once the shelter was a week away from closing, the administrators called around to other shelters and begged and pleaded with them to take the remaining soon to be homeless.

Chloe ended up in New Hampshire, not far from the border of Maine, with a couple of other cats, one dog, and the rabbit and the guinea pig, and it was at that little New Hampshire country shelter that Judy found the love of her life.

As soon as she walked in and looked to her right, she saw Chloe.

Chloe was a silvery stripy colored Maine Coon with green eyes, and Judy had honestly never seen any being so beautiful.

The shelter manager came over and introduced herself.

Hi, I'm Sue. May I help you?

Judy asked if it would possible to hold this amazing cat and secretly wondered why she hadn't been adopted.

Sue said, Sure. I'll be right back.

She went to the back to get the key to the cage, which frankly, wasn't quite large enough for Chloe.

As she opened the cage, she explained that Chloe had come from a shelter in Maine that had to close down, and she had been with them for about two months.

Judy had to ask.

Why hasn't anyone adopted her?

Honestly, people want kittens, and we estimate this big girl to be close to three years old already. Also, as you can see, she's the size of a small to medium dog, and that's not what most people want when they decide to adopt a cat.

The manager handed Chloe to Judy, and it took Judy a moment to get over the shock of Chloe's girth and weight. But then something amazing happened. Judy looked right into Chloe's eyes and asked her if she wanted to live with her. Chloe let out the loudest purry meow. The other potential adopters in the shelter actually turned to see what was making such an interesting sound. Chloe then licked Judy right on her nose, and Judy swore she saw just a momentary smile.

Wow! The manger said. In the two months she's been here, she's never let anyone touch her much less react with such love. I didn't want to say anything initially because I was afraid you wouldn't give her a second look.

Judy literally started to cry, and Chloe began rubbing and nuzzling Judy's cheek as if in an attempt to wipe away her tears. She then reached up with both front paws and hugged Judy.

At this point, the manager was weeping, and a couple of people close by were digging in their pockets for tissues. It was truly quite a moment.

The manager said, I am really hoping that you're ready to adopt Chloe. I have never seen anything like this introduction, or should I say reunion. It sure does seem like you two are meant to be together, and for those of us who believe in reincarnation, I'd say you two knew each other before.

Judy asked if she could hold Chloe while filling out the paperwork. She couldn't bear the thought of putting her down; although, she eventually had to sit her on the counter because her weight was becoming just a bit unbearable.

Once all the paperwork was done, Sue took Chloe in the back to weigh her and get her medical paperwork.

Sue returned to the front desk with Chloe. As she handed her back to Judy, she informed her of Chloe's status.

Chloe was spayed and vaccinated at the other shelter, and she's been given a clean bill of health by our vet, but she's weighing in at over twenty pounds which is over where she should be, so feed her the special diet I wrote on her paperwork, and she should live a long and healthy life.

Judy hadn't brought a cat carrier with her, and frankly, there wasn't one that Chloe could fit in, so the shelter lent her a medium size dog carrier for the ride home.

The drive home was a little confusing for Chloe, but basically uneventful. She felt happy with this new person and more so, felt this was a person she could really love and take care of.

When they pulled into the driveway, Judy said, Here we are, Chloe. Chloe looked up through the bars of the dog carrier.

Judy parked her car, got out, and walked around to the back-seat passenger's side.

Ok Chloe, welcome home.

Judy carried the carrier into the house with Chloe in it and thought to herself that she would have to find a better way to transport her because Chloe and the carrier were just way too heavy for her to carry any distance.

She put the carrier down and opened the wire door.

Okay Chloe, this is your new home. Make yourself comfortable.

Chloe didn't hesitate. She quickly exited the carrier, looking back briefly as if to say, Good riddance.

Being as big as she was, she found living in a cage to be very uncomfortable and distasteful.

Chloe walked leisurely around the little cottage sniffing everything as she went. She checked out her food and water bowls and a very snuggly bed that Judy made out of an old blanket. She noticed a litter box in the bathroom and then went directly to Judy's bedroom and jumped up on Judy's bed. She let out a very content "meow". At that point, Judy knew this was going to be a love affair to remember.

As the days turned into weeks, Chloe was very pleased. She took to Judy and her new surroundings right away, and she liked Judy's style. They were both independent ladies who respected each other's space, and she was happy that Judy didn't require much training. Chloe recognized that Judy knew her place as Chloe's person. Judy was completely dedicated to giving Chloe the life she deserved with fresh water every day, very yummy breakfasts, the most delicious snacks, wonderful belly rubbins and of course, eventually, their walks in the woods. In Chloe's opinion, Judy was perfectly trained, and Chloe planned on keeping her.

3
The Bubble

Judy had been living in an emotional bubble of her own design-safe but alone, and her challenge, she realized, was to find a balance, to learn how to "be" in the world around her. She could easily continue to live a quiet and even solitary life, and would that be so bad? After all, she had Chloe. This was how she rationalized her current situation.

But something was shifting. Judy could sense a need to step out of her comfort circle. She wasn't sure yet what that meant exactly, and the thought alone caused anxiety, so she knew it was time. The signs were popping up all around her.

She did some research about offerings in her quiet town and found a Tai Chi studio nearby. She had been studying Tai Chi on and off for about ten years, and the studio was about to start a new session.

This seems like a sign, Judy thought to herself. I love Tai Chi. Maybe this is a good place to start my transition. I'll sign up tomorrow.

Judy felt a slight rush of excitement mixed with anxiety. This was truly a big step, and it was scary stepping into the unknown. She hoped she was ready. She would, as her mother used to say, put her big girl pants on. She had to draw from an unfamiliar source though. Confidence was not an apparent strength for Judy, but something deep inside was stirring, and she felt, on some level, that she should trust her instincts.

That night, Judy had a dream. She was standing at one end of a bridge looking at the other end. Her surroundings were gray and somewhat stormy. She began to walk across the bridge and felt a lot of resistance. Eventually, she crossed to the other side where she saw a bunch of people, blue sky, and a rainbow. It was the kind of dream that feels so real, and Judy wasn't sure it wasn't. She had trouble shaking it off the next day, like a spider's web that you don't see but walk right into; she felt a lingering something.

She drove into town to the Tai Chi class and parked right in front. Judy loved this small quiet, even sleepy town. The buildings were old but quaint. The movie theater only showed one movie at a time; the sweet shoppe was one of two daytime hangouts; the little cafe was the other. There were two bars, a gas station, a small market, and a couple of small office buildings. The bowling alley doubled as a laundromat, and there was one elementary/middle school and one high school. It reminded her of a long-ago place. It was almost as if she had been there before. She had hazy memories of traveling with her dad to someplace like this town but couldn't really remember much else.

Judy got out of her Prius, took a very deep breath, and walked into the studio.

4

New Friends

The studio was small but nicely done. The room had a pretty big, open floor space with a couple of shoji screens, some bamboo furniture, and art work on the walls. She walked over to the reception area.

Hi, said a friendly voice. May I help you?

Judy didn't know if it was the lingering memories of the dream, the fact that she was starting a new adventure, or a combination of things, but the girl at the desk seemed almost hauntingly familiar.

Have we met before? Judy asked her.

I don't think so, said the girl at the desk.

Huh, thought Judy. Anyway, I'd like to sign up for Tai Chi.

Sure. Have you taken classes here before? By the way, my name is Meg.

I'm Judy.

Nice to meet you, Judy. Welcome to Half Moon Studio.

Once Judy filled out the paperwork and paid the registration fee, Meg showed her where she could leave her stuff. The class would be starting in ten minutes, so Judy had a few minutes to look around. She was feeling pretty nervous and even debated just walking out and going home to the loving purrs of Chloe but had a back and forth with herself and decided to push through the angst.

Just then, the instructor entered the room. He was a little

older than Judy and about six inches taller. She noticed that he had blue eyes and soft brown, slightly wavy hair that was so shiny, Judy was tempted to reach out and touch it.

I wonder what kind of shampoo he uses? she thought to herself while standing in the dojo. He was fit but not super muscular, and he had a smile that just made everything seem like all was okay in the world. It had been a long time since Judy had felt the feelings that were suddenly stirring. She was immediately smitten. She wasn't sure if her attraction to Steve, the Tai Chi instructor, was a good thing or not, but standing there in the room, she could do little more than try to gather all focus on what he was saying. When she came out of her reverie, she looked around and realized the class was actually pretty full. It was nice to see all different ages, sizes, and ethnicities coming together to learn what Judy thought was the best activity ever.

Steve began the class by telling everyone about himself. He explained that he had always loved martial arts and that his parents encouraged him to study because he was so puny as a kid and was often picked on. Taking martial arts definitely helped build his confidence and physique, but after many years, he felt something was missing; he wanted something less aggressive, something that would help him tap into his inner self, so he started learning Tai Chi, and "The rest is history", as they say. Steve then asked if they could go around the room and give a brief introduction. He said he believed that a group works better as a unit if the group has some familiarity. With that he smiled a smile that took Judy's breath away. Here she was, standing in this Tai Chi class, at a loss. The controlled, organized, intelligent part of Judy had gone right over one of the Shoji screens and out the open window. She was just standing there, in a total daydream. Next thing she knew, the entire class was looking at her. She was able to surmise that they were all waiting for her to introduce herself and so what seemed like a lifetime, was actually seconds. She apologized for not paying attention, made a joke about getting off on the wrong foot, and told everyone her name. She realized then that she was in the class, communicating and participating, but part of her was somewhere else. Something about Meg, and of course, there was Steve. She told herself to pull it together and focus on the Tai Chi.

Once it got started, the class was really good. Steve took them through some breathing exercises and basic moves. One of the essentials with Tai Chi is repetition, which one may think is boring, but the truth is that once you're in the zone, the Chi starts to flow, and there is a sense of universality and oneness. Judy felt like it was just what she needed to help her refocus and come back to present. She was glad she had pushed herself to sign up, and the others in the class were all very nice. She was proud of herself and looked forward to coming back the next week. As she was walking out the door, Meg caught her and asked her how she liked the class.

I really enjoyed it, Judy told her. I had forgotten how nice it is to do Tai Chi with a group.

I know what you mean, Meg said. If I didn't have this job, I might spend all my time in my little apartment not seeing or talking to anyone.

Judy was surprised to hear this confession from Meg. As she looked at her, she felt haunted. Something was really, really familiar.

Meg then asked, would you like to go get a smoothie? There's a really good place about three blocks away, and I'm done working in about ten minutes.

Judy hesitated. This was turning out to be quite a day for her. She felt like she needed to go home and recharge but decided to push herself a bit more.

Sure, she said. I'd love to.

5
Unfolding

That night, Judy fell asleep and dreamt. Her sleep was restless and unsettled. Nothing made sense. She awoke feeling a deep grief, and she had tears in her eyes.

Much of the next day, her parents were on her mind. She felt a sense of both melancholy and mystery mixed with anticipation. She thought about the day before. She had clearly broken through her anxiety of getting out into the world and had had a very nice time with Meg, so why was she so sad?

Chloe jumped up onto the bed and nuzzled her. Chloe always knew when Judy was out of sorts. Judy envied Chloe's ability to sense beyond the senses. Cats just seem to be intuitive and present. She yearned to have those abilities. She craved the insight to know beyond her physical world.

Well, she thought, perhaps one day I'll see beyond sight, hear beyond hearing, and have an internal knowing.

She sat quietly with Chloe and went into a deep meditation.

At first, her mind raced. There were thoughts of Meg, then Tai Chi, next a flash of her parents, then more Meg. Eventually, Judy's mind quieted, and she went into a self-guided meditation to one of her favorite places -"her" meadow. The colors were particularly vibrant, and the air felt extraordinary. Her meadow always had an abundance of brilliantly colored flowers from goldenrod yellow to lilac purple. There was a ton of Queen Ann's Lace, Dianthus, and lots of green weed-like stuff. The sky was a perfect blue, and the sun shone brightly. Judy walked down a path, through the woods and entered the meadow. She asked what she needed to know, to see, and sat down amongst the flowers and grasses. Crickets and various other bugs were chirping. She breathed in deeply and breathed out, repeating the process slowly and deliberately. Then there were glimpses of her childhood. She couldn't have been more than maybe eight or so, and there was another little girl with her. They were playing and laughing. She came out of the meditation, got a drink of water, and went to sleep.

The next day, Judy was a bit off, discombobulated. She went about her routine, but she wasn't really present. She felt distracted and couldn't figure out why she was so turned around. She sensed there was something coming on the horizon but had no idea what. She tried to comfort herself.
Stay in the moment, she told herself. Keep your focus. Allow things to unfold.

6
An Offer

The week flew by, and Judy found herself driving into town for her second Tai Chi class. She felt excited to see Steve, and she thought about her outing with Meg. They hadn't spoken since then, and she wondered if a friendship might develop. They had kept the conversation very casual last week, mostly talking about Tai Chi, and so Judy really didn't learn much at all about her.

Judy arrived just on time, waved at Meg on her way into the room, and found a place to stand on the floor. When Steve walked in, Judy's heart rate immediately increased, and she felt herself blushing slightly.

Wow! she thought. What is going on?

The class went well, a lot of exercises and basic movements again, and that was fine with Judy. She was beginning to relax a bit when, at the end of the class, Steve called her over. Judy could barely catch her breath. As she walked toward Steve, she was overwhelmed by his amazingly good looks and felt very attracted to him in a lusty way. Then she heard a voice in her head tell her to get control of herself.

Why would he have any romantic interest in you? You don't even know if he's married, or in a serious relationship, or gay. You know nothing about him and have nothing to bring to a relationship.

Hi, she said, as she approached Steve. I'm really enjoying the class.

Steve said, I'm glad. Actually, I'm curious. It seems like you have some experience with Tai Chi.

Judy told him she'd been studying for ten years but mostly on her own.

Steve hesitated before asking. Would you be interested in a more advanced class?

I didn't see that on the schedule and figured I could use a refresher on the basics, Judy said.

It's not on the schedule, but I'd be happy to work with you if you'd like.

Judy wasn't prepared for this offer. Of course, she would love to expand her Tai Chi abilities, but was suspicious.

What did Steve really have in mind? On the other hand, it would mean spending more time with him, and why did she immediately question his motives? Paranoia didn't run in her family, so why did she feel so untrusting?

I would love that, she heard herself say, despite the protestations from her inner self, generated by her fears and insecurities.

Great, Steve said. How about right after this class each week? Do you think you can handle two hours in a row with me? He smiled, and Judy thought she might pass out right there on the spot.

Instead however, she smiled back and simply said, Sounds good. I'll see you next week.

It's a date, Steve replied.

When Judy got to her car, she had to sit for quite a few minutes to collect herself. She knew going into this that change was going to happen in her life, but somehow, it all felt kinda fast.

Okay, she said out loud, take a deep breath.

Judy didn't feel like going home yet, so she drove out of town to the mall. She needed to feel the comfort of the anonymity she used to feel when she lived in the city. She walked the mall for a while, browsing in and out of the different stores, checking out the new fiction at Barnes and Noble, and then treated herself to Chinese food. She was beginning to feel calmer and was ready to head back home.

7

Reflection

On her drive home, Judy thought about her life. She had learned to be independent at a very early age due to the loss of both parents in a car crash, and although her adopted grandma took her in, she had depended on no one since the age of seventeen. Trust didn't come naturally, perhaps because she had experienced such a great amount of loss when she was so young. She always waited for everyone she got close to to leave. She had become very good at repressing feelings and desires, and now, within just a few days, so much had begun stirring. She wasn't sure what to make of these unfamiliar feelings. Her bubble had definitely broken, for better or worse. She always saw herself as alone, a loner. She wished she had someone to talk to besides Chloe.

Tuesday finally arrived and with it, some new and unnavigable feelings. She prepared herself for a two-hour Tai Chi session and gave herself a pep talk.

Let whatever will be be, Judy. Don't assume outcome. Allow this story to play out. Be open to new possibilities. You can handle yourself.

But she certainly didn't foresee how this particular Tuesday would change her life forever.

She entered the studio with a smile on her face and an openhearted attitude. Meg was at the desk and greeted her with a smile.

Hey, Judy, how's it going? I heard you are going to do double time today.

Yes, Judy replied. I hope I can keep up.

You'll be fine, Meg assured her. Steve is a great teacher. If you're up to it after your classes, do you want to go out and get something to eat?

Sure, Judy said.

Judy got through the first class with no problem. Once the other students left, Steve said, Give me a minute, and we'll start. Be right back.

Judy took the opportunity to regroup. She did a quick meditation and told herself to stay focused and present. This would be a learning experience, and it would be good for her. When Steve returned, Judy looked confused.

Everything ok? Steve asked her.

I thought there would be more people, Judy said.

Oh, Steve said. I really just wanted an opportunity to work with you alone. I see a lot of potential in you and want to get a better feel for your capabilities.

Ok, Judy said hesitantly, not really understanding.

Ok, Steve said. Let's get started. Show me your 24.

And so, they worked, Judy doing form, Steve correcting minute details in her movement. Frankly, it was exhausting, but it was also invigorating. Judy had been doing Tai Chi for a long time, but Steve's instruction took her to a whole other level, and it felt good. She was finally learning the discipline component.

At the end of the hour, Steve praised Judy's commitment and asked if they could talk.

The dialogue in her head kicked in full force.

Oh, here it comes. He's going to ask me out. Am I ready for this? I mean, yes, he's attractive, but do I want this kind of complication in my life? On the other hand, what if he's my Prince Charming? I already have the fairy tale cottage. Or, what if he's a murderer, secretly stalking his victims through Tai Chi instruction? Wow, Judy, get a grip. WHAT IS WRONG WITH

YOU?

So, Judy, as you know, this is a pretty small town, and the studio has only been open for a few months. We are doing pretty well and beginning to grow. So, at this point, I could use another instructor. I'm finding it challenging to run the Center and do all of the teaching. Although your movements are rough and definitely need some polishing, I think you have what it takes to make a great teacher. You are clearly committed to the art, and your broad movements are good. I'm willing to continue working with you to tweak your skill if you would consider taking on some of the very basic beginner classes. This would then free me up to do more outreach and expanding of the school. What do you say?

Well, Judy couldn't believe what she was hearing. This wasn't at all what she was expecting. Did Steve just offer her a job as a Tai Chi instructor? Had this actually been a tryout? She was trying to process but was having some trouble.

Hello? Judy? Are you in there?

Oh, sorry, Steve. You took me by surprise. I wasn't expecting this at all.

Well, go home and think about it. I do believe you would be the right fit for this school. If you decide to come on board, we can discuss salary and hours. Otherwise, I'll see you next Tuesday.

Thanks, Steve. I'll let you know by tomorrow.

Sounds good, Judy.

As Steve left the room, Judy's head began to spin a little. What just happened? She had been sensing some pretty big changes were coming into her life, but she never foresaw a job offer. Wow! She really needed to ponder.

As she walked out, Meg said jokingly, Oh, there you are. I thought you had snuck out the back to avoid me.

Judy had completely forgotten about their "date". No, Meg, I'm here and ready to go.

They headed a little ways out of town to a popular diner. Since it was mid-afternoon, it wasn't that busy, so the server told them to sit anywhere. They found a booth, which would become "their" booth at "their" diner for years to come. Neither realized it yet, but this lunch date would be the beginning of a new chapter for both of them, but I'm getting ahead of myself.

Judy ordered one of her very favorites: tuna melt with cheddar and avocado and a fresh brewed iced tea no lemon, no straw- because straws choke the sea mammals.

Meg ordered a veggie burger, loaded, with crispy fries on the side with a promise from Judy that she would help her eat them.

As they waited for the food, Judy found herself staring at Meg. She hadn't even realized it until Meg asked her if she was ok.

What do you mean? Judy asked.

Well, you've been staring at me for the past five minutes.

Ohhh sorry, Judy responded. She felt awkward and uncomfortable but actually really appreciated Meg's direct honesty.

Judy decided to go for it. It was already that kind of a bizarre day, so why not?

You seem really, really familiar, Judy said to Meg. It's been haunting me since we first met.

Meg thought about this for a while, and then their food arrived. The distraction of really good fries was welcome for both of them but once they were eating, Meg began to think out loud.

Let's see. I was born not far from here. Have lived here my whole life. I went to Disney a few years ago but otherwise, haven't really traveled.

When I graduated from high school, a bunch of us saved up to go to Disney World instead of the prom. It was a blast!

Then I got my Associates degree in Business at the community college.

Judy couldn't put her finger on it but wasn't willing to let it go. Her sense of something was just way too strong.

Meg asked, What about you?

Judy took a second to gather her thoughts. This story was a painful one. Did she want to go there? On the other hand, maybe she'd find an answer...

Welllll, Judy started. I was born south of here near Manhattan in upstate New York. My mom was a teacher, and my dad was a salesman. He used to travel a lot - mostly up and down the east coast, so we didn't see him that much. He was a good dad, but he was sort of distant. My mom and I were close. We used to joke that it was really just the two of us and that once in a while, we'd have a man in our lives. We were happy.

Then, when I was about eight, both my mom and dad went out to a show. On their way home, they were hit head on by a drunk driver and were killed instantly.

My next-door neighbor, who became my adopted grandma, took me in till I was a senior in high school. She was very nice, and we had a great relationship. She helped me through the loss of my parents. Then in the summer of my senior year, she passed away. I was completely devastated! I've kind of been a loner ever since.

I went to college in Manhattan and lived there for a while because I could be one amongst many. I like the city because nobody stands out. It's easy to just blend in there. I loved the anonymity. It's so much different than here. I did meditation and took some Tai Chi classes to help me stay focused during the tough times. It's really saved my sanity.

Judy intentionally left out some big parts of her life. She just wasn't ready to share.

Wow! I am so sorry, Judy. You've really had a tough life.

Neither of them could connect their life stories but did feel a connection with each other and agreed to try to make getting together a regular thing.

That night, Judy did a couple of chores: cleaned Chloe's litter, vacuumed, and straightened up. She decided that a meditation would help her make a decision about becoming a Tai Chi instructor. So, she settled in, and started deep breathing. A peacefulness came over her. She felt this was the right move. She sensed a positive energy around the decision. As she came out of the meditation, she felt comforted and settled. She would call Steve in the morning.

Judy slept well but dreamt about her parents. It must have been because of the conversation she had had with Meg.

8

Judy Takes the Job

Judy dialed Steve's number using her old flip phone. As the phone was ringing, Judy felt strangely calm.

Hi, Judy.

Steve had a nice voice. It was a voice that portrayed a person of confidence and kindness. She felt comfortable around Steve and was looking forward to spending more time with him in perhaps a variety of capacities.

Hi, Steve. If the offer still stands, I would love to give it a try.

Great! Steve said. Can you come in today to fill out some paperwork? We'll talk details.

Sure, how's around one?

Sounds good, Judy. I'll see you at one.

Judy hung up and realized she was smiling.

Huh, she thought.

She had a couple of hours, so invited Chloe on a woods walk. She and Chloe often went out exploring their big and beautiful backyard. The woods went on for miles, and the two of them always discovered something new. As they walked, well Judy walked, and Chloe darted about, climbing half way up a tree and then shimmying down and pouncing on a pile of leaves then darting out ahead of Judy while making a chirpy happy sound. Judy talked, sort of to Chloe, sort of to the nature around her, about thoughts, occurrences, desires, and wishes. She felt she was in a good place. It was now late spring; the thaw had come early, and the days were warming up nicely. Judy had hope for an exciting future. She was looking forward to the adventure of being a teacher, and the timing was good. Although she was still okay financially, some extra money would give her a cushion that she never had before. She felt proud of herself for finding the courage to make this move to the country. It seemed to be paying off.

Once back at her little cottage, Judy gave Chloe some fresh water and changed clothes. Although the entire interview process had been pretty casual, she wanted to dress professionally for the second half of it. It just seemed appropriate.

She got to the studio about ten minutes early and went in. Meg was at the front desk and broke into a huge smile when she saw Judy.

Hiiii, she beamed. That was so much fun yesterday. Of course, I had to run an extra 3 miles this morning to burn off the fries, but it was totally worth it. My dad always used to say, do something fun every day, and yesterday definitely applies.

Judy stopped in her tracks. What did you just say?

What do you mean? Meg asked.

What did your dad used to say?

Just at that moment, Steve came out of his office.

Hi, Judy. Right on time. I like that. Come on in to my office, and we'll work out the details.

The meeting lasted about thirty minutes. They agreed that Judy would start with two beginner courses: both starting at 10:00. One would be on Monday, and the other one would be on Wednesday. That way, Judy could continue attending her refresher class and keep working with Steve on more advanced Tai Chi. If that all worked out, he would add classes to her schedule. He offered her $20.00 per class and the ability to take her own class at no charge. Judy liked the arrangement, and so she filled out the paperwork, and they shook hands. She noticed that Steve's hand was really soft and warm. She felt some electricity between them with the hand shake but decided it wouldn't be professional to say anything.

Anyway, she was really excited about starting to teach the next Monday and wanted to head over to the local library right away to get some books out on teaching techniques.

As she walked out of Steve's office, she saw Meg and remembered the start of their conversation.

How'd it go in there? Meg asked.

Great, said Judy. I start Monday.

Hey, that's terrific! I think you'll really like it here. My brother is a great guy!

Your brother? Judy had a really confused look on her face.

Oh, I'm sorry. Technically he's my stepbrother, but we are pretty close.

I had no idea. That's cool that you guys have such a good relationship.

Judy felt a pang of envy mixed with sadness. Her self-reliant, independent, don't really need anybody identity was rising and feeling confused and insufficient.

Well, she said, I better get going. I have a lot of preparation to do. I'll see you on Monday at 10:00.

Sure thing. I'll see you on Monday.

Meg waved as Judy headed out the door.

9

Bruce & Rachel

Meg was two years younger than Judy and grew up worlds apart from her. She was a small-town girl, sweet but not particularly experienced in life. Meg's mom wasn't actually married when she became pregnant with Meg. She was pretty young and had a history of making bad decisions. She met Meg's dad in a bar just a couple of towns from the town Meg currently lives in, and hooked up, as they say. Although the encounter started as a one-night stand, the two of them kept in touch. Bruce wasn't from the New England area but frequently did business there, so at least a couple of times a month, he would show up and visit Rachel.

They had been seeing each other for five or six months and had been having a really good time together hopping from bar to bar. Life was quite the party until Rachel realized that she was pregnant.

The next time Bruce came to town, Rachel told him that she was pregnant and wanted to keep the baby.

Bruce didn't take the news well and went on a real bender. He had a drinking problem already, and Rachel's news set him right over the edge. The tension was palpable, and frankly Rachel couldn't figure out why Bruce was so out of control. They had been happy, had a good time whenever they spent time together.

Rachel was ready for a next step. She wanted the stability of a family and was pretty upset and confused by Bruce's reaction. Bruce, I don't get why this is so upsetting, Rachel said with tears of confusion and frustration running down her cheeks. I have feelings for you, and I thought you had feelings for me.

I do have feelings for you, baby, but I can't be tied down. We've been having a good time, so why ruin it?

His words cut like a knife. Rachel realized they were in completely different places.

Bruce felt panicked. He tried to talk her out of keeping the baby, but Rachel wouldn't have any of that. She wanted this baby and was hoping Bruce would be a part of the picture. After a few days of arguing and lots of tears, Bruce had to get back on the road.

Before leaving and after a lot of thought, he decided to be honest with Rachel. It was either that or just disappear for good. The thing was, he had real feelings for her, and after he processed the whole situation, he felt a responsibility and some desire to play some kind of a role in Rachel's life and the baby's life. So, he told her that he needed to talk and that he had something really tough to say.

I'm sorry, Rachel. I haven't been honest with you.

What is it, Bruce?

Rachel looked at Bruce and felt her heart start pounding. She wasn't sure she wanted to hear what he had to say, but there was no turning back at this point.

Bruce took a deep breath in, held it for what felt to Rachel like an eternity, and then exhaled. Rachel continued to stare at him, feeling the anticipation rising. She wanted to say, just spit it out already, but she couldn't form words.

I'm actually married and have a family, a little girl. They live in New York. He explained that he couldn't leave them and felt shame for being a cheater and an alcoholic. He hugged Rachel and promised he would try to help support the baby financially, but that was about all he would be capable of.

Rachel was stunned. How could she have been so stupid? How

did she get involved so blindly? This was a lot to wrap her head around, but she really wanted to keep this baby. She needed something to take care of, to ground her. She believed that this child would make her a better person. She felt ready for the responsibility.

She sat alone at home that night and thought and thought. She concluded that, with or without Bruce, she would keep the baby, and she would be the best mom she could be.

The next time Bruce was in town, she told him she would appreciate his support and that he was welcome to visit their child whenever he was in the area.

Rachel was still pretty angry at Bruce and herself but decided to take a positive attitude and that having a father around would be good for her baby.

10

Meg & Steve

Meg's birth was easy and relatively painless. She was just six pounds – a little peanut is how Rachel described her to people. Rachel didn't think she could love another person as much as she loved Meg. Meg was an easy and happy baby and never gave Rachel any trouble.
She and Meg had a good life together. They didn't have much, but Rachel showered Meg with love.
Bruce was true to his promise. He sent Rachel money every month and would spend what time he could with them. Life wasn't bad, but as time went by, Rachel saw less and less of Bruce, and when he did show up, he was almost always drunk.

On Meg's 5th birthday, Rachel took her to the Aquarium. She was hoping that Bruce would be there for Meg's sake, but held little expectation, and was in fact relieved when he told her he couldn't make it. She wasn't in the mood for a big drunken scene, and lately, that's how each visit had ended between them. When Meg asked about her daddy, Rachel explained that he had to work but that he loved her very much. She wanted Meg to have a good feeling about her dad, despite his weaknesses.

So, Rachel and Meg watched the sea lions play and the penguins swim. They went to the dolphin show and were invited to come down and participate in the show. Meg had the best time.

They then went to the aquarium's cafe for a special birthday dinner. Rachel had planned to have some of the staff come to the table with a cake. They gathered around Meg and sang a rousing rendition of *Happy Birthday*. Most of the room joined in. It was memorable for Meg.

At the next table was a man and his son. The boy was 10 years old and also celebrating his birthday. After the singing, the man and boy came over to Rachel and Meg's table to wish Meg a very happy birthday. The man, Matthew, told them that it was his son, Steve's birthday also. He said it was their tradition to come to the aquarium each year.

Rachel invited them to have some cake with them. So, Matthew and Steve sat down at Rachel and Meg's table.

Matthew and Rachel hit it off immediately. There was so much electricity; they could have lit up the aquarium dining room. Rachel realized she was smiling like a crazy person but couldn't help herself. How could she fall so quickly for this man who told her he was a single dad?

Rachel told Matthew that she is a single mom and found herself sharing many details of her life. She felt so comfortable with Matthew and almost forgot about Meg. When she looked over at Meg, she was contently eating her birthday cake and chatting away with Matthew's son. Wow, Rachel thought. How sweet!

After a bit, Rachel said it was getting late and she and Meg needed to get going. Matthew asked if it would be possible to call her to go out for coffee, and although Rachel briefly thought about all of the bad decisions she had made in her life, this felt so right.

Yes, I'd like that.

So, they exchanged numbers, and Matthew told her he'd call her later.

As Rachel and Meg were walking into the house, the phone was ringing.

Okay, okay, I'm coming said Rachel to the phone. Hello?

Hi.

Rachel heard a hesitant voice on the other end of the phone.

Hi, Rachel said back. Then there was silence.

Umm, it's Matthew, from the aquarium.

Ohh, Rachel said. Hi. I wasn't expecting you to call so soon. We actually just walked in.

I hope I'm not being too forward, but I had such a nice time and can't wait to see you again.

Rachel's crazy grin came back, but she didn't care, and besides, Matthew couldn't see it through the phone.

I'm glad you called. I had a really nice time too.

Do you think I could take you on a proper grown up date? Maybe this coming Saturday night?

There were a few seconds of silence - because Rachel didn't want Matthew to know that she was about to pass out from excitement.

Are you there?

Yes, sorry. I'm here. Saturday would be great. But, could I meet you?

Sure, Matthew said, but I don't mind picking you up.

I appreciate that, but I'd feel more comfortable meeting you. I hope you understand.

Completely, Matthew said.

Why don't we meet at Riley's at seven? Do you know the place?

Yes, Rachel said. Sounds perfect. I'll see you then.

When Rachel hung up, she immediately called Mrs. Miller, her next-door neighbor. She tried not to ask too often, but Mrs. Miller was always happy to watch Meg for her if needed, and Meg loved spending time with her. She was like the grandma Meg didn't have. They would often play games together while Mrs. Miller told Meg about the good old days. She was now a widow for more than ten years, but she had had a lot of adventures and a great zest for life. Meg loved being around her.

11
The Proposal

Rachel was in a good place, feeling really good about herself, her life. After spending so much time feeling inadequate and undeserving, she had finally met a great guy who respected her and cared deeply for her daughter. The year passed quickly, and Meg asked if they could all go back to the aquarium for Steve's eleventh birthday and her sixth. Although this wasn't Steve's idea of a great way to spend his birthday, after all, he was almost a teenager, he agreed, and to show his appreciation, Matthew agreed to take Steve on a weekend trip to Boston to see a Celtics game, so Steve was pretty happy.

What Rachel didn't know was that Matthew had a really big surprise planned and swore both Meg and Steve to secrecy.

When Meg found out that Matthew was going to propose to her mom, she almost wet her pants. The thought of having a dad who would actually be around, and a big brother to boot was almost too much to stand. She didn't think there could be a better birthday present.

Saturday afternoon finally arrived, and the four almost to be a family headed out to the aquarium.

Rachel noticed that Meg was kind of quiet and asked her if she was okay. Meg looked at Steve with wide eyes, and Steve immediately came to her rescue.

She's fine, Steve said. She's just excited to see the dolphins.

Rachel thought that was a little strange but let it go. You have to choose your battles, and this one didn't seem worth the push, she thought to herself.

After walking around the aquarium for a while, Matthew suggested they all go over to the giant tank with the rainbow assortment of fish. It was an impressive tank, so beautiful, even mesmerizing.

Steve had a camera at the ready, and when Rachel and Matthew were just centered in front of the tank, Matthew got down on one knee and pulled out a little box.

It all happened so fast, but what Meg remembers is starting to squeal loudly. She couldn't contain herself any longer. She remembers seeing her mom start to cry and Steve's camera flashing away.

Then Matthew said, Rachel, our love started here one year ago, and it's my hope that we will spend many, many more years loving each other. Will you marry me?

Well, at this point a crowd had gathered, and it was quite a moment. Rachel, of course, said yes; the crowd burst into applause and cheers, and Matthew stood up, kissed Rachel, and then came over to Steve and Meg and gave them a big group hug. I'm so happy Meg heard Matthew say as the crowd began to dissipate.

He then asked one of the people who was still lingering if he would mind taking a picture of the four of them in front of the fish tank to mark this momentous occasion.

C'mon, Matthew said. We have two birthdays to celebrate. Wow! What a great day!

So, they all went to eat in the aquarium's dining room and laughed and talked - one big happy family.

That night, Rachel and Meg sat together on the couch at home. Rachel told Meg she loved her very much and asked her how she felt about the day. Meg told her she was really happy. She loved Matthew and Steve and was excited to be getting a dad and a big brother she could spend time with.

It then occurred to Rachel that she needed to tell Bruce. But for the moment, she was going to just enjoy.

12

Young Judy

About a week after getting engaged, Rachel picked up the phone and called Bruce.

Matthew knew all about Bruce, and although they had never met, Matthew was cautiously respectful of Bruce's place in Meg's life.

Hello?

Rachel froze for a moment then took a deep breath.

It's Rachel, she said. Are you sober?

What kind of a question is that? Bruce said defensively.

I have something important to tell you, and I want to know that you'll remember our conversation tomorrow.

Bruce's drinking had increased in the past two years, and he had admitted to Rachel and his wife, Marilyn, that he believed he had blacked out a few times because he couldn't remember days at a time.

Fine, Rachel. What is it?

I got engaged.

Silence

Bruce? Are you there?

Silence

Bruce?

I'm here. Congratulations, he said sarcastically. Have you set a date? he said with very little affect.

Probably sometime in the fall.

How's Meg taking it?

She's thrilled. Matthew has a son who is five years older than Meg, and they get along great.

I'm happy for you, Rachel. And, by the way, I'm in AA. I'm trying to make amends to the people I've hurt and so told Marilyn about you and me and Meg.

What exactly did you tell her?

I told her about our relationship. She said she would like to meet Meg.

I don't know, Bruce. Let me think about that.

Marilyn and I are going to start couples counseling to see if we can't salvage our marriage.

Good for you, Bruce. It sounds like you are really trying to get your life together.

A few weeks later, Bruce and Marilyn were on their way to their first therapy session. Neither felt any great expectations. After all, there were many years of unspoken anger and disappointments, so it would take an awful lot of work to find their way back to each other. Marilyn felt betrayed and didn't know why she was putting the effort in. Bruce was a cheater and an alcoholic. Boy could she pick'em, she thought. She also realized that she was pretty disappointed in herself. How did she not see what was going on all these years? On the other hand, maybe she did but chose not to acknowledge Bruce's behavior. After all, it wasn't like he hit her. He always provided for them financially. It's just that he had a problem with alcohol and loyalty.

They were silent during much of the drive, and you could cut the tension because both knew, on some level, that this trip to a therapist would be a pivotal one, that their relationship was about to change for better or worse when....

Bruce, LOOK OUT! Marilyn screamed.

The crash was a bad one, and it happened so fast that neither Bruce nor Marilyn had time to react. The irony of it all was that the man who hit them was drunk and had just had his license taken away. He had borrowed his son's car to go to the liquor store thinking he would get himself straightened out right after this bender. He just needed to party one more time. He wasn't quite ready to feel the feelings. He wanted to be numb a little while longer before facing the inevitable.

Bruce and Marilyn were pronounced dead at the scene.
Judy was with her babysitter, Kay Hutchins, at Kay's house when the accident occurred. Kay had picked her up from school just about an hour before when the phone rang.
Hello? Kay said. Speaking. Who's calling? Uh huh. Oh my. Oh dear.
She hung up the phone without even looking. She had a very strange look in her eyes and walked out of the kitchen without saying anything to Judy, who was stirring the chocolate chip cookie batter.
The two of them had a routine when together. They would make chocolate chip cookies, sometimes with walnuts, and then play Yahtzee and eat the cookies. Judy loved this time with her babysitter/neighbor.
Mrs. Hutchins, Judy called from the kitchen. The batter's ready.
Judy wasn't allowed to use the stove without Kay there to supervise.
When she didn't come in, Judy left the batter and went to find her. She felt a little afraid.
Mrs. Hutchins, she called out as she went room to room in the little house.
Kay was sitting on the edge of her bed. She was crying.
What's wrong? Judy asked.
Come sit next to me, Judy.
Kay patted the bed by her right side.
Judy scooched up onto the bed. Her feet hung far from the floor.
Judy, she began. Something terrible has happened.

There was silence that seemed like it lasted for hours.

What? Judy finally asked, feeling some strange and unexplainable emotion starting to rise up in her.

Your parents have been in a car accident, Kay said as calmly as she could.

Judy stared straight ahead.

So, will they be okay? she asked, almost anticipating the answer.

Kay turned toward Judy and gently took her by the shoulders. She turned her so that they were looking at each other.

No, honey. I'm afraid they aren't okay. They didn't survive the crash.

Judy didn't know how to react. She didn't have any experience with such grown up things. She was only eight. Her biggest worry in life up to now had been homework and making friends. Hers was an average childhood. She had a mom and a dad, her own bedroom, and Mrs. Hutchins to play with.

The two of them sat silently on Kay's bed for a while.

Then Kay went into a semi-manic "do" mode.

Okay, she said out loud to no one in particular. Let's get out of here.

This startled Judy a little bit.

But what about the cookies? Judy asked.

Never mind the cookies.

Kay started digging around in her dresser drawer. I know it's here somewhere, she said.

What? asked Judy.

Your house key. We need to go to your house and wait for the police. They are going to come over to talk to us.

Now Judy was beginning to panic. This was really all too much.

Mrs. Hutchins, Judy said in a pretty sobby voice. I don't understand what's happening.

Kay stopped her flurry of activity for a moment and looked at Judy. She realized that she needed to pull herself together and focus all of her energy on this eight-year old child because

Judy's life was about to change in a very big way.

She held Judy's cheeks in both her hands and looked her straight in the eye.

Judy, she said with conviction. I need you to be strong right now. I'm not going to lie to you. What happened to your parents is one of the worst things that could happen, and your life is going to change a lot.

I promise you this though. I will do everything in my power to make sure that no harm comes to you. I will not leave your side. Let's have a pinky promise, okay?

Judy really had no idea what Mrs. Hutchins was talking about, but she knew pinky promise, and to her, that meant the world.

So, the two of them took a moment to collect themselves and some things and headed next door to Judy's house.

The house of course was empty, and there was an eeriness to it. The emptiness was palpable, particularly for Mrs. Hutchins, who frankly wasn't sure how she was going to get through this for herself or Judy.

The gravity of the situation was starting to sink in.

Okay, lady, she whispered to herself. Get a grip here.

About ten minutes after they walked into Judy's house, the police arrived with Social Services.

The police officer identified himself as Officer Mac. He was a big guy with a gentle smile. It was clear that this wasn't his first time dealing with such a tragic situation.

He introduced Mrs. Smith from Social Services and asked if the four of them could have a seat.

Mrs. Hutchins introduced herself and Judy and suggested that they go to the kitchen and she would make some tea. She felt this setting might be a little easier on Judy.

C'mon Judy. Let's make some tea for Officer Mac and Mrs. Smith.

They all went into the kitchen, and Officer Mac and Mrs. Smith sat down at the small round oak kitchen table. Mrs. Hutchins made sure to keep Judy close to her and used the most soothing voice that she could muster. She also forced a smile.

Judy was pretty confused by the whole situation and became very withdrawn and more quiet than usual. She attached herself to Mrs. Hutchins' side despite Mrs. Smith's efforts to connect with Judy.

So, Mrs. Hutchins asked Officer Mac. What exactly is your relationship to the child?

Hmmm, Judy thought. Is he referring to me?

I'm Judy's babysitter, and I live a couple of doors down.

Do you know of any relatives in the area? asked Mrs. Smith.

I know that Marilyn has a sister in Manhattan, but we've never met. I don't think they were particularly close.

Well, continued Mrs. Smith, in this type of circumstance, we will place Judy in foster care until we can locate a relative.

Mrs. Hutchins presented both of their guests with tea and then asked if she could speak to Mrs. Smith in the other room.

This left Judy with Officer Mac, which didn't make her all too comfortable.

As she stared at Officer Mac, who was busy writing in his pad, she remembered being in first grade when the class had a visit from a police officer. He was there to assure them all that the police are their friends. He called on Judy to come up so that he could demonstrate how his handcuffs worked. Judy was a shy child and did as she was told, so it never even occurred to her that she could have said no thank you. She walked up to the front of the room and looked up at this man in his uniform with shiny buttons and medals pinned all over it.

Put out your hands, young lady, the officer said in a authoritarian tone. You're under arrest.

Judy almost wet her pants!

She put her arms forward and heard a clink, clink as the handcuffs locked around her little wrists.

Okay, she thought. You can take them off. This isn't fun.

The officer was explaining the arrest process to the rest of the class and not paying much attention to Judy who was standing next to the officer at the front of her entire class cuffed and mortified.

After only a few minutes, that felt like an eternity, Judy became a little agitated.

Ok, said the officer. If there are no more questions, I'll get going.

Finally, Judy thought.

He turned and looked at Judy who was standing to his side trying not to cry or pee.

Oops, he said. I almost forgot. Let's see, where did I put the keys?

He searched and searched, tapping each pocket of his uniform.

I may need to leave those cuffs on you and bring you down to the station.

The officer gave Judy a big toothy grin.

By now, Judy was trying not to pass out.

He patted a small front chest pocket.

Ohh, here they are. I found them.

Well, this was certainly not Judy's best day. When she got home, she broke down.

What's wrong? her mom asked.

Judy told her what had happened.

I'm sorry, honey.

Marilyn knew that Judy was sensitive, but she had no idea the extent of it. She made a mental note to read up on how to handle a sensitive child.

As Judy was rehashing her very bad first grade memory in her head, Mrs. Hutchins was in the living room with Mrs. Smith.

I may not have any right in the world to ask this, but is there any way I could keep Judy with me until her aunt is located? I have been her babysitter and neighbor since she was an infant and so although I'm not family by blood, I'm probably the closest thing to it at this moment. I love Judy dearly, and I promised her I would take care of her.

Well, said Mrs. Smith. This is not the usual protocol, but the circumstances are certainly unique, and I think DSS would want the child to be with a familiar and safe guardian. Let me talk to Judy and make some calls and see what I can do.

Ohhh, thank you, Mrs. Smith. I think Judy and I really need each other's support right now.

The two women went back into the kitchen.

Mrs. Smith looked at Judy who was trying so hard not to have an eight-year old's nervous breakdown.

Judy, may I talk to you in private?

Judy looked at Mrs. Hutchins who gave her a loving smile and nod.

Without speaking, Judy followed Mrs. Smith into the living room.

For a brief moment, Judy looked around at all of the familiarity. She saw the tv, and the old but comfortable couch where she and her mom would watch jeopardy at night. She saw the shelves where her mom kept her precious collectibles, as she called them. There was the picture window that looked out at the front yard and driveway, and the painting of the lily pond and flowers that hung perfectly centered on the side wall. Judy saw all of these things every day, but now, on this day, somehow it all seemed unfamiliar and distant. She almost felt like she was in a dream. Yes, she was standing in her living room, but it didn't feel like her living room.

Judy?

Judy was pulled out of her reverie by the sound of Mrs. Smith's voice.

Yes? Judy responded.

As you know, I just had a talk with Mrs. Hutchins. Now it is my job to find a family member who is willing to take you in. Mrs. Hutchins has asked me if it would be okay for you to stay with her while we locate your family. How do you feel about that?

Judy wasn't feeling much of anything at that moment, but she was sure she didn't want to leave Mrs. Hutchins' side.

I would like that, she said almost in a monotone.

Okay, Mrs. Smith said. Please understand that I need to ask you a few questions to be sure that you will be safe with Mrs. Hutchins.

Okay, said Judy, still in a stupor.

Have you seen Mrs. Hutchins drink alcohol, smoke, or take any pills while she was with you?

No, Judy said.

Okay. Has Mrs. Hutchins ever yelled at you or touched you in a way that made you uncomfortable?

Judy looked up at Mrs. Smith in disbelief.

Of course not. Mrs. Hutchins is my best friend. She's like a grandma.

Okay, Mrs. Smith said with a little chuckle.

I just needed to ask because, like I said, your safety is my number one priority. Let's go back into the kitchen.

Judy was happy to do so. This whole thing was just too difficult to comprehend.

Well, Mrs. Hutchins, I am so very sorry for your loss.

Mrs. Smith then turned to Officer Mac and told him that she had some business to take care of before they could proceed.

Officer Mac nodded and said, I understand.

Mrs. Smith then told Mrs. Hutchins and Judy that she would be in touch soon.

Thank you, Mrs. Smith. Thank you, Officer Mac. Judy and I appreciate your kindness and understanding.

Mrs. Hutchins was standing with her arms around Judy who had her face partially buried in Mrs. Hutchins' stomach.

I'll see you soon Judy, Mrs. Smith said.

Judy peeled away from Mrs. Hutchins and shyly said, okay.

As Mrs. Smith and Officer Mac closed the door and headed to their cars, Judy and Mrs. Hutchins stared at them from the picture window in the living room. They stood there for quite a while, both silent, both staring.

Mrs. Hutchins broke the silence.

Well, Judy. Let's pack a bag, and we'll have a sleepover at my house. Sounds okay?

Judy nodded. She was lost. She had no sense of time or circumstance and was really glad that Mrs. Hutchins was there with her.

They went down the hall to Judy's room and packed just enough for an overnight.

It happened to be a Friday, so there was no school for a couple of days. Mrs. Hutchins made a mental note to ask Mrs. Smith who would contact Judy's school.

For the time being she thought, let's just get through the night.

Judy and Mrs. Hutchins left the house, and Mrs. Hutchins made sure to lock the front door.

Are you hungry, Judy?

Judy didn't really answer. She didn't want to think or make any decisions. She just wanted Mrs. Hutchins to take care of everything.

Mrs. Hutchins must have sensed this.

I get it, honey. You have a lot to process.

Let's go to the diner and try to eat something. Sounds good?

Judy nodded.

Then we'll go back to my house and get you settled in.

Neither of them was particularly hungry, but they picked and munched a little and asked for two doggie bags.

On the drive back to Mrs. Hutchins' house, Judy began to cry. This then turned into sobbing with loud deep, heaving breaths and coughing.

It's okay, Judy. You just go ahead and let it all out.

That's why Judy loved Mrs. Hutchins so much. She never made her feel stupid or told her what to do. They just connected with each other.

Once at the house, Mrs. Hutchins fixed up the guest bed for Judy. This wasn't Judy's first sleep over at Mrs. Hutchins' house. Sometimes, when her mom had teacher conferences and then would go out with the other teachers for a social time, Judy would just stay over. She really loved sleepovers with Mrs. Hutchins, but this one wasn't a fun one.

Mrs. Hutchins helped Judy into her pajamas and tucked her in. She sat on the edge of the bed and stroked Judy's hair. When I was a little girl, my mom used to recite a poem to me about family. Would you like to hear it?

Judy nodded.

It's entitled, *Where Family Lives.* It was written by Alice Wills.

Where family lives am I there.
As you are, we are.
From the start
Within my heart
Remains thee
Remember we
Where family lives.

Do you know what it means?

Judy had no idea.

It means that no matter where the people you love are, they are near as you are near to them, so even if you can't see them, they are close because they are in your memories and your heart.

Try to get some sleep. If you need me, I'll be right in the next room. Good night, sweetheart.

Good night, Mrs. Hutchins. Mrs. Hutchins?

Yes?

What's gonna happen to me?

Judy felt the tears coming again.

Well, we are going to talk to Mrs. Smith to find out what the next step is. For now, I think we could both use a good night's sleep. This has been an awful, awful day. We have both lost very special people that we loved so much, but don't forget that we pinky promised, and so we will stick together.

Mrs. Hutchins bent down and gave Judy a super tight hug. They rocked back and forth for a few minutes, and frankly, Judy didn't want to let go.

Okay, said Mrs. Hutchins.

She kissed her forefinger and middle finger and tapped Judy's forehead while making a kissy sound. I love you, Judy. No matter what happens going forward, don't forget that.

Okay, was all Judy could choke out.

Once Mrs. Hutchins left the room, Judy closed her eyes and tried to process this terrible day as best she could from an eight-year old's perspective.

No child should have to lose their parents at such a young age. Judy's thoughts drifted for a bit until she finally fell asleep.

Judy, Judy.

Was Judy dreaming? She knew she heard her name, but it was like the voice was far, far away.

It's mom. I love you forever. And I will watch over you from heaven.

Judy bolted upright.

Wow, she thought.

And then she lay back down and was asleep within seconds.

Meanwhile, Mrs. Hutchins finally had some alone time to grieve and think. She sat on her bed and wept as quietly as she could. She knew she had to be strong for Judy, but now was her time to break down.   After a good thirty minute or so cry, she grabbed some tissues from her night stand, blew her nose, wiped her cheeks, and took some really deep breaths. She thought about Marilyn and the friendship they had. She had thought of her like a daughter and a confidant. She had never been blessed with children of her own, and after her husband passed, she was kind of lost. She moved into this suburban neighborhood, not a particularly high end one, but very sweet, and on her second day there, a very pregnant Marilyn rang her bell. When she opened the door, she could smell the cinnamon wafting from the freshly baked apple pie, and she knew they would be instant friends. Now, a little more than eight years later, here she was with Judy.

Life can be funny, she thought. From one day to the next,

boom, everything changes.

It was at that moment that she had a realization. She needed to fight for Judy. She would raise her. That way, Judy could stay in her school and familiar surroundings.

But hold on. What was she thinking? She was seventy-two, soon to be seventy-three. She was still in good health, but this would be no small undertaking. Could she really handle an eight-year old?

As she pondered this, she thought out loud.

Kay, this is Judy. She's not just some kid down the block. She needs you now. This is absolutely not the time to abandon her, and frankly, it's what Marilyn would want.

With that thought, she realized she hadn't once thought about Bruce. Honestly, she didn't know him well and didn't like what she knew, not that his goings on were any of her business, but she knew he had hurt Marilyn, and that was enough for her not to like the guy.

In the morning, she would call Mrs. Smith privately and ask if there were any way she could keep and raise Judy. Let the chips fall where they may. She was up to the challenge.

The morning came fast, and Mrs. Hutchins had trouble rousing Judy.

C'mon, honey. Wake up.

Judy was exhausted. She just wanted to go back to sleep because maybe her mom would come to her again.

C'mon, Judy. We have a day ahead of us. I'll meet you in the kitchen.

Judy got up and rubbed her eyes. They were red and scratchy from all of the crying she had done the day before. She was still quite numb.

As she walked down the hallway to Mrs. Hutchins' kitchen, she stumbled a little.

Hi, Judy. Did you sleep okay?

So, so, Judy replied.

How about some pancakes with real maple syrup? I think we both need a hardy breakfast today.

Okay, Judy said. Can I help?

What a sweet girl, Kay thought to herself. How could I doubt my ability to raise her? We'll be like the dynamic duo, conquering the world together. Hell, lots of grandmas raise their grandchildren. If they can do it, so can I.

They sat and ate pancakes with syrup, and then Kay washed the dishes while Judy dried them.

Hey, Kay said. We're a really good team, aren't we?

Yes, Judy said. And she actually smiled just a little bit.

Just as they finished, the doorbell rang.

Judy sucked in her breath.

Kay told her not to worry. She had a good feeling about today despite the circumstances.

They went to the door together. Mrs. Smith was standing there. Good morning, ladies, Mrs. Smith said. May I come in?

Kay collected herself and apologized. I'm so sorry. Please come in. Would you like some coffee?

Oh, that would be lovely, thank you.

The three of them headed to the kitchen. After Kay poured some coffee for Mrs. Smith and herself, she sat down at the table. I wasn't expecting to see you so soon, said Kay. I was actually going to call you a bit later. At that point, Kay looked at Judy and said, Judy, why don't you go get washed up and dressed while Mrs. Smith and I talk?

K, said Judy.

Okay, said Kay and Mrs. Smith simultaneously.

Kay cleared her throat a couple of times. She didn't know how to ask.

Oh, what the hell, she finally said. Mrs. Smith, after much consideration, I would like to know how to go about adopting Judy.

Oh, said Mrs. Smith. Well, there is of course a lengthy process. We first must locate Judy's relatives to find out if they have the ability and willingness to take her in. For better or worse, this is our policy. Hypothetically, if there is no viable living arrangement for Judy with family, we would then search for a suitable guardian/foster family.

Kay, if you are truly serious about this, I can get the paperwork started. We will do a background check on you, and there will be some court appearances. It's hard to say how long the process will take because the courts are pretty backed up. I did manage to reach my manager yesterday after I left you and Judy, and she agreed that staying with you would be the best scenario for Judy for the time being. So, let me work on finding Judy's aunt, and we can go from there. Okay?

Kay exhaled deeply, realizing that she hadn't breathed during the conversation. It occurred to her that this is really serious business, and she was in it for the long haul. Yes, she responded. I will do whatever it takes to keep Judy with me. I want her to be able to remain in her school and in a familiar setting. I believe that will give her the best chance at living a steady and stable life.

I can't argue with that, said Mrs. Smith.

Thank you, said Kay.

I'll be in touch once we've located any relatives.

Kay and Mrs. Smith walked to the front door as Judy was coming down the hallway.

Judy, Kay and I have agreed that for the time being, it would be best for you to stay here with her. Sound okay?

Yes, Judy said, feeling some sense of relief.

You'll hear from me soon. Thank you for the coffee.

As Kay closed the front door, she looked at Judy. Let's get your hair brushed. Did you brush your teeth?

13

Social Services

By the middle of the week, Mrs. Smith called.

Hello?

Hi, Kay. It's Alice Smith from Social Services.

Oh, hi. We're you able to locate Judy's aunt?

Well, Kay, said Mrs. Smith. We have a lot to talk about.

Kay asked Mrs. Smith if she would hold on for just a moment. She then told Judy she was going to take the call in her bedroom and would be back in about fifteen minutes.

Uh huh, Judy answered. I'll wait here in the living room.

Judy really didn't mind. She liked the quiet alone time. She sat and thought about her mom.

When Kay came back into the room, she was smiling, and that seemed like a good sign to Judy.

Judy, Mrs. Smith would like us to go over to her office to work some things out. Can you be ready to leave in about ten minutes?

Yes, said Judy.

They arrived at Social Services about an hour later and waited in the waiting room. They had never been in the building before, and both felt a little overwhelmed by all of the different people waiting to be seen. There were people of all ages and ethnicities, and Kay realized how lucky she and Judy were to have each other, a nice home, and the ability to live comfortably. It made her sad to see so many people struggling. Some seemed to virtually have nothing.

As Kay sat, she felt very blessed and decided that once everything was worked out, she would volunteer some time at her local soup kitchen and explore some other ways to give back. She would also teach Judy about charity. Maybe they could even get involved in some community efforts together.

Mrs. Hutchins and Judy Tanner?

Kay jumped a little. She was so deep in thought, she forgot where she was for a minute.

Judy looked at Kay. Are you alright?

Yes, I'm fine, honey. Come on, let's go in.

They were led down a dreary hallway. It was poorly lit and institutional looking, but they soon came to office number 5. They knocked and heard a voice say, come in.

They opened the door.

Mrs. Smith was sitting behind an old wooden desk with piles of papers surrounding her.

Hi. Please have a seat. Thank you for coming over on such short notice.

Mrs. Smith looked at Judy. I have some news and a very big question to ask you.

Mrs. Smith seemed tired and a little overwhelmed.

Judy, we located your aunt, your mom's sister. She lives in Manhattan, which is about an hour or so away from here. She told me that her apartment is very small, and she isn't really able to take in a child, but if it were absolutely necessary, she would try to make some adjustments.

Do you remember ever meeting her?

No, said Judy.

So, normally, in a situation like this, we like to place children with relatives. Do you understand what I'm saying?

Yes. Judy took a quick deep breath in an attempt to hold back tears.

How would you feel about going to live with your aunt in Manhattan?

Judy looked at Kay.

Kay said, Judy, just tell Mrs. Smith the truth. Would you like to go live with you aunt?

Judy didn't have to think about it.

I'd rather not, she said.

Okay, we'll then, fortunately, we have another option.

Kay couldn't keep quiet anymore.

Judy, would you like to live with me? I'll take care of you if that's what you want.

Judy burst into tears. That's what I want. She jumped up and wrapped herself around Kay. She sobbed and sobbed while Kay held her.

Mrs. Smith had to take a moment and find a tissue. This whole ordeal was really emotional.

Mrs. Smith explained that there would be a process they had to follow and that it moves kind of slowly and that there would be a couple of court appearances. She also told Kay that she herself would put in a good word to the judge and would be making periodic visits to the house to make sure Judy was well provided for. She said she would be in touch. She gave Kay Judy's aunt's phone number so that they could be in contact and said she would call her to let her know what was discussed at the meeting.

Kay filled out some forms to start the process of officially becoming Judy's guardian; they thanked Mrs. Smith and made their way back down the dreary, institutional hallway, through the waiting room, and out the door. Once outside, Kay stopped in her tracks, looked up at the sun, and took a very deep breath. She wasn't sure how to feel but tried to stay focused on the tasks at hand.

We have a lot to talk about, she said to Judy.

They were standing on the third step of Social Services, and Judy looked up at Kay and whispered, thank you, Mrs. Hutchins.

You are very welcome, and I think since we are going to be roommates, you should call me Kay.

Judy nodded in agreement.

Now, we need to contact your aunt to introduce ourselves. We then need to take a trip to see Mr. Kramer, so that we can give your mom and dad a proper burial.

Kay was pretty direct with Judy, and some may think it was inappropriate to talk about such matters with an eight-year old, but Judy appreciated being included in the decision making.

14

Aunt Maddie

Aunt Maddie was much older than her younger half-sister, Marilyn. Her father left his family for another woman many years ago, and so the relationship was never a great one. Actually, Marilyn barely knew her sister because after their father left and remarried, Maddie's mother told him to stay away from her and his daughter.

Kay had to make a decision. Despite the distance, she felt it should be Maddie's choice whether she wanted to say goodbye to her sister, so she called her.

Kay got Maddie's answering machine and left a brief message. She didn't want to go into detail on a machine.

In her day, that just wasn't proper etiquette.

Maddie called back, more out of curiosity than anything else. She hadn't had any communication with anyone from her sister's side of the family in so many years.

Hello? answered Kay.

Hi, this is Maddie. I believe you left me a message?

Yes, said Kay. Thank you for calling me back.

Kay gave Maddie a complete update on what had happened and assured her that Judy was doing relatively well considering the circumstances.

I thought you might want to know.

Maddie thanked her. Despite the fact that she didn't feel any connection to her half-sister or her half-sister's family, she was interested in meeting Judy. After all, Judy is an innocent in all of this drama, she thought. And, she is family.

Water under the bridge and all that.

Let bygones be bygones.

Time for a fresh start.

Okay, she said to herself after hanging up. Enough with the idioms. I don't need to convince myself.

The service was planned for the following weekend. Kay made all necessary arrangements asking for Judy's input every step of the way.

On the Monday after the tragedy, Kay called Judy's school to let them know what had happened. She explained that she was going to keep Judy home for a week or so to help her adjust and make sure she was okay.

The school understood and offered condolences. Kay told them she would keep them updated.

On Monday evening, after Judy had gone to bed, Kay went next door to start going through papers. Thankfully, Marilyn had been very organized, must be a teacher thing, Kay thought to herself. She found two file boxes completely labeled. They weren't particularly heavy, so she carried them back to her house. She was relieved to find everything so quickly because she wasn't comfortable leaving Judy alone for too long.

She made a cup of tea and set herself up in the living room. She opened the first file box and found mortgage papers, the family's medical history, banking info, some life insurance policies, and the name of an attorney. This was all a great relief to Kay. Tomorrow, she thought to herself, I'll call the attorney and find out how to sort all of this out so that Judy is protected financially. She then read through all of the papers late into the night. She felt a huge responsibility. She was, for all intents and purposes, all Judy had, and she would do her damndest to make sure this precious child was taken care of, even if it killed her.

She went to bed feeling exhausted but determined. She fell

asleep quickly and slept hard.

Next thing she knew, her alarm was going off.

That can't be, she thought, still mostly asleep. I just lay my head down.

When she opened her eyes and focused on the clock, she was shocked to see that it was eight o'clock.

Well, I guess four or five hours is better than nothing. Maybe I can talk Judy into taking a nap with me later today.

She put on her bathrobe and shuffled down the hall to the kitchen. All she could think about was coffee.

Good morning, Kay.

Kay looked up to see Judy sitting at the kitchen table eating a bowl of cereal.

Hi, sweetie. You're an early bird today. How did you sleep?

Okay, Judy replied.

Kay noticed a little pout.

What's the matter, honey?

I was hoping my mom would come to visit me last night.

Kay was confused and a bit alarmed.

What do you mean?

A few nights ago, when I was sleeping, my mom came to me. It seemed so real. I miss her so much, Kay. I feel like my heart is broken.

I completely understand. And I wish I could bring her back. She will remain a very special person to both of us. So, what we need to do is get on with our lives as best as we can. She would want us to. And it won't be easy, but we have each other.

Yeah, said Judy.

Kay realized that although she had the best of intentions for Judy, it might not be a bad idea to find some professional help for her. She made a mental note to research child psychologists who specialize in trauma and loss.

But today's priority was to talk to the attorney.

I'm going to make some calls, Judy. Will you be okay for a few minutes?

Uh huh, said Judy.

Ok. I'll be back in two shakes.

Ice cream? Judy asked.

Kay chuckled. No, two shakes of a lamb's tail. You never heard that expression before?

No, Judy said. What does it mean?

It means I'll be back very soon. Like as long as it takes a lamb to shake its tail two times.

That's pretty fast, said Judy.

Meanwhile, clean up your dishes and wash up and get dressed, okay?

Okay.

We'll meet back here in about fifteen minutes.

Kay left Judy in the kitchen finishing her cereal.

She walked down the hall to her bedroom and dialed the number on the paper she had found the night before.

15

Attorneys

The phone rang about five or six rings. Kay was about to hang up when she heard a voice on the other end of the line.

Watkins and Watkins, said a female voice.   How may I help you?

Hi, Kay said. I am looking for Mr. Watkins. Is he in?

May I ask who's calling?

He doesn't know me, but I found his name and number on a piece of paper.

What is thus in reference to?

I am trying to locate Marilyn Tanner's attorney.

Oh, regarding the pending divorce proceedings?

Oh my God! I didn't realize. I just assumed Mr. Watkins was handling Marilyn's daily affairs.

Please hold.

Kay waited, thoughts circling around in her brain.

Their on-hold music is nice she thought, getting lost in a jazzy version of an old classic.

Hello?

The voice on the other end was a male's, and it jarred her.

Hello.

May I help you?

Yes, I'm looking for Marilyn Tanner's attorney.

This is he.

Oh, Mr. Watkins, my name is Kay Hutchins, and I lived next

door to Marilyn. I don't know if you heard, but Bruce and Marilyn were in a fatal car crash this past weekend. I'm taking care of their daughter, Judy, and while going through Marilyn's papers last night, I found your name.

Oh my, I'm very sorry to hear about this tragedy. I was actually representing Mrs. Tanner in her divorce. If I understand correctly, you need an estate attorney.

Yes, said Kay.

Actually, my wife practices that type of law. Would you hold on for just a moment?

Yes, of course.

Kay hummed along to the on-hold music for a few minutes.

Hello?

This time there was a female voice on the line.

Hello? Kay responded.

Hi, Mrs. Hutchins. My name is Nancy Watkins. I was Mrs. Tanner's attorney.

Finally, thought Kay.

Ohhh, okay.

My husband just filled me in on the tragedy. I'm so very sorry to hear about this.

The two women spoke for a few minutes and Kay made an appointment to meet Nancy that afternoon at three o'clock.

Watkins and Watkins was a well-established law firm and one whose reputation was solid. Kay and Judy arrived at two fifty-five with the file boxes in hand. Kay took great care to make sure nothing was missing because she knew this was Judy's future.

After sitting for about ten minutes in the waiting room, they were escorted down the hall to a conference room.

Please make yourselves comfortable. Nancy will be right in.

Kay had explained to Judy what they would be doing, but it was a little bit over her head, so she just sat quietly.

Nancy walked in a couple of minutes later.

Hi. I'm Nancy. You must be Kay, and you must be Judy. She took Judy's hand and said, Judy I'm so very sorry about what happened to your parents.

Judy looked up at her from her seat.

Kay interjected.

Thank you for seeing us so quickly, Nancy.

Of course, said Nancy. I understand the urgency with circumstances like this. So, let's see what we have.

Kay handed Nancy the file boxes.

My. This paperwork is really well organized. That's going to make everything easier. Let me spend the next few days reading through everything and I'll give you a call, if that's okay?

That sounds fine, said Kay. Judy, okay with you?

Yes, said Judy.

Good, said Nancy.

Kay then said that she was planning a service for Marilyn and Bruce to be held on Saturday.

She explained that she had some money saved but was hoping that there would be some way to be reimbursed for expenses once everything was figured out.

Nancy understood and assured Kay that she would be very thorough.

All right, said Kay.

Then we'll speak soon. Let me show you out.

They all shook hands and went their separate ways.

Judy, how about an early dinner? I'm pretty tired and need to get to bed soon.

Shall we take out some Chinese food and bring it home?

Okay, said Judy. She hadn't ever had Chinese food before, but she was curious to try it.

Kay chose a few different dishes and made sure they got some fortune cookies.

At home, Judy set the table for dinner, and Kay pulled out the containers. Judy tried some fried rice and some sautéed vegetables. She also ate a couple of shrimp. She really liked the food.

Okay, Kay said. Now read your fortune.

Kay handed Judy a cookie.

Break it open and tell me what it says.

Judy cracked open the cookie and found a little piece of paper inside.

She read it out loud to Kay: "You make your own happiness."

Hmmmm, said Kay. That is something to ponder.

What does ponder mean? Judy asked.

It means to think about.

Judy liked the word ponder. She would try to remember it and use it.

The next day, Kay and Judy took a walk and then spent the rest of the day in the house relaxing. They were both very emotionally tired and so napped for much of the afternoon.

Kay was awoken by the phone at about five-thirty.

Hello?

Hi, Mrs. Hutchins. It's Nancy.

Hi, Nancy.

I've started looking over the paperwork and wanted to set up an appointment for you and Judy to come in so we can get everything in order. Would you be able to come in next Monday morning at say, ten?

Yes, that would be fine.

Okay, see you then.

Thank you.

Kay hung up and lay in bed for a few minutes. The reality of her life was beginning to hit her, and she panicked. She became dizzy and felt as though she was going to vomit.

Just breathe, she said to herself. This is all going to work out.

On Wednesday, Kay got Judy up and dressed. She made them both scrambled eggs with rye toast- one of Judy's favorite meals. Kay then contacted the funeral home to make sure all arrangements were in place. She was determined to make this week about Judy as much as possible. She decided to try to talk to her about her parents to get a feel for where she was emotionally and to prepare her for the funeral.

Hey, Judy, would you like to go shopping for clothes with me today? I thought we could drive over to the mall and look for a few things.

Judy wasn't that familiar with the mall. It was a few towns away, so this sounded like a fun adventure.

That sounds pretty fun, said Judy.

Once at the mall, Kay explained that Judy needed to find an outfit for the funeral.

It doesn't need to be black, but it should be a darker color. Do you prefer pants or a skirt?

Judy definitely preferred pants, so they went to the children's section in Macy's and found a pair of black pants. They then found a nice blouse – it had blue and green and black flowers on it, and Judy felt pretty in it.

My mom would like this top, Judy said.

Kay smiled. You just keep her close in your heart. If we remember her often, then she will never really be too far away.

After purchasing their outfits, they wandered around the mall for a little while and went to the sweet shop to have some lunch.

Kay looked at Judy.

How are you holding up, Judy?

I'm really sad, but I'm really glad that we're together.

After lunch, they headed home.

Saturday was soon upon them. Kay tried to explain what to expect and encouraged Judy to allow any feelings that may come.

There weren't many people, but those who came were very sweet. Many gave Judy hugs and told her how very sorry they were. Most of the people were from the school where Marilyn had worked. There were even a couple of students who came to pay their respects.

Then a woman came over to Judy.

Kay said, You must be Maddie. I'm Kay Hutchins, and this is Judy.

I'm your Aunt Maddie, your mom's older sister.

Maddie was very fancy. She wore makeup and high heels. She had bright red nail polish that matched her lipstick.

They talked for a little bit, and then Maddie said she had to catch the train back to the city. She gave Kay all of her contact information, kissed Judy on the forehead, and was gone. It was like a dream.

The entire day had been a long one and once Bruce and Marilyn had been buried, Kay and Judy sat for a while at the cemetery, quietly remembering.

Finally, they both got up and walked to the car, holding hands. This is the start of a new chapter in both our lives, Judy.

Judy didn't really understand. It was only much later, when she was an adult, that she realized the great loss Kay experienced, as well as the sacrifice she had made for Judy.

The next Monday they were out the door to go see Nancy.

Once at Watkins and Watkins, they were greeted and asked to have a seat.

It'll just be a few minutes, said the receptionist.

As they sat, Kay realized how surreal this whole situation was. Boy, she thought to herself. You just never know what turns life will take. I never thought I'd be raising an eight-year old in my seventies.

Nancy came into the waiting room.

Hi, Kay. Hi, Judy. Come on in.

They followed Nancy down the hall and around the corner to an office. It wasn't the same space they had been in during the first visit. It was much smaller but beautifully decorated.

This place is so different from Mrs. Smith's office, Judy thought to herself.

So, Nancy began. I've reviewed all of the papers and accounts. Bruce and Marilyn were well prepared. They established a trust for Judy when she was an infant. It has been accruing interest over these past eight years. Judy will be able to access the funds upon her eighteenth birthday, so the money will continue to grow for another ten years. This trust will cover college expenses and a bit more, helping Judy get started on a career path. As well, Judy is the beneficiary of both parents' life insurance policies, and this money should be sufficient to cover all immediate costs incurred as well as Judy's needs until she is eighteen.

I suggest that we set up a monthly stipend with you as the guardian. We can figure a rough estimate of need. This way, the money will earn interest as you go.

Well, said Kay. This is really quite a relief. I'm relatively comfortable financially speaking, but to be honest, I was a little nervous about how I was going to support Judy.

Oh, said Nancy. There's also the matter of the house. I'm assuming you are inclined to sell it?

Well, I don't know, Kay responded.

Would it be okay if Judy and I talk things over tonight and get back to you?

Yes, of course. I'll be here all day tomorrow. Just let me know. But I will tell you that it is my opinion that you sell the house rather than rent it out.   That way, any monies from the sale could be added to Judy's account leaving you both in a pretty good financial position.

Nancy looked at Judy. Do you have any questions for me?

Judy shook her head no.

Okay. I look forward to hearing from you both, tomorrow. Again, I am so sorry for your loss.

Kay and Judy thanked Nancy and left the office.

That night, Kay made spaghetti and salad. Judy and Kay sat silently at Kay's kitchen table, eating.

Out of nowhere, Judy looked at Kay.

Are you going to sell my house? Judy asked.

Kay was caught off guard.

What do you think we should do, Judy?

Well, can't we keep it? It has all of my stuff in it, and plus my mom's garden is in the backyard.

Kay explained that they didn't have enough money to maintain both houses.

I think the best thing to do is sell your house, and we will live here together.

How about if we go to your house tomorrow and start going through things. We can make piles: things you want to keep, things you aren't sure about yet, and things you can give away. Sounds okay?

Can I think about it, Kay?

Yes, of course. This is a really big decision, so you take your time.

After dinner, they watched Jeopardy. Judy then went to her room.

I just need some alone time, she said to Kay.

I totally get it. I'll be in to say goodnight in a little while.

16
The Library

At the library, Judy walked up and down the stacks looking for the books on teaching. She suddenly felt melancholy. She remembered being a little girl in New York and going to the library with her dear, dear friend, Kay. They were frequent visitors to the library and would often wander through the stacks looking at different genres of books. They would then select one or two books to read together at home. She hadn't been in a library since college, and childhood memories kind of took her by surprise. She sat down in the middle of a stack and sobbed. She was surprised how the feelings came welling up, but she just let it all out. A few minutes later, the librarian approached her and asked her if she was ok.

Yes, thank you. I'm sorry. I was just overwhelmed by a childhood memory.

I see, said the librarian, and she walked away and back to her desk.

Judy dried her face, blew her nose, and took a breath.

Okay, kiddo. Focus. If Kay were here with you now, you know she'd say, put your big girl pants on and deal with it.

Judy felt Kay's presence and said out loud, I miss you so much. How am I going to get through my life without you?

At that moment, a book tumbled off the shelf. Judy bent down to pick up the book entitled, *I'm Ok, You're Ok,* by Thomas Anthony Harris.

Hmm, she said. That's interesting. I'm glad you're okay, Kay. And, I actually feel you watching over me. You taught me to be a strong and independent woman with compassion and humility. You also taught me that it's okay to melt down sometimes as long as I don't wallow in the pity. So, with that said, my pity party is over. Thank you for helping me through it.

As Judy exited the stacks, she heard a distant, you're welcome. Wow, she thought. This is getting creepy.

Just then she realized it came from the librarian who had been helping someone, but even still, Judy had to wonder…

She pulled herself together and refocused on the task at hand. She found some books on basic teaching techniques as well as a book on how to create lessons. Although the references were all academically based, she figured she could create plans using these as a guide. She had four days to prepare, so she would be okay. She knew in her heart that Kay was by her side, and that comforted her.

While walking out of the library, she decided it might be a good idea to get an iPad. This way, she could research Tai Chi techniques on line and keep her notes right on the tablet. She went back into the library and asked the librarian if there was an Apple store nearby. The librarian explained that there was one about 45 minutes north in Portland, Maine. She printed out directions for Judy. Judy thanked her for her help and headed north.

It was a gorgeous late spring day. Judy had a sweater with her, but the air had warmed up to close to 70 degrees and the sun was shining brightly, so by the time she got to the Apple Store, she didn't even need her sweater. As she pulled into the parking lot, she felt a pang of reality excitement. She also began to question herself.

Can I afford a new IPad?

Judy had the original one at home, but it didn't work well anymore. It had gotten her through college, helping her graduate with a B.A. in Sociology, but she hadn't really used it much since then. She also had an old flip phone because why did she need a fancy smart phone? She had resisted giving into the technology trends, but perhaps it was time. So many aspects of her life and herself were changing.

Why not go full out.

So, in she walked. The store was actually really amazing.

Oh my God! She thought. Have I been living under a rock?

While waiting for a sales person, Judy wandered around the store playing with the various devices. She was in awe of how far technology had come.

Can I help you? asked a voice behind her. My name is Henry. I am an Apple sales associate.

Hi, Henry. Have patience with me. I am a tech ignorant.

Henry smiled. Okay, he said. What are you looking for?

Well, I have been doing fine without much technology, but I've just been offered a job teaching Tai Chi, so I think it's time to get something so that I can do research and create lesson plans. I don't need a lot of bells and whistles, just something basic.

I think you should go with the iPad. It's a great tablet for the money. It'll give you internet and the ability to write. It's completely touch screen with a full size on screen keyboard. And if you decide you need a separate keyboard, you can easily add that right onto the iPad..

What does this amazing machine run?

The basic iPad is $350.00.

Oh, thought Judy, that's not so bad.

Okay, wrap it up, Henry. You've sold me on it.

Henry gave Judy some pointers and helped her with some of the applications. He also gave her his cell number, just in case she might have some questions later on. He winked at her as he handed her his card.

Judy thanked him and headed home not thinking much of it.

By the time Judy got home, she was hungry. She took out a pan and chopped some veggies for a sauté. She made some rice in her little rice cooker that she had found in a second hand store and mixed the whole thing together. Chloe sat with her while she ate dinner, and Judy told her all about her day. Chloe mostly purred as her tail gently moved back and forth, but she occasionally meowed as if to say, Uh huh.

Judy spent the next few days at home preparing for her classes. She and Chloe took walks, and Judy meditated. She read and planned and practiced form. By Monday, she felt prepared.

17

Teaching Tai Chi

Judy bolted awake at 7:00 am Monday morning. She was disoriented for a moment. She took a few deep breaths and closed her eyes. She couldn't remember details but felt a presence around her.

Wake up, Judy. You're being silly, she scolded herself.

Chloe jumped up on the bed and meowed.

Good morning, my baby. How did you sleep?

Chloe gave Judy a big lick on her cheek and then tapped her nose with her paw. She looked intensely into Judy's eyes. Judy got a chill. There was depth. It was as if Judy was looking through Chloe's eyes into another world.

It was too much to process, and within a moment, Chloe was off the bed and heading to the kitchen to wait for her breakfast.

Stay present, said Judy out loud to herself. Stay focused. You have a big day ahead. You're going to be great!

She went into the kitchen, fed Chloe, and made some tea. She decided to have her favorite breakfast: scrambled eggs with rye toast. This gave her comfort. She thought about all of the times she and Kay sat together at breakfast making plans, giggling like little girls. Judy felt very grateful for her years with Kay.

We just never know what direction life is going to take. The trick is to accept whatever comes along with grace and love, she thought.

Judy did some stretches, took a shower, and got her notes together.

Wish me luck, Chloe.

Chloe looked up from her napping chair but went right back to sleep.

Judy noticed how beautiful she looked with a sun ray gliding across her body.

You are something, my Chloe. Okay, then. On that note, I'll see ya later alligator.

Judy stopped at the florist on her way to bring Steve and Meg a lucky bamboo plant.

New beginnings, she thought.

She got to the studio at about 9:30. She was intentionally early. She wanted to be in the space and get herself centered before the students arrived.

Good morning, Meg. Judy beamed as she walked in. Good morning, Judy. How was your weekend?

Really good, said Judy. How about yours?

Pretty quiet. Not much happening in this sleepy town.

Judy smiled. I brought you and Steve a gift. She presented Meg with the bamboo.

Ohhh, that's so nice, Meg said. Thank you.

You are very welcome, said Judy.

Just then, Steve came into the studio.

Good morning all, he said. How are we doing today?

Judy and Meg gave a simultaneous, good.

Judy, are you ready for your class?

Yes, sir, Judy said playfully.

Okay, said Steve. Do you mind if I peek in periodically?

Not at all, Steve. And don't hesitate to offer some pointers.

Sure thing, said Steve, but I have a feeling you're not going to need them.

On that note, Judy said, I'm going to get ready.

See you guys in a bit.

Break a leg, so to speak, called Meg.

Judy entered the class space and looked around. She wanted to be really comfortable with the environment.

After about two or three minutes, Meg came in with a class roster.

You have six students today. The class will probably be a little bigger going forward, but a couple of people aren't able to attend today.

Thanks, Meg.

Sure thing.

Judy walked around the place a few times, getting a feel for the physical energy.

She took a look at the roster. She wasn't surprised that there were more women than men, but she was happy to see that a couple of men had joined.

Just then, two women entered the classroom.

Good morning! Judy said with a smile. I'm Judy, your Tai Chi instructor. It's nice to meet you.

Good morning said the women. We're a little bit nervous. We've never done Tai Chi before and don't really know what to expect.

No reason to be nervous, said Judy. I'll go easy on you.

The three of them laughed.

The other four students came in.

Hello, said Judy. Welcome. I think we're all here now. My name is Judy, and I am your Tai Chi instructor. I've been doing Tai Chi for close to eleven years, and I have found that it gives me balance, focus, core strength, and confidence. I look forward to working with each of you and truly hope that you will find the same qualities that I've found over the years.

Does anybody have any questions or concerns before we begin?

One of the men raised his hand.

Hi, yes –

I'm not very flexible and am worried about hurting myself.

Okay, said Judy. That brings up a good point. In order to have the strength and balance to do the Tai Chi forms properly, we will spend a good part of each class stretching and building muscle. We will end each class with ten or fifteen minutes of actual form. I encourage you to pay attention to your body. You know your limits, so go gently. You will find that over time, your body will become more flexible and stronger, but please start out slowly.

Any other questions?

Okay, let's begin.

The class stretched and moved in a variety of postures with traditional Chinese music playing in the background.

Judy then showed the class some of the more basic moves to begin to prepare for the form.

They ended the class with Judy showing everyone a warm up form.

To end, she turned to the class with her left hand over her right fist, thumbs pointed downward in a triangle, bowed, and said, Xie' xie'.

She explained that Xie' xie' means thank you in Chinese and that the left hand over the right fist is a ritual of respect often done before commencing exercise and then once again at the end.

The left palm (with 4 fingers) symbolizes Virtue, Wisdom, Health, and Art, which are also called the "4 nurturing elements", symbolizing the spirit of martial arts.

The left thumb is slightly bent to mean that one should not be arrogant.

The right fist symbolizes rigorous practice. Since the right fist is clenched, it means a form of 'attack' but with the left palm wrapping it, it means "discipline" and 'restraint/control in order not to abuse the practice".

Let's try it. Judy faced the class, and they all bowed with left palm wrapped on right fist.

Xie'xie, they said in unison.

See you next week, Judy said.

Thank you, the class said.

A couple of students came up to Judy to tell her how much

they enjoyed the class.

Judy was pleased. Once everyone had left, she took a deep breath and sat down on the floor. She closed her eyes and did a quick five-minute meditation.

She walked out and almost bumped into Steve.

How'd it go? he asked.

Well, Judy responded with a big smile.

I agree, said Steve. I like your teaching style. You are gentle but disciplined, and very organized. Your movements are clean and precise. I think you could have a future in this. Something to think about.

Thanks, Steve. I'm pretty pleased with the class too.

Um, Meg and I are going to grab some lunch in about ½ an hour. Would you like to join us?

Oh, that sounds great. I'm going to do some errands, and I'll meet you back here in about twenty minutes.

Great, said Steve.

Great, said Judy.

She left the studio feeling really good. She had pushed through her fears and stayed in the moment.

I can do this. I can actually do this. She smiled to herself.

She entered the local market not realizing the smile on her face. As she went to pick up some organic bananas, a man approached her.

Hi, he said.

Judy was taken by surprise.

Hi, she said back.

I haven't seen you around. Are you new here?

Judy wasn't sure what he was talking about.

Umm, no, not really. Hey, it was nice talking to you, but I have to run. I have an appointment.

Judy grabbed her bananas and headed to the cashier.

She could feel the man staring at her, and it made her pretty uncomfortable.

Is that man bothering you, sweetie? the cashier asked.

I wouldn't say bothering, but the encounter was a little

strange.

He's in here all the time trying to meet women. So far, he's harmless, but don't let your guard down. Listen to your instincts. That'll be $3.49, hon. The advice is free.

The cashier smiled.

Thanks for the advice and the bananas, Sherry. Judy smiled back.

You have an exceptional day.

You too.

Judy walked out and got in her car. She did look around and in her back seat to make sure that the guy wasn't stalking her.

She headed back to the studio, looking forward to having lunch with Steve and Meg.

When she walked in, Steve was on the phone.

Steve'll be ready in a minute, Meg said. He's taking us out special to a Japanese restaurant across town. I can't wait. I love the place. Have you ever been there, Judy?

No, but it sounds good.

Steve came over and said, are we ready?

Definitely, Meg said.

Steve chuckled. Meg loves this restaurant. Okay, let's go.

They all got into Steve's car and drove for about 20 minutes or so.

Here we are, said Steve. I hope you're both hungry.

They were greeted as they entered the restaurant.

Konnichiwa, Steve San. Okaerinasai.

Konnichiwa, Hirohito. Domo arigato.

Judy was impressed.

They took off their shoes and sat at a table in a cut-out space.

It was a really beautifully decorated place.

Judy, do you drink?

It's a bit early, isn't it?

Generally, Steve said, but I feel like celebrating.

You wanna share, Steve? Meg asked.

Not yet. Let's just have a good time.

Hirohito

Hai

Three hot sakes, dozo.

Hai, Steve San.

Domo, domo.

Do itashi mashite, Steve San.

Once the sake was served, Steve said, a toast.

He raised his sake cup, so Meg and Judy did the same.

To us. A team of three. And to new beginnings.

Meg looked at Steve as if he had lost his mind but went with it. Judy didn't know what to think, so raised her cup and took a sip.

Wow! That's strong!

Steve smiled. It does take a bit of getting used to.

They all laughed.

Judy loved the joviality and playfulness of Steve and Meg. She could see that their's was a long-time brother/sister relationship. It was easy and familiar to both of them. She felt a little bit like an outsider but reminded herself that Steve had invited her.

After scanning the menu, they were ready to order.

Have you had sashimi or sushi before, Judy?

Yes, a couple of times, but I tend to be more vegetarian.

No problem, Steve said.

He ordered a bunch of different things from the menu, including, as Meg reminded him, tempura because that's her very favorite, Steve said bumping gently against Meg.

Stop teasing me, Meg whined.

Ahh, c'mon. You can take a little bit of teasing.

Meg smirked, and in that moment, looked like she was five years old.

She had a cute way about her, Judy thought.

As Judy drank her sake, she noticed Steve. As she observed him, she started having some uncomfortable feelings. She was getting stirred up – hot and bothered, she thought to herself. But hold on, Judy. Steve is your boss. Stop thinking about him in any other way.

Whatcha thinkin about there, Judy?

Judy was startled. She was having a little fantasy and dialogue with herself in her head and lost her sense of surrounding for a minute.

Not too much, Steve. Just enjoying the sake and the company.

Meanwhile, she was in a whole other naughty place in her head. It must be the sake, she thought. I'm going to stop drinking right now. Well, after one more sip.

With that, she began to feel very frisky and silly. She felt herself flushing and started jabbering about nothing in particular. Steve first looked at Meg who was chowing down on the tempura. He then looked at Judy. He realized that she had probably had a little too much to drink because her face was red, and she was telling some story about bananas and a stalker. He couldn't quite follow what she was talking about but liked how cute she was telling her story in a really animated way.

Every couple of minutes, Meg would say, uh huh with her mouth full of tempura.

Steve suddenly felt like a bit of an outsider because Meg seemed to understand what Judy was talking about.

Hold on, Judy. Slow down. I'm having trouble following you.

Judy looked up. Really? Sorry about that.

She then started to laugh uncontrollably.

Oh my God, Meg said. Steve, I think Judy's drunk.

Ya think? Okay Judy, I'm cutting you off.

They finished lunch and went back to the studio. Meg made some coffee and insisted that Judy drink it.

She did and then passed out on the couch in Steve's office. Two hours later, Judy heard a voice in her head.

Judy, wake up. I'm gonna drive you home.

Her eyes popped open, and she realized what had happened.

Steve, she yelled. Oh no! I am so sorry. How long have I been here?

A couple of hours. I think the sake hit you pretty hard.

Steve, I am so embarrassed. I'm so sorry.

Don't be. C'mon. I'll drive you home.

Not necessary, Steve. I'm fine.

Are you sure?

Yes, but thank you for everything. I had a really nice time.

You're welcome. Drive safe, and would you do me a favor?

Sure.

Call me when you get home, so I know you're ok, promise?

Okay. Will do.

See you Wednesday.

Yes, Judy replied as she crawled out of the office.

She made it home and called Steve. I'm home safe and sound. Thanks again for a very cool day.

My pleasure, said Steve.

After she hung up and said hello to Chloe, she went directly to the medicine cabinet.

Where is the aspirin? she whined out loud. My head is about to explode!

She lay down on her comfy couch that she had gotten at the Salvation Army and began to doze. Chloe jumped on top of her and nuzzled. She then curled up on Judy's stomach.

Boy, Judy thought. Cats really know how to be in the moment. They both fell asleep in the early evening, and Judy dreamt.

18

Goodbye Kay

Judy was eight when her parents were killed in a car crash, and it was a life-changer. She and Kay got through it together, but it certainly wasn't always easy. As the years passed, Judy and Kay found a rhythm, and things were good for the first seven to eight years or so.

Judy did well in school, and Kay became the grandparent/parent/best friend that Judy so desperately needed. Kay found Judy a wonderful psychologist whom she saw for a few years. Dr. Savoy taught Judy how to allow and feel her feelings and face situations head on in the moment. She also taught her how to separate subjective and objective. Judy was always a natural observer, so the tips that Dr. Savoy taught her worked well for her.

As she entered high school, Judy began to do meditation which made it even easier to apply the techniques she had learned as a child.

But, as Judy finished her junior year in high school, something shifted. She noticed that Kay seemed to be getting more and more confused. She was also a little bit short-tempered.

Judy was becoming concerned. One Saturday, Kay was sitting at the kitchen table – the two of them called it the pow wow table because over the years, this is where they had all of their serious talks with each other and made plans for their future together. They also would pretend and play – making up creative scenarios for each other and then laughing till they were crying.

So, Judy said as she sat down. Kay, I'm worried about you.

What do you mean?

You don't seem like yourself lately. Is everything ok?

I'm fine, Sarah

Who's Sarah?

Who's Sarah? I don't know. Why do you ask? Are you trying to confuse me? Hey, don't you have to get to school? What time is it anyway?

That's it, Judy thought. I need to talk to somebody about this. Now Kay seems a little bit paranoid as well.

On Monday, Judy went to her guidance counselor who then took her to the school nurse. They were both at the school working during summer school.

Judy explained what she'd been noticing at home with Kay. They all agreed that Kay should be checked out.

It could be a number of things, said the nurse. How old is Kay?

She's almost eighty-one, said Judy.

Do you think you can talk her into going to see a neurologist? asked the nurse. I'll give you the name of a really great woman in Portland.

Well, I'll try.

Judy felt panic welling up inside of her. What is happening? Kay has been my angel, my guardian, my friend for all of these years. Am I going to have to be her guardian? Okay, she thought. Don't get ahead of yourself. Just have a serious talk with Kay and convince her to see a doctor. You can do this. After all, it was Kay who taught you to be strong.

Later that week, Judy called the neurologist's office and explained the situation. They gave her an appointment for three weeks from Saturday at 11:00.

So, the Friday night before the appointment, as Kay and Judy were cleaning up the dinner dishes, Judy broached the subject.

She had noticed a pretty rapid decline already.

Kay, could we talk about something serious for a minute?

Sure, Judy, what's on your mind?

Well, this isn't easy. Judy felt tears coming.

Kay knew Judy really well and could see that she was pretty upset.

Put the dish towel down and let's sit. Tell me what's going on.

Hmm, Judy thought. She's pretty clear right now. Maybe everything will be okay.

Judy started by telling Kay how much she loves her. She then explained that over the past few months she had been noticing some changes in Kay's personality and behavior.

Fortunately, Kay was in a pretty clear place while they were having the talk and admitted that she herself had noticed some things that were a little bit off. She had been dismissing them, but now that Judy was talking about it, she realized that maybe it was more serious than she wanted to believe.

Judy, I don't think it's anything to worry about, but I'll go with you tomorrow just to make you feel better, k?

Okay, Kay. Thank you.

That night was hard. Neither of them slept much in anticipation of the next day.

They got up and went through the motions, neither saying much. On the ride to Portland, Judy put in one of Kay's favorite cd's. So, Benny Goodman entertained them on their trip to Maine.

At the office, they were greeted by the receptionist who gave them a clipboard full of papers to fill out. They sat down and proceeded. Kay was actually having a little bit of trouble filling out the forms, so Judy took them.

Some of these can be confusing, Judy said, despite the fact that they were only asking for name, address, etc.

Once done, Judy brought them up to the desk. She was told it would just be a few minutes.

Judy and Kay sat side by side, and at one point about five minutes later, Kay took Judy's hand.

Thank you, she whispered.

Judy looked at her and gave her a little smile, masking the fear, panic, and upset she was feeling.

Kay Hutchins, a voice called from a door across the waiting room.

Kay looked at Judy and said, Come with me. I need you for support.

The two of them walked down a hallway and were escorted into a doctor's office. They had a seat on one side of the desk and waited.

Soon the doctor entered and sat on the other side of her desk. She reached her hand across the desk.

Hi, I'm Dr. Mujeed. You must be Kay.

Kay shook Dr. Mujeed's hand.

Judy then reached out her hand. I'm Judy, Dr. Mujeed. Kay is my adopted grandma.

It's nice meeting both of you. So, tell me what's going on.

Judy began. She talked about the past few months and the changes she had noticed in Kay.

Kay remained quiet, which in and of itself, was unusual.

Well then, said Dr. Mujeed. Why don't we do a preliminary exam, and I'll schedule some tests, and we'll see from there, sounds okay?

Judy turned to look at Kay. It was as if she were in a coma. She was staring straight ahead with no affect.

Kay? Judy said.

Kay? Dr. Mujeed said.

Judy put her hand on Kay's arm. Kay?

Kay slowly turned to look at Judy. It was as if she was seeing her for the first time.

What? Kay asked abruptly. What do you want?

Judy and Dr. Mujeed looked at each other.

Judy was pretty freaked out.

Dr. Mujeed already had a suspicion of a diagnosis but said

nothing. She wanted to be sure.

Let me show you to the exam room.

They followed Dr. Mujeed across the hall to exam room 1.

Kay, I need you to remove all outer wear. You can keep your under garments on. I'll be back in a couple of minutes.

Thank you, said Judy.

Judy helped Kay get undressed and helped her get seated on the exam table. Kay was off balance and seemed confused.

Why are we here, Judy?

Before Judy could answer, Kay asked, Where are we?

Judy tried to make light conversation, but Kay wouldn't or couldn't engage.

Dr. Mujeed knocked and entered the exam room.

Okay, she said. Let's get started.

Kay looked at her. I don't need my hair done today.

Dr. Mujeed looked at Judy who had tears in her eyes.

Alright, Kay. I am going to ask you to do some tasks for me.

The exam was incomplete because Kay just wasn't able to follow instructions.

Dr. Mujeed then had Kay taken to the room down the hall for an MRI.

Once done, Kay and Judy were escorted back to Dr. Mujeed's office.

It appears that Kay has Alzheimer's Disease. It is relatively far along from what I can tell.

The disease is a mysterious one, but some people do progress rapidly. I'm very sorry.

Judy asked a bunch of questions about what to expect.

Kay sat quietly.

Dr. Mujeed suggested that Judy look into having a caregiver in the home or placing Kay in a facility designed for dementia.

At the end of the visit, Judy thanked Dr. Mujeed, and Dr. Mujeed gave Judy some information on facilities.

I would like to see Kay in three months, so please make an appointment on your way out.

Judy barely remembered the drive home. She was in shock. She tried to talk to Kay to no avail.

How can this be? She's like a completely different person.

When they got home, Kay went straight to her room.
Judy knocked on her door a few minutes later. Kay? May I come in?
Kay said weakly through the door. Very tired.
Then there was silence.
Judy tried to console herself.
She just needs to sleep. She'll be better tomorrow.

Judy made herself some dinner and went to bed. The day had caught up with her, and she realized she was wiped out.

Sunday morning came quickly. Judy got up and went directly to Kay's room. The door was closed since last night, which was strange because Kay never closed her door. She had made it a habit to always leave it open after Judy moved in with her, in case Judy needed her. She would say, we have no secrets. Just two gals living in a house together.
Judy knocked on the door. Kay? Nothing. She knocked a little louder. Still nothing. Judy felt tears running down her cheeks. She didn't want to open the door. She didn't want to face her fear.
After a couple of minutes, she took a very deep breath and opened the door. Kay was laying in her bed on her back. She looked so beautiful and peaceful.
Judy walked over to her.
Kay, it's time to get up. Let's make Sunday pancakes.
Kay didn't respond.
Judy had taken a first aid class at school and so knew how to check for a pulse. She put two fingers on Kay's neck near her carotid artery. Kay was cold. Judy couldn't find a pulse.
KAY!!!! Judy screamed. She burst into hysterics. KAAAAAY!! WAKE UP!!!!

NOOOOOOOOOOOOOOO. NOOOOOOOOOO, KAY.

Judy collapsed on the floor.

What was happening? How could she lose more people she loved? It just couldn't be possible.

After sobbing heavily for a few minutes, Judy attempted to compose herself. She stood up and walked down the hall to get her phone. She dialed 911 and could barely explain.

Within ten minutes, the ambulance and the police were at the door. Judy let them in but couldn't really speak. She pointed to Kay's bedroom.

Coincidentally, the police officer who accompanied the ambulance was Officer Mac. When the call came over the radio, he recognized the address. He had been keeping distant tabs on Judy over the years and felt a bit like a very distant uncle or some other relative.

Judy, he said when he walked through the door.

Judy looked up at him with a puzzled look on her face.

It's Officer Mac, Judy. Do you remember me? I was here when your parents passed away.

Oh yeah, Judy said in a whisper.

C'mon, Judy. Let's have a seat in the kitchen, and you can tell me what happened.

Meanwhile, the EMT's were checking out Kay. She had been dead for a few hours. It appeared to be a heart attack, so they had contacted the coroner and were waiting for her to arrive.

Judy told Officer Mac about Kay's behavior and that they had just gone to a neurologist yesterday. She told him the doctor did a bunch of tests and thought it might be advanced Alzheimer's.

Just then, the Chief EMT came into the kitchen. She said it appeared to be a heart attack.

Judy said, I thought she had Alzheimer's.

It isn't unusual for some Alzheimer's patients to experience heart attack and even stroke. The brain is a very mysterious organ. We're waiting for the coroner to arrive to officially pronounce. I'm so very sorry for your loss.

Those words left the EMT's mouth, and Judy swore she could see them floating around the kitchen. They echoed as they travelled.

Officer Mac took Judy's hand and said, if it's okay with you, I'm going to hang out for a little while.

Officer Mac had never married or had any children, but he had a soft spot for Judy and felt like if he had had a daughter, he would have wanted her to be like Judy.

Judy looked at Officer Mac and began to cry again. She folded into his arms, and he held her and rocked her.

He had a fleeting thought that this would totally ruin his tough guy reputation, but Judy's heartache in this moment trumped that.

After about thirty minutes, the coroner arrived. She pronounced Kay dead, and the ambulance took her to the hospital.

Officer Mac asked Judy if she knew Kay's wishes.

Judy said, I have to call Nancy. She's our attorney.

Judy went to Kay's important papers box and looked for Nancy's cell number.

Hello? Nancy said. Hello? Is someone there?

Judy couldn't get any words out, so Officer Mac grabbed the phone.

Hi, Nancy. This is Officer Mac. I'm here with Judy Hutchins.

Oh my God. Did something happen?

Kay passed last night. I was hoping she had made some kind of arrangements with you about her wishes upon her death.

Nancy sighed. Well, I need about an hour. I'll go over to my office and pull out her file. Could you meet me there? And, Officer Mac, could I speak to Judy?

Officer Mac handed Judy the phone.

Hello? Judy's voice trembled.

Judy, I am so sorry. Will you come with Officer Mac to my office? You can show him where it is, okay?

Uh huh.

I'll see you there in an hour.

Judy heard a click but continued to hold the phone.

Officer Mac realized that she was in shock and took the phone out of her hand.

Judy, how about we go get some breakfast before we head over to Nancy's?

Judy just stared up at him.

Why don't you go get out of your pajamas and throw on some comfy clothes. I'll be right here.

Without a word, Judy walked down the hall. She felt as though she were floating in a dream.

She re-joined Officer Mac within five minutes, and he grabbed the keys that were hanging from the hook by the front door.

As they walked out, Judy's knees buckled. Officer Mac caught her.

Whoa, steady there, girl! Just put one foot in front of the other.

At the diner, Judy had some rye toast. She really couldn't eat but did make an attempt.

The two sat in silence. There just wasn't much to be said. Finally, Officer Mac stood up from the booth.

Well, Judy. I guess it's time to go. I'll go pay the check and meet you at the front door.

About five minutes went by, and Judy hadn't come over to the register. Officer Mac made his way to the back of the diner where they had been sitting and saw Judy still in the booth with her head on the table. He could see she was sobbing by the way her head bobbed.

He gently touched her shoulder, and in a whispered voice said, C'mon, honey. I know this is extremely difficult, but we need to go see Nancy.

Judy got up from the booth and followed Officer Mac. By now, her eyes were so puffy, she could barely see.

They arrived at Nancy's. She was waiting inside the door for them.

She pushed open the door and unnecessarily explained, we aren't open on Sundays, so I want to keep the door locked. As she said it, she realized how impertinent it was.

Once they were all in the building, Nancy wrapped her arms around Judy who was standing there looking lost and so very sad.

I'm so, so sorry, Judy. What an awful thing!

They went into Nancy's office. She had already pulled the file on Kay.

Nancy went into a business mode because she knew she would break down if she didn't stay focused on the task at hand.

So, she said. Kay was very prepared and explicit in her wishes. Judy, you are the only family she had in this world, so she happily and lovingly wanted you to have all of her possessions. We'll go into the details at a later date.

Officer Mac, I am assuming that Kay has been taken to the hospital?

That's right, he responded.

Okay. I will contact the hospital and the funeral home and make sure they connect with each other. I will also ask about a service date. Judy, Kay wanted to be buried in Simpson's Cemetery with her parents and husband. Do you have any questions at this point?

Judy looked at Nancy. What am I going to do now?

Oh, said Nancy. Well, I will contact your aunt in Manhattan. In the meantime, do you have any friends you can stay with?

Judy had some acquaintances but no one she felt comfortable asking.

I want to sleep in my own bed.

Oh, Judy. I'm not sure that's such a good idea.

Judy insisted that she would be fine, and Officer Mac said he would check in on her, so he took her back home.

Judy thanked him for being so kind, and he said he would be back with some dinner in a few hours. Lock the door, and if the doorbell rings, be sure to ask who it is.

Okay, said Judy. She was seventeen after all, but today she reverted back to the eight-year old who had just lost her parents. Judy walked from room to room as if she were in a museum. She observed the furniture, touched the tchotchkes, and spent quite a while staring at the varied art work on the walls. She had lived here for the past almost nine years, but never truly noticed all of the stuff that Kay had.

When her parents died and she and Kay were selling her house, Judy walked around there too, but it was more like a shopper trying to decide what she wanted to acquire.

Now was much different. She felt like she didn't want anything in the house. She would give up all possessions to have Kay back. They weren't finished. They still had much to do together. They had just started talking about college for Judy and were going to take a very big trip together next summer.

Judy began to feel cheated and angry.

This sucks! she said out loud. Am I just meant to be alone for the rest of my life?

She plopped down on the floor in the middle of the living room, and as the brain tends to do to distract, began thinking.

What an interesting perspective, she said out loud.

She then started talking to herself.

Well, Judy, here you are. You're seventeen. You have one more year of high school. Then off to college.

I don't think money will be a problem. I know my parents left me some, and I guess Kay did as well. Could I manage to live here in the house alone for the next year? Put on your big girl pants- as mom used to say.

Just then, the doorbell rang. Judy got up off the floor and went to the door.

Who is it? she asked, even though she already knew.

It's Officer Mac, Judy. I brought us some dinner.

Judy unlocked the door. She was really happy to have the company.

Hi, Officer Mac. Please come in. I'm glad you're here.

I know how tough this is for you. You've been dealt a shitty hand, pardon my French.

Judy smiled. Officer Mac, do you kiss your wife with that mouth?

Officer Mac let out a howl. That's very funny! C'mon, let's eat. I hope you like turkey burgers and fries. I need to cut back on red meat, so I'm giving this a try.

They went into the kitchen, and Judy set the table.

As they started to eat, Officer Mac looked at Judy.

I'm here for you, kid. Whatever you need.

Judy welled up and almost choked on her burger.

I appreciate that, she was finally able to get out.

After dinner, Officer Mac told her that if there is ever anything she needs, she should call him. He gave her his cell number.

Thanks, Officer Mac. You've been a real support for me today.

Officer Mac bent down and kissed Judy on the forehead. I'm just a phone call away. Try to get some sleep.

Good night, Judy said, as she closed and locked the front door. It was only eight o'clock, but Judy suddenly felt exhausted. She decided to take a hot shower and get into bed. On her way to her room, she pulled Kay's door closed. She knew she would have to deal with going in there eventually, but not tonight.

After her shower, she climbed into bed. There was something so comforting about being under her covers in her familiar space. She had a little tv in her room, so she clicked it on and found a sappy movie.

The next thing she knew, she opened her eyes and saw the Monday morning news on the tv.

I must have fallen asleep pretty quickly, she thought. I don't even remember the name of the movie.

She stretched and got out of bed. She began going through the routine motions of the morning. She got dressed and walked down the hall to the kitchen. She treated herself to a hot chocolate and made her favorite breakfast of scrambled eggs and rye toast.

As she sat eating, the feelings started returning, and the reality of the day before hit her like a ton of bricks. She was starting to melt down when the phone rang.

Hi, Judy, it's Nancy. How are you doing today? Scratch that, stupid question. Judy, can you come into the office this morning? I want to go over some things with you.

Okay. What time?

Any time is fine. I've cleared my schedule.

I'll be there soon.

They hung up, and Judy felt grateful for the distraction. She cleaned her dishes, brushed her teeth, and pulled her hair back into a pony tail. She grabbed her bag and the keys and headed to Nancy's office.

Once there, Judy told the receptionist that Nancy had asked her to come.

One moment. She intercomed Nancy.

Okay, Judy. You may go in.

Judy walked down the now familiar hallway to Nancy's office.

Hi, Judy. Please have a seat. As I mentioned yesterday, Kay has left all of her belongings to you. She had me draw up a will, and since there are no living relatives, there won't be anyone to contest it. Kay has left you the house, her jewelry, and her savings which totals $30,000.00. She also made you the beneficiary of her life insurance policy. The cash value comes to $70,000.00, so there is $100,000.00 and the money from the sale of the house. What we need to subtract is the cost of the funeral, any mortgage, loans, or other debt Kay may have had, and my fee.

So, one question you need to consider is where you are going to live. It is my professional opinion that you sell the house and find a little apartment. Between your trust, the sale of the house, and your inheritance, you'll be able to live comfortably, pay for college, and have a cushion to get you started once you graduate from college. I'm assuming you are planning to go to college?

Judy shook her head yes.

Okay, so I will work on the paperwork for all of this, and I can give you the name of a good realtor who can help you with the sale of the house. Take a few days to process this.

Meanwhile, we have to talk about the service for Kay. I know it's really soon, but have you had a chance to think about what you would like to do?

Where is Kay's body?

At the funeral home. I suggest a one-day wake and then a morning burial service. You can then host a small lunch at a local restaurant. I can help you with the arrangements if you'd like.

Judy had no idea about any of this, so she gratefully accepted Nancy's offer.

They called the funeral home and set up a wake for Thursday with a burial on Friday morning.

And yes, Judy said when they hung up with the funeral director; I would like to talk to a realtor.

Well then, I think that covers just about everything. Do you need an advance for the time being while I work out the inheritance?

Judy realized she never really dealt with money. She received a monthly stipend from her parents' estate, but never paid attention to paying bills or anything like that.

Nancy could see Judy was a bit perplexed.

Judy, do you know who Kay's accountant was?

Judy thought for a moment. Yes, I think his name is Mr. James.

Okay. Call him and explain what happened. He can help with the bill paying while everything gets settled. Give him my number.

Judy left the office, her head spinning. The business of death, she thought. How strange.

She decided to go to the park nearby and sit for a while. She found a bench near an open space with a stream on the other side of it. There was a group of people gathering.

Judy was naturally curious about human behavior, so she watched in anticipation.

After about ten minutes, the group of fifteen or so started doing the most beautiful movements in unison. An older man sat down on the next bench.

Excuse me, Judy said. The man looked inquisitively.

Yes? he asked.

Do you know what those people are doing?

That's Tai Chi, he said. Beautiful, isn't it?

Yes, she said. It's captivating.

Judy watched while they moved ever so slowly and amazingly gracefully. She wished she could join them. They were so focused and seemed so at peace.

When they stopped and were breaking up, she walked over to the guy who was leading the group.

May I ask you where one could go to learn Tai Chi?

I'm an instructor. I would be happy to teach you. My dojo is just around the corner. If you follow me back there, we could get you signed up for classes.

Bo held out his hand in an introduction.

Bo, he said.

Judy reciprocated.

Judy, she said.

Judy walked with Bo back to the dojo. She was excited to learn something new and so beautiful. She couldn't wait to tell Kay. Then she remembered.

The instructor took out an application. Are you okay? he asked.

Yes, Judy said. I will be. I just lost someone very close to me, and it's still very fresh. I was just thinking about her.

I understand. I think Tai Chi will be helpful in your healing process. Fill out this paperwork, and we can get started.

Oh, Judy said. I didn't realize you meant right now.

Bo looked her straight in the eye. His gaze was intense and gave Judy goose bumps. It was as if he was looking into her soul.

I can see a lot of sadness within and surrounding you, and I really believe that practice and movement of your chi would help you in this moment.

Judy thought of her former therapist, Dr. Savoy. Maybe that's what she meant when she told

Judy to stay focused and present. What the heck, she thought. What else am I gonna do? I don't want to sit in the house by myself.

Okay, said Judy. I'm in. But what about payment?

Bo explained that each class is one hour long. Private lessons are $35.00 for the hour, and group class is $15.00 per class.

I don't have any money on me, but I am happy to come back with money after the class.

That's fine, said the instructor. He wasn't the suspicious type, and he could tell that Judy was sincere. Besides, he had all of her contact information on the application.

As they entered the dojo, Bo faced Judy. By the way, Bo stated. For the purpose of instruction, you may call me Sensei which means teacher.

Judy nodded. Okay, Sensei.

It felt good not to think about the last couple of days for a little bit. For the first time in a long time, Judy felt focused and centered. She wasn't thinking or grieving or wondering. She was simply being.

So, when you enter a dojo, it is proper to put your left palm over your right fist and bow. By doing this, you are showing respect to the space you are about to enter.

What does that mean?

You mean the hands?

Yes.

The fist is a symbol for attack or fight. The left hand goes over it with fingers straight which indicates peace. So, you are indicating that you do not want a fight. You are saying you desire peace.

Ohh.

They stood side by side, bowed with hands in fist and palm

form. Then Bo explained that Xie' xie' means thank you in Chinese. This is generally spoken when one bows. Let's try it. Xie' xie', they said together while bowing.

Okay, we are ready to enter the space.

Bo started with some stretching and very basic movements. Judy liked the structure, discipline, and repetition.

After the hour, they stepped off the mat and once again bowed in humility and gratitude. She asked Bo how long he would be there.

Do I have time to run home and get your money?

Yes, he said. No problem. I have classes till 9:00 tonight, so I'll be here.

Judy told him she'd be back in an hour.

When she got home, she was hit by a wave of grief. The reality of everything that had happened, the loss of past and present rolled over her like a tsunami. She collapsed on the floor of the entrance way and sobbed. Then, she heard a voice. She stopped crying to listen more closely.

Am I completely losing my mind? she thought to herself. No, I'm sure I heard something.

She sat a while longer in the silence. She became aware of her breathing and its rhythmic pattern. It felt soothing to sit in the quiet just being. Her thoughts slowed down, and she closed her eyes. She continued to pay attention to her breathing and went into a meditative state. She found herself in a meadow. It was breathtaking! There were wild flowers of every color; the sun was shining super brightly, and the sky was a blue like she'd never seen before. She wanted to stay there forever. She was safe and felt loved. In the distance, she saw a person. There was a familiarity about her, but she couldn't place her. She reached out for her, but the woman walked away into the woods just off the edge of the meadow.

Who are you? Judy cried out. Please come back. Don't leave me alone. I'm so alone. Please!

Judy came out of the meditation sobbing. She laid down and

pulled her knees to her chest and rocked. I don't want to be alone. I can't be alone. I'm so scared.

She sobbed for a bit longer and then the tears stopped. She was dazed and realized how exhausted she was.

Okay, she said. Go pay Bo, get some groceries, and come home. Big girl pants, Judy.

See, Mom? I did listen to you when you gave advice.

Judy felt a gentle stroke on her cheek. She figured it was from all of the tears.

She went to her room, grabbed some money, and headed back to Bo's dojo.

He was in between classes, so she paid him for the hour, and signed up for two group classes a week starting the next week.

See you then, Bo said.

Thank you, Bo.

Judy left and headed to the health food store to get some fruits and vegetables, and went next door to get take out Chinese food.

At home, she set one place, took the food out of the containers, and broke open her chopsticks. She sat down and picked up her glass of Honest Peach Tea, and said, To you, Kay. You sacrificed everything for me, tolerated me when I had tantrums, became my confidant, therapist, mother, and best friend. I love you forever.

Judy ate a little bit, cleaned up, and went to bed. She cried herself to sleep.

Tuesday morning, Judy woke up but didn't feel like getting out of bed. She fell back asleep for a while, woke up, then fell asleep again. When she finally really woke up, it was dark out. She got up, had some fruit and actually went back to bed.

On Wednesday morning, the phone woke her up.

Hello?

Hi, Judy, it's Officer Mac. Just checking in. How are you doing?

Oh, hi, Officer Mac. Umm, okay. I actually slept all day yesterday and just woke up.

Really, Judy? Okay. I'm off today. Can I pick you up and take you out for a little while?

Oh. Probably not a bad idea. I just need to take a shower.

Not a problem. It's ten now. How about I pick you up at noon?

See you then, Officer Mac.

Judy stretched, got out of bed, and took a very long, very hot shower. She threw on some clothes, went into the kitchen and grabbed a banana.

She also drank a ton of water because she felt pretty parched.

She grabbed her phone and decided to wait for Officer Mac out on her front steps. It was a gorgeous day. It was about 80 degrees with a gentle breeze. Judy imagined Kay was sitting next to her on the front steps enjoying the weather, and she was talking to Judy about flowers.

Officer Mac pulled up twenty minutes later, got out of his car and gave Judy a big hug which felt so comforting. Actually, Judy realized she really needed the affection.

He said, c'mon. Get in the car. I have a surprise for you.

They drove for a while and ended up at a wildlife rescue farm about an hour north. Judy was fascinated. They walked around and learned about the different animals living there. They were amazing. So beautiful. Judy related to these injured and abandoned wild animals. They were living in a place different from their natural environment without family and friends. She wondered about their sensibility. Did they feel sad? Lonely? Angry? Lost? Or perhaps she was personifying.

Officer Mac pulled her out of her reverie. Are you hungry, Judy? You wanna get something to eat?

Just like that, they were on the road heading to a restaurant.

Judy thought, boy, life just changes in an instant.

19

We Are Not Alone

The summer passed quickly and at the same time, slowly. Judy buried Kay, sold the house, and moved into a cute little one-bedroom apartment right in town. She also got more involved in Tai Chi at Bo's dojo.

Nancy called her periodically just to check in, and Officer Mac took her out every few weeks.

She appreciated their concern, but it didn't take the pain away.

School would be starting in a couple of days, and with the dust settling, she decided to contact Dr. Savoy. She felt like she needed someone to talk to her knew her and "got" her.

This is Dr. Savoy speaking. How may I help you?

Judy hesitated. She didn't expect Dr. Savoy to answer the phone.

Hi, Dr. Savoy. It's Judy Hutchins. I was a client of yours about eight years ago.

Judy, Judy; oh yes. Judy, how have you been?

That's why I'm calling. I know that you are specifically a child psychologist, but I was wondering if I could see you.

There was silence. I had a cancellation for 4:00 today. Why don't you come in, and we'll get caught up.

Thank you, Dr. Savoy. I really appreciate this.

See you at 4:00, Judy.

Judy hung up and felt some relief. She felt good advocating

for herself and liked that she was able to recognize that she needed the support. She thought of herself as a strong young woman, but also realized that sometimes being strong meant reaching out for help.

She got to Dr. Savoy's about fifteen minutes early and sat in the familiar waiting room. Not much had changed, except maybe the paint color on the walls; she couldn't remember.

Dr. Savoy came into the waiting room.

My, Judy. You've certainly turned into a beautiful young woman. I'm glad you called. Let's go into my office and talk.

Judy followed Dr. Savoy into her office. It wasn't real fancy, just a big chair and a couple of comfortable smaller chairs placed facing the big chair. In the corner to the right were some toys and a drawing pad on a small table. Judy remembered sitting there as a child, playing with a Barbie doll while talking to Dr. Savoy.

So, Judy, catch me up.

Judy started at the beginning and talked for close to 45 minutes without hardly taking a breath.

Well, you've certainly not had an easy life. I am very sorry for your loss. I remember meeting Kay a couple of times, and she was a lovely woman.

Are you going to stay in the area to finish high school?

Yes. I sold the house and moved into a little apartment in town.

Okay, good. I think it would be a good idea to start working together again if you'd like to. I applaud you on having the insight to realize that you need some support to help you navigate all of the emotional stuff.

They set up a Saturday morning appointment, hugged, and parted.

I'll see you next week, Judy.

Judy walked out into the daylight feeling unburdened. She was also pretty hungry.

She decided to treat herself to some maki two towns over.

She sat in a booth and ordered a bento box for $9.99. It came packed with rice, vegetable maki, shumai, and tempura.

She knew she was experiencing "eyes bigger than stomach" syndrome, but she didn't care. She broke open her chopsticks and picked up a piece of maki. As the food was going into her mouth, she heard a voice.

Judy? She looked up from her bento box and noticed Bo standing there.

Hi, Bo, she said with a mouth full of maki.

Bo smiled and giggled. I can see you like your maki.

Judy giggled, a little embarrassed.

May I join you? I would love some company.

Sure, Judy said, feeling pleased that he wanted to sit with her.

Judy wasn't the best at socializing and didn't see herself as someone others would want to spend much time with. Maybe it was because she had mostly been with adults her whole life.

This place is so good, don't you think?

Judy said, Yes, I come here a lot. I like getting out of our small town and being somewhere less conspicuous.

I get it, said Bo. Sometimes, you just want to blend.

YES, exactly, said Judy emphatically.

A couple of people turned to look.

Sorry, she whispered. It's just that it's nice to talk to someone else who feels the same.

Bo smiled.

The waitress came over.

Bo said, I'll have what she's having, pointing to Judy's bento box.

The two talked for a bit about Tai Chi and life. Judy was really enjoying the company.

As she was talking, she looked at Bo. He was sweet, smart, and cute, and way too old for her. She couldn't tell, but he looked like he was at least twenty-three or more. Like a big brother, she thought.

Bo talked about his life. He was a military brat, and so lived all over the world. He said, it made it hard to establish roots, but the plus was that he knew a lot of different cultures and had met a lot of interesting people. He started doing Tai Chi when his dad was stationed in China. He found it to be a constant element in his life. No matter where they were transferred, he could do his Tai Chi. It gave him a sense of stability.

This made a lot of sense to Judy. Although she hadn't traveled, much of her life was turned upside down. She could see the Tai Chi being the constant force.

After dinner, Bo said he had to run. He had a couple of classes to teach.

Let's do this more often – I like your company.

Judy smiled. I'll see you next Wednesday evening, she said.

It's a date, said Bo.

Judy assumed he meant that as an expression.

Senior year began that Monday. Judy wasn't real excited about going back to school, but she had put some support systems in place that would certainly make it easier. She had her therapy, and she had her Tai Chi. She could get through this year, and soon, she'd have to think about college.

Judy had been in touch with her Aunt Maddie. They weren't super close, but Maddie was open to having some kind of a relationship. Judy had actually gone to Manhattan a couple of times to visit her. The city was so different from Judy's home town upstate. It took some getting used to the sounds and the crowds and the general hub bub.

Judy and Maddie would walk all around the city, window shopping, and sometimes really shopping. It actually made Judy feel very cosmopolitan. They would go to restaurants and shows. Judy did enjoy this time with her aunt, and slowly but surely, they got to know each other and began to care about each other.

As summer became fall, Judy and Maddie talked about college. Maddie suggested that Judy attend right in Manhattan.

There are excellent schools right her in the city, and that way, you and I could spend more time together.

What Maddie didn't share with Judy was that she'd just been diagnosed with cancer. Although it was only stage two, it was a more aggressive form, and as her only relative, Maddie wanted to spend as much time with Judy as possible. She realized she couldn't take this opportunity for granted. Suddenly, her life had a ticking clock attached to it, and there was a very finite label stamped upon her forehead. Maddie was going to make the most of the life she had left, and a big part of it would be spending time with her niece.

They went to check out NYU, and then went up town to see Columbia.

Something clicked for Judy at Columbia. She could see herself there. It felt right.

So, she made an appointment with her guidance counselor to find out how to apply. The process was somewhat arduous, but Judy was kind of determined.

The next time she was in the city, she had an interview at the Admissions Office.

Her grades were good, and the finances were in place. She tried for early acceptance and was successful. She would live at school. Maddie's apartment was too small for the two of them, and Judy was used to being independent anyway.

The rest of the school year went by. She was taking three Tai Chi classes per week and seeing Dr. Savoy on Saturdays. She and Bo had the occasional Japanese lunch two towns over, and she saw Officer Mac about once a month. She managed to get through the holidays and spent New Year's Eve with Maddie. The city was out of control! The decorations were amazing, and they went to see the Nutcracker ballet at Lincoln Center. Judy was becoming more comfortable with the city. She liked that she could just blend into the mass.

During one of her visits to Maddie's in the spring, Judy asked Maddie if they could talk. Maddie was doing okay and still hadn't told Judy about her illness. The treatments were keeping things at bay, and she didn't feel too awful. She felt that Judy had been through enough, and so wanted to keep this from her as long as she could.

What's up, Judy?

Kay and I used to talk about taking a trip together after my graduation. We hadn't decided on a place but wanted it to be a really special trip. I was wondering if you would consider going with me?

Maddie was up against it now. She would never be able to travel. She knew she didn't have enough strength for that.

Judy. Maddie took Judy's hands in hers.

Judy didn't know why, but she started to cry. Nooo.

No what, Judy? I haven't said anything yet.

I know, but this feels bad.

Listen, I didn't want to tell you because you've been through so much.

Judy stared at Maddie with tears running down her cheeks.

Judy, I have cancer. I've been getting treatments, but the cancer is aggressive, and I'm not sure how much time I have. I would love to go with you on an adventure. I would love to do that more than anything else, but I'm afraid I don't have the strength.

Judy was speechless.

I'm sorry, honey. Maybe I should have told you sooner, but you've been through so much.

Judy stood up and walked out of Maddie's apartment.

She walked down the street and kept walking. She didn't have a destination; she just needed to walk and think and process.

What is going on? Why do I keep losing the people I love?

She walked into the night and ended up back at Maddie's apartment well after ten.

Are you okay?

I guess, said Judy.

I know you must be feeling so many things. You've had so much loss in your short life. Judy, I can't even imagine. But, hold this...you have also been loved very deeply, first by your parents, then by Kay, and now by me. You are lucky to have had so much love. Some people spend an entire life wishing for that.

Maddie started to cry.

Judy came over and sat next to her on the couch.

I've spent my life looking for that and have only found it with you in these past months, Maddie shared through her sobs.

Judy cried.

Maddie continued to cry.

Okay, Maddie finally said somewhat abruptly. Enough with the pity party. We are strong women, and we will live to the fullest for as long as we can. Also, I've been thinking. Even though I can't go with you, you must travel. This is going to be my gift to you. But promise me you'll call me from each destination and describe everything in vivid detail. Deal?

Judy was silent.

Judy, this is my dying wish. Please don't deny me this.

What could Judy do?

Okay, deal, Judy agreed hesitantly and with a pout.

Good, said Maddie.

So, plan on coming to the city right after graduation. We'll celebrate and then plan your trip.

Now, let's go to bed; I'm tired.

Judy went back upstate the next morning to study for her finals.

She got through them relatively well and graduated with honors.

She then packed a bag and headed to Manhattan. It was mid-June, and she didn't have to be at Columbia till the end of August. She would visit with Maddie for a few days to plan her trip and then go back home to settle up her apartment and let Bo and Dr. Savoy know that she would be moving.

Hey, Maddie, how are you feeling?

Okay.

Judy knew that wasn't the truth, but she went along.

Judy, I've made a reservation at Ko for 6:00. Did you bring anything dressy?

Sounds exciting! Yes, I have a summer dress.

Good. I also called my travel agent, so we'll meet her in about an hour. Do you want to get some brunch first?

That sounds good. I just need to make a pit stop, and then I'll be ready.

Out they went, Judy and her Aunt Maddie. Two gals in the big city.

They brunched and then went over to Travel Time on Fifth and 49th.

Jessica was waiting for them.

Welcome, welcome, she said.

Please have a seat. Maddie, it's great to see you. It's been ages.

She and Maddie air kissed, which Judy found fascinating.

She loved observing human behavior. That's why she chose Sociology as a major.

So, Jessica began. Tell me what we're thinking.

Maddie looked at Judy. May I?

Sure, Judy said, thinking to herself: this should be interesting.

Jess, I want Judy to take a trip of a lifetime. I was thinking the month of July.

Judy looked at Maddie in disbelief.

Maddie said, oh Judy, stop. Remember, you are doing this for me.

Wow! Judy thought. She's good at the guilt.

So, Maddie continued. Judy should begin in Europe. I want her to stay at interesting places. Money is no object.

Then, maybe she could get on a cruise around the Greek Islands.

Then, she should...

Wow, Maddie. That seems like a lot, Judy chimed in.

Jessica looked at Judy. Where would you like to go?

I like seeing a bit of Europe, but I've also always been fascinated by Asia.

Interesting, said Maddie. Perhaps a tour of Southeast Asia?

Okay, said Jessica. Give me a day to work on this. I am going to create an itinerary for you.

Can you both come back tomorrow around 2:00?

Sounds like a plan, said Maddie.

Okay, I'll see you two tomorrow. Judy, you won't be disappointed; I promise you that.

The two walked out of Travel Time feeling pretty excited.

Maddie, this really seems like...

Ta,ta,tatatata, don't you burst my bubble, niece of mine.

20
Steve

Steve's childhood was pretty average. His parents seemed happy; his home life as relatively uneventful. He grew up in New Hampshire, had some close buds, played baseball, and loved to travel. Each summer, he and his mom and dad would go camping all around New England.

Then when Steve was seven, they took a trip to Walt Disney World.

It was just after they returned home that Steve's parents had a huge argument. Steve was in his room and didn't know what to do. He heard his dad yelling that he couldn't take it anymore and wanted his mom to get some help. She was crying and pleading. But then her voice changed. She started cursing at Steve's dad, Matthew. Steve didn't understand.

He came out of his room.

What's going on? He asked with trepidation in his voice.

In complete and utter frustration, Steve's dad responded.

Your mom's a drug addict, and I can't live with her anymore. I also don't want her around you. I'm filing for divorce, Steve.

Whoa, Steve cried. I don't understand. Tears were now freely flowing down Steve's cheeks.

Steve's mom came over to Steve. She bent down and reached out to hug him, but he backed away.

While still on her knees, she presented a defense.

Steve, honey, your dad's exaggerating. I have a bad back and need pain pills to help me, she told him in a not so convincing voice.

Matthew interjected. Oh, please, Sylvia. You're an addict. Admit it. You need help.

Steve looked at his mother. She was shaking and crying.

Mom? Steve was sooo confused and upset.

It's okay, sweetie. Mommy's going to be okay.

She reached out to Steve, but Matthew stepped in between them.

C'mon Steve, I'll tuck you in to bed, and we'll sort this out tomorrow.

Matthew walked Steve to his bedroom.

I love you, my baby boy, Sylvia called out to Steve. Remember that.

Matthew tucked his son in.

Mom's been suffering from depression for a long time and is really good at pretending that everything's okay.

Matthew told him that they both loved him very much, and he would get her the help she needed. Good night, son. Try to get some rest.

Good night, daddy.

Matthew walked out of his son's room and down the hall to his and Sylvia's room.

Sylvia, can we talk this out rationally? Matthew was talking to the en suite door. Sylvia?

What are you doing in there?

Matthew suddenly panicked and broke down the bathroom door.

Sylvia was on the floor; an empty pill bottle lay a few inches away.

Jesus!! Matthew screamed.

Steve came running in.

Dad??

Steve, call 911, NOW!

SYLVIA!!!

Matthew was slapping her cheeks trying to get her to wake up.

C'mon Sylvia. Can you hear me? C'mon. WAKE UP, DAMNIT!

Steve could hear sirens in the distance. He was in a bit of shock. Why was his mom lying on the bathroom floor? Did she fall asleep? Why was his dad slapping her and yelling at her?

The ambulance and police pulled up out front. Steve went to the front door and let them in.

My mom's in the bathroom down the hall.

Steve followed them. There were EMTs all around her doing different medical things.

Matthew grabbed his son, and the two of them sat down on the bed to be out of the way. The medical people put his mom on a gurney and told Matthew they were taking her to Portsmouth Regional Hospital.

Matthew grabbed Steve and the two followed the ambulance to the hospital in Portsmouth.

They sat in the Emergency Room waiting area for what seemed like forever. Finally, a doctor came out. Matthew Williams?

Yes, I'm Matthew, and this is my son Steve.

Doctor Thompson – they shook hands.

Your wife is alive, but she's in a coma from the pills. We'd like to admit her and keep a close eye on her. It appears she's been on this medication for a very long time, and it's broken down her system tremendously. I'm honestly not sure she'll wake up.

Matthew was hugging Steve as if to protect him from this news.

Can we see her?

We're preparing a room upstairs for her, but you may go into the ER for a few moments if you'd like.

Matthew and Steve went into the room. Sylvia was on a ventilator and hooked up to a whole lot of machines.

Oh my God! Matthew covered his mouth with both hands. Why, Sylvia? Why?

Steve was sobbing.

Daddy? What's wrong with Mommy?

Matthew picked up Steve. Listen, kid, Mommy's not in good shape here, but the hospital is going to keep her and try to make her better. He picked Steve up and held him close to his mom.

Give her a kiss, Steve. Steve kissed his mom on her cheek.

The two then walked out of the room and drove home.

At about 4:00am, the phone rang.

Matthew was jarred out of a hazy sleep.

Hello?

Mr. Williams?

Yes?

Mr. Williams, it's Doctor Thompson. I think you should come to the hospital.

Why? What's going on?

There was panic in Matthew's voice.

Mr. Williams, I'm very sorry. Your wife suffered a massive heart attack while we were transporting her to a room. We did everything we could. We're going to need you to come back to the hospital to fill out some paperwork. I'm sorry to have to ask you, but do you have any idea if your wife was an organ donor?

Ummm, I'm not sure. I could check her license. So, Sylvia is dead?

I'm very sorry for your loss. Perhaps we could talk more once you get here?

Matthew hung up. He stayed in bed under the covers and tried to understand the past few hours.

We were arguing, he said out loud. I wanted her to stop using the pills. They were destroying her and our relationship. I just wanted her to stop. I had no idea she was that desperate.

Matthew started to cry. He cried and screamed, NOOOO!!!

This woke up Steve. He sat up in a daze.

Daddy?

Steve got out of bed and walked down the hall to his dad.

Daddy?

Matthew looked up and heaved a couple of times.

Come here, my baby boy.

Steve walked over to his dad and climbed up onto the bed.

Matthew wrapped his arms around Steve. They rocked and rocked.

After about twenty minutes, Matthew whispered into Steve's ear.

I have to tell you something, Steve. Mommy took a lot of pills, and they made her heart stop beating. She's gone to heaven, Steve.

Steve pulled away from Matthew. He looked up at his father.

Why would she want to leave us, Daddy?

I don't know, baby. She was feeling very sad for a long time. We need to go back to the hospital. Can you put your clothes back on for me and meet me by the front door in five minutes?

Okay, Daddy.

They drove back to the hospital in silence. One of the nurses took Steve to get a hot chocolate while Matthew filled out the necessary paperwork.

The two were exhausted by the time they left the hospital for the second time. Matthew took Steve to the diner to get some breakfast. He couldn't bear to go home yet.

They ordered pancakes and sat silently. Steve watched the other people eating and talking, laughing, and reading the newspaper. He saw life all around him. He looked up at his dad.

Don't these people know how sad we are, daddy? They're all laughing and smiling.

Matthew was caught a little bit off guard. He looked around the diner. He had no response.

He thought about Steve and how this loss might affect him. He would have to pay extra attention to him to make sure he got through this.

My son is a sensitive kid, he thought to himself. And he's really pretty aware of his surroundings.

Ready, big guy? his dad asked?
Steve shook his head yes.

When they walked into the house, they quietly both went to their rooms and closed the doors. Steve lay down. He was in need of sleep. He fell asleep quickly and slept and slept.

By early afternoon, Matthew peeked in on him. Steve was still asleep, so Matthew let him.

Meantime, Matthew called the funeral home and made all necessary arrangements.

He also called relatives to let everyone know. Sylvia's drug addiction had not been a secret, so no one was really surprised by the news.

As the days, weeks, years passed, Matthew and Steve picked up the pieces and got on with their lives. Matthew tried to provide as much normalcy in the home as possible. The two of them went to counseling together, and Matthew spent as much time as possible with Steve.

Matthew started traditions.

One of Steve's favorites was spending his birthday at the aquarium. They would look at all of the mammals and fish, watch the dolphin show, and then have dinner right at the aquarium. The routine and expectation were good for Steve. It was a necessary constant in his life year after year.

Another tradition that Matthew created was taking trips. Matthew wanted Steve to be exposed to other cultures and languages, so he made sure that they went to a different country each year. They ate exotic foods, tried to speak to the natives wherever they were, and went to all of the places of interest. These trips made Matthew and Steve very close and helped Steve mature into a well-rounded young man.

Steve was particularly enthralled by their trip to Southeast Asia. He was fascinated by the traditions. He loved touring the temples, and he thoroughly enjoyed the traditional dances and music.

Matthew was so happy to see Steve take such a huge interest in a culture so different from their own. He hoped that this experience would help to mold Steve as he evolved.

21

Summer Travel

About ten days before the Fourth of July, Judy walked out of Travel Time with an itinerary and all the other documents she needed to go to Europe and parts of Asia. She was starting to get really excited, but it was bittersweet. Maddie's cancer was progressing, and this scared Judy.

She entered Maddie's apartment and found Maddie with her head over the toilet.

Aunt Maddie, are you okay?

Not at the moment, hon, but I will be. Did you get all of the paperwork?

Yup, but…

There was a hesitation in her voice.

What? Maddie asked.

I'm having second thoughts. I don't want to leave you.

Listen girl, you're getting on that plane in five days and flying to London come hell or high water. Do you feel me?

Yes. Judy silently laughed. Maddie was probably the coolest person she had ever met.

But, Maddie.

No buts. This is a chance of a lifetime. Don't worry. I'll be right here waitin for you when you get back. I am going to fight this cancer with everything I've got. I'm not ready to leave this world, believe me.

They hugged and cried a little.

Okay, Judy said. I'm going to go home and pack for this trip of a lifetime.

Okay, what's today? Oh yeah, Tuesday. I'll see you back here on Sunday. We'll go to the airport together. We should leave the apartment at around 3:30 for JFK.

It's a plan, said Judy. See you Sunday.

Judy kissed her aunt goodbye and headed back upstate to get ready.

The few days there flew by.

On Sunday morning, Judy loaded her car with suitcases, locked her apartment door, and drove to Manhattan. She made really good time, probably because so many people had already left the area to celebrate the 4th somewhere else.

As Judy entered Maddie's apartment, she felt some trepidation.

I'm here, she called out.

Maddie came out of the bedroom.

She looked pretty good.

You look much better, Maddie.

I'm feeling better than the last time you saw me. Fingers crossed. Let's get some lunch and then we'll come back and head to the airport.

After lunch, Judy and her aunt headed back to the apartment to freshen up.

Judy brushed her hair and her teeth in preparation for an all-night flight to London. What she didn't realize was that Maddie had called Jessica and told her to book Judy first class all the way.

Hey, Judy, you ready? called Maddie from the living room.

Yes. Judy walked out of the bathroom looking pretty excited.

Now remember your promise to me. You have to call me each night and describe your day.

I promise, said Judy. They hugged, and Judy whispered, thank you, Aunt Maddie. I'm so glad we got to know each other.

Me too, honey, me too.

They carried Judy's luggage down to the street where a limo

was waiting at the curb.

Aunt Maddie!

Hush – my niece is going in style. Don't fight it. Enjoy it.

The limo ride was a blast, and they were at the airport in no time.

There were more hugs as Judy got out and a few more tears.

I'll see you in four weeks, Aunt Maddie.

You bet your ass you will, oh, and Judy, I've hired a personal guide for you to take you all around Europe. Her name is Catherine, and she will find you at the hotel. Give her my love.

Judy headed into JFK and turned back to see Maddie leaning against the limo waving.

Judy blew her a kiss.

The airport was bustling with the so many travelers going here and there.

Wow! Judy thought.

The energy was palpable. So many people going to so many places. And all of the different languages...she recognized Spanish, Italian, and a little French, but the Asian languages sounded like a jumble. Then she saw a group who might have been speaking a Slavic language.

Communication is so interesting, she thought.

Judy got on the check in line at British Airways and checked two suitcases. She then went through security, taking off her shoes and jacket. All was going relatively smoothly.

On the other side of security, she checked the clock. Okay, she thought. I have about an hour and a half. I'm going to get something to eat and then go to the gate.

The restaurant choices were quite amazing. This wasn't her idea of what an airport would be like, but she actually felt kind of sophisticated.

She then remembered Aunt Maddie telling her to exchange some money at the airport for the variety of countries she was going to.

She said, most countries happily take the American dollar, but it's not a bad idea to have some local currency in your pocket. So Judy went over to the exchange counter and got a bunch of very funny looking coins and paper money. This is already a fascinating experience! she said to herself.

She thanked the teller and found a little café near her gate. Judy ordered a tuna melt and club soda. She figured she would get something else after eating to take with her on the plane. She really didn't know what to expect, but that made it fun.

Once she finished, she went to the ladies' room to freshen up and then sat down at the gate.

She had about 30 minutes till boarding. While looking around at the other passengers who would be taking this flight to London, she wondered. Were they going for business, pleasure? Did they have families? Were they rich, poor?

She began constructing stories about certain people. Who would meet a long-lost lover by chance at the theatre in London and have a wild affair? Who was planning a meeting with the Queen? Who was desperately trying to find himself by leaving everything he ever knew behind?

A British accent blared from above.

Flight BA112 to London Heathrow will be boarding in approximately ten minutes. Please have your boarding pass accessible. Thank you.

Judy was feeling more and more international and realized that she had lived a relatively sheltered and simple life.

There was nothing wrong with that, she thought, but there's a whole big world out there, and here I come!

She got up and got on the line to board. Her heart was racing.

Deep breaths, deep breaths, she whispered to her self.

She handed her boarding pass to the flight assistant and heard her say, enjoy your trip.

Thanks, Judy responded.

She walked down the jet way and stepped onto the plane.

What is your seat number, please? The flight attendant asked in a British accent.

Judy showed her her boarding pass.

Follow me.

They walked just a few steps, and the flight attendant pointed to a seat by the window in the third row.

Judy looked confused. Are you sure? she asked.

Yes, the flight attendant replied. Why?

I didn't know I was in first…Judy realized how stupid she must have sounded. Never mind, thank you.

She sat down and tried to take it all in.

Aunt Maddie, she thought. She really is special!

Judy watched as the other passengers boarded. There was a seat in between her and the aisle seat where a business-type looking man sat down, opened his laptop, and began working even before they had taken off.

Once in flight, exhaustion took over. Judy hadn't realized how much adrenaline she was burning. She pushed her seat back, and to her delight, a foot rest popped up. She was given a blanket and a pillow and was asleep within five minutes.

After about two hours, she was awakened by the flight attendant.

Would you care for some tea and dinner?

Sure, Judy said sleepily.

She was served a beautiful meal. It was quite delicious.

She thought to herself, yeah, I could get used to this.

Once done and cleaned up, Judy closed her eyes again.

The plane landed a little before seven am England time, and Judy wanted to try to stay up till bedtime and hope her body adjusted.

She went through Customs, and then grabbed her suitcases and a taxi. The Wellesley, please.

Yes mum, toot sweet.

Once there, the Concierge helped Judy with her luggage. She was already beginning to regret how much she had packed. The saving grace was that wherever she went, her aunt knew there would be people to assist.

As she entered the hotel, she almost dropped. It was spectacular with its chandeliers and marble everywhere.

Wow!!

The concierge smiled.

Judy blushed. No worries, mum. We get that a lot.

Judy chuckled. She realized she couldn't help who she was, so why not just enjoy the experience.

Once in her room, she unpacked and showered. It was mid-morning England time, so she dressed and headed downstairs to look for a map.

As she was wandering the lobby, she was approached by a woman who seemed to know her.

Judy? she asked in a British accent.

Yes?

Good day. My name is Catherine, and I've been hired by your Aunt Maddie to show you around England. How was your trip?

It's nice to meet you, Catherine. I have to admit, I'm a little bit relieved. I wasn't quite sure what to do or where to begin.

No worries, Catherine said with a smile. Leave it up to me. It's a bit early for lunch. Are you up for a bit of touring?

Yes, that sounds great.

Okay, then we'll plan out an itinerary and then get some fish and chips. If it's okay with you, I'll be your guide all around Europe.

Oh, yes please. That would be fantastic! Oh, by the way, my Aunt Maddie sends her love.

Judy felt really comfortable with Catherine and was happy to have someone take charge of the traveling.

They walked out of the lobby of the hotel, and Judy felt like she was having an awakening.

Catherine told her to just soak it all in and feel free to ask any questions that might come to mind.

I'm at your service, she said with just a slight curtsy.

They walked around Knightsbridge for a little while and then down a block to a local pub and ordered two plates of fish and chips with vinegar.

Judy looked skeptical.

Give it a try. It's simply the best!

Judy heard her mom's voice in her head – put your big girl pants on.

One bite, and Judy was hooked.

Oh my God!!

Catherine gave her a huge grin.

Do you know the origin of the pubs?

No, Judy said with interest. She loved learning factoids.

Back long ago, it wasn't proper to have liquor in the home, so each street corner had what was called a Public House where folks could gather to have a pint and socialize. This was then shortened to the word pub.

They ate and talked – getting to know a little about each other and what Judy hoped to do and see while in Europe.

Catherine suggested that they start right away so that they could get it all in. They would have about ten days to cover a lot of territory. They started walking and went all around London. They saw Buckingham Palace, Piccadilly Circus, London Tower, the Thames, Harrod's and more. It was a whirlwind.

They found a local type of a restaurant for dinner and a pint.

Catherine dropped Judy back at the hotel.

I'll see you tomorrow morning. Nine too early? I was thinking we would head south west to Stonehenge and parts and then the day after, we could make our way to Canterbury and Dover if that sounds okay?

I am happy to go wherever you think.

Tally ho, Judy

Tally ho, Catherine.

Judy walked through the lobby of the Wellesley. She wasn't ready to pack it in so decided to sit for a bit and do some people watching. She pulled out her phone and figured out the time in New York. It would be around one am, but she promised her aunt so gave her a call.

Maddie picked up right away. I'm so glad you called. I've been on pins and needles waiting.

Sorry it's late, Aunt Maddie. Do you want me to call you tomorrow?

Are you out of your mind? Tell me everything.

Judy talked about JFK, the flight, the hotel, Catherine, and the day.

If I died right now, I would feel content. Aunt Maddie, my only regret is that you're not here with me.

I know, honey. I feel the same, but I'm glad you like Catherine. She was my guide a few years ago, so I knew she'd be great for you. Send her my love and tell her I expect her to take very good care of you.

I will.

Okay, I'll await your call tomorrow. Have a great second day, kiddo.

Judy felt tears coming but choked them back. I love you.

I love you too, Judy.

She heard the phone click and suspected Maddie was struggling from the same "teary eyes" syndrome.

Judy sat for a while and listened to the pianist across the lobby in the corner. She felt so fortunate and sophisticated.

Maybe I should pinch myself, she thought.

Instead, she went into the bar and ordered a pint and enjoyed the music.

By eight, her body was clearly telling her it was time to go to sleep. Between the travel, the alcohol, and the touring, she was really done.

She hit the pillow hard and was glad she thought to set her alarm for eight because she could have easily slept through.

Next morning, Catherine was in the lobby at nine.

Good morning, sunshine. How'd you sleep?

Like a rock.

Have you eaten?

No, Judy said. I wasn't sure what the plan was.

Okay, let's have some breakfast, and we'll hit the road.

They ate in the hotel's restaurant. Judy couldn't get enough, but what the hell, she thought.

They left by ten and got in Catherine's car to head to Stonehenge.

The drive will take about two hours, but if you want to stop at any point, just let me know.

Judy was enthralled with the countryside.

This is a really beautiful country, Catherine.

Yes, I agree.

They stopped in some of the little towns along the way and wandered a bit.

They arrived at Stonehenge by about 1:00. Judy was once again amazed. Catherine gave her a full tour and told her the history and belief behind this really unique rock formation.

How did I get through my sheltered life? Judy thought. This is such a huge world with so much to see and learn.

They lunched nearby and then got in the car.

Catherine drove to the Close where they walked around for a few minutes. She then took Judy to Arundells. After that, they headed to the Salisbury Museum and then did some shopping at Fisherton Mill. At that point, Judy felt she should call Maddie. She didn't want her to wait up again.

Hey, Judy, so how's your second day going?

Fantastic! Catherine and I went to Stonehenge and then toured some cathedrals and a museum. We've just finished some shopping at Fisherton Mill in Salisbury and are going to get something to eat at a wine and cheese bar. Oh, Aunt Maddie, there aren't words. Do you want to say hi to Catherine?

Sure, put her on.

Hi, Maddie, how are things in New York?

Things are pretty good here, my dear. When are you coming for a visit?

Oh, I hope to in the next couple of years. Will you be my tour guide?

It would be my pleasure.

Maddie, it's been lovely talking.

Catherine handed the phone back to Judy.

Hi, Maddie. Tomorrow I will check out of the Wellesley, and we'll go down to Dover and across to France. I'll talk to you tomorrow, okay?

It's a date, my love.

They hung up, and Catherine and Judy ended the tour at Maul's Wine and Cheese Bar.

Another fabulous day, Judy said.

Let's head back to London, Catherine suggested. We've got a two hour drive ahead of us and a pretty full day tomorrow.

They arrived back at the hotel at about nine that night.

Judy went straight to bed.

In the morning, she checked out and met the concierge in the lobby. He put her luggage in Catherine's car, and they were off to Canterbury.

The entire day was great. Judy couldn't get over the architecture in Canterbury and was thrilled to be standing in the place of Chaucer's great work.

The beauty of the White Cliffs of Dover was incredible, and Judy was speechless when they toured a castle.

They then drove onto the ferry which took them to Calais. As they left England, Judy stared out at the cliffs. She felt as if she could live in each place they had been. She was so comfortable.

This has got to be a dream, she thought.

Once in France, they headed to Paris. Judy was sad to leave England but really excited to see France and the rest of Europe. The two girls drove down to Paris. The sun was just beginning to set as they entered the city of romance. It was breathtaking! They checked into the Radisson Blu Hotel Champ-Elysees and walked out to get some dinner. The night air was warm, and the energy in Paris was indescribable.

Catherine and Judy found a little café about three blocks from the hotel. This was Judy's first true French meal, and she loved it! They had baguette with cheeses, escargot, frites, and a chocolate mousse that Judy would dream about for years to come.

They decided they had better do some walking or they wouldn't be able to fit into their clothes the next day, so they rambled along the River Seine looking over at the Eiffel Tower and watching lovers kiss and stroll hand in hand.

Back at the hotel, they sat in the lobby and planned. They would see the Eiffel Tower up close, the Louvre, and some other sights before heading out of Paris toward Belgium.

They went up to their suite and wished each other a good night.

Judy slept like a baby. She was so content. She loved spending this time with Catherine and anticipated each day and its adventures.

The next day, the two girls had breakfast and bid adieu to Paris. They drove through really quaint little French towns, stopping along the way to shop and sight see here and there. They got to Belgium by late afternoon and found the bed and breakfast where they would spend the night.

Then, it was time to party a little, so after dinner, they found a very cool nightclub where the beer was flowing, and the music was blaring. People from all over the world were speaking in a multitude of languages, but they were all enjoying dancing - a universal language, thought Judy.

A local guy came over to Judy and asked her to dance. Catherine winked at her as if to say, go ahead, I've got your back.

Judy really had the best time. They didn't get to the B&B until well after midnight, but it was okay. They slept in the next day and then went sightseeing around Belgium.

They were then off to Germany, Switzerland and finally, Italy. Each country was more fantastic and exciting.

They hiked through the Black Forest in Germany, climbed an alp in Switzerland, and toured the cities of Italy. Each afternoon, Judy called her aunt.

Well, Maddie, today I climbed an alp.

You don't hear those words very often, chuckled Maddie.

Maddie, it was amazing! We drove up to a spot that leveled off. There was a small park area and a café. We started walking up on the grass. It was about seventy-five degrees. About four or five yards up, there was snow. We were hiking in the snow in shorts and t's. I turned around and looked out. Maddie, I was literally on top of the world. What an experience! I just don't have the words to describe the trip.

Catherine bid farewell to Judy at the Rome International Airport. She had to drive back to London, and Judy was heading to China and Indonesia. They hugged and exchanged contact information. Judy hoped that Catherine would remain a friend. It had been so easy spending time with her.

Judy checked her luggage at the British Airways desk and headed for security. She got to the gate with about forty minutes to spare and so sat and processed her European trip.

She couldn't imagine it getting any better, but she was looking forward to seeing parts of Asia.

22
Asia

Judy landed in Taiwan in the late afternoon. She picked up her baggage at carousel number three. As she walked through the airport, she looked for her guide. She just assumed. Finally, she saw a group waving at her.

Are you Judy?

Yes, hi

We think you're with us.

There were three couples and two other women, perhaps also a couple? They were all older than Judy.

I don't know, said Judy.

The tour guide came over to the group.

Okay, are we all here? he asked in broken English.

Judy asked if he had her name on the sheet.

Judy, Judy Tanner, yes, right here.

Okay. She realized she would be traveling with a group this part of the trip. This could be interesting. Actually, she thought, it will give her more time for self-reflection and some alone time.

So off they went. They all traveled together in a microbus. Since Judy was solo, she sat up in the front seat with the tour guide/driver. It was pretty comfortable.

At the Mandarin Oriental Hotel, the tour guide told them they had the rest of the day to themselves and he would pick them up at nine am.

As Judy's group dispersed, she got a sudden pang of anxiety. She felt very alone.

Who would she eat with? Who would she talk to? Big girl pants, Judy, big girl pants.

She went up to her room and took a deep breath. She didn't feel like napping, so she showered and went back down to the lobby to create a plan for the evening. She found the concierge, an older man, and asked if he could recommend a nice Taiwanese restaurant. He looked at her a bit alarmed.

Where is your companion? he asked.

Judy was confused.

What do you mean?

It's not proper for a young lady to go out at night alone.

Is this guy for real? she thought.

Ohhhh, she said with a smile. You're joking, right?

The man looked offended.

Not joking. Proper lady should have proper escort.

Judy wasn't sure how to respond.

Well, I am here alone, so I will escort myself. Please call me a taxi, Judy said emphatically. Thank you.

The concierge shrugged his shoulders and went outside and hailed a taxi. He held the door for Judy.

Thank you, she said, a bit exasperated.

In the cab, Judy asked for a nice Taiwanese restaurant recommendation. She figured when in Rome...

The cab driver had a little bit of English and recommended Din Tai Fung.

Okay, Judy said. Let's try it.

The drive was quick.

As Judy paid him, she said, Xie' xie'.

Bu' ke' qi, he responded.

As she walked into the restaurant, she said to herself, you go girl! Look at you, speaking Chinese in Taiwan.

Huan ying. You duo shao?

Judy looked at the host.

Ok, ok. How many?

Oh, Judy said. It's just me tonight.

This way.

They walked across the dining room which was humming with conversation in a variety of languages. The host offered her a seat at a table for two and went back to the front of the restaurant. Within minutes, a waiter came over.

You have partner?

No, Judy responded. It's just me.

The waiter cleared the second setting and gave her a menu. Fortunately, everything was listed in both Chinese and English.

Oh, thank God, Judy said under her breath.

She perused through the menu and realized that she was pretty hungry.

The waiter returned. You ready?

Yes. May I have boiled vegetable dumplings and rice noodle with shrimp and broccoli?

To drink?

Do you have club soda?

No response

Seltzer?

Oh, sure.

The waiter walked away leaving Judy alone.

Okay, you can do this, she mouthed to herself.

She watched the other diners around her and noticed that there were a few others eating alone.

The dumplings came within just a few minutes, and they were delicious! Judy had never tasted anything like them. She could hardly contain herself from inhaling them. It must have been pretty obvious.

You really like those dumplings, huh?

She looked up.

I noticed you were sitting alone and thought how sad for such a pretty young woman to be alone.

Judy continued to stare at this guy who was standing at her table. She wasn't sure what to do. She didn't really know about social mores in Taiwan and didn't have any romantic experience to speak of anyway.

Hello? she said.

I'm sorry, he said. How rude of me.

He held out his hand. I'm Vihaan; lovely to meet you.

Judy noticed a British accent.

With a mouth full of dumpling and her hand over her mouth, she mumbled, Judy.

Vihaan smiled. Would you mind terribly if I joined you?

Judy could only nod. She figured there were enough people in the restaurant that she would be safe, and she was happy to have the company. She observed Vihaan. He was slender but athletic with beautiful olive skin and big brown eyes. He had a charm about him that portrayed culture and education.

Vihaan sat down and waved a hand in the air. The waiter came right over and set a place.

Have you been in Taiwan long? he asked Judy.

By now, Judy had finished chewing.

I just got here this afternoon.

First time?

Mmmhmmm.

You?

I'm just traveling around while on break.

What are you taking a break from?

School.

May I ask you a personal question?

Of course.

Is that a British accent?

You have a good ear. Yes, it is. I'm studying in England.

Oh, I just came from England.

Really? What part?

London, Canterbury, and Dover. I really loved it!

Where are you studying?

I'm at Oxford.

Wow! That's impressive.

How about you, Judy?

I just graduated from high school. I'm going to attend Columbia next month.

This is also quite impressive.

Judy liked Vihaan's accent. He sounded so scholarly.

What are you studying, Vihaan?

Law.

Also very impressive. Do you like it?

That is an interesting question.

Do you have an interesting answer?

Vihaan laughed.

The waiter then brought Judy's dinner.

May I take your order, please?

Vihaan, would you like to share my dinner? This is way more than I'll ever eat, and I can't take it home with me.

I would love to, said Vihaan. He looked at the waiter and asked for another plate and a Windmills.

What's a Windmills?

It's a dark Indian beer – very popular there.

Ohhh. Where is there?

In India, where I'm from.

The waiter placed an empty plate in front of Vihaan.

Thank you.

Judy passed her plate across the table. Help yourself.

You have a very generous nature, Judy.

I also ate too many dumplings.

They both laughed.

Judy liked Vihaan's laugh. It felt sincere.

So, Vihaan, why did you come over to my table?

Well, I walked in to have a drink at the bar, having just come from a concert and noticed you sitting here by yourself. Frankly, you looked a bit uncomfortable, so …

Oh, so this is a pity visit?

A pity visit?

You know, you felt sorry for me?

I see. Well, partly, I guess, but something else drew me to you.

Hmmm, should I be afraid?

Vihaan laughed so loudly that some of the other diners turned to see what was happening in the back corner.

Tell me about Judy.

Judy was having a nice time, and she wasn't in the mood to go into her long and sad life story.

I'd rather not, if you don't mind.

Okay, keeping some mystery. That's fair. Are you going to be in Taiwan for a while?

Just a week. Then I'm flying to Bali. Have you been there?

Oh yes, it's beautiful!

They ate and talked for the next two hours.

Judy looked at her watch. I have to get back to the hotel. I have an early tour.

Where are you staying?

Judy wasn't sure if she should tell Vihaan, although she figured if she stayed where there were people, she would be okay.

I'm at the Mandarin Oriental Hotel. Do you know it?

Yes, I am actually staying there as well.

Come on, Judy said in disbelief.

I am, said Vihaan. Really. May I give you a ride back?

Ohh, I don't know. Thank you, but I think I'll take a cab.

Please allow me to escort you. It's only proper.

Judy remembered the concierge.

You're the second person tonight to say that to me.

The first must be a true traditional gentleman, responded Vihaan.

I thought he was being an old fashioned fuddy duddy.

A what?

Never mind.

Shall we?

Oh, just a moment. I need to pay the check.

It's been taken care of.

Oh, that's not necessary.

Judy, it's my pleasure.

Well, thank you very much. The food was really excellent, and the company wasn't so bad either.

Well, thank you very much, replied Vihaan with a smile.

As they walked out of the restaurant, the host bowed to Vihaan and thanked him for his business.

Judy was fascinated. Why did the host bow to you?

I'll tell you later.

Outside, the air felt so warm, and there was still a lot of bustle. Judy looked to her right and noticed a market.

Would you like to walk through the night market? Vihaan asked.

I would, said Judy.

They headed down the street and entered a tented type of area.

This is like a flea market, he explained.

There were all kinds of things for sale from jewelry to a variety of foods, clothing, and so much more.

After a while, Judy told Vihaan she was starting to feel pretty travel weary.

I think the flight from Rome is catching up with me. If it's okay with you, I need to go back to the hotel.

Absolutely. Vihaan raised a hand, and within seconds, a limo pulled up down the road.

After you. Vihaan opened the back door.

Judy thought to herself, this is really a limo level trip – how nice!

Okay, Judy said. You need to give me some deets.

Deets? Vihaan looked confused.

Details. I am dying of curiosity right now.

What are you doing tomorrow, Judy?

Ohhh, I have the tour with the group at nine.

Allow me to give you a tour. We can go anywhere you'd like, and you can sleep a little later.

Can this be for real? Judy thought. Her New York instincts were kicking in.

I don't know, Vihaan. We just met. I hardly know you, although the sleeping later is tempting.

I'll take care of everything. What's the name of your tour

group?

Collette Small.

Done.

Vihaan then spoke to the driver in what Judy assumed was Chinese.

Okay, Judy thought. Why not?

Okay, Vihaan. I'm going to take a chance on you and accept your offer. You won't do me any harm, will you?

Absolutely not.

By now, they were at the hotel. Vihaan spoke to the driver again.

Vihaan then got out and walked around to open Judy's door.

They walked into the hotel.

The concierge bowed. Good evening, Dian Xia.

Judy looked at Vihaan.

What did he just say, Vihaan?

I'll tell you tomorrow. Shall we meet in the lobby at eleven for brunch?

I like the way you think. Thank you again for a really nice evening. I'm glad you took pity on me. Judy smiled.

As am I. Vihaan smiled back. Sweet dreams, as they say.

Same, Judy said as she got into the elevator.

She hit the button for the fourth floor and waved as the door closed.

Judy entered her room and noticed she was smiling.

She was happy, and it felt really good. She liked Vihaan. She had no expectations, and there was mystery about him. She was definitely having an adventure, and it was exciting and international. Life was good.

The next morning, she got up at about nine-thirty, showered and dressed, then called her aunt.

Good morning, she sang into the phone.

Good morning to you, Judy. Why do you sound high?

I am high, Aunt Maddie. I'm high on life.

Okay, said Maddie. Tell me everything.

Judy gave Maddie the details of the night before.

Wow! Sounds like you've met your Prince Charming.

They both laughed.

Have a wonderful time today. I can't wait to hear all about it tomorrow.

I love you, Maddie.

I love you too, my niece.

At 10:45, Judy went down to the lobby. She half expected that Vihaan wouldn't show – maybe it was her New York skepticism. She created a story in her head that she would have to spend the day on her own. She should have stuck with the group. Why is she so naïve? She shouldn't just trust the way she does. How stupid could she be? He was thinking she's so sophisticated. Boy, what a fool!

She hopped up out of the chair to go back to her room.

Where are you headed?

She turned to see Vihaan coming into the hotel with a bouquet.

Hi, Judy said with surprise in her voice.

Good morning, Vihaan said. These are for you.

Vihaan bowed as he handed Judy the bouquet.

Judy stood stunned. She felt very ridiculous for letting her insecurity get the best of her.

Thank you, Vihaan. They're really beautiful! And I didn't get you anything.

Not to worry. Are you hungry?

Yes, Judy said. She decided to make a conscious effort to keep her head drama to a minimum.

Let's get some brunch and then go touring. It's a gorgeous day.

In the hotel's restaurant, they ate and talked and laughed.

We have a nice chemistry, Judy thought to herself. And, Vihaan is actually pretty cute.

What are you thinking about, Judy?

Oh, not much. Just wondering what we'll see today.

Well, no need to wonder any longer. If you would allow me to, I would like to be your host on an overnight stay to Sun Moon

Lake. The drive takes a little over four hours, but I thought we could stop along the way to see the different towns.

Judy thought for a moment and decided this is probably a chance of a lifetime.

I'm in, she said. I'll just run up to my room and pack a bag. I'll meet you here in the lobby in twenty minutes.

Judy grabbed a few things, hardly paying attention to what she was doing.

Is this really happening? Am I being stupid? But it feels right. I think it'll be okay.

She headed down to the lobby. Vihaan was waiting for her by the entrance.

A man in a black suit walked in behind Vihaan and took Judy's bag.

Vihaan could tell that Judy was a little uncertain. It's okay, said Vihaan. He's my driver.

They stepped out of the hotel, and the sun hit Judy with the warmest, most comforting rays she had ever felt.

This must be right. It sure feels right, she thought to herself.

Wow! What a day! she exclaimed.

The man in the suit held the door for Judy and then walked around to the other side of the car and held the door for Vihaan.

Vihaan spoke to the man in Chinese, and the limo pulled out onto the road.

Okay, Judy said. It's tomorrow.

Vihaan looked at her with confusion.

You told me you would explain some of the things that are going on tomorrow, and it's tomorrow.

Ohhh, Vihaan laughed. You're right, I did. Well, where to start...

Start at the beginning.

Okay. My name is Vihaan Singh. I am of the Mewar Family from Rajasthan, India. My family is one of eight royal families. They own many hotels and resorts.

Judy was staring at him.

Are you making this up? The next thing you're going to tell me is that you are a prince or something.

Not the something.

Get out of here, Judy pushed Vihaan's arm. His body jerked to the left and back.

Judy, why did you hit me?

That wasn't a hit. That was a push. I'm sorry, but I'm having trouble processing this. I am riding in the limo of a prince from India. That's what you're telling me right now?

Yes, that's right.

All righty then. Would somebody please pinch me?

What do you mean?

You know. When you think you're dreaming? When you can't believe your reality is your reality, you need someone to pinch you and wake you up.

I've never heard of that before, but I can assure you, you are very much awake.

Why me, Vihaan?

I'm not sure I understand your question, Judy.

You're a prince.

Yes, that's true.

So, you could be with any girl you want. Why me?

Oh, I see.

From the outside, one might think it's easy to be with girls, and it is, but many just want to be with me because I'm royalty. You didn't know anything about me and yet you invited me to sit down and shared your meal with me. I was very touched by your kindness and generosity. I could tell that you are genuine.

I guess I can understand that. I am sorry I pushed you, but you have to see it from my perspective. This is a lot to hear, and I'm just a gal from New York. I'm not rich or royal. I'm just a simple American.

Vihaan laughed and laughed. His laugh was contagious, and Judy began laughing. She actually laughed so hard, she cried.

Okay, Ms. Simple, I understand. There is no need to cry. Are you okay?

Judy took a few breaths. I'm fine. Oh boy, that felt good.

Vihaan handed her a handkerchief.

Thanks, Judy said while wiping her cheeks. That was really cathartic.

So, I don't think we could be more different, and yet, I feel really comfortable with you, Judy shared.

As I do with you.

Well, then, that's that. Let's just be comfortable with each other and have a nice time.

Vihaan leaned over and kissed Judy. It was like the feeling of Christmas and the Fourth of July rolled into one.

Was that ok, Judy?

That was very okay, said Judy. Wow!

They sat quietly while holding hands. The car sped along, and Judy realized she hadn't been paying any attention to the scenery, and frankly, she didn't care. What was happening in the limo was way more interesting. She was having some very real feelings already and didn't truly understand them.

Judy remembered being in twelfth grade when Willie Carson took her to the school dance. As he dropped her home, he kissed her, but then he tried to grope her. She pushed him back and told him she wasn't that kind of a girl.

Whatever, Willie said as he got in his car and left.

Jerk! Judy yelled as the car zoomed away.

She vowed then that she had no interest in boys – until now.

Vihaan was mature. He was a gentleman, and she was loving the attention.

After about two hours, Judy asked if they could stop to stretch their legs.

That's a good idea, said Vihaan.

They were in a little town. The driver parked on a side street, and Vihaan told him they would be back in about thirty minutes.

They walked to the main street and found a café.

Shall we have a drink?

Yes, that sounds good.

They ordered a couple of sodas and used the restroom.

Judy asked if they should bring the driver a drink.

Vihaan looked at her.

What a nice gesture. I will do that.

They went back to the limo and got back on the road. The driver was very appreciative of the drink and turned and smiled at the two of them before pulling out.

We have about two more hours. Tell me something about you now.

Judy started from the beginning and told Vihaan her whole story.

My, said Vihaan. You certainly haven't had an easy life.

No, that's true, said Judy, but you know what? I have been loved by my parents, by Kay, and now by my Aunt Maddie, and I feel very blessed for that.

Vihaan smiled at her. You are a really special person.

I think you're pretty special too.

Vihaan kissed Judy again, and they sat closer to each other, embracing.

23

Sun Moon Lake

They pulled into Sun Moon Lake at about four, jumped out of the limo and stretched. Vihaan thanked the driver and told him to return the morning after next. The driver bowed and left.

Judy stood and stared out over the lake. She had never seen anything so beautiful.

Vihaan came up from behind her and wrapped his arms around her. Do you believe in love at first sight?

Judy almost wet her pants.

Ummm, not really, but I am open to the possibility.

Vihaan laughed.

Well, I do, Ms. Simple, and I know the feelings I'm having are not whimsy.

Whimsy, said Judy. I like that word.

She turned around to face Vihaan and smiled. They kissed and embraced for what felt like a while. Then they stood looking at the lake.

Shall we check in and then take a walk?

That's a perfect idea, Vihaan.

The Sun Moon Lake Hotel was exquisite.

Judy looked panicked.

What's wrong?

I'm not sure I have the proper outfits for this place.

Okay, Vihaan said. Don't worry. We'll do a little shopping in the gift shop.

Judy pursed her lips and had to hold back tears. Are you sure I'm not dreaming you?

Vihaan said, I don't think so, but go ahead and pinch me if it makes you feel better.

Judy burst into laughter.

Not necessary, she replied.

They walked up to the reservation desk to check in.

I reserved a two-bedroom suite for us, Judy, if that's okay.

That sounds more than okay.

They got their room keys and went up to the penthouse suite.

Vihaan!

What's the matter?

You forgot to mention that the suite is the penthouse suite!

Oh, oops!

He raised his shoulders and smiled at her.

They both started laughing again until they were doubled over.

Once they finally composed themselves, they keyed into the suite.

Judy had to catch her breath. She couldn't believe where she was.

What do you think?

This is way better than the tour.

Well, I should hope so, Vihaan said.

Judy turned to Vihaan and whispered, thank you. She kissed him pretty passionately.

Let's go out on the veranda, he suggested.

The view of the lake was amazing. There was a light fog drifting just above the water giving it an almost eerie feel. They stood for a while, both losing themselves in the beauty.

Shall we walk?

Vihaan broke Judy's reverie.

She shook her head as if coming back to present. Yes.

They left the suite and went outside. They meandered around for about an hour then sat on a garden bench. Vihaan took

Judy's hand.

Judy, I don't want you to worry that I am some kind of a play-boy. I know that is the reputation of many royals. I haven't had a girlfriend in quite a while because I've been very focused on my studies. My parents wanted me to marry a girl from home, and she was nice, but I didn't have those kinds of feelings for her. It was then that I decided to move to England to study. I needed to separate from my family to figure out what I wanted. I must admit that I have some serious feelings for you already. I hope that doesn't intimidate you.

Judy looked at Vihaan.

I haven't ever had a serious relationship before, and this is moving very quickly, but frankly, it feels so right. I am really enjoying myself with you.

Vihaan smiled. I'm glad. I have never met anyone like you before. I think you are very special.

They hugged and rocked.

Judy just wanted to melt into his arms.

Vihaan suggested they get ready for dinner. We'll make a stop in the shop and get you some proper clothes.

Judy chose a couple of pretty dresses, not too fancy, and a pair of nice shoes with a heel. Vihaan had about six inches on her, so she could wear heels and still look up at him, which she liked.

Back in the suite, they each showered and dressed for dinner.

Judy put her hair up with just a few strands dangling down. She looked at herself in the mirror. She certainly wasn't model material, but she thought she had a nice look. She had always been pretty plain but put on a little blush and a lip gloss.

She walked out to the living room. Vihaan was there. Judy took a step back. Vihaan was dressed in a nice long sleeve shirt and slacks.

Man, is he good looking, Judy thought.

She smiled at him.

Judy, you look beautiful.

Thank you, Vihaan. So do you.

Hmmm, Vihaan responded. Shall we go?

Vihaan held out his arm, and Judy wrapped hers around his.

They entered the dining room and were greeted by the host. Dian xia, the host said as he bowed to Vihaan, and showed the couple to a table raised up on a slight platform.

This is nice, Judy said. What do the hosts keep saying to you when they bow?

Your highness.

Ohh, said Judy awkwardly.

Does it make you uncomfortable?

I'm not sure, she said.

You'll get used to it.

Judy smiled. Okay, she thought to herself. That's future talk – interesting.

Would you care for a drink, Judy? Perhaps some red wine?

Sure, Judy said. She was up for a new experience.

Vihaan raised his hand, and the waiter came over. We'd like a bottle of Chateau Lafita Rothschild, please.

Wow! That sounds fancy.

Once the wine was approved and poured, Vihaan asked Judy if she minded if he ordered for them. He ordered a dumpling appetizer and shrimp with rice noodles.

The meal was extraordinary. Judy ate way too much.

The two drank and ate and laughed and talked. Judy didn't want the night to end.

They made their way back to the suite and sat out on the veranda. The moon was full and shone brilliantly over the lake.

This is like a fairy tale, Judy whispered.

Judy?

Vihaan?

Would you like to share my bed?

Oh boy, Judy thought. That awkward moment. Judy was grateful for the amount of alcohol she had consumed at dinner.

I have actually never had sex before.

She felt herself blushing.

I understand.

But, I think I'm ready.

Are you sure? Why don't we see where the night takes us?

They showered and got into Vihaan's bed. They lay naked next to each other stroking and kissing. Judy felt very excited.

Oh Vihaan, this feels amazing.

Vihaan kissed Judy on her forehead, then her cheeks and lips. He kissed her breasts and stomach and the inside of her thighs. Judy thought she would explode!

He then looked up at her.

They looked into each other's eyes and melded into each other.

Vihaan was so gentle and loving. Judy knew that this moment would remain with her forever.

They fell asleep, spooning.

The sun shone brightly through the bedroom window, and Judy awoke to the sound of a tropical bird in the tree below.

Good morning, she heard Vihaan whisper. She realized he had been watching her.

Good morning, she said sleepily.

How are you this morning?

Man, she thought, he is chipper in the morning.

Having lived alone for the past year or so, Judy wasn't used to morning conversation.

I'm great, she said. How about you?

I'm feeling quite well.

Vihaan leaned over Judy and kissed her. She remembered some of the passion of the night before, but the alcohol had definitely been an influence.

Vihaan wrapped himself around Judy, and she felt the stirrings again.

They made love – she noticed that the morning sex was different from the night before but still really nice!

After a few minutes, Vihaan spoke.

I really enjoy being with you.

And I do too.

Would you like to spend the day on the lake?

Ohhh, that sounds great!

Vihaan rolled over and picked up the suite phone. He ordered breakfast for two and a boat with a captain to launch at eleven.

Done, he said.

Judy had to admit it was nice having the world at your fingertips. She had never had to worry about paying the rent, but this lifestyle was on a completely different level. She could only imagine what his home life was like. Opulence is one word that came to mind. But he certainly was humble and very sweet.

Judy got out of bed and took a shower. While dressing, she heard voices in the living room.

Must be breakfast, she thought.

When she came out, Vihaan was a speaking to a man who didn't look like hotel staff, and it was clearly not Chinese. They quickly ended their conversation, and the man left when Judy walked in.

Everything ok, Vihaan?

Judy felt a little bit uncomfortable.

Yes, fine.

Vihaan was short and went into his room without elaborating.

Judy stood in the middle of the room wondering what to do. Where was the charming, self-confidant Vihaan she knew?

She knocked on his door.

Vihaan? Are you okay?

Yes, Judy. I'll be out in a minute.

Judy left it at that.

She turned and took a juice out of the mini bar when she heard a knock at the door.

Would you get that, Judy? It's breakfast, Vihaan yelled from behind his door.

Judy opened the door and watched the waiter bring in a cart with more food than she could ever imagine eating. There was a single red rose in a bud vase. She signed for the meal and thanked the waiter. Xie' xie', she said.

The waiter bowed. Xie' xie'.

He left the room, and Judy called to Vihaan.

Are you hungry? Breakfast is served.

Vihaan came out dressed for the day. Judy sensed some tension.

Hi? she said.

She looked at Vihaan, who was clearly perturbed.

I owe you an apology. The man who was here was sent by my family back home. They have summoned me to return. Some family business. I was so hoping to spend much more time with you.

Ohh, well, family is important. I understand.

They ate in silence, and Judy was feeling a whole lot of mixed feelings. She had a little talk with herself in her head.

Meeting Vihaan was great. What were you thinking; he was going to get down on one knee and propose? You would live the rest of your life as an Indian princess? Nice fantasy, but you have Columbia in a few weeks and your Aunt Maddie to watch over. Chalk it up to a very cool international experience.

So, Vihaan, when do you need to leave?

This afternoon. My sister is marrying – it's an arrangement, and

He stopped short.

I've just had a thought. Come with me, Judy. You can meet my family.

Vihaan suddenly came back to life.

Oh, Vihaan. I don't know. I'm supposed to be in Bali in a few days.

Not a problem. We'll attend the wedding, and I'll fly you to Bali.

Is this guy for real? He has every single resource at his disposal.

Could I give this some thought for a few minutes?

Sure, of course, Judy. I almost forgot that we just met. I feel so comfortable with you, and I don't want our time together to end.

That was really sweet, she thought to herself.

Would your family mind my coming to your sister's wedding?

I will prepare them. They'll love you.

I'm going to call my aunt and talk it out with her. I'll be back in a bit.

Judy went into her bedroom and called Maddie.

Hi, hon. So tell me everything.

Judy gave Maddie the highlights and then got to the part about going to India.

Okay, well, how do you feel about all of this?

I like him, Maddie. And it would be a fascinating experience.

It sounds like you've made a decision. Go for it. Take lots of pictures and call me when you get there.

I love you, Maddie.

I love you too, my princess. They both chuckled and hung up.

Judy found Vihaan picking at some eggs in the living room.

Okay, Vihaan. I'll be your date if you still want me to.

Vihaan lit up. That's great! I will call my parents and let them know. Oh, I'm sorry about the boat ride. I owe you a ride around Sun Moon Lake.

Deal, Judy said. She smiled, but there was a little bit of anxiety behind it.

Vihaan?

Yes?

I only brought a few casual things for this trip. I was expecting that we would be back at the hotel by tomorrow.

Not a problem at all. We don't leave until seven tonight for India. Let's go shopping.

Do I need a plane ticket?

No. We will be flying in my family's jet.

Of course we will, thought Judy.

Vihaan excused himself to call home. He was gone for about fifteen minutes, so Judy picked at the breakfast.

Okay, he said when he returned. All is set.

Okay, Judy said. Then I guess we're going to a wedding.

They headed out of the hotel and into the shops around the lake. Judy allowed Vihaan to select some clothes for her based on what she would need for the different occasions during their few days in India.

We'll get you some traditional clothing once we are home.

Hmmm, once we're home? Okay, Judy, don't overthink this. What about my stuff at the hotel?

I will have my driver pick up your luggage and meet us at the plane.

Judy couldn't get over having so many people to do for them. It really is convenient, she thought.

Once back at the hotel, Vihaan told her he needed to talk.

Okay, said Judy. What's up?

Well, this is a bit awkward.

Just go fo it, Vihaan. Jeez, she thought. We've just slept together and now you're taking me to meet your royal family on the family jet.

I would like to review some proper etiquette.

Okay.

So, guests are treated with a great amount of respect in India. Have you heard the word Namaste?

Yes, sure.

When you meet my family, each member will put their hands together in front of their chest and bow while saying, Khamaghani. This is the Rajasthani way of greeting. It is similar to saying Namaste, but because my family is descended from the Mewar Empire, a different dialect is used. Khamaghani means 'many greetings' in the local dialect, and it is accompanied by the gesture of folding hands in front of one's chest and bending at the waist. In the days of Maharajas, the expression was used to greet the royals as well as friends. It still holds an important place in the heart of my people, and we prefer it over saying Namaste, which is more common in the other parts of the country. My people are from Rajasthan state in western India, and traditions are similar but not exactly the same as in the other parts of India.

To each family member you meet, simply do the same. Shall we practice?

I'm feeling a little bit nervous. I don't want to do the wrong thing.

Not to worry. I will not leave your side. You are going to be greeted and fawned over.

They faced each other and, with palms together, bowed and said, Khamaghani.

Judy put the word in her phone so that she could practice during the flight.

Perhaps we should have some lunch and then rest for a while. The plane will leave at seven, and the flight takes about six hours. It will be four-thirty when we arrive, and our drive is only thirty minutes to the compound.

Judy started to panic a little. What was she getting herself into? This all sounded good, but she didn't really know Vihaan that well and suddenly, she is going to be immersed in his family life, language, culture. Talk about jumping in with both feet.

They found a little restaurant on the lake. It was so beautiful. Although I didn't give you the boat ride I promised, at least we can enjoy the beauty from here.

Judy smiled.

It's spectacular. Thank you for everything. This is quite the adventure!

And it's only just begun. Vihaan took Judy's hand in his and gazed at her.

Their lunch arrived, and she pulled away instinctively. She had ordered prawns and rice in a brown sauce, and it was really delicious.

Enjoy, my sweet Judy.

Thank you, my darling Vihaan, Judy said in a joking tone.

They ate and chatted about the upcoming trip.

Judy decided to have a beer. She thought it might relax her and help her sleep.

Once back at the suite, Vihaan excused himself. Why don't you rest a bit, he suggested. I have some family business to take care of before we board the plane.

Judy didn't argue. She was feeling pretty wiped out from the traveling and emotional toll.

I'll wake you in a couple of hours.

As soon as Judy lay her head down on the pillow, she was out. It felt like minutes, but she was awoken by Vihaan who had climbed into bed and wrapped himself around her. It felt so good. She realized that she was really turned on by him. This wasn't a feeling she was used to. She felt a little bit naughty.

Once she was completely awake, they made love passionately. She couldn't hold back. She loved the way Vihaan touched her and kissed her. He whispered sweet words in her ear, causing her to explode with desire and a lust she didn't realize she was capable of. The entire world around them disappeared when they were making love. There was only the two of them in the moment, and it was magical.

After basking for a while, they both agreed it was time to shower and dress for the flight.

I'll meet you in the living room in an hour.

See you in an hour, Judy smiled. Boy did she feel good!

She took a leisurely shower, singing to herself. She got dressed, did her hair, and put a little bit of makeup on. She was still flying when she entered the living room.

Vihaan came out shortly after. Judy wanted to leap into his arms and tear his clothes off, but she knew they didn't have time. Instead, she sat on the couch gazing lustily at him. He had awoken something in her, and she felt almost like an addict. She wanted more, more, more.

They headed down to the lobby, checked out of the hotel and stepped outside. Vihaan's limo was waiting right in front, of course.

Judy chuckled to herself. Limos all the way, she thought, from NYC to India and beyond-

The ride to the plane was pretty quick, and Judy took a breath when they got out of the limo and were standing right in front of a Pilates PC24. It was exquisite. There was no security, and the best part was that she didn't have to drag all of her luggage by herself. Everything was done for them.

They climbed up the steps into the plane, and her knees buckled. Vihaan was behind her and caught her as she dropped.

Whoa, are you okay?

Yes, I'm sorry. I'm not used to all of this opulence.

I guess I'm so used to it. It's cool to watch you experience all of this for the first time.

They got seated and buckled in. Within ten minutes, they were up in the air, jetting off to India.

24

India

About an hour into the flight, Judy felt her eyes get really heavy.

Vihaan, I'm going to shut my eyes for a little bit.

Vihaan looked up from his laptop. Please, be my guest.

She pushed back the executive seat, put some headphones on, and slept like a baby.

Three hours later, she heard Vihaan's voice.

Judy, wake up. She felt him jiggling her, and even that touch turned her on.

She opened her eyes and smiled at him. He must have realized what she was thinking.

Are you a member of the mile-high club, Judy?

What's that?

Allow me to show you. He took her hand and led her to the back of the plane and into the restroom.

Twenty minutes later, they emerged.

I like the mile-high club, she said, cheeks flushed and hair a mess.

Vihaan laughed. I could tell.

As they took their seats, a flight attendant entered and offered them something to eat and drink.

They were enjoying their snacks when Judy looked at Vihaan.

Yes? he asked.

Do you ever feel bad for the many, many people who don't

have enough to eat or have a place to live?

That's an interesting question. In the Hindi religion, there is what is called a Caste system which divides people based on their birth. There are scholars, then soldiers, then merchants, then at the bottom are the laborers, also referred to as the untouchables. The problem with this way of thinking is that the level that one is born into is the level he or she will die in. India has modernized in its thinking, but there is still an attitude of elitism. The belief is that one's karma drives one's place in life. Although no one wants to live a life of poverty and hardship, it is not necessarily seen as a bad thing the way you are thinking of it. We are given our lot and must do the best we can with it.

Well, you've given me something to think about.

Vihaan smiled.

I like the fact that you are open to new ideas. It's a sign of intelligence.

Thank you, Vihaan. I consider that a real compliment coming from you.

For the rest of the trip, Judy and Vihaan held hands and made small talk.

The trip was very comfortable.

Once in India, they got into the limo and off they went to meet the family.

Judy started feeling nervous. Vihaan, what if your family doesn't like me?

That's not possible. I'm a pretty good judge of character, and I'm not worried.

Judy heard his words, but she didn't find them to be very comforting.

As they pulled into the driveway, Judy looked out the window and could not believe what she was seeing. She had seen what she thought were big houses back in New York, but this was a whole other ball game. The palace was incredible.

Holy cow!

Vihaan smiled. Yes, cows are very holy.

Judy looked at him. Are you making fun of me?

No. Cows are considered sacred in India.

Really?

Yes, and although there are a few interpretations, one of them is that that is where the expression comes from.

Fascinating.

Vihaan explained that his family's home is typical of the historic royal palaces but on a smaller scale.

A smaller scale? Judy asked. Really?

They both laughed.

Come on, I want you to meet my family.

Oh shit! Judy thought. I forgot the word for greeting.

They entered the palace and made an immediate left into a very large room that looked like a museum but was actually the library. Everyone was there.

Vihaan! Welcome home!

They all came over.

Vihaan's parents approached Judy and in ritualistic fashion, palms together, bowed and said, Khamaghani.

Judy reciprocated and then realized she was the object of what looked like a receiving line. One by one, family and friends faced her and greeted her.

She in turn modeled the greeting.

Once she had officially greeted everyone, the family pulled the two of them into the back yard where a party began. There was music, food, dancing, and drinking.

Judy was very impressed. Everyone was so welcoming and friendly. Some of Vihaan's sisters took Judy upstairs to show her her room and offer her some traditional clothing.

The chiffon sarees were so beautiful! They explained which were more for daily use and which were for special occasions, and that all of them are designed for simplicity and elegance.

They then all went back down to the party.

Meantime, Vihaan was fielding a number of questions from his parents and one of his brothers. He had been taught to be practical, a role model. As a royal, it was expected that he behave in a proper manner, following tradition and family values. Bringing Judy home to meet the family didn't exactly meet those expectations. The thing was though, that he really liked her. He realized how complicated this could be, but his heart was overriding his judgement, and he was going with his feelings.

The party went on well into the evening. Everybody had a very good time.
Finally, at about one in the morning, Judy found Vihaan and told him she had to go to bed. She was exhausted.
I will escort you to your room.
Judy said goodnight to everyone, and the two went upstairs to Judy's bedroom.
Once there, Vihaan explained that although he wanted nothing more than to stay with her, it wouldn't be proper, so he was going to sleep in his room.
Judy completely understood. Actually, she was glad for the privacy. She liked Vihaan a lot, but hadn't had any alone time for days, and was in need of some personal recharge time.

The next morning, there was a knock at Judy's door. Come in, she called. Vihaan entered. Judy was still in bed. She was enjoying the king size four post bed with the veil around it. She felt as though she could get lost within the blankets.
Good morning, Vihaan. You're up early.
I couldn't wait to see you. I missed you last night.
Ahhhh, poor you. Judy smiled.
Vihaan looked at her.
You are really adorable, he told her with a loving expression.
He climbed into bed and kissed her all over. She simply couldn't resist him. She was so attracted to this man she hardly knew.

They made passionate love in her four-post king size bed at the palace and then snuggled with each other for what must have been close to an hour.

We should probably get up, he finally said.

I'm going to shower. What can I expect today?

Well, tomorrow is the wedding, so today will be much preparation. I think my sisters want to take you in and get you ready right after breakfast. Are you okay with that?

Yes, of course. Judy was a little hesitant but reminded herself to go with the flow. I'll meet you downstairs in about thirty minutes, ok?

Vihaan gave Judy a very passionate kiss and said, okay, see you downstairs.

Once he was gone, Judy showered and called her aunt. She filled her in on the past couple of days. Maddie couldn't even believe what she was hearing.

Don't you go falling in love and becoming a princess on me.

Judy chuckled. I'm sure I'm very far from that, Aunt Maddie. I love you, and I'll talk to you tomorrow or the next day.

Judy then made her way down the grand staircase and located everyone out on the back veranda having breakfast.

Good morning, Judy. Vihaan's mother was right there waiting for her. Please join us for some breakfast.

Judy thanked her and sat down next to her.

So, Judy, tell me a little bit about yourself.

Mother!

Judy turned around to see Vihaan standing behind her.

Let her have her breakfast in peace.

I just want to get to know your girlfriend. Is that so bad?

Judy smiled politely, but thought to herself, girlfriend? Is that what he's telling his family?

Is that what I want him to tell his family? Maybe he's just saying that because they wouldn't understand otherwise.

Judy? Are you with us? Vihaan was rubbing her shoulders from behind.

Oh, yes, sorry. I was lost in space for a minute.

Judy looked around and realized that the conversation had already gone in a different direction. She relaxed a little bit and enjoyed her breakfast while observing the family's interactions and dynamic. They were very sweet and playful with each other.

She suddenly felt a little bit weepy. She particularly missed her mother and Kay. They would have gotten a kick at her sitting in a palace in India.

Are you okay, my dear?

Oh, I'm sorry. Judy was suddenly embarrassed. I'm fine.

Are you sure? Vihaan's mom asked. You look upset.

Judy looked at Olivia. She couldn't hold back her tears. I miss my mom.

In her head, Judy heard a voice say, what are you doing? You sound like a three-year old. Pull yourself together. You're being ridiculous.

Oh, honey, is she back in the states?

No, Judy looked down. She passed away.

I'm so very sorry, my dear.

Olivia took Judy's hand in hers.

In our culture, we believe in reincarnation. Do you know much about that?

Judy shook her head no. She feared she wouldn't be able to produce words, she was so choked up.

Hinduism is the belief in a supreme being that watches over an endless cycle of creation, preservation, and dissolution. Reincarnation, a major tenet of Hinduism, is when the soul, which is seen as eternal and part of a spiritual realm, returns to the physical realm in a new body. A soul will complete this cycle many times, learning new things each time and working through its karma. This cycle of reincarnation is called samsara.

Reincarnation in Hinduism is not limited to being born as human. You may have had prior lives as animals, plants, or as divine beings who rule part of nature. If it has life, then it is part of the cycle. Remember that, the next time you step on and crush a bug; according to the idea of reincarnation, it could be your great uncle or future grandchild.

So, you see, your mom is not really gone. Just as you and I will, she will return again.

Olivia smiled, and Judy felt better. She wanted to hug Vihaan's mom but wasn't sure that it would be proper, so she just said thank you.

You are most welcome. Now, I must attend to some wedding business. Will you be alright?

Yes, I'm fine.

Olivia went into the house leaving Judy alone at the table. The others had already finished eating and gone about the duties of wedding preparation, so Judy decided to take a walk around the property. She headed deeper into the backyard and found a really beautiful garden. She had never seen such magnificent flowers. There were roses and jasmine, marigold and chrysanthemums. She sat down on a bench to meditate. After a few minutes, Judy heard the strangest sound. She opened her eyes, and about two feet away from her were three peacocks with their feathers fully spread. She blinked a couple of times. She couldn't believe what she was seeing.

There you are.

She looked to her left and saw Vihaan coming toward her.

Look, she said, pointing to the peacocks. Aren't they fantastic?

Yes, they are, Vihaan said, chuckling a little bit. I love how excited you get when you experience something new. It's part of your beauty.

Have you finished your wedding prep?

Yes, for now. Would you like to have a tour of the area?

Oh, yes, that would be nice.

The day flew by, and there was yet another party that night. Judy was so impressed by Vihaan's family. Yes, they had their spats, their pushes and pulls, but all in all, they loved each other and were loyal to each other. It made her feel good to watch their interactions. It also made her a little bit sad that she didn't, for all intents and purposes, have a family of her own.

The day of the wedding arrived, and Judy was made to feel a part of the ceremony, which was really gracious of her family to do. She had a beautiful chiffon saree to wear, and some of the girls taught her about henna. She felt very exotic.

The wedding itself was fascinating to watch. Judy realized the importance of centuries old traditions, and she was touched by the fact that cultures around the world carried on the traditions of their ancestors. Maybe, she thought, she would start some of her own traditions to be handed down to future generations.

The after party went on into the morning hours, so Judy slept in the next and last day of her visit to India. She and Vihaan would be jet-setters once again and fly over to Bali.

Judy knew that ultimately, she would have to make a tough decision, but for now, she was going to stay in the moment and enjoy the fun.

The next day, she was packed and ready. She thanked Vihaan's parents for including her in such a special event, said goodbye to all of her new friends, and made her way out the door.

The limo was waiting, of course, and Judy wondered how she would possibly get by without all of the luxury and convenience of others doing for her..she chuckled to herself.

Once on the plane, Vihaan took a very deep breath and sighed. He looked tired.

Are you okay?

Yes, just tired. It's been quite a whirlwind, and I want to thank you for being the perfect guest at my family's home. They all loved you.

And I had a really great time. Your family is the best!

The two of them became quiet. The flight would take about eight hours, so sleep seemed like a good option. They both slept peacefully until the plane hit some turbulence five hours

163

later.   Vihaan and Judy were jarred awake and looked at each other.   There was a look of concern. Vihaan grabbed Judy's hand as if to say, don't worry, I'll protect you.

After about twenty minutes, the plane leveled out, so the flight attendant came out and asked if they wanted anything to eat.

They were served a wonderful meal. After resting and eating, both were feeling more relaxed and started to talk.

So Vihaan, do you have a plan for us once we're in Bali?

As a matter of fact, I do. I would love to show you some of the highlights of Bali.

Okay. She looked closely at Vihaan. She was only eighteen and certainly not looking for any kind of a commitment for a long time, but perhaps if she were older when they met, Vihaan could potentially be a serious partner. Oh well.

25
Bali

They landed in Bali and were picked up by a car service. They pulled up at the The Seminyak Beach Resort & Spa.

Wow! Judy whispered, her mood lifting even more.

Yes, said Vihaan.

The tropical beauty was indescribable. The palm trees were swaying gently, and the aroma of the tropical flowers wafted through the air.

In the distance they could hear tropical birds squawking back and forth.

Excuse me, Judy stopped a hotel employee. What kind of bird is that squawking?

Oh, that's either a Black Drongo or an Oriental Magpie-Robin. I get them confused.

Huh, said Judy. Fascinating!

Once settled in, Vihaan said, Judy, let's go for a swim.

They headed out and jumped right into the water which was the clearest water Judy had ever seen. The temperature was about eighty-five degrees, and it was delightful. They swam around with the tropical fish, turtles, eels, and starfish. It was an experience that Judy knew she would never forget.

When they came out of the water, Judy said, I think I could just live here forever.

I understand, said Vihaan.

They lay on the beach for a while soaking in the tropical energy. It was really relaxing.

Finally, Vihaan asked, are you hungry?

Judy hadn't realized, but she was pretty hungry. They went back to their room, changed clothes, and headed down to the dining room. They tried mixed rice with banana, grilled tuna, and for dessert, they had banana fritters. The different flavors and seasonings were so unique and delicious.

They then took a stroll along the beach, which was really very romantic. They came to a pretty rock formation and sat down in the sand to stare out at the sea.

Judy?

Vihaan?

I very much enjoy being with you.

Judy took a very deep breath. She felt the same but wasn't sure how this relationship was going to end up. She was intent on attending Columbia in just a few weeks, and she knew Vihaan would have to go back to England soon. She wasn't experienced with long-distance relationships, frankly she wasn't experienced with any relationships. On the other hand, perhaps they could maintain some sort of a romance from afar. Vihaan had the means. He could fly to New York once in a while, and she certainly wouldn't mind jetting to Oxford occasionally, especially, if it were on Vihaan's family's jet. She chuckled to herself.

What? Vihaan asked.

What? Judy replied. She had gotten lost in her thoughts for longer than she realized and didn't notice that she was laughing out loud.

Oh, sorry Vihaan. I was daydreaming.

Do share.

Well, Judy thought. Now is as good a time as ever, I guess.

Vihaan, obviously, we've only known each other a short time. And, we have had a great time these past couple of weeks!

Stop right there. Are you breaking up with me?

Ohhh, nooo. On the contrary, I was just trying to figure out how we might make this relationship work with me in New

York and you in England. I think it's definitely worth a conversation.

I see, said Vihaan. You think you're up to a long-distance love affair?

To be honest, it's not my first choice, but I'm willing to give it a try. I really don't want to call this quits. I have had such a good time with you, and I believe we have a connection.

Are you planning on dating other boys at Columbia?

Judy was taken a little by surprise.

I hadn't thought about it. You are my very first relationship, unless you count Tommy Sherman in the first grade. We held hands for a couple of days, and then her left me for Sherry Alberts.

Oh, Vihaan smiled. And I thought I was your very first.

I'm sorry, Vihaan. Tommy will always have a piece of my heart.

They both turned and looked directly at each other and burst out laughing. They laughed and laughed till they had to hold their stomachs.

Oh, man, that felt good, Judy said.

Vihaan grabbed Judy and kissed her hard. She actually had a little orgasm right there on the beach in Bali. Vihaan then took her hand, and they went behind the rocks where there was some privacy. The sun was setting, and they made passionate love over and over, rolling around in the sand, kissing, stroking, sighing, and moaning.

Vihaan whispered, I think I'm falling in love with you, Judy.

They held each other till the dusk blanketed them.

Vihaan gazed into Judy's eyes for a long moment.

Shall we head back to the hotel?

Sounds good, Judy replied, still in a semi dream-like state.

Vihaan, I've never been in love before, but I can imagine that this is what it feels like.

Vihaan wrapped his arms around Judy. Let's talk about it later, he said. For now, let's enjoy this amazing place.

Judy smiled in agreement.

Back at the hotel, there was a Balinese band and dancers. Vihaan and Judy sat towards the back feeling the glow of their lovemaking and moving to the music.

Judy felt as though this really had to be a dream. Who lives like this? Can anyone possibly be this happy?

By around ten, they headed up to the room, opened the veranda's sliding glass doors, and both crashed, sleeping soundly to the sound of the waves hitting the shore.

Judy woke up first, thanks to the Oriental Magpie-Robin.

She quietly got out of bed and went out onto the veranda.

If I died right now, all would be okay. I don't know how my life could get any better.

After about thirty minutes, she felt a kiss on her head.

Here you are.

Here I am. How did you sleep, Vihaan?

Like a baby. I don't think I've slept so well in years. Must be the company.

I agree, said Judy.

So what would you like to do today?

I was just reading about some of the excursions. They all sound really great.

Name some.

Okay, but don't laugh.

I promise, I won't.

I would love to go to the Mandala Suci Wenara Wana.

Really?

Yes. Do you know what I just said?

No idea.

It's the Ubuntu's Monkey Forest Sanctuary. You probably don't know this about me, but I am a huge animal lover, and it would be a total thrill to walk amongst the long-tailed monkeys.

Well, you probably don't know this about me, but I happen to be a long-tailed monkey.

Judy burst out laughing. In that case, I should return you to your habitat.

Sounds like a plan. I'm going to grab a shower and will be ready in twenty.

Vihaan.

Yes?

Judy gave him a look that didn't require words.

Right here?

Judy smiled.

The next thirty minutes were as passionate as ever. Both had let go of any inhibitions and made wild, passionate love completely naked on the veranda.

Boy, are we good together, exclaimed Judy as she put her pajamas back on.

That's no lie, said Vihaan. You're going to completely wear me out if we keep going like this, and I won't make it through the monkey park.

Well, in that case, go take a shower so that we can get going.

While Vihaan was in the shower, something came over Judy. She couldn't help herself.

She snuck into the bathroom, took off her pajamas (again) and got into the shower with Vihaan.

Hello, she said.

Oh my God, Judy. I realize I'm pretty good, but really?

What can I say? Vihaan. I can't get enough of you. You are really sexy.

Well, I certainly don't want to disappoint.

The lovemaking was wonderful in the shower, and the two of them embraced while the hot water poured over them.

26

The Monkey Park and More

As they strolled along the paths, Judy read the brochure that they received at the entrance. Did you know that Mandala Suci Wenara Wana is the sanctuary or natural habitat of the Balinese long tailed monkey? It's scientific name is Macaca Fascicularis.

Really, Judy? I didn't know that.

Well, you should, since it's your habitat. There are around 749 monkeys living in the sanctuary. They are divided into 6 groups. Ubud Monkey Forest also has 186 species of plants and trees so you will have plenty to eat when I leave you here.

Vihaan made monkey noises and started dancing around Judy while scratching his right side.

Ha,ha. Very funny, my monkey man.

They walked and admired the beauty and fed the monkeys along the way. Although the monkeys are considered wild animals, living freely, they are used to the many tourists who visit and are happy for any handouts, Judy explained.

I guess a free meal is a free meal, Vihaan joked.

They visited the three temples, and while standing in front of the Holy Spring Temple, Judy said,

Did you know that the Ubud Monkey Forest describes its mission as one of conservation of the area? The mission is based upon the Hindu principle of Tri Hata Karana which means three ways to reach spiritual and physical well-being. I love that! Do you know that principle, Vihaan?

Actually, I do. I am not super religious, but I do know the basic Hindu principles.

Tri Hata Karana seeks to help people live harmoniously during their lives. The "three ways" to this goal under the Tri Hata Karana doctrine are harmonious relationships between humans and humans, between humans and the natural environment, and between humans and The Supreme God.

Well, we're at least a third of the way there.

Judy smiled at Vihaan, and his heart actually fluttered.

Wow! he thought. That's never happened before. Maybe I'm truly in love.

Judy continued reading to him.

The Monkey Forest has a philosophical goal of creating peace and harmony for visitors from all over the world. It also seeks to conserve rare plants and animals for use in Hindu rituals and to provide a natural laboratory for educational institutions, with a particular emphasis on research into the social interaction of the park's monkeys with one another and their interaction with the park's natural environment. That's so great; don't you think so, Vihaan?

I do, Vihaan said.

There's a bench up there on the left. Could we sit for a bit, Judy?

Of course, Judy said. Are you okay?

Yes, I'm fine. Just a bit worn out.

I can't imagine why, Judy smiled.

After about fifteen minutes, Vihaan said, Okay, let's carry on.

Right here? Judy joked.

Oh, you are funny.

As they exited the park and headed to the limo, Judy stopped Vihaan. She looked directly into his eyes. Vihaan, I don't think I can ever thank you for this amazing trip, time with you, day. She kissed him and held him for a couple of minutes.

It has been my pleasure.

Back at the hotel, Vihaan told Judy he needed to go take care of some errands. Judy couldn't imagine what errands he had to do, but she told him she'd see him in a bit.
On his way out the door, he said, do you have a nice outfit for dinner? I want to take you out.
Umm, not really super fancy.
Go down to the hotel's boutique and pick something out.
Okay – will do.
See you later
Alligator.
Vihaan wasn't sure why Judy called him an alligator. He made a note to ask her when he got back.
Down in the boutique, Judy meandered around admiring the clothing and the jewelry. She loved imagining herself in the different outfits and maybe being at a party or on a yacht or even in a business meeting. She had always had a great imagination, maybe because she spent so much of her life with adults and often had to entertain herself.
She tried on a few dresses. They all looked ok, but there was one that she thought really looked fabulous on her. It was a traditional Balinese outfit - an orange sarong with blue flowers on it, and the top was a soft blue low cut with orange flowers on it. There was a green tree coming up the middle of the top, and the top was cut so that it came down over her hips and ended at a point in front.
She asked the clerk what she thought.
Oh yes, beautiful! You need shoes?
Vihaan hadn't given her a spending limit, so she hoped this purchase was okay. The dress was about three hundred dollars US, and the shoes she chose were about seventy-five. Well, she thought, she would offer to pay him back. She has already, in just those few minutes, fallen in love with the whole outfit.
She went back up to the room and stretched out in the lounge chair on the veranda. She was staring at the sky, singing

quietly to herself, and feeling awe. Could she see herself just staying in Bali? Forget Columbia. She could always go to college later. But what would she do?

Hey, Alligator. I'm back.

I'm out here on the veranda, Judy called.

Vihaan came out and joined her in the lounge chair.

Hey, why did you just call me an alligator? Judy asked.

Because you called me one, Vihaan responded.

I did? When?

When I left before.

Judy thought for a few minutes.

Ohh, ohh, ohh. She laughed. I didn't call you an alligator.

Yes, you did.

No. You said see you later. I said alligator.

I don't get it. Vihaan frowned.

It's an expression. See you later, alligator. After while crocodile.

Well, that's a very silly expression.

Yeah, maybe, but when you said see you later and didn't say alligator, I just finished the expression for you.

Boy, if I stick with you, I can learn a lot.

Oh yeah, Judy said, some really useful information.

She laughed and kissed Vihaan.

Did you miss me, my alligator?

So much, said Judy.

Did you find a dress for tonight?

I sure did, but listen Vihaan, I want to pay you for it. It wasn't so cheap.

It's my pleasure, Judy. I don't want you to think about money, not this trip. Okay?

Okay. Well thank you very much. I can't wait for you to see it. Where are we going?

It's a surprise. I can't tell you. But we need to leave here in about forty-five minutes. Will you be ready?

I will.

They both got busy getting dressed for their big night out.

Judy was excited. She loved spending time with Vihaan, and the thought of going to a fancy restaurant together made her so happy.

Vihaan was dressed and ready before Judy and so was just hanging out in the living room. He seemed a little edgy, but Judy dismissed it.

She came out of the bedroom fully made up with her new dress on and her hair done.

Vihaan stood up. Wow! Judy!! You look absolutely beautiful!

Thank you, Vihaan.

At seven forty-five, they went downstairs and got in the limo. The restaurant wasn't far away. It only took about twelve minutes to get there.

When they walked in, Judy was dumbstruck.

Vihaan, this place is gorgeous. I have never seen anything like this.

They were greeted by the hostess.

Good evening. Welcome to Merah Putih. Do you have a reservation?

Yes, under Singh.

Oh yes, here we are. Please follow me.

They followed the hostess to a beautiful, candle lit table for two in the back.

Your waiter will be right over. Enjoy your meal.

Thank you, they said in unison.

Oh, Vihaan, I can't get over this place. I love everything about Bali. How amazing!

I'm glad, Judy.

Vihaan took her hand across the candlelit table. I am having a great time too.

Just then, the waiter came over.

Good evening. My name is Kadek, and I will be your server this evening. Would you like something to drink?

Vihaan ordered a bottle of wine.

Very good, sir. I'll be right back.

The waiter was back in no time. He poured just a little bit of wine in Vihaan's glass for him to taste. Vihaan nodded his approval, and so their glasses were filled.

A toast, said Vihaan as he lifted his glass.

To you, Judy. In this short time, I have gotten to know a woman who is intelligent, very sexy, and extremely fun to be with.

They clinked glasses and then looked at the menu.

The meal was extraordinary.

Judy thought, here's another reason to stay in Bali. She smiled to herself.

So, Judy, would you like dessert? They have a really special dessert here.

Sure, Judy said. She wasn't one to turn down a good dessert.

About ten minutes later, Kadek brought over a beautiful dessert of fruit, chocolates, and coconut ice cream with a sparkler in the middle of it. He placed it on the table and walked away.

Judy noticed that Vihaan was digging in his pocket for something.

Are you okay, Vihaan?

Just then, Vihaan went down on one knee.

Judy wasn't sure what he was doing.

Judy, you've added sparkle to my life. I realize we haven't known each other for long, but I know that I want you in my life. Judy, would you do me the honor of being my wife?

Well, between the wine, the atmosphere, and her feelings for Vihaan, Judy didn't take a beat.

Oh my God, Vihaan. She was crying and slid off her chair and wrapped her arms around him.

Is that a yes?

Yes, Judy said.

Well, try the ring on.

The ring was magnificent. Vihaan had chosen a ring from the Harry Winston collection. It was a Winston Blossom 3.00

carat diamond ring, and it was unlike anything Judy had ever seen.

The ring fit perfectly, and Judy felt like a queen.

Is this really happening?

Yes ma'am.

Vihaan, are you sure? After all, you are a prince attending school in England. I'm just a simple girl from New York.

Well now you're my simple girl from New York. Let's have some dessert.

They dug into the sparkling mass of ice cream and chocolate.

Mmmmm, this is exquisite.

As are you, Judy.

As they walked out of the restaurant, many of the diners congratulated them. Judy was floating on air.

In the limo, Judy asked Vihaan, have you told your parents?

I did, said Vihaan.

They're okay with this?

They are. And how do you think your aunt will feel?

I'm not sure. We've only just gotten to know each other, but I think if I'm happy, she'll be happy.

And are you happy?

Vihaan, do you really need to ask that?

I guess that's the answer.

Judy kissed him, and they melted into each other in the limo.

Once upstairs, they undressed and made love for the first time as an engaged couple.

This has been a very special day.

You deserve to have all special days, Judy.

I do love you.

And, I love you.

They fell asleep in each other's arms and slept through the night.

The next morning, Judy got up and went out to the veranda. She was dying to call her Aunt Maddie.

Hi, my niece. I was hoping to hear from you.
Hi, Aunt Maddie.
So, what's new in Bali?
Well, Vihaan proposed to me last night.
There was silence.
Aunt Maddie?
I'm here. Just a little in shock. What did you say?
I said yes.
Judy?
I know, Aunt Maddie. We only know each other for a couple of weeks, but you know when you know?
I do, actually. So, he's good to you?
He treats me like a queen.
And what about school?
We haven't talked about our futures yet, but I think we'll do that today.
Well, if you're sure.
I am.
Then I'm happy for you. And remember, I'm here for you. You can always come home to me.
I appreciate that, Maddie. How are you feeling?
I'm doing okay. I'm on an experimental drug that seems promising.
Oh, that's great! I'll call you tomorrow. I'm going to take a shower.
Okay, my love. I'll talk to you tomorrow.

Judy went back into the bedroom. Vihaan was just waking up.
Come here, my bride to be.
I like the sound of that, my husband to be.
Judy got into bed and they kissed and snuggled.
Vihaan, we need to talk about the future.
I know, he said. This is a little bit complicated.
That's an understatement, said Judy.
Let's go get some breakfast and take a walk and talk, okay?
Good plan, said Judy.

They showered and dressed and went downstairs for breakfast. They sat outside and ordered eggs, fruit, and tea.

Another perfect day in paradise, Judy said dreamily.

Yes, said Vihaan.

They ate mostly in silence, both processing the reality of the prior night's events.

Shall we walk on the beach?

Oh, that's a nice idea, but I make no promises that I won't attack you at the rocks.

Vihaan looked at Judy. I am capable of protecting myself, he said. But I probably won't.

They smiled at each other and walked down the path to the beach.

So, Judy began.

Yes, interrupted Vihaan. I would never deny you your education. I think education is very important. And, I have two more years at Oxford.

But, how are we going to maintain this relationship so far away from each other?

Judy, would you consider moving to England to attend school?

Wow! Judy thought. That's a big ask. But then I would be near my fiancée.

I guess it's something I could look into. I guess the other option is to travel back and forth whenever we can.

Honestly, I would very much like to be near you, Judy.

Me too.

We do have a dilemma. Perhaps I could start at Columbia and work on transferring in the spring. That way, I'll have some college done and can spend some time with my aunt.

Let's pick this up later. Where shall we go today?

Judy kind of felt like Vihaan was avoiding the conversation, but she figured one more day wouldn't really make much of a difference.

Let's go to Mount Batur, Vihaan suggested.

Oh, that's a good plan.

They made their way back to the hotel to prepare for a hike up the volcano.

Once there, they both stood staring up at the monstrous mass. We can do this, Judy said, trying to convince herself of the climb and their future.

Vihaan looked at her.

There's no time like the present, he said.

About half way up, Vihaan had to sit down.

Are you okay?

I don't know. My heart is fluttering. Maybe it's because I love you.

Ahh, that's so sweet, but should we turn around and head back down?

Give me a minute to catch my breath.

Vihaan, you don't look so good. I'm honestly a little bit worried.

They sat for a while. Judy was staring at Vihaan whose color was a little bit ashen.

Vihaan, I think we should go to a medical station, okay?

Vihaan was also concerned. There was a ranger station just a few feet up, so Judy left Vihaan to find some help.

She returned with a ranger who called for an ambulance because by then, Vihaan had laid down and was having some trouble breathing.

Vihaan asked the ranger to call for a helicopter instead.

Ten minutes later, they were in the air and headed to the hospital.

The doctors were standing by and rushed Vihaan inside. They hooked him up to a bunch of machines and drew blood. Judy was trying to stay out of the way but felt so helpless and wished there was something she could do.

Vihaan weakly called her name.

I'm here, she said, trying to sound calm.

Please take my phone and contact my family. The number is in my contacts.

He handed her his phone as they were wheeling him down the hallway.

Please stay here, one of the nurses told Judy.

Judy sat down in the waiting room and began to cry. Not again. This cannot be happening.

Okay girl, pull yourself together. You have to make this call.

Judy called and got Vihaan's mom. She explained what had happened and then remembered that this wasn't the first time Vihaan seemed to have an issue.

Vihaan's mom thanked Judy for calling and said they would fly to Bali immediately.

Judy sat – in a daze. She lost track of the time.

Eventually, a doctor came out and told Judy that Vihaan had a congenital defect in his heart. His heart is enlarged, and he has suffered numerous small heart attacks. He is resting comfortably, but it's only a matter of time. You may go in to see him if you like.

Judy followed the doctor down the hall to Vihaan's room. She was in a fog.

What happened? We were so happy, climbing the volcano, getting engaged, making life plans. And now, Vihaan is dying in a hospital bed.

She entered his room and was grossly unprepared for the sight. She expected her smiling Vihaan to sit up and say something sweet, or maybe even funny, but instead, he lay still with tubes and machines. His eyes were closed.

Vihaan, Judy whispered close to his face. It's Judy.

Vihaan slowly opened his eyes, looked at her and gazed as if to say, my love.

He then closed his eyes.

Judy sat next to the bed, holding his hand for hours.

At around nine o'clock, Judy was sitting half in the chair by the bed with her upper half slumped

over and her head on the bed. She was holding Vihaan's hand in both of hers. She wasn't awake or asleep but was in an in between state. As she was lying there, she heard a tapping which caused her to stir. She sat up and tried to stretch and focus, she noticed a black form at the window. Tap, tap, tap. The noise was coming from the window not, as she first thought, in a dream. As she stared intently at the window, she realized it was a raven.

Oh, that's not good, Judy thought. That's not good at all.

This took her back to her tenth grade English class. They were required to read Edgar Allan Poe, and the teacher selected "The Raven". Now, she thought, I am living in a Poe novel.

By a little after nine, she heard shuffling and voices out in the otherwise quiet hallway.

Where is my baby, my sweet baby boy? cried a distraught female voice.

Judy recognized the voice. Vihaan's family had arrived.

Judy leaned over and kissed her fiancée, knowing that it was now her time to step back and let the family say goodbye to this amazing person.

They all came rushing in.

Judy hadn't moved away yet. She felt that as long as she held onto to Vihaan's hand, he would stay with them.

Oh, Judy, Oh my God! What happened?

Judy was sobbing and so couldn't really speak.

The family gathered around Vihaan. There were tears, and wailing, and even praying.

Within about thirty minutes, the doctor came in and took Vihaan's father into the hallway.

The family was silenced by the base, deep, guttural scream that came from outside the door.

Vihaan's father walked in and spoke in Hindi to the rest of the family. En masse, they went silent. They didn't pace, speak, or sit. They all just stood in a group looking at each other.

It was unsettling, to say the least. Judy didn't know what to do. She really didn't know these people that well, nor did she know their rituals or behavioral patterns in a situation like this. Besides, she was losing the love of her life, and that was bringing up all of the other losses she had already experienced in her short lifetime. So, she just stood in the corner, crying silently.

After fifteen minutes or so, Vihaan's mom, Olivia, turned around and noticed her there.

Oh, my dear, I'm sorry. She walked over to Judy and wrapped her arms around her. Together they sobbed and sobbed.

Meanwhile, the rest of the family left to bring back chairs for everyone.

They all sat vigil over Vihaan while his breathing got slower and slower.

Well into the early hours of the morning, when it was just Vihaan's mom, dad, and Judy, and they were all in a state of fatigue, and spiritual haziness, they looked over at Vihaan all together, at the same time.

He opened his eyes and gazed at the three of them. Judy thought she detected the slightest smile.

Then, there was a very deep breath, and his eyes closed for the last time.

Judy noticed she had been holding her breath and finally let out a sigh.

Vihaan's parents broke down from extreme grief and exhaustion.

They sat for a while, until a nurse came in and realized that Vihaan had passed.

I'm so sorry for your loss.

She turned off the machines, and the room became very silent. The words and silence shook them all out of their grief-stricken stupor.

Vihaan's parents got up very slowly and left the room.

Judy was left sitting by the body of her fiancée.

She crawled up in the bed with him.

Take me with you, Vihaan, she whispered. I can't bear this pain again.

She openly sobbed and sobbed, holding onto to his limp arm.

Please don't leave me. Everyone I have ever loved has left me. Please......

Just then, Olivia came in.

She touched Judy's shoulder.

Come with me, honey.

Judy blindly obeyed. She was in such a state that she would have gone anywhere with anyone. She was exhausted and was feeling the greatest depth of grief she had ever experienced.

The family gathered in the waiting room.

Judy didn't realize that Vihaan's father wasn't there.

She didn't ask questions. She didn't really need to know or even care in that moment.

After a while, Vihaan's father returned.

Olivia quietly whispered to Judy that they were all going to get on the jet and fly back to India for a burial ceremony. She told Judy they would like her to join them because she is part of their family now, and their son loved her so deeply and wanted to spend the rest of his life with her. Judy's knees buckled. This was all way too much.

One of Vihaan's brothers was near and caught her as she dropped.

Judy then heard Olivia tell Bandhupala to help her to the plane.

They all boarded; there wasn't much talking.

Bandhupala helped Judy to a seat. She crunched herself up into a semi fetal position and closed her eyes. The last thing she remembered was the sound of the engines revving.

Judy, we're here.

She opened her eyes and saw Bandhupala.

She thought, I guess he has taken the responsibility of watching over me.

She stood up and went back down immediately.

Wow, easy, he said. Let me help you.

Vihaan's brother held out his hand, and Judy grasped it.

He gently pulled her up and held her as she stumbled out of the plane and over to one of the limos that was waiting.

Back at the house, one of Vihaan's sisters took Judy up to a room and encouraged her to bathe. If they gave her any information on the ceremony, she didn't remember.

She turned on the shower and got in. She stood for a while and cried, her tears mixing with the spray of the shower water.

Once downstairs, she noticed a lot of people mulling around. She later learned that Vihaan's body was flown home when they all came to India. The funeral would be held right in the home, and they all would go to the pond on the property to spread his ashes. She was introduced to the Hindu Priest and told that the eldest brother, Bandhupala, would be spreading the ashes.

This was pretty different from what Judy was familiar with, and if it weren't so personal and painful, she thought, she would have found the whole experience to be fascinating.

The day passed with chanting and other death rituals. Judy sat quietly observing and crying. At one point, Bandhupala came and sat down next to her. He explained that in the Hindu religion, the belief is that when someone dies, the soul passes into another body. We hope to cleanse our negative karma so that eventually, we do not need to reincarnate, but instead may move on to spiritual enlightenment.

As Bandhupala was speaking, Judy realized how much Vihaan looked like him. She also realized that she wasn't the only one grieving.

Bandhupala, I am so sorry for the loss of your brother. I didn't know him long, but he was already very special to me. Thank you for being so kind.

Bandhupala said, I believe this wasn't the first time you two were together. A love that is that strong so quickly is something that only two old souls who have been together before could discover and endure. One day, you too will realize this.

Bandhupala hugged Judy and walked away.

The next day was the spreading of the ashes. All who had been in the house at the funeral attended plus some others. There was a lot of wailing and hugging. Judy was still pretty numb and stood toward the back trying to feel Vihaan around her.

She remembered the dream she had had as a little girl the night her mother died and came to her. Maybe, she thought, Vihaan would come to her as well. She was totally open to the possibility that there are different levels of energies and that maybe we don't just vanish but can communicate in unconventional ways from beyond and even, as Bandhupala explained, we can return.

That evening, Olivia asked Judy to come into the parlor. She asked her what she wanted to do.
Judy hadn't thought about it but realized she was supposed to start Columbia in less than three weeks.
You are more than welcome to stay here in our home for as long as you would like, and Judy, you are always welcome here. I do hope you will consider returning at some point in your life, and please keep in touch with us, my daughter.
Olivia had no idea how much this meant to Judy, but all she could manage was a thank you.
I think I should head back to New York. I was supposed to start college there in a few weeks, and my aunt is ill, so I would like to spend some time with her.
That sounds like a very good idea, my dear. I will make all of the arrangements for you. What do you think about leaving in two days, just to give you both time to rest and to get to know your Indian family a little better before you fly back.
That sounds perfect. Thank you so much for everything you've done for me. I'm so very sorry for your loss. Vihaan was a really special person.
Thank you, my love. I agree. And I would be honored if you would keep the ring. It's quite lovely. Vihaan had excellent taste in rings and wives. Olivia smiled at Judy, and she felt a chill run through her body. There was a strange familiarity.
Hmmm, reincarnation, hmmmm.

In the next two days, Judy slept a lot and got to know her brothers and sisters better. She fell in love with each and every one of them and told them that they are always wel-come in her home, wherever she ends up. They promised to keep in touch, and all accompanied her to the airport for her flight back to New York. There were hugs and kisses and tears, and then Judy was walking through the airport on her way back home.

27

Back to New York

The flight was long, but Judy didn't mind. She cherished the quiet alone time to process everything that had happened.

When she landed at JFK, she picked up her luggage, went through Customs, and headed out to catch a taxi. Across the lobby area, Judy thought she saw her Aunt Maddie, but no, how could that be?

She stopped for a minute and focused. Sure enough, Aunt Maddie was waiting for her with a "Judy" sign as if she were a limo driver.

Aunt Maddie, Judy shouted.

She dropped her luggage and ran to her. The tears flowed.

Oh, Aunt Maddie.

I know, honey. I know.

After a couple of minutes, they collected Judy's things and headed outside. Maddie had hired a limo to take them back to Maddie's apartment.

Once inside, Maddie said, okay, tell me everything.

So, Judy went through the entire trip beginning in Taiwan and ending in India.

Well, you certainly have been through it. I am so sorry, Judy. I would have loved to have met Vihaan. It sounds like he truly was very special.

Judy took a very deep breath. I don't know how to move forward, Aunt Maddie. I feel really lost and somewhat numb.

That is perfectly understandable. If I may, I would suggest you go for some grief therapy. I think it might be the extra support you need.

I agree. Do you have any recommendations?

I actually know someone that I think would be really good for you. I'll call her tomorrow. Also, why don't you stay here with me till it's time to move into Columbia. I would love the company.

That's an offer I can't refuse. Thank you, Aunt Maddie, for everything.

Meantime, are you hungry? Shall we head down the block to our regular?

Yes, that sounds really good. By the way, how are you feeling?

I'm really good, Judy, really good.

For the next couple of weeks, Judy and Maddie went to shows, museums, shops, and restaurants. The distraction helped a little, but she carried her grief with her as if there were a cloud of sadness enveloping her. She was just going through the motions of everyday life, so she started therapy, and day by day, started to feel some semblance of normalcy.

Judy went to Columbia a couple of times to register for classes and get her residence secured. Then the time came for her to move into the residence hall. She liked the fact that her aunt was only a quick subway ride away – a safety net, so to speak. They promised to get together the next weekend and do something, so Judy had something to look forward to.

Judy was placed in a suite with two bedrooms, each with its own bathroom, a kitchenette, and a living room type of common space. There were four of them, two in each bedroom. She liked her roommate and thought the other suite mates were okay but didn't feel like she could be really close friends with them. The two of them had come from the same high school and had history. They also liked to party pretty hard. Fortunately for Judy and Sarah, her roommate, the other two girls did most of their partying in someone else's suite, so Judy and Sarah had the whole suite to themselves. When classes began, Judy felt a little bit reenergized. Schoolwork was something she could put her attention in, and she liked all of her classes. She also knew pretty quickly that she wasn't going to have any problem keeping up with her school work, so she would be able to visit her aunt and get involved in some of the social activities. She and Sarah attended some of the extracurricular lectures and other events on the campus, and Judy found an intramural Tai Chi class. The familiar was comforting, and although it had been a while, she hadn't lost her muscle memory.

She also discovered that she liked to walk the streets of Manhattan. She liked being just one of many different people. The anonymity gave her some comfort. She was slowly putting the broken pieces of her life back together, little by little.

As the first semester was coming to an end, Judy was feeling a bit melancholy. The weather had turned cold, and there had already been a couple of snow flurries. She was missing her mom, Kay, and Vihaan, and wasn't much looking forward to the holidays.

One Saturday afternoon, while Judy was at Maddie's studying for her last final, Maddie came into the living room.

Hey Judy, I have some wander lust. What do you think about spending the holidays with me in Cancun? We could veg out on the beach, see the ruins, and eat lots of Mexican food.

Maddie figured this would be an easy enough trip for the both of them, nothing too far or complicated.

Judy looked up from her Sociology text book. She was envisioning the two of them hanging out in Mexico, and it didn't sound so bad. Actually, she had always been interested in learning more about native cultures, and Mexico was as good a place to start as any.

Aunt Maddie, I think that's an excellent idea.

Okay. Maddie clapped her hands together. I will call Jessica tomorrow and have her set it all up.

Two weeks in Mexico was really good for Judy. She and Maddie went on a few excursions, swam in the beautiful Caribbean Sea, ate way too much food, and had a very fun time. They both felt a little bit sad about flying back to New York, but Judy was also looking forward to her second semester. She missed Sarah and was excited to hang out and get a little bit more involved in campus life. So, once they were back, it didn't take her long to get back into the swing.

She moved back into her residence hall, and it was as if she and Sarah hadn't even been apart. They picked right back up where they had left off during finals and were really thrilled when they discovered that their suite mates had moved on and nobody else had been assigned to their suite. They were able to use the second bedroom as storage, which was very nice.

About three weeks into school, Judy was walking out of her English class one afternoon, not paying attention, and bumped into a guy coming out of his history class. Her books went flying, and he was startled.
I'm so sorry, said Judy.
No worries. Aren't you in my Soc 2 class?
Um, I'm sorry; I'm not sure.
Maybe you'd like to go out some time?
Boy, he was kind of direct, and it made Judy uncomfortable. She still felt a bit like a widow and hadn't had any interest in guys since the loss of Vihaan.
Oh, thank you, but I'm really just focused on my studies.
Well, if you change your mind, feel free to bump into me again.
Judy smiled politely but was sure she wanted to stay away from guys. She still had way too much to deal with scholastically and emotionally.

The rest of the semester went smoothly, and Judy was faced with summer. She was approaching the one year anniversary of Vihaan's death, and Aunt Maddie was very aware that this would be a pretty tough time. One afternoon, Maddie decided to go out on a limb.

Judy?

Maddie?

Do you have any plans for the summer?

I don't know. I was thinking about looking for a job.

Oh, why? That's no fun.

Okay, Judy chuckled. What do you have in mind?

Well, since you asked, how about traveling with me around the Greek Isles. It's been ages since I've been, and I would love to go with you. You are great travel company.

Oh, Aunt Maddie, I don't know. That's an awfully big trip.

Well, will you at least think about it?

I promise I will think about it.

The next day, Judy brought it up in therapy. Together, she and her therapist went through the pros and cons of going to Greece instead of staying in New York, and frankly, the pros outweighed the cons by a lot. So, when Judy left the therapist's office, she went to Maddie's to tell her she was in.

That's great news! I'm calling Jessica right now. Oh Judy, we are going to have the best time. I promise.

So, an itinerary was created, and a date was chosen.

The two packed way too much and headed off to the airport. They flew into Athens, spent a couple of days and then got on a boat and went to four of the Greek Isles.

The trip was fantastic, and although Judy had some blue days around the anniversary of Vihaan's death, for the most part she did her best to stay focused on where she was and with whom.

They returned home with a couple of weeks left before school and spent the rest of the summer enjoying Manhattan.

Second year was better than the first. Judy was in a few Sociology courses and loved them. She knew she had chosen the right major and was grateful for all of her traveling because she was able to apply cultural experiences to the theories and concepts she was learning in her classes. The semester flew by, and before she knew it, it was the holidays again. She wished Sarah a happy holiday and headed to her aunt's apartment.

As she walked in, she asked, so Aunt Maddie, where are we going this time?

Maddie asked her where she would like to go.

Hmmm, how about Spain? That way, I could practice my Spanish. I've completed three semesters. That's got to count for something.

Bueno, said Maddie. Vamanos.

Judy smiled. Let's call Jessica.

So, once again, they spent the winter break overseas, and neither was disappointed. They traveled from Madrid to Barcelona and then over to the Canary Islands. By the time they returned, Judy's Spanish was much improved, and she had gained a little too much weight.

That's it, Maddie. My New Year's Resolution is to lose all of the weight I've gained.

Okay girl, but it was so worth it, wasn't it?

Yeah, it was.

Judy hugged Maddie and headed back to school. She was entering the end of her second year and had been through so much. She was proud of herself for working through her grief and doing well in school. She and Sarah got even more involved in groups and made a few other friends, but then something changed.

In the early spring, Sarah met a guy in her Political Science class, and she was smitten. Her personality began to change. She's wasn't around as much, which was okay, but when she was in the suite, she wasn't her normal self.

What's going on Sar? Judy asked one Saturday morning.

What do you mean? Sarah replied.

Well, is everything okay?

Yeah, everything's fine.

Are you sure?

What's your problem, Judy? Are you jealous or something?

I don't have a problem, Sarah. It's just that your personality has changed, and I'm worried about you.

Well, just because I have a boyfriend and you don't, you don't have to be like that.

Like what? Concerned?

You're not my mother.

Obviously.

At this point, Judy realized this conversation was going nowhere.

You know what Sarah? Never mind.

Judy grabbed her jacket and left. She couldn't figure out what the heck was going on.

As she walked across the campus, she saw Phil, Sarah's boyfriend. He was with a group of guys, had his arm around a girl, and they all seemed high.

Hey Sarah's roommate, come here, Phil yelled across the quad.

Judy wasn't sure what to do. She didn't get a great vibe from Phil.

Can't right now, she yelled back and waved.

Ohhh, cmon. Don't be like that.

Although she had no interest in socializing with Phil and his friends, she figured maybe it would give her a clue about what was going on. She walked over to the group.

Hello, she said.

They all laughed.

What's so funny?

Oh, it's nothing, Phil said. Inside joke. You want a toke?

No, thanks. I don't use drugs.

Oooohhhhh, Phil said. Miss Goody Goody. So where's your nerdy roommate?

Do you mean your girlfriend?

This really cracked up the group.

What's going on, Phil? What are you doing with Sarah?

Well, Sarah, my sweet Sarah. We have lots of fun together.

Judy glared at him. I gotta go.

As she walked away, she heard Phil yell, hey, where are you going? The party's just starting.

They all laughed again.

What a bunch of losers, Judy thought.

Back at the suite, Judy found Sarah stretched out on the couch in their living room.

Hey, Sarah.

Sarah didn't respond.

I just saw your boyfriend and his friends.

So?

This peaked Sarah's interest.

He had his arm around another girl, and he was pretty high.

You go to hell, Sarah yelled at her. You're just jealous that I have a boyfriend.

Sarah, I'm not jealous; I'm concerned; I care about you.

Just because you had your prince on a white horse...It's not my fault he died.

Sarah! Judy exclaimed. Why are you being like this?

Judy burst into tears and ran into the bedroom.

Sarah didn't know how to correct this, and so instead dug herself deeper in. Just stay away from my boyfriend, she yelled through the door.

Judy then heard the suite door slam. She lay on her bed for a while, crying on and off and thinking about this situation. Sarah had become a really good friend, almost like a sister. She didn't want to lose her friend, but she couldn't live with her like this. She texted her Aunt Maddie to see if she was home, then packed a few things in case she decided to stay at her apartment.

Judy left campus, jumped on the subway, and headed downtown. She had a key, so just unlocked the door to her aunt's apartment and walked in.

Maddie? You here?

In here, hon.

Judy went into Maddie's bathroom.

Are you okay?

I'm okay. It's just the residual from my treatments, but all is well. So tell me, what's going on?

Judy went through the whole thing with Maddie.

Oh man, girls can be so brutal sometimes.

Maddie, could I stay here with you for a few days? With finals coming up, I can't deal with Sarah's drama. I need to focus.

You know you are always welcome here, baby. Mi casa es su casa.

They both laughed.

That's really good, Maddie.

Gracias, replied Maddie.

28
Graduation

Judy finished out the spring semester at Maddie's and stayed for the next two years. The apartment wasn't that big, but they figured out how to stay out of each other's way. Judy spent a lot of time in the library or getting involved in school activities and ultimately lost touch with Sarah. She often wondered if she could have handled things differently but felt like she needed to take care of herself, as did Sarah. While she was at school filling out her paperwork for graduation, she bumped into one of her original suite mates.

Hey, Judy, right? We were suite mates for like five minutes freshman year.

Oh yeah, hi. How have you been?

Cool, I'm actually going to graduate, which is kind of a freakin miracle considering everything I got mixed up in.

What do you mean?

Well, I was kinda wild, if you remember. And then there were all of the drugs. Actually, I guess you know about your friend Sarah, right?

No, we lost touch a couple of years ago.

Ohhh.

Why?

She overdosed about six months ago. She was running with a really tough crowd. I never would have guessed she would hook up with them, but I guess you never know about people.

Judy was in shock.

Is she okay?

No, Judy, like I said, she overdosed. She didn't make it. I was actually at that party, but I wasn't doing anything but weed. Anyways, I gotta bounce.

Bye, Judy said, somewhat in a daze. She felt so sad. She had abandoned her friend. If she had tried harder, maybe she could have helped her see the decisions she was making were so bad for her.

Later that week, she talked it out with her therapist. Her therapist helped her see that she's not responsible for other people's choices or actions. And doing the "If only, woulda, shoulda, coulda" is pointless.

Her therapist looked directly at Judy.

I'm going to be Captain Obvious for a moment. You have had an awful lot of loss in your life, and it's natural that you may feel responsible, but newsflash, you are not responsible. Come on, say it with me.

They chanted together – I am not responsible; I am not responsible; I am not responsible.

Good. Now, please let go of all that ugly, nasty guilt you have been carrying around with you. K?

K.

Judy left feeling better and would make an effort to let go of wanting to control everything around her. She made a resolution to start meditating and doing more Tai Chi. She found that the Tai Chi kept her pretty focused and present.

Back at Maddie's, Judy started thinking about what she was going to do next in her life. She was now a college graduate, from Columbia, no less, with a degree in Sociology. She still really loved people watching and learning about other cultures, languages, and traditions.

She wondered if it was time to go back to India to visit "her Indian family". Was she ready to face that pain again? Would they be so welcoming all of these years later? She had kept up some correspondence with Olivia, but Vihaan had been the link. Would she be moving in a backwards direction by going back? On the other hand, something was pulling on her to go. She couldn't get a tangible read on it, but she had a really strong sense that she needed to be in India at this point in her life.

When Maddie came home, Judy asked if she could take her out to dinner. She told her she had something big to talk about with her.

I never refuse a free meal, Maddie said with a grin. Just give me thirty minutes to get my shit together, and we can head out.

Judy felt like a big change was coming, in a good way.

They headed out to their favorite corner restaurant near Washington Square Park and ordered their usual.

So, what's on your mind, kiddo?

Maddie had the cutest pet names for Judy.

I've been doing a lot of thinking about what my next steps should be, and there is something drawing me to return to India.

Wow! I'm not sure what to think about that. Won't that stir up all the pain?

That's kind of the point. I think I may be ready to move past it once and for all. I don't know. I can't explain it, but I really feel like it's my next step.

Well, you have always had a very good head on your shoulders. I have never worried about you getting into trouble or making bad decisions. You've kinda been my measuring stick in a lot of ways, so if you feel like this is what you need to do, then I think you should do it. You are a bright and very intuitive person, Judy, so listen to your heart.

This was exactly the affirmation that Judy needed.

And, if you want, I'll go with you to Travel Time tomorrow to talk to Jessica.

Thank you, Aunt Maddie. I don't know what I would have done without you for all of these years.

Yeah, well, life sure can be funny, can't it? Who knew that you and I would become so close? It sure didn't seem to be in the stars for us early on.

After dinner, the two walked around the East Village for a while. Judy realized that one of the things she liked so much about Manhattan was the energy and the beat. There was so much creativity and life there, and you could be anyone or anything you wanted, and no one would blink an eye.

The next day, she and Maddie headed over to Travel Time to make arrangements. Judy felt excited about this trip. She felt as though there was something over the horizon, just beyond reach, and she needed to push through to get to it. She would leave in the morning for Mewar.

Back at the apartment, she packed and texted Olivia.

The response was a positive one. Actually, it was a little freaky. It was as though Olivia knew before Judy that Judy was planning to return.

Judy remembered their conversation from those years before – reincarnation, she thought.

Maddie rode with Judy to JFK the next morning, hugged her hard, made her promise to keep in contact, and held both her cheeks in her hands, looking directly in her eyes.

I love you sooo much, Judy. Go find yourself and then please come back to me.

Judy kissed Maddie right on the lips.

I'll see you soon, Maddie.

As she got out of the limo, Maddie called through the open window. Text me when you get there.

Judy raised her right hand up as if to say will do and goodbye, all with the same gesture.

29

Searching

The flight was long but uneventful. No surprise to Judy that there was a limo waiting for her at the airport in India. And, she realized, she had never taken off her engagement ring. It had become a part of her, and she didn't even notice that she was wearing it.

The driver took Judy's bags and opened the car door. Inside were Olivia and Bandhupala.

Ohhh, Judy cried out. What a wonderful surprise! They all hugged and rocked and cried.

This was the start of a journey, Judy thought.

Welcome home, my child, Olivia said with tears in her eyes. And congratulations on graduating from Columbia. Vihaan would be so very proud.

Judy gave her a tear-filled smile.

I miss him so much, Olivia.

I know, my dear. I know.

The drive to the palace was quick, and everyone was standing out front when they pulled in.

There was cheering and clapping and a big congratulations banner.

Judy felt this was way more than she deserved, but she remained ever polite.

Come, Olivia said. You must be hungry.

They ate and talked and laughed.

Some of Vihaan's siblings had since married and had children, adding an adorable youngest generation to the family's legacy. At one point, Bandhupala sat down next to Judy.

So, he said. Have you found another mate? I noticed you are still wearing your engagement ring.

Judy thought this was a strange question, but maybe something was getting lost in the translation.

Actually, no. I've spent the past four years focused on my studies. I haven't had any interest in dating. After knowing your brother, the boys at college seemed so inappropriate, do you know what I mean?

I think so. Perhaps I could take you out to dinner while you are here?

Judy stared at Bandhupala. She was taken by surprise and took a moment to respond.

Bandhupala, what are you suggesting? She asked with some hesitation.

Bandhupala blushed a little bit.

Judy read his body language and tried to ease the tension he was feeling with his question to her.

Bandhupala, you were so kind and supportive to me four years ago, and I love you for that, but, and I hope this doesn't offend you - I am not looking for a relationship.

Bandhupala let out a deep sigh. Honestly, I have been missing my brother so deeply and felt that I could somehow fill the emptiness by taking over as your partner. I've waited to marry because I felt a responsibility to you and most importantly, to my brother Vihaan.

Oh, my goodness, Bandhupala. That is so very sweet, but not at all necessary. I wish we had had this talk four years ago. I'm sorry you waited so long.

It was my pleasure, Judy. I don't think I would have been ready for a serious relationship before now anyway. Perhaps now, we can both begin to move forward in our lives.

Judy hugged him and kissed him on the cheek. You will always be my brother, she whispered in his ear.

He looked at her and said, and you will always be my sister.

This encounter meant a lot to Judy. It confirmed that she was supposed to be there in India, and she already felt as if the healing had begun, not just for her, but also for Vihaan's family.

Bandhupala walked away, leaving her amongst this wonderful family. She sat for a while, watching the interactions, and then excused herself. The trip had caught up with her, and sleep was just about all she could think of.

Olivia showed her up to her room, the same room she had stayed in four years ago.

Do you have any plans, Judy?

No.

If you are up to it tomorrow, I would like to introduce you to a friend of mine.

That sounds good, said Judy.

Good. Sweet dreams, my dear. Welcome home.

Olivia closed the door, and Judy began to cry. She had anticipated that this would be an emotional trip, but there was something else too. There was something about Olivia.

Well, let it go, Judy, she said to herself. Let go; let God.

She fell into a very sound sleep. She had vivid dreams that were peaceful and comforting. She was in a meadow, filled with wildflowers and birds. She felt whole and loved. Then there was a stroke and a whisper.

You are loved.

This jarred Judy out of her dream. She sat up thinking someone was there.

As the cobwebs cleared, she remembered the dream she had had of her mother coming to her. This felt very similar.

Judy looked at her phone. It was already mid-morning, so she got up and dressed and headed downstairs.

She found some of the family in the kitchen.

In unison they greeted her. Good morning, Judy.

Judy couldn't help but smile. She had spent so much of her life alone or mostly alone, so having all of these people around felt really good.

Good morning, she chirped.

Are you hungry?

Oh yes.

Okay, please have a seat.

The small group ate and chatted and laughed. They caught up on boyfriends and husbands and the latest fashions.

Then Olivia said, Okay. Judy and I have an appointment. We will be back later.

They headed out and got in the limo.

Where are we going? Judy asked out of curiosity.

She trusted Olivia with her life and so knew that this was going to be a great adventure.

You will soon know, was Olivia's response. And as you already know, you are ready to take the next step.

Judy stared at Olivia. How did she know her thoughts, her desires? They had written back and forth a bit but nothing in depth.

Olivia?

Judy, allow.

Those words penetrated into her soul. What was happening? She felt a little strange and just a tad uncomfortable.

After about twenty minutes in the car, they turned off of the main road and headed down a dirt road. The foliage was so beautiful, and Judy got lost in the energy of the trees and flowers.

After another fifteen minutes, they pulled into a small driveway that led to a few very simple buildings.

Judy was intrigued.

Olivia said something to the driver in Hindi, and then she and Judy got out of the car.

They walked over to what looked like the main building and entered through a big, old, ornately carved wooden door. Judy immediately smelled incense and heard chanting somewhere in the distance. She followed Olivia down a short hallway and into an office. They both sat down but said nothing. The wait seemed like forever, but finally a very elderly man with a long white beard came in. Olivia placed her hands together, palms facing, stood, and bowed. She said, Khamaghani.

Judy followed suit.

Judy, it is my humble honor to introduce you to Swami Ravi Baba Singh. He is a very revered Guru in this part of India and is a distant relative. It is time for you to learn from him. You are ready.

Judy looked at Olivia.

I'm confused, she said. With all respect, Olivia, I don't understand.

I know, my child. I know.

Olivia said something to Swami Ravi Baba Singh, bowed, and left.

Ummm,

Swami Ravi then spoke.

Please follow Dasa. She will show you to your room.

Judy was confused, but something deep inside felt right.

Dasa, that's a pretty name. What does it mean?

Dasa is the term for servant. We are all referred to as Dasa to teach humility.

Oh, said Judy.

You may sleep here, Dasa pointed to a small, simple cot like bed. We will share the space. Please keep it clean and show respect.

Dasa walked out leaving Judy alone in the small room. As she looked around, she noticed one of her suitcases sitting in the corner.

Olivia, Judy thought.

Okay, so this is my path. This is what the calling was. Judy, step up to the plate. Put your big girl pants on and buckle your seat belt; you're in for a ride.

Judy left the space and wandered around the small complex. It was so beautiful.

She came to a structure and walked in.

Namaste, she heard from behind a counter.

Namaste. I'm new here and not really sure what to do. Is there someone who could help me?

Yes, of course. I'm Katie.

Judy.

Welcome, Judy. Did you just arrive?

Yes. A friend dropped me off. She told me we were going to meet a friend of hers, but when we arrived, she left me here. I realize that this is where I should be right now, but I wasn't expecting to be here, and so am a little lost.

Okay. It's no problem. Have you been shown your room?

Yes, that I know.

Good. That's a good first step. I'll show you around, and we'll find out what your work assignment is.

What does that mean?

Everyone here is given a job to do. It helps us stay humble and appreciate the simpler aspects of life.

Boy, I've kind of gone from riches to rags, Judy thought. This should be interesting.

Judy was assigned the task of helping prepare meals. Once she got to know her way around the kitchen and became friendly with the other kitchen workers, she actually really enjoyed working in the kitchen. Everyone was very nice and pretty calm.

There must be something to this whole meditation thing, she thought.

Judy arose each day at four-thirty to attend morning meditation. She found the chanting to be comforting and predictable, but it took her quite a while to learn the words in Sanskrit.

After morning meditation, she headed over to the kitchen to help set up for breakfast. There were about ten participants plus five sort of staff people and of course Swami Ravi Baba

Singh, when he was there, so sixteen people in all to cook for three times a day. It did keep her busy, but she learned a lot about preparing very simple, tasty vegetarian meals using lots of grains, vegetables, spices, and beans. She enjoyed the meals.

During the little bit of free time they were all given, Judy wandered around the property. She participated in a walking meditation amongst the trees and plants. She often sat right down on the ground, took some deep breaths, and allowed herself to go, often to her meadow. She secretly hoped that Vihaan might appear to her, to reassure her, and maybe even give her some guidance.

One day, while she was sitting in the woods in her usual meditative state, she felt something on her shoulder. She opened her eyes and turned to look at her left shoulder. To her surprise, there was a butterfly just sitting there. It was a Tree Nymph Butterfly, which is very rare in India.

Hello, she said. You are welcome to sit on my shoulder as long as you like. I am honored that you have chosen to sit with me. The butterfly sat for quite a while, and Judy went back into her meditation. She traveled through her meadow, breathing steadily, enjoying the flowers and watching the multitude of butterflies that suddenly filled the meadow. It was like watching a rainbow. The colors were extraordinarily sharp and bright. They took Judy's breath away.

Then, suddenly, she heard a flurry of flutter. She quickly opened her eyes and could have sworn that she saw Vihaan flying away.

But that can't be, she thought. That was a butterfly on my shoulder, certainly not a person.

She stood up and walked back to the kitchen to help prepare dinner. As she was working, she shared her experience with Valerie, who was also assigned to the kitchen.

Well, said Val, the butterfly is the symbol of rebirth, so maybe it was Vihaan's way of letting you know that he is reincarnating. Who knows, you may end up finding each other again.

This concept was comforting for Judy. She liked to think that he was okay and that maybe they would see each other again. It gave her the motivation and determination to continue meditating and serving with the goal of gaining more insight.

As the days came and went, Judy got better at sitting for long periods of time in meditation, chanting, and devotion. She began to have really vivid dreams, some making sense, others simply leaving an impression.

Occasionally, Olivia would stop by for a visit. On one of her visits, she told Judy that she grew up at this particular Ashram. It was like a second home to her, and so she knew Judy needed to spend time here as well.

Olivia, may I ask you a question?

Of course.

It seems like you knew before I did that this would be my path.

I see.

How?

In this physical world, we live within time constraints, in a linear fashion. As you free yourself, dissolving ego, you will find that time is ultimately an illusion. It serves a purpose in a practical sense, but the truth is nonlinear, and in fact is not bound by time the way we understand it.

You really have insight.

I was orphaned as a very young child. Swami Ravi found me in the street and took me in. He knew I would never survive on my own at such a young age. I grew up right here in this Ashram, and because of that had the opportunity to live a life of service and meditation for almost my entire life. In essence, Swami Ravi is like a father to me. He saw my true self well before I had any idea of who I actually was. When I met you the first time, I saw much the same in you. I knew that we were destined to walk the path together, that part of my mission would be to help you find your way. It was just a matter of time, so to speak. You see, my child, you and I are not stran-gers. We have been together in other lifetimes, but this is a conversation we will have at a later date. I must return home. We are hosting guests who cannot be left unattended.

Olivia looked Judy straight in the eyes.

Trust your heart, even if things seem as though they can't pos-sibly be.

She kissed Judy on the forehead and was gone.

My, Judy thought. She is one cool lady!

Judy continued to serve, even leaving the Ashram to help the less fortunate.

Lessons of humility may be found in all corners, said Swami Ravi at one of his rare public appearances. Do what must be done.

Judy liked Swami Ravi. She wished she could talk with him about so many things, but she learned early on that that was not how things worked here.

Val explained one afternoon while they were peeling carrots that Swami will come to you if there is a need for him to share something with you. He is aware of all of us and where we are in our process. His is not to control us but to guide us. It's up to us to commit to enlightenment.

And so Judy did. She chanted, meditated, and served each day. One day blended into the other.

After about eight months, she was beginning to feel frus-trated. She expected there to be something. She thought she would perhaps see the future, or hear the dead, or something.

She looked forward to another visit from Olivia so that she could get some clarity on when changes might happen.

A month or so later, Olivia did return to visit Judy.

So, it seems you are feeling stagnant in your process.

Judy half expected that Olivia would know Judy's struggle be-fore she told her.

Yes. I just thought I would have some great insight or under-standing. I have been sitting in meditation for months now and have peeled a ton of carrots and potatoes. I've washed the feet of the homeless, scrubbed floors, and chanted with the best of them, and still I don't feel as if any change has occurred. Let go, Judy. Let go. Be not the seeker. Allow the universe to teach you and support you. Let go.

Olivia turned and walked away.

But…oh, okay.

Judy went into the garden of trees away from the buildings and the others at the Ashram and sat. Let go, she chanted. Let go, let go. Get out of your head. Let go. She listened to her breath – in and out and in and out. She sat for hours, missing dinner. The day turned to night, and Judy sat within the trees. Breathing, breathing, in and out, let go.

After about eleven hours of meditation, she heard the slightest whisper say, yes.

Yes what? she asked from within.

Yes.

Mom? Is that you? Vihaan? What do I need to know?

Yes.

Okay, she said. She gave up wanting to understand and stood up slowly and made her way back to her bed. She fell into it without washing, and she slept.

She jerked awake at four-thirty the next morning expecting to feel exhausted, but instead, she had an energy that she had never before experienced. She dressed and went to morning meditation. She noticed that she was barely touching the ground. Hmmm, she thought.

Okay. Once again, she let it go.

As she was meditating, she remembered the day before. She went deep and realized that the answer was so simple. Yes. Of course. Forgiveness is acceptance. Yes, is the answer. Acceptance to all things.

It made so much sense. She had had an epiphany.

I've got it Olivia, she said out loud.

The tricky part was to live it.

30
Where is Home Now?

One year to the day that Olivia brought Judy to the Ashram, she felt it was time to rejoin the world. She was under no false illusions that she had much training still to go, but that awareness in itself was an indicator of how far she had come.

She spent a couple of days at the palace visiting and soaking up Olivia's insight, and then she was on a plane and heading back to New York.

Judy made her way across town to Maddie's. She had missed her and was excited to spend time with her.

Maddie, Judy called as she keyed into the apartment. You home?

Judy walked through the apartment and into Maddie's bedroom.

Hi, honey. She heard a very weak voice coming from the darkness.

Maddie?

I'm here.

What happened?

My cancer has come back with a vengeance.

Oh, Aunt Maddie. I'm so sorry I haven't been here for you.

Then Judy heard the toilet flush.

Oh, that's my nurse, Lila. Lila, this is Judy.

It's very nice to meet you. Maddie has told me so much about you.

Judy didn't even acknowledge her.

But, Maddie.

Judy, come sit here next to me on the bed. I do not, I repeat, do not want you to feel that you should have stayed in New York. First of all, I was fine when you left.

Yeah, but why didn't you call me when you got sick again?

You had important self-reflection to do, and I was on my own path. I feel exceptionally blessed to have had the time I had with you. You are an amazing young woman with unbelievable strength, and I know that you will be fine in this life. Now listen, my time is very limited. Please promise me that you will not carry guilt. You've been through enough, and I need to leave this earth knowing that you are okay.

Judy was sobbing.

Aunt Maddie...!?!

Judy, we had some good times, didn't we? I will hold you in my heart now and forever, my love. Please smile when you think of me. I don't want any lingering sadness. Celebrate me. That is the best way to keep my spirit alive. Promise?

Judy nodded.

Judy took Maddie's hand in hers. They sat in silence for a while, then Lila asked Judy if she could get her anything.

No thank you, Lila. I'm just going to sit here with Maddie for a while.

Okay. I'll be in the living room. Let me know if either of you needs anything at all.

Judy sat with Maddie as she slept. Her breathing was strained. Apparently, the cancer had just spread everywhere, but Maddie swore she wasn't in any pain. After a few hours, Judy lay down by Maddie and fell asleep.

Something caused her to stir at about four the next morning. Judy sat up.

Maddie?

She looked over to the other side of the bed. Maddie was there but there were no breath sounds. Maddie? Tears started forming. Lila!!! Judy yelled.

Lila came running into the bedroom.

I don't think she's breathing.

Lila put her stethoscope to Maddie's heart.

She's gone, Judy.

Judy was frozen. She couldn't move.

Judy?

Judy looked at Lila.

She got out of Maddie's bed and walked like a zombie to the bathroom. She locked the door and got in the shower. She wailed and sobbed for at least thirty minutes.

Meanwhile, Lila called an ambulance and her agency to let them know.

Maddie had already made all arrangements and had asked Lila to contact her lawyer once the time came, so that was the third call Lila made. She let the attorney know that Judy was back in town, and the attorney said he would contact her in a day or so.

Lila then knocked on the bathroom door.

Judy? Are you okay? Can you come out?

Judy was just drying herself off. She wrapped the towel around herself and opened the door.

I've called the ambulance to come and also spoke to the lawyer. He will call you.

Your aunt made specific arrangements, so you won't have to take care of anything.

Judy stood there with a towel around her listening to Lila. She stared blankly at her.

I'm so very sorry, Judy. Maddie loved you so much. You were her world.

Judy put on some clothes and sat with Lila in the living room waiting for the ambulance.

As they carried Maddie's body away, Judy thought about "yes".

Yes is not always easy, she said out loud.

What, honey? Lila asked.

Nothing, Judy responded.

Well, again, I am so sorry for your loss. Your aunt was a special person. Is there anything I can do for you? Anyone I can call?

Judy then realized that she was completely alone.

No, Lila, thank you.

Okay. Then I'll be going.

Lila collected her things and left.

Judy sat down in the middle of the living room and tried to draw on the past year's experiences. What is the meaning of all of this? How many losses can one person endure? Is my karma so bad that I am destined to spend my life alone? Why does everybody I love leave me? This really sucks. SUCKS!!!

Okay, breathe, Judy. Meditate, breathe, meditate, breathe.

Judy went in. She went to her meadow. She sat there for a while amongst the flowers. This was her familiar place; it was safe and calm and beautiful. Her breaths were steady. She looked across the meadow and way off in the distance, she saw a form.

Who's there? she asked.

The form was coming toward her very slowly.

Who are you?

As the form got closer, Judy recognized him. It was Vihaan.

Vihaan, she cried. She stood up in the meadow and ran toward him. He held out his hands.

Vihaan, I miss you so much.

He didn't speak but instead just held her hands in his.

I can't go on alone, Vihaan. I can't.

He looked at her with so much love. Although he didn't verbalize, she understood that she had to carry on. It wasn't her time. She also understood that they would be together again. He released Judy's hands and turned and walked away.

Instead of collapsing, Judy felt an internal strength rise up in her. She came out of the meditation with a renewed sense of peace.

In the next days, Judy buried her aunt, met with the lawyer, and tied up loose ends. She decided to stay in the apartment for a while to figure out a direction. Between the trust left by her parents and a small inheritance from Kay and now from Maddie, she was okay for a while, and Maddie's apartment was paid for – her stepfather bought it for her as a graduation gift when real estate was reasonable in the City. School was also completely paid for, and she thought about maybe going to graduate school, but she didn't feel particularly motivated to do so.

Frankly, Judy was pretty lost. She continued working with her therapist and continued doing Tai Chi and meditating. She missed her family in India, but that didn't seem like the answer either. She took long walks in Central Park and eventually got a job as a waitress in a local diner near her apartment, just for some socialization. She enjoyed serving customers and got to know the regulars and their stories. She had learned while at the Ashram that no job is greater than another and the purpose was to serve, whether bringing someone a cup of coffee or lending a shoulder.

She also liked that there wasn't a lot of responsibility being a waitress. She walked out the door at the end of the day and left it all behind her - a lesson in staying present and not carrying baggage around.

The days ran into weeks which ran into months, and after a while, Judy felt a shift. It had been a year since her return to the city, and it was definitely time for a change.

31
New Hampshire

After much contemplation, Judy realized that she was still living in an emotional bubble of her own design. It was safe, but she was becoming tired of being alone, and her challenge, she now understood completely, was to burst the bubble.

No more ostriching, she said to herself. That's why you left Manhattan.

One year ago, she had taken a deep breath, bought a used Prius, sold her aunt's apartment in the city, and drove north. She had settled down in a small New England town and was beginning a "new" life.

Meeting Steve and Meg would prove to be life changing. Judy was on a path that felt right, and forward was the only direction she wanted to move in. She had been teaching at the studio now for a couple of months and was finding a nice rhythm and routine to her life. Her goal was to keep her stress level at a minimum and stay open to whatever might come.

She had found a good therapist just three towns over, a referral from her Manhattan therapist, and they seemed to click. Judy was only seeing her about once a month or so; they called it maintenance visits. She also called Olivia periodically, just to stay connected.

As she was coming out of her morning meditation one Sunday, her cell phone rang.

Hi, Steve.

Hey, Judy. Meg and I thought we'd head out to Janson's pond for a swim since it's going to be ninety today. Would you like to join us?

Oh, that's so nice of you to ask. It sounds fun. Should I meet you there?

If you want, we'll pick you up. I would love to see your Snow White cottage.

Oh, okay.

Judy's heart started pounding. She hadn't had anyone over since she had moved in over a year ago. Maybe it was time to break through that resistance.

What time are you thinking?

How does an hour sound?

I'll watch for you. You have the address, right?

Sure do.

See you then.

Judy hung up and went into action. Chloe lifted her head and let out a little meow as if to say, what's all the flutter? Come nap with me.

Can't baby, I've got to straighten up. We're having company.

Chloe didn't have any idea what Judy was talking about and frankly, didn't care. She fell back to sleep in a sun spot that was shining through the sliding glass doors overlooking the backyard.

Meanwhile, Judy rushed around putting things away and wiping down her countertops. Her home was hardly a pig sty, but she had her standards.

She put on her bathing suit and then a tee shirt and shorts over it. She packed a hat, sun block, sunglasses, and extra tee shirt. She dug under her bed and found a pair of flips.

Okay, she said to herself. I'm ready.

She sat down in the living room and worked on centering herself.

C'mon Judy. It's just a social outing with two people you know and like. Piece of cake.

She closed her eyes and breathed. Chloe must have sensed her anxiety. She stood up, stretched in a downward dog pose and jumped up onto Judy. She bumped against her and purred and kneaded her.

Judy opened her eyes and stroked Chloe.

Thank you, Chloe. You are very helpful.

Judy wasn't kidding. The distraction took away her anxiety.

Within ten minutes, the doorbell rang.

Okay, girl, here we go.

Judy got up and opened the door.

Hi, guys, she said. Please, come on in.

Oh, Judy, Meg exclaimed, I love it. It's sooo cute. How did you ever find this place? And if you ever move out, you have to let me move in, deal?

Judy smiled. Deal.

She showed Steve and Meg around and took them out to the backyard.

So this is all yours? Steve asked.

Well, I don't own it if that's what you mean, but the property is private and can't be built on. Chloe and I often take walks for hours at a time. The woods go way back.

That's fantastic, said Steve. By the way, whose Chloe?

Oh, she's my cat companion. I'm her person.

Meg giggled. That's funny.

Well, you girls ready?

Ready, they said together.

I'm just going to grab my bag. I'll meet you out front.

Judy went through the house, grabbed her bag and kissed Chloe on the head. See you later, my baby.

Kneow was the response.

Judy came out the front and jumped into the back seat.

Okay, drive away, Steve. Where did you say we are going?

Janson's Pond. You've never been?

Never.

Oh, you're in for a treat.

Good. I like treats.

The pond was about a thirty-minute drive. There were a few others there, but it was surprisingly quiet.

It's big enough to give us some privacy, Steve said with authority.

Steve parked by a tree about thirteen yards from the pond. He knew the best spot because he had been coming to Janson's since he was a kid.

Judy grabbed her bag and jumped out of the car. It was really hot out and a little muggy, so the pond looked very inviting. She applied some sun block and asked Steve and Meg if they wanted any. Meg put some extra on her face. She said she was so fair and had to be really careful.

Off they went down to the pond. As they got closer, Judy noticed a tire swing hanging from a branch over the water.

Oh wow! That looks really fun!

C'mon, Steve said in some disbelief. You're not going to tell me that you've never been on a tire swing. What kind of sheltered life have you been leading?

His smile was infectious. Judy really liked Steve and Meg. They felt like family, and that was a welcome and needed feeling.

I wouldn't say I've lived a sheltered life, but it's true that I've never been on a tire swing, particularly one that swings over the water.

Okay, Steve said. Allow me to baptize you.

Steve jumped into the water and grabbed the tire.

While he was getting the tire, Judy took off her shorts and top so she would be ready.

He swam, pulling the rope to shore.

For you, my queen, he said jokingly.

Judy realized he was playing, and knew he had no idea about that part of her past, but it still stung a little.

Shake it off, girl. Stay present. Yes, yes, she said to herself.

Yes had become a strong and meaningful mantra for Judy, and she found herself saying it more and more often.

She grabbed the swing. Here goes nothing, she called.

Judy jumped onto the tire and let it go out over the water.

Wooooooo, she yelled as the tire swung back and forth. On about the third time out, Judy let go and splashed down into the pond. The sensation of hitting the water and sinking down was refreshing. She opened her eyes for just a moment while under the water and tried to focus. The water was a little murky, but as she adjusted, she could have sworn she saw Vihaan a few feet in front of her under the water sitting by some water reeds, just swaying and smiling. She inhaled from the shock, took in way too much water, and surfaced quickly, gasping and choking.

You okay,? Steve shouted from the shoreline.

Judy couldn't speak because of the water in her windpipe, but she was able to lift a hand as if to say all good.

Steve wasn't convinced. He jumped in and swam to her. Here, he said, let me pat your back. That might help. They stood in the shallow part of the pond. Judy gagging and coughing, and Steve patting her back. She noticed a little sensation when Steve touched her bare skin but was too busy trying to recover to pay much attention.

After about five minutes, Judy was fine. Thanks, Steve, she said raspily.

You sure you're okay? Steve asked. I don't want to lose my prize teacher. He grinned.

Something about that struck Judy. She started laughing and couldn't stop.

Oh my god, Judy. What is going on?

I don't know, Steve. That just struck me as really funny. No explanation.

None needed. Steve smiled at her in a way that moved her.

Hmmm, she thought.

Maybe you should take a break from the tire swing, he said.

Maybe, she said.

At that point Meg showed up.

Where ya been, Sis? You missed all the excitement.

I walked around the pond to get us some orange ices. Why, what did I miss?

Oh nothing, Judy and Steve answered simultaneously.

Okay, well then, here take your ices. They're already melting.

Meg handed Steve and Judy their ices in a white paper cup.

There was orange juice running down the sides of the cups.

Judy licked around the edges.

Wow, is that good! Judy proclaimed.

Oh no, Steve said. You are not gonna tell me that you've never had an orange ice.

Sorry, Judy said with a smile, but I have had a Balinese Long-tailed monkey on my shoulder. Does that count for something?

Oh, do tell.

That's a story for another day.

They finished their ices and all jumped back into the pond. They splashed and swam and laughed. A couple of times, Steve and Judy crashed into one another, and it wasn't so bad. On the contrary, it was actually really nice.

After about two hours, Steve asked if they were hungry.

Yes. Both girls responded emphatically.

They all got out of the pond and dried off, sitting on towels in the late afternoon sun.

The conversation was light and cheerful.

Judy then asked about Steve and Meg's childhood.

Did you come to Janson's a lot together?

Actually, Steve did more than I did. He's five years older, and we didn't meet until I was six.

Judy had a confused look on her face. But aren't you brother and sister?

We sure are Steve said, pushing Meg so that she almost tipped completely over in a sitting position.

Hey, stop Steve, she cried out in a whiny voice.

Judy smiled. You two are very cute.

Ahhhhhh! Steve said. We're so cute.

They all three laughed.

Come on you cute girls, let's eat. My stomach is growling.

Steve has a rumbly in his tumbly, Meg teased.

Ha ha, Steve mocked.

Okay you two, don't make me have to discipline you, Judy said sternly.

They all laughed again.

I like her, Meg said out loud to Steve.

So do I, Steve said.

Judy blushed a little bit.

They all got dressed and hiked back to the car.

Okay, where to? Steve asked.

You guys chose, Judy said, and it's my treat.

Well, in that case, Meg said.

Meg, be nice. Steve looked at Meg with a serious face.

Okay, Meg said in a pouty voice.

No, Judy said. Where do you want to go Meg?

The Copper Door.

Oh, Meg, stop, Steve scolded.

No, Judy said. It's okay. I would love to take you both to the Copper Door. It sounds intriguing.

Judy, that's really not necessary.

Listen. You guys are my only friends here, and it took me over a year to find you. That means a lot to me. Not to be over dramatic, but I don't make friends easily, and I really appreciate how easy you both are to be with. So, please, let me do this for you. You would be giving me the gift of being able to say thank you.

Steve smiled. Well, that's very zen of you.

Judy smiled.

I knew you'd understand. Do we need to change clothes?

The restaurant is nice but not super fancy, Meg said.

We should change, Steve said. He looked at Judy. How about I drop you home so you can change?

Then Meg and I will go change and pick you back up.

Are you sure you don't want me to meet you at your house or at the restaurant?

No, at least allow me to be your chauffeur.

Judy had a quick flashback. She shook her head as if to clear her thoughts.

You okay? Meg asked.

Yes, fine. Okay, I think we have a plan.

After I drop you off, I'll call and make a reservation, Steve said more to himself than to the girls.

Steve and Meg dropped Judy off and told her they'd be back in under an hour.

Sounds good. I'll be ready.

Judy fed Chloe and changed her water. I'm going out tonight baby, so you're in charge.

Chloe meowed and rubbed against Judy's leg.

As Judy headed to her bedroom to get undressed and shower, she heard a whisper.

Yes.

She stopped in her tracks.

She hadn't turned the light on yet in her bedroom and when she looked in, she thought she saw a figure.

Vihaan? she whispered.

Yes.

Then the figure was gone.

Okay, acceptance. Yes, she said to herself. Yes.

She got in the shower and enjoyed the hot water beating down on her.

She then went over to her closet to pick out something nice but not super fancy, as Meg described.

She fixed her hair and even decided to put on some makeup. It had been a long time, but she was in a pretty happy place at the moment and so went for it.

Steve and Meg rang the bell about ten minutes after Judy was finished getting ready. She grabbed a light sweater, just in case the restaurant was blasting their air conditioning, and opened the door.

Hi, I'm ready to go.

I can see that, Steve chuckled. You must be as hungry as I am.

They got in the car and headed off to the Copper Door. The drive took about forty minutes, but Meg assured Judy that it was so worth it.

Once there, Steve handed his key to the valet and in they went. The restaurant was very New England with its beautiful stone fireplace and dark wood. It was cozy and comfortable.

The three were seated at a table and handed menus.

Would you like to start off with a beverage?

Steve looked at Judy.

Are you remembering the last time? she asked.

He laughed.

Judy started the ball rolling.

Do you have Stella on tap?

Sure do.

I'll have a Stella please.

That sounds good, said Steve. Two Stellas. Meg?

Ummm, may I have a glass of Shiraz?

Okay, said the server. My name is Angela, and I will be right back with your drinks.

Angela left, and Steve started looking around.

Man, I haven't been in this place in ages. I guess my business has been kind of consuming me.

Yeah, Judy said. It's important to find your balance.

They all picked up menus and scanned through.

What looks good? she asked to no one in particular.

Meg said, I know what I'm having.

Steve then said, I bet I know too.

Judy asked, what am I missing here?

Go ahead Steve, tell her.

Meg's most favorite thing in the whole wide world is shrimp. She'll eat it prepared anyway; she's not picky.

So, what are you getting Meg?

Oh, the creamy shrimp and veggie pasta. I can already taste it.

Steve handed her a napkin.

What's this for? she asked.

You're salivating.

Judy laughed. That's funny. Steve, what are you getting?

Let's see, hmmm. I think I'll go for the Moroccan spiced swordfish.

What about you, Judy?

I think the arugula and roasted beet salad, asparagus, and roasted garlic smashed potato, so nobody try to kiss me tonight.

I make no promises, Steve said with a big smile on his face.

Interesting, Meg said.

Just then the drinks came.

A toast to our new friend, Judy.

The three clinked glasses and sipped.

Boy, is that good, Judy said. It's been a really long time since I've had a beer.

Yeah, Steve said, but not that long since you had sake, right?

Oh yeah, Judy laughed. Don't worry, there won't be a repeat performance.

Okay, but just in case, I got your back.

Ahh, that's my big brother, ever the gentleman.

Shut up, Meg.

Meg stuck her tongue out at Steve.

It's fascinating how the two of you can revert back to when you were children.

Well, I guess there's habits that we never lose.

Angela then came over.

Okay, you guys ready?

Hey, Judy said, do you want to share an appetizer?

Good idea, Steve said.

What about the Mediterranean hummus?

Yeah, that sounds good.

Okay, one Mediterranean hummus, please.

All right, and for your entrees?

They all ordered and drank and talked.

Judy was having a really nice time.

Do you guys go out together a lot?

Not if we can help it, Steve teased.

Meg slapped him on the arm.

But seriously, we actually don't socialize that much. Maybe because we work together. Outside of work, I think I see you at Mom and Dad's more than anywhere else.

Yeah, that sounds right.

Meg, do you have a boyfriend?

Steve looked at Meg.

Yeah Meg, do you have a boyfriend?

Meg blushed. I've been seeing someone for a few months. It's still pretty casual.

Have Mom and Dad met him?

No. We're not anywhere near there yet.

Angela placed the hummus on the table.

Enjoy, she said.

That looks really good, Judy said.

They each took some and dipped the pita that came with it.

Yummy! Meg exclaimed. I didn't think I would like hummus. It just seems so exotic.

Well, it's good to try new things. It's how we expand our comfort circle.

Right on, Judy. I like your way of thinking, Steve affirmed.

They ordered another round of drinks when their entrees arrived.

Anyone want to try my pasta? Meg asked.

No thanks, Judy and Steve responded.

Bon apetit, Judy told them.

Mercie, Steve replied.

They ate and talked about nothing in particular.

Then Meg asked Judy if she was dating anyone.

The table got quiet.

No, Judy said. It's actually been a while since I've been in a relationship.

She left it at that.

Then Meg turned to Steve. How about you, Steve?

No, Meg, as you already know. I have been busy growing the business.

Huh, Meg said.

What does huh mean?

Nothing. Meg smiled at Judy.

Meg, what are you doing?

I'm having a nice dinner and drinks with my brother and my friend. Why?

Judy dropped it.

Well, dinner was fantastic!

Angela came over. Can I start clearing plates? And, did you leave room for dessert?

Before anyone could answer, Angela left three dessert menus.

Well, Judy said, it never hurts to look. I think I'm in the mood for an apple crisp. I haven't had one of those since I was little.

I like the sound of the salted caramel cheesecake, said Meg. Steve you wanna share?

Why don't we all share the two desserts? Judy suggested. That way, we can feel better that we each didn't eat a whole one.

Steve smiled. It sounds like a plan.

He looked around and then raised his right hand into the air to get Angela's attention.

Judy had to catch her breath. She flashed back to her time in Asia with Vihaan.

Judy, you okay?

Yeah, Judy. What just happened?

Judy shook herself out of the memory.

I'm fine, sorry guys. Would you excuse me? I'm gonna hit the restroom.

Sure, Steve and Meg said.

Be back in a flash.

Judy left the table, attempting to stabilize herself. She wobbled her way to the ladies' room and locked the door.

Deep breaths girl, slow and steady. You're fine.

She looked in the mirror. You're okay. Yes, yes, yes. Breathe.

After a few minutes, Judy felt back to normal.

She rejoined Steve and Meg.

Sorry about that. I just needed to regroup.

Steve looked at her with some concern.

If you ever want to talk, I have two very well working ears and two very strong shoulders.

Judy teared up a little bit.

Thank you, Steve. I appreciate that, and I just might take you up on your offer one of these days.

Deal, he said.

Angela came over.

So, what's it gonna be? Devil or angel?

Judy smiled.

We are going to share an apple crisp, Steve winked at Judy. And a salted caramel cheesecake, so three forks, please.

Excellent choices. Give me a few minutes to warm up the crisp. Would you like that a la mode?

Oh yes, Judy said with some excitement.

Everyone chuckled.

Steve felt it was time to change the subject, so he started talking shop.

So, Judy, do you feel ready to take on another class or two? Personally, I think you're a wonderful instructor, and I would love a little more free time.

Can I think about it for a day or two?

Of course.

Meg, Judy asked. Why don't you do any teaching?

Well, I actually just started learning Tai Chi. When Steve opened the business, what's it been now, Steve? Like a year?

A little more.

Over a year ago, he asked me if I would handle the front for him. I have an Associates Degree in business, so I thought it was a great opportunity.

And, Steve added, it keeps it in the family.

Yeah, that too. Although we kid around a lot, we trust each other with our lives. I never really had much interest in actually doing the Tai Chi until a few months ago. Maybe one day, I'll be good enough to teach. How long have you been doing Tai Chi, Judy?

Ohh, let me think. I started when I was in senior year of high school. Then I stopped for a while and went back to it when I went to Columbia. I've kind of done it on and off since then. For me, it's been a stable in my life, and I haven't had much stability or predictability for a very long time.

That sounds tough.

Yes, it certainly hasn't been easy, but I do believe that everything we are faced with molds us into who we then become, and we have the choice to go in a negative direction or a positive one. Sort of glass half empty or half full. Life happens with or without us, and it is up to us to choose how we react.

Wow! Steve said. You're deep, man!

Judy smiled. It must be the beers.

Angela brought the desserts, three forks, and three plates.

Enjoy, she said.

Oh boy, this looks amazing!

I like your style and energy, Judy. You have a really nice aura about you.

Thank you, Steve.

You guys, please carry on with your mutual admiration society. I'm digging in.

Steve and Judy laughed, and simultaneously said, after you, Meg.

They laughed again, and then Steve took Judy's plate and served her.

Thank you, Steve.

My pleasure, said Steve.

Oh brother, said Meg, rolling her eyes. Could you too be more obvious? Maybe I'll go sit over at that empty table and give you two some time alone.

Steve and Judy blushed.

What are you talking about, little sister?

Okay, Meg said. We'll go with denial. It's not just a river in Egypt ya know. Meg broke into a Cheshire cat grin.

The three of them burst out laughing, then got quiet, but for some moans of joy while they devoured the desserts.

Angela put the check on the table. Take your time, I'll just leave this here with you. It's been a pleasure serving you this evening. You all get home safe.

Thank you, they mumbled with mouths full of sweet.

Steve instinctively reached for the check.

Uh uh uh, Judy shook her finger at him. This is my treat, remember?

I have to admit, this isn't easy for me.

Well, get over the old-fashioned man always pays attitude. I'm a modern and independent woman.

You tell him sister, Meg applauded.

Judy looked at the check, did some quick math, and put her credit card in the check holder. She took out some cash for the tip and placed it under the sugar dish.

I don't think I've had this much fun being out with my sister in a long time, and that's thanks to you, Judy.

Thanks a lot, Meg pouted.

Just teasin ya.

Watch out, Steve, revenge is a bitch!

Ewwwww, I'm so scared.

Wow, you guys really are so cute together!

I think it's because of our parents. Steve's dad and my mom love each other sooo much. They still act like two teenagers in love, and they made sure that we stayed very close as a family, right Steve?

That's right. They are pretty special people.

Judy teared up again.

Judy, what's wrong? Meg asked.

I never really had a family like that, and I guess I'm holding some sadness.

I'm sorry, said Meg. Hey, I have a fabulous idea.

Meg's eyes lit up.

We'll adopt you, right Steve? You can be a part of our family.

Judy couldn't hold back any longer. She burst into tears.

Oh my God, I'm so sorry.

Steve grabbed some napkins from the next table and handed them to her.

Well, I think I'm going to have to cut you off. You definitely can't hold your dessert.

With that, Judy's tears continued but she went from crying to laughing.

Thank you both. I'm so sorry. I'm not usually so out of control.

No problem, Steve said. It's entertaining, to say the least.

They headed out to the parking lot and got in the car.

I hope you both don't think I'm a total whacko, Judy said apologetically.

Nope, Steve answered, not a total one.

Steve, Meg slapped him again.

No, Judy said. I deserve that. It's fine.

They drove back to Judy's little cottage in the woods.

I love this place, Steve said again. I really love it!

Would you guys like to come in for a little bit? You can officially meet Chloe.

Ummm, not tonight, Judy, but could we take a raincheck? I have some paperwork I have to finish tonight.

Of course. You're welcome any time.

Judy opened her car door and started getting out.

I had such a good time tonight, and please don't worry about the tears. One day, I'll share my story with you guys.

Meantime, I like the mystery, Steve said.

Night, Judy. See you tomorrow.

See you tomorrow.

Judy got out and walked to her door. She unlocked it, turned on the light, and turned to wave at Steve and Meg.

That's nice that they waited for me to get inside. They are

really special people, Judy said to herself.

As she walked into the house, she received a little attitude from Queen Chloe.

MEOW, MEOW! MEOW!

Hi, my baby. I know. I left you for such a long time. I'm sorry.

With that, Chloe rubbed against Judy's leg as if to say, all is forgiven.

Hey Chloe, how about a make-up snacky?

Judy went into the kitchen and got out Chloe's favorite snacks. Here, baby.

Chloe never refused a snacky. She gobbled it up and licked her lips, then licked her paws, and washed her face.

All was once again well in the world of Chloe.

Judy went into the bedroom, with Chloe in tow, to get into her pajamas. There was no way Chloe was leaving her sight. She needed her Judy time.

The two stretched out on the bed, Judy stroking Chloe, and Chloe happily receiving strokes.

Judy told Chloe about the night with Steve and Meg and how she became so emotional a couple of times.

I guess I still have some "stuff" to work on, huh Chlo?

Chloe purred and bumped against Judy. For her, there wasn't stuff. She had already let it go.

You are one of my most important teachers, Chloe. Please be patient with your student, okay?

Chloe looked Judy straight in the eyes and squished hers together as if to smile.

Judy gave her a kiss on the head and got under the covers.

Good night, my baby.

Chloe curled up on her pillow next to Judy's and kneaded and purred until they both fell asleep.

32

A Visit

The next morning, Judy woke up at about eight. Chloe was already awake and curled up in her favorite spot in the living room. The morning sun was shining in through the sliding glass doors, and Chloe was bathing in the rays. She looked so beautiful.

Good morning, Chlo, Judy sang.

Chloe lifted her head half-heartedly. Sun bathing would take precedence.

Judy sat near Chloe and did her morning meditation. She went in slowly and headed down into her depths then over to her meadow. It was wonderful, as usual, to be in her meadow. It was the safest space she knew. The birds were singing, the sky was bluer than blue, the sun shone brightly but wasn't hot, and butterflies were all over the place. It was as if she were back at the Ashram. She sat down in the meadow and focused on her breathing while saying her mantra – yeeeees, yeeeeees, yeeeees. A slight breeze picked up and felt delightful. Judy then sensed a presence. She couldn't feel who was with her in her meadow, but there was definitely another being. She remained open and sent out an energy of welcoming.

Judy, she heard a familiar voice, but it took her a minute to recognize it.

Judy.

Swami Ravi Baba Singh. I am honored and humbled, she sent

out telepathically. She bowed.

Stay open. There is no future nor past. Stay open.

The breeze returned, and she could sense that Swami Ravi had gone.

She remained in her sitting posture for a while, and then heard a faint chime sound. As she returned from her meadow, she realized it was the alarm she had set. She took a few moments to come back to her living room, stood up, and stretched.

She made a bowl of cereal with some blueberries and poured cranberry juice on it. This would get her through the morning. She got dressed and reviewed class notes.

You can do this, girl; you can.

She kissed Chloe on the head. Goodbye, my baby. I'll see you later.

Chloe let out a little meow, but she was too relaxed to put much effort into it.

While driving to the studio, Judy decided to pick up two bouquets of flowers for the front and the work out space.

It will bring the earth inside, she thought.

She chose two lovely bunches of sunflowers that were already in vases, paid the cashier, and went on her way. She noticed she was humming a non-descript tune on the way to the studio.

As she walked in, she greeted Meg in a sing song voice and placed one of the vases of sunflowers on the counter where Meg was sitting.

Wow! Those are really beautiful! Meg said. You're sure in a good mood.

I am, aren't I? she said walking past Meg and smiling.

She entered the inner space and found a little platform area to place the second vase.

What's the occasion? Steve asked, following Judy in.

Judy jumped a little bit.

Oh, Steve. You scared me.

Sorry. Why the flowers?

I don't know. I was driving over and decided it would be nice to have flowers in the space today. You don't mind, do you?

Actually, they brighten up the room. Thank you, Judy.

You're welcome.

Judy began stretching and mentally preparing for her class.

Steve then asked, Have you had a chance to think about my offer?

Yes and yes.

Fabulous! Steve said. Come find me after your class today, and we'll work out the details.

Will do.

The class went really well, and Judy was feeling more confident than ever.

After the students left, she sat down in the middle of the room and closed her eyes. She felt the need to re-center herself and offer gratitude for her earlier meditation and life in general. She spent about twenty minutes in a semi-meditative state and was brought back by a ringing phone. She got up, bowed to the room, and went to find Steve.

Meg was just hanging up when Judy came out.

All good? Judy asked.

Yeah. A little busier than it's been. Steve put an ad in the local paper, and we're getting some responses.

That's great, Judy said.

We may need to expand our hours.

Hey, Judy. Steve peeked out from his office. You ready?

Sure thing. See you later, Meg.

Judy walked into Steve's office and sat in the chair in front of his desk. She noticed that there were a bunch of papers, not in any particular order.

Steve followed her in and sat at his desk. Sorry about the mess. I'm not the neatest to begin with and it's been challenging teaching and administering at the same time. I'm really glad you said yes to taking on a couple more classes. What I'd like to do is hand over all of the beginner classes to you. So, your schedule would be Monday, Tuesday, Wednesday from 10:00 till 11:00, and then Thursday from 6:00 till 7:00. Sound okay?

Um, yes, that's fine.

Great. I will continue with the more advanced classes and the private lessons, but you will be freeing me up three mornings a week and Thursday evening. That should make a big difference.

And Steve, if you ever need some admin help, I'm happy to lend a hand. Please just let me know.

Will do, thanks. I just might take you up on that.

Steve was smiling and looking directly into Judy's eyes.

She was looking back at him, and for a second, she felt as if they were having a moment.

Well, Judy said while standing up. I better get going.

Yeah, Steve said, and I have a bunch of work to finish here. He looked at the mess on his desk.

As Judy was leaving, Steve said, Judy?

She turned. Yeah, Steve?

He stood, unable to form words.

Time felt frozen to Judy.

Thanks again.

Sure, Steve, no probs.

Judy walked out.

Hmm, she said under her breath. Was that something or was that something?

She wasn't paying attention and bumped into Meg who was just coming out of the restroom.

Whoops, Judy said. I'm sorry. I guess my head's in the clouds. Are you ok, Meg?

Oh yeah, I'm fine. I'm tough. I can take the occasional bump. Just don't make it a habit.

Meg smiled.

Judy smiled.

So, Judy, are you gonna take on more classes?

Oh yeah, Tuesday morning and Thursday evening.

That's great! I'm glad we found each other.

Me too, Meg.

Hey, what are you doing later?

Ummm, I don't know. No particular plans.

You wanna get some dinner? Meg asked hopefully.

That sounds nice. Want me to pick you up?

No, let's meet at the diner at about seven?

Sounds good. I'll see you then.

Judy left the building and got in her Prius. She wasn't in the mood to go home, so she drove around for a while and ended up near Portland, Maine. She parked her car in a garage and started strolling around. She found her way to a nearby marina and realized it was way past lunchtime so went into a little café and got some shrimp salad and a fresh brewed iced tea, no straw. It was her policy to always say "no straw" because she had read that the accumulation of plastics in the oceans was becoming way out of control and can be very detrimental to the sea life.

She sat at a little table out on the deck overlooking the water and ate and thought about Swami Ravi.

There is no past or future. Stay present. Huh. Easier said than done, Swami Ravi.

She smiled remembering her days at the Ashram.

I owe Olivia a call, she thought to herself.

After eating, Judy got up and went inside to pay the bill.

She decided to take a walk along the beach. It was a beautiful day. The humidity had dissipated, and it was a comfortable eighty-four degrees.

It's cooler here in the summer than it was in New York, she said half out loud.

Oh yeah? said a voice behind her.

Judy turned and looked.

Howdy, said James.

Hi? said Judy, feeling a little bit stalked. How long have you been walking behind me?

Since you left the café.

Now Judy felt uncomfortable. She quickly scanned the area. Well,

James. My name's James.

Well, James, I have an appointment, so bye.

Wait, can't we hang out for a while?

Judy started walking quickly and made it to the boardwalk to see James heading toward another girl.

She noticed that her heart was pounding and that she was ill prepared if she were ever attacked.

Maybe I should sign up for some self-defense classes.

She checked her watch and realized she'd better head back to New Hampshire. The afternoon had gotten away from her, and she probably wouldn't even be able to stop home before meeting Meg at the diner.

She made pretty good time and got to the diner just a couple of minutes after seven. She went in and scanned the room. Towards the back, she saw a hand waving at her. She headed toward the booth and noticed there were three people there.

Hi.

Hi, Judy. I hope you don't mind. When I told Steve I was meeting you here tonight, he asked if he could join. I told him it was supposed to be a girl's night out, but he insisted. So then, I texted Charles to see if he wanted to join us, and here we are.

Charles, this is my friend, becoming like a sister, Judy.

Hi, Charles, nice to meet you.

Judy put out her right hand to shake Charles' hand. His grip was firm which she believed was an indicator of someone with some confidence.

And, of course, you know Steve.

Judy chuckled. You do look familiar.

Steve smiled and laughed. So, do you, he played. Haven't we met somewhere before?

Judy sat down next to Steve and looked across at Meg and Charles.

I'm sorry I'm a couple of minutes late, she said. I lost track of time and then actually had a little bit of a scary thing happen.

Steve turned and looked at her. Are you all right?

Oh, I'm fine, really. But I have to admit, it shook me up and made me think.

Oh, now you have to tell us what happened, Meg said.

Just then, the waitress came over.

Okay, I will, but let's order first.

They all ordered beers and dinner.

Okay, Steve said, spill.

Judy looked at him. She realized how really attractive he was.

Well, after I left the studio, I decided to take a drive. I ended up in Portland, so I parked and started wandering around. I came to a marina got some lunch and then went for a walk on the beach.

This is very exciting, Meg said jokingly.

As I was walking, I guess I was thinking out loud, which I do a lot, and I heard a voice behind me comment on what I was saying, so I turned around, and he introduced himself. But you know how some situations just don't feel right? He was kind of creepy.

So, what did you do? Charles asked.

Meg looked at Charles with some amusement.

You're really into this story, huh?

Judy smiled.

I told him I had an appointment and had to go. I started walking really fast to get to the boardwalk, and he followed me, but once I was off the beach and on the boardwalk, I turned around, and he was already bothering another girl.

Did you call the police? Steve asked.

No, he didn't touch me or threaten me. It's not illegal to be creepy.

Meg and Charles laughed, but Steve looked concerned.

I did, however, notice that my heart was pounding, and it made me think. I don't know that I could have defended myself if I had needed to. So, on the drive over, I decided I am going to find a self defense class.

Good for you, Meg cheered.

I can teach you, Steve said.

Judy looked at Steve.

I took martial arts for years. I have a black belt in Aikido.

Oh, Steve, that's really nice of you, but I don't want to take up more of your time. You're already so busy.

No, it's settled. We can work on Sundays. I'll have you kicking ass in no time.

Meg was staring at Steve. She knew her brother well enough to know that he never gave up his Sundays unless it was for something that meant a lot to him. Although this was a prime teasing opportunity, something made her keep quiet. Her initial suspicions seemed to be accurate.

The food arrived, and everyone dug in.

So, Charles, Steve said. What did you say you do?

Steve, Meg whined.

I didn't say, Charles said. But I am currently working at my dad's financial advising firm, and I'm studying to take my Series 7 Exam.

Charles is a math whiz, Meg bragged.

Well, I don't know about that, Charles said with a smile on his face.

You two are very cute together, Judy chimed in. Don't you think so, Steve?

Steve didn't say anything. He was dealing with enough between being worried about Judy and the feelings he was beginning to feel for her and being a big brother to Meg.

As they all ate, they talked and laughed.

Who's having dessert? Meg called out.

Not me, said Judy.

Me neither, said Steve.

Oh, come on you party poopers. Charles, you have to have dessert with me.

I can't refuse an offer from such a beautiful lady.

Ohhh, Judy said. On that note, I think I'm going to head home.

Do you think I could catch a ride with you? Steve asked. Meg drove us here, but I need to get back, and I think she and Charles might like to be alone with their dessert.

Meg and Charles both blushed and giggled a little.

Sure, said Judy.

Meg, I got this, said Steve. You guys enjoy dessert. Charles, it was nice to meet you.

Yes, Charles, Judy chimed in, it was very nice to meet you. Drive safe.

Bye, Meg called after them.

33

A Surprise

By the time Judy and Steve left the diner, it was almost eight-thirty.

This is my favorite time of the day, Judy said as they walked to her car. It's not completely dark, but the daylight is gone. It's the dusky part of the day, when everything starts to settle down for the night, and there's still a hint of color in the sky.

Steve took Judy's hand.

She stopped and looked at him.

Steve?

Steve kissed her right there in the diner's parking lot, then pulled away quickly.

I'm so sorry, Judy. I don't know what came over me. Oh my God. I'm so embarrassed. That was completely inappropriate.

Judy stared at him as he fumbled for words.

Steve, this is complicated.

No, I know.

The thing is that I really like you too; I have since the first Tai Chi class, but when you offered me a teaching position, I told myself that I had to stay professional.

Of course. You are absolutely right, he said.

He then grabbed her and kissed her long and hard.

Steve!! Judy said half laughing. I think we are both having a head and heart conflict.

Steve smiled. Right now, the heart is winning.

They got in Judy's car and headed back toward their little town.

Judy followed Steve's directions to get him back to his house. Once there, she pulled into his driveway.

This is cute, Judy said.

It works for me. It's small, but it's affordable and convenient. Would you like to come in?

Okay, just for a few minutes.

They went into Steve's condo, and Judy noticed that it looked somewhat like his desk at work. She smiled to herself.

Can I get you something to drink?

Sure, water's great.

Okay, two waters coming up.

Judy sat down on the couch and was watching Steve. He seemed nervous.

Okay, here you go.

He sat down next to her, and they both half turned to face each other.

So, he said.

Well, maybe we should talk about this?

That's probably a good idea.

They looked around the room a bit, and then Judy said, okay, I'll start.

Are you seeing anyone?

No. I was, but it ended about a year ago.

You?

No.

Silence

How do we make the boss and employee thing work if we become romantic?

Here's the thing, Judy. I like you, Steve pauses, a lot. And I believe we are both mature and professional enough to not let a relationship get in the way of work.

Do you agree?

I would like to think so, but I'm afraid I'm not real objective on this topic because I like you too, and I want to get to know you better.

I think we should give this a try, Steve said, his eyes gazing at Judy with intensity. What do you say?

Okay, but let's take it real slow.

Good idea.

Are you going to tell your sister?

I think she already knows that I like you, and to be fair, I think she should be told since she works at the studio too.

By the way, Steve, what did you think about Charles?

He seems okay. He's a little nerdy but harmless.

I think Meg really likes him.

Yeah, well, we'll see how long they last.

Wow! You're a real romantic.

Judy looked at Steve and smiled.

He leaned in and kissed her for a long time. They held each other, and it felt so nice.

Then Judy whispered in his ear. I should go. I have a class in the morning.

That's right, Steve said. I forgot you're taking over tomorrow. Come on, I'll walk you to your car.

Steve kissed Judy one more time before she got in her car and then waved as she backed out of the driveway.

On the drive home, Judy processed this new relationship.

Am I ready for this? God, I wish Maddie were here to talk this out with me. Maddie, are you watching over me? Am I making the right decision? It feels right, but I'm scared, too. I guess that's normal. Stay present. Stay focused.

She chanted her mantra: Yes, yes, yes.

Judy pulled into her driveway, got out of the car, locked it, and went into her cottage.

Chloe? I'm home, baby.

She flipped on the lights and saw Chloe on the couch. Chloe wasn't acknowledging Judy which meant that she was upset with her.

Okay, I'm sorry. Come, I'll give you some snackies.

Judy went into the kitchen and opened the bag of Chloe's most favorite snackies. C'mon my girl. C'mon. Pleeeeaaase?

With that, Chloe jumped off the couch with a little purry mumbly sound, as if to say, this doesn't mean I'm not still upset with you.

She came over to eat her snack.

Judy went into the bathroom to shower and get ready for bed. She climbed under the covers and grabbed a book.

Chloe came into the bedroom and jumped up on the bed. She bumped against Judy's chest as if to say, no reading; pay attention to me.

Okay sweetie, okay.

She put the book down and stroked Chloe. Chloe settled down on Judy's stomach and purred happily.

Judy turned off the light and began telling Chloe about her day and about what happened with Steve. She then yawned, closed her eyes, and was asleep within minutes.

The next morning, Judy jerked awake. She thought she heard something but looked over to Chloe who was sound asleep on her pillow next to Judy. Hmmm, Judy thought. That sounded so real.

She got out of bed and did her morning meditation. She made herself some breakfast, fed Chloe, and got dressed for class.

I'm kind of liking this routine. I have two more classes each week, Chloe. This is good. Chloe looked up and licked her chops.

Judy checked the time. She still had about a half an hour before she had to leave.

Chloe, you want to take a woods walk?

Judy walked over to the sliding glass doors and opened them. Chloe shot out.

I'll take that as a yes, Judy chuckled.

They walked for about fifteen minutes, and then Judy called to Chloe.

Come on girl, we have to turn around.

Just as Judy was turning to go back to the cottage, she thought she saw movement from behind the tree ahead. She stopped in her tracks and looked. There was nothing there, but she had a sense. She wasn't far from home, and so picked up the pace.

Come on Chloe, she called with some anxiety in her voice. She had never felt afraid before walking in these woods, but something just seemed off, and after what had happened yesterday with James, her senses were heightened. She turned to make sure Chloe was with her.

Chloe, she yelled louder. Where are you? She stood for a minute looking back.

Finally, Chloe appeared, a dead mouse in her mouth.

Oh Chloe, put the mouse down.

Chloe wasn't having any of that. This was her mouse, and she was very proud of it.

And actually, the distraction took the edge off of Judy's worry. The two headed back to the cottage, and Judy had to wrestle with an unhappy Chloe because there was no way she would allow a dead mouse in the house.

She picked Chloe up, shook the mouse out of her mouth and brought her in. She locked the sliding glass doors, gave Chloe some water, and headed out to teach.

34

A New Class

Judy got to the studio just five minutes before the class was supposed to start. She was a little bit upset with herself because she liked to be in control and prepared, and she was feeling a bit discombobulated.

Okay girl, focus.

She ran into the studio.

Whoa, Meg said. You okay?

Yes, Judy said in an exasperated voice. I don't like to be late. It throws off my rhythm.

Well, take a deep breath. Because it's almost the school year, the class is smaller than usual; a lot of people are getting in their last summer vacation. You only have three students.

Judy entered the class space.

Hi, I'm Judy. I'm going to be taking over for Steve.

Hi, Judy, the three students said in unison.

Judy called the roster. Mark – here. Sandi – here. Eileen – pretty much here.

They all chuckled.

I can relate, said Judy. So, tell me where Steve left off.

Is he okay? asked Eileen.

Oh, yeah, he's fine. His studio is expanding, so he asked me to take on a couple more classes to free him up.

The students gave Judy a summary of what they had learned so far.

Okay, very good. Let's do some stretching.

The class went off without a hitch.

Thanks everyone. I'll see you next week.

They all bowed, Xie', xie'.

Judy lingered for a little bit to regroup. She sat in the center of the space and did some breathing.

She muttered, centered, focused, yes, yes.

After about fifteen minutes, she stood up.

Steve was standing in the doorway. Hi, Cutie. He was beaming.

Hi, Steve. Judy felt better already.

How did it go?

Good, really good. There were only three students today because the others are on end of summer vacations, but we all worked well, I thought.

Great. And it was nice having the morning to start catching up on some paperwork.

Hey, Steve, I had an idea for the studio this morning. Do you have any time that I can talk it out with you?

Yeah, sure, no problem.

Actually, what are you doing tonight? You wanna come over, and I'll cook dinner?

Wow! Steve said with surprise. What about taking it slow?

This is a business meeting, right?

Hopefully, there'll be a little pleasure too.

Oh, Steve. Judy was flummoxed.

Just then, Meg came in.

Hey, you too. She looked at both of them. What's going on in here?

Nothing, they both said. We're just talking about work.

Uh huh. Meg said. Oh, Steve, you have a phone call.

Steve went to his office but turned and said, how's seven?

Perfect, Judy said. See you then.

Once Steve was in his office and out of range, Judy noticed Meg was staring at her.

Okay, spill. What's going on here?

Judy just looked at Meg. She was hoping Steve would have told her, but he either forgot or hadn't had a chance.

I think you should ask your brother.

I'm asking you.

Judy bit her lip. This was feeling uncomfortable.

Could we wait for Steve to get off the phone?

C'mon, Judy. Now you're freaking me out a little bit.

Okay. Let's sit down.

They went into the entrance waiting room and sat down.

The other night, as Steve and I were walking out of the restaurant, Charles is great by the way.

Don't change the subject. Talk!

Steve kissed me.

Meg gasped and put her hands over her mouth. There was a little squealy sound coming from behind her hands and she had started tapping her feet really quickly.

Are you ok, Meg?

I'm so excited. Meg jumped up and started bouncing up and down and all around.

Just then, Steve came out of his office.

I guess you just told her.

I was hoping you would, but she twisted my arm.

Yeah, Meg has a way of getting info out of people.

Oh Steve! Meg ran over to him and wrapped her arms around him.

Wow! Steve said. What exactly did you tell her?

I only got as far as the kiss in the parking lot.

Okay, sis, relax, please, calm down.

I'm sooo excited!!

Meg, your brother and I agreed that we would take it slowly and see where it goes. And, we will be professionals here at the studio.

Ohhhh, you guys are sooo cute! I love this.

Meg was bouncing up and down again and clapping her hands.

Hey! she shouted. We can all go on official double dates. It'll be a blast.

Slow down there, slicker.

Meg looked at Steve with the hugest grin on her face.

I am very happy for the two of you. After you guys left the other night, I told Charles that I was really hoping you guys would hook up.

Oh you did, did you? Steve retorted. And pray tell, what did Charles have to say?

Come to think of it, he didn't have any comment about it. Hmmmm.

Well, Judy jumped in. I hate to break up the party, but I have some errands to run.

See you tomorrow, Meg.

See you at seven, Steve.

See you later.

Bye, Judy, Meg said in a teasy flirty way.

Judy went out and got in her car. She sat there for a few minutes thinking about what to make Steve for dinner.

Okay, maybe arugula salad, broiled salmon with a creamy dill sauce, asparagus, and wild rice. Yes, that sounds really good.

She drove over to the Whole Foods about three towns away and got everything she wanted.

Oh, we need dessert. Hmmm, let's see.

She noticed a bakery two doors down from Whole Foods.

As she perused the pastry case, she became a little bit stuck. Everything looked so good.

May I help you?

Yes. Were the chocolate eclairs made today?

Yup. Everything is made fresh daily.

Okay. May I have four chocolate eclairs?

Judy left with groceries and eclairs in hand and was getting excited about entertaining Steve.

Back at home, she checked the clock. It was just a little after three, so she put the groceries away and worked on some lesson plans for a while.

At about 4:30, she and Chloe went out for another woods walk. Judy decided to pay extra attention to her surroundings. She listened closely to the birds chirping and the squirrels running along the branches. She looked up at the trees against the blue of the sky and down at the ground shrubs. Judy loved the woods. She always felt energized by the trees. So many people love to be near the water, she said out loud to no one, but I think I will always need to be near woods.

They walked for a while, Judy in a daydream state.

There was a sudden crack. The noise pulled Judy out of her daze and scared Chloe. Chloe ran under a nearby bush, and Judy looked around to see what had happened. Up ahead, she thought she saw a pretty large branch on the ground. She walked toward it to see. As she got closer, she thought she saw the hint of a person off in the distance, running away from her. Instantly, her heart started pounding again.

Okay, she said. This is more than a coincidence. Chloe, baby, come on.

Judy turned and walked rapidly back toward the house. Because she had been daydreaming, she hadn't realized how far she and Chloe had gone.

She kept up a quick pace, calling for Chloe every few steps.

Once Judy got back to her cottage, she looked around to see if there was anything off. Everything seemed to be the way it was when she had left.

She unlocked the sliding glass door and entered the cottage. She called for Chloe and waited.

Her heart was racing, and she began to panic. At the top of her lungs, she yelled, Chloe! Chloe!

She began to tear up. Come on, Chloe, please, she cried.

Judy looked as far out into the woods as she could. Off in the distance, she saw something moving around.

She ran to the kitchen and grabbed Chloe's snacks. She stepped back outside and began shaking the bag. Come on, Chloe; come on.

Chloe shot back to the cottage like her tail was on fire. Something was strange, to say the least.

With all of the drama, Judy had lost track of time and realized she needed to start cooking.

She went into the kitchen but had to stop a few times to refocus and catch her breath.

She got out all of the ingredients and started working.

Fifteen minutes later, the doorbell rang. Judy was so wound up that she screamed and dropped a dish, which sent Chloe fleeing into the bedroom.

She opened the front door and was relieved to see Steve standing there.

Hi, he smiled. Are you okay?

I am really glad to see you.

Okay, tell me what's going on.

They sat down together on the couch, and Judy told Steve about the two walks.

She said, It may be paranoia, but...

Steve said, well, we'll see, but I trust your instincts, and I think if you feel that something is off, then something is off. How about if I start taking some walks with you? We can figure out times that work for both of us.

Thank you, Steve. Normally, I would tell you it's okay, but honestly, this is really shaking me up.

It's set then.

Now, is dinner ready? I'm starving.

Oh, not quite yet. Would you like something to drink?

Yes, how about a beer?

Done.

Steve hung out in the kitchen while Judy worked. They chatted about the studio.

While Steve was talking, he thought, this is nice. I like this domestic feeling.

He was looking at Judy, watching her, and feeling feelings he wasn't so sure about. It had been a long time.

How long? he thought. Wow! Has it been over a year? Yes,

it must be because I opened the studio over a year ago, and I haven't dated since then.

Steve? Hey, Steve; you here with me?

What? Oh, sorry, Judy. I was lost in space.

Here, take these plates and silver and set the table, k?

Judy put the dinner on the table and sat down across from Steve.

Steve lifted his beer glass. A toast to a beautiful woman and a wonderful dinner.

Here here, Judy said.

They clinked glasses.

Dig in, Steve.

Everything looks really good, Steve said. I haven't been eating a lot of home cooked meals.

They ate and chatted, getting to know each other a bit better.

So, tell me something about you, Judy.

Hmmm, she thought.

Is this a game? I tell you then you tell me?

Okay, Steve said. I wasn't thinking that, but it's a good idea. You go first.

I love Chloe with all of my heart.

Okay, not what I was going for, but

You go now, Judy said.

Hmmmm, Steve thought.

At some point, I would like to have three or four children.

Whoa! Judy said. I sure wasn't expecting that.

Your turn, Judy.

K, ummm. Okay. My parents were killed in a car accident when I was eight.

As soon as she said it, she regretted it.

Judy, Steve said, the mood suddenly becoming really sullen. I'm so sorry. I had no idea.

Well, how could you? Listen, of course, it was really really hard, but I'm okay. I'm doing okay.

Steve stood up and walked around the table. He held out his hand to Judy. She took his hand and stood up. Steve hugged

Judy for a very long time. Judy started to sob. They rocked and hugged.

Steve whispered, it's okay. You're okay.

Judy apologized. I'm sorry, Steve. It seems like whenever we're together socially, I start crying. It can't make for a very good impression.

You know what kind of impression it makes? Steve asked. It tells me that you trust me, that you're carrying around a lot of hurt, and I am honored to be able to help you through it.

Judy pulled away from Steve, and they looked at each other. They kissed and held each other until Judy suggested they finish dinner.

She excused herself to wash her face and came back to the table.

They finished eating. Steve told her the dinner was delicious. But wait, she said. We're not done.

She went into the kitchen and plated the éclairs.

She brought them over to Steve. Steve looked at the eclairs and then looked at Judy.

How did you know?

How did I know what?

How did you know that eclairs are my most favorite dessert?

Get outta here. You're full of it.

No, really, Steve said very seriously. He pulled out his phone and held it out to Judy.

Here, call my stepmom and ask her.

Judy laughed seeing Steve so serious about éclairs.

No. That's okay, Steve.

She picked up an éclair and brought it to Steve who took a bite.

Ohhh, that's sooo good.

Judy then bit into the same éclair.

Hey, Steve said. That's mine.

Oh, sorry. Judy handed Steve the rest of the éclair.

She grabbed one for herself and then gave Steve another one.

Man, these are good! she said. I haven't had an éclair since, I can't remember.

After dessert, they sat on the couch for a while.

I really like you, Steve said.

And I really like you too.

I look forward to getting to know you better and spending time with you.

Me too, said Judy. She smiled.

After some kissing, Steve told her it was time for him to go home.

Judy walked him to the door.

Make sure you lock your door when I go, k?

You bet, Judy said.

35
Thanksgiving

As the days passed, Judy continued teaching at the studio and dating Steve. They began taking woods walks with no incidents. Judy was definitely falling in love. It wasn't like the romance she had had with Vihaan. They were moving super slowly emotionally and physically, and Judy loved that Steve respected that need.

They also worked really well together, and more and more, Judy was feeling like a part of the studio.

She and Meg were also becoming closer. They would go out for lunches and then occasionally double date.

Life was good. The summer was over, and fall was definitely present. The leaves were changing, and Judy and Steve's walks were reduced by the change in the weather.

Before she knew it, Thanksgiving was just around the corner.

Steve and Judy were out on a dinner date one evening when Steve looked at Judy very seriously.

What's up, Steve? Why are you looking at me like that?

Okay, Steve said. I think's it's time.

What's time? Judy asked while she was crunching on some carrots.

Well, you know that Thanksgiving is pretty soon.

Yes, I know that.

Would you consider joining me at my family's house?

Judy looked up from her carrots and dip. She stared for a few minutes.

Thanksgiving, as well as the other holidays, had been days that she tried to just get through. She had often spent them alone year after year and had gotten to a place where that was okay.

Now, she was being asked to attend a real family Thanksgiving, and not only that, meet the parents of the man she was falling in love with.

What are you thinking, hon?

How could she verbalize all of this to Steve?

Umm, I would love to, Steve. It's so nice of you to invite me. Are you sure you're ready for me to meet your family?

Oh, honey. I am so ready.

Okay then. If you're ready, then I'm ready. Do they know that you've been dating? And, do they know that you're inviting me?

They know that I have been seeing you because I told them that I've met a very special person and have been dating her for a few months. The other day, my stepmom called to ask if I would be coming for Thanksgiving dinner and would I like to invite the person I've been dating.

In that case, I would be honored, said Judy.

Good, said Steve.

Good, said Judy.

Their dinner came, and they ate in silence.

Finally, Judy broke the silence.

Steve?

Yes?

Maybe it's time to tell you my story.

Okay.

Judy took a deep breath.

Okay.

She started at the beginning and told Steve everything.

Steve listened without interrupting.

There were tears and pauses, but Judy got through it.

Steve pulled his chair around to Judy and took her hand.

He looked intently at her.

I don't have words, Judy. You have really had a hell of a life. I can tell you that I am exceptionally happy to be a part of it now, and I hope you feel the same.

I can also tell you that I will do my very best to never hurt you. On the contrary, it is my current mission to take care of you as best as I can.

Oh, Steve, Judy cried. She hugged him.

I guess it wouldn't be a date without you shedding tears.

They both began to laugh and laugh, holding their bellies.

The server came over. I guess you guys are having a good time. Would you like dessert?

They ordered a hot fudge sundae to share. The evening ended on a high note. Judy felt quite unburdened after sharing her life's struggles with Steve.

She woke up on Thanksgiving morning and did an extra-long morning meditation. She wanted to be as centered as possible because this would be a huge day for her.

After meditating, she had Olivia on her mind and so called.

Hi, honey.

Khamaghani, Olivia.

So, this is a holiday for you, isn't it?

Yes. Today is Thanksgiving.

How are you doing, Judy?

I'm doing really well. How's everyone there?

All is as it should be. We do miss you, though. Do you think you might make a trip to India any time soon?

It's possible, Olivia. I've met a very nice man, and our relationship is progressing. I recently told him about my past.

And how did he respond?

He told me that he is happy to be a part of my life now and that he sees himself as my protector.

That sounds very charming. How do you feel about him?

I will always hold Vihaan in my heart, Olivia.

My dear, you don't need to feel guilty about finding another love. This is what life is about. I am happy for you if you have found love again. This is a blessing, and I would be honored to one day meet this wonderful man.

That means so much to me, Olivia. As a part of your special family, I would never want to do anything that seemed hurtful or inappropriate.

I don't think that's possible, but I appreciate you checking in. You must walk your path, wherever that may lead you. It is not for me to judge that.

I love you, Olivia.

I love you too, my dear. Please don't be a stranger. You are always welcome here.

Judy hung up feeling better about her circumstances. She was falling for Steve but was conflicted about her family in India. She felt very fortunate to have Olivia as a friend.

She showered and dressed for the meeting of the parents.

This is a big day, Chlo. I'm going to meet Steve's mommy and daddy.

Chloe sat looking up at Judy. Did she mention snacky? Chloe was hoping.

Judy must have picked up on the vibe.

Okay, Chloe, here you go.

She then took the apple crisp out of the refrigerator. She had made it to bring to Steve's parents because one thing Kay taught Judy very early on in their relationship was never to go to one's home empty handed. Kay used to describe it as one of the world's greatest faux pas.

Steve was picking Judy up at one o'clock, so Judy got her coat out of the closet, checked her teeth and hair in the bathroom mirror, and waited for him. She was sitting on her couch staring out at the back when she could have sworn she saw something again. She leapt up. Did you see that Chloe?

Chloe looked up, unsure what it was Judy was asking.

Judy went to the sliding glass doors and looked intently into the woods. The day was kinda gray, so the view wasn't as clear as it could have been.

As she was staring, the doorbell rang.

She unlocked her front door and let Steve in.

Hi. What's wrong?

I just saw something out in the woods again.

Why were you out in the woods?

No, I wasn't. I was sitting on the couch, but I swear I saw a movement of some sort.

Okay, stay here.

Steve, no.

I'll be right back. Lock the glass door behind me.

Steve headed out down the path looking to his right and left and up ahead of him.

Judy could hear him yelling-

Hey, is anyone there? Anyone out here? Hey!

Just as he was about to turn around, he saw movement out of the corner of his eye.

Son of a gun, he thought. Maybe she wasn't hallucinating.

He sped up his pace and yelled again, Hey!

He saw a man running away from him.

Hey, stop. What are you doing?

The guy kept running and disappeared into the gray.

Steve turned and went back to the cottage.

When Judy saw him, she unlocked the glass door and slid it open.

Well, you weren't hallucinating. I did see a guy out there, but when I called to him, he ran, and I lost him. Hopefully, he won't come around now that he knows we are aware of him, but Judy, do me a favor – please don't go out walking in the back woods without me – deal?

Okay, Judy said. She liked that Steve wanted to protect her. She had been so independent for so long that it wasn't easy giving that up, but she figured she could still be independent and have someone watching over her.

Thank you, Steve. You're my hero.

Happy to serve, ma'am. Steve tipped a pretend hat.

Judy giggled.

You ready to head out?

Yes, let me just get my pie.

What pie?

I made an apple crisp.

Oh, that was nice of you.

Well, Kay taught me early on never to show up at a person's house empty handed, and apple crisp happens to be something I make really well, if I do say so myself.

They left the cottage and got into Steve's car.

The drive was quick, just twenty minutes or so.

I'm nervous, Steve.

No need to be. My parents are really excited to meet you. Oh, I should tell you that they also invited Charles.

Really? Judy asked. Does that mean that Meg is getting more serious?

I don't know. You never know with Meg.

Judy was glad that Meg and Charles were going to be there. Maybe it would take a little bit of attention off of her and Steve.

Once at Steve's parents, Judy took a deep breath.

You ready? Steve asked.

As I'm gonna be, Judy responded.

You'll be fine.

Steve opened the front door and held it for Judy. Once inside, he yelled, We're here.

They heard a voice yell back.

We're in the kitchen.

Steve took Judy's coat and hung it up on the hook in the entry.

Judy followed Steve into the kitchen. Meg and Charles were already there.

Mom, Dad, I'd like you to meet Judy. Judy had the pie in her hand, so Steve took that so that she could shake hands with Rachel and Matthew.

It's really nice to meet you, Rachel said.

Yeah, Matthew interjected. We've heard a lot about you.

Dad!

Uh oh, Judy said.

Everyone smiled.

No, all good, Matthew assured her.

Please come, have a seat.

Judy sat down and said hi to Meg and Charles who were sipping some wine.

Can I get you anything to drink? Rachel asked.

Oh, no. I'm fine. Thank you.

Okay, well you let me know if you change your mind. We'll probably be ready to eat in about forty minutes.

Can I help with anything? Judy asked.

Umm, for now, I think we're covered, but thank you for offering.

Rachel picked up her glass of wine.

So, Judy, Steve tells us you've been in New Hampshire for a couple of years?

Yes, I moved here from New York.

My dad was from New York, Meg chimed in.

Really, Judy said.

Yes, he was a salesman.

Huh, Judy thought. That's odd.

Steve said you are a very good Tai Chi instructor, Rachel said to Judy.

Judy looked at Steve. Thank you, Steve.

She then turned back to Rachel.

I'm really enjoying teaching.

Matthew had left the kitchen and just returned.

Boy, babe. It smells awesome in here.

Judy watched Rachel and Matthew. They really were in love.

How did you guys meet? Judy asked.

Oh, that's a story for when we have more time, Matthew answered.

Okay, Rachel said. Let's all go into the dining room. Dinner is ready. Everyone grab your glass.

Judy, are you ready for a drink?

Water's great, Judy said.

Rachel gave her a glass of water, and Judy headed into the dining room.

When Rachel came in with a huge bowl of mashed potatoes, Judy said, you have a beautiful home.

Thank you, Judy. We've been here since Matthew and I got married. Boy, time sure goes fast.

Once everything was on the table, Matthew said a quick grace about his appreciation for his family.

Steve glanced at Judy to make sure the water works hadn't started up.

I'm fine, she mouthed to him.

Steve winked at her.

For a few minutes, there was passing and clinking, slicing and serving. Plates were filled with all kinds of yummy stuff.

And then the eating commenced.

At one point, Judy stopped and sat back and observed. She was so happy to be here with this family, having a Thanksgiving meal. She felt content.

Once everyone was pretty much finished, and Rachel got up to start clearing dishes, Judy jumped up to help. It just wasn't in her nature to sit back watching others work.

She carried a pile of plates into the kitchen.

Oh, thank you, Judy. Just put them in the sink. Matthew and I will wash them later.

Okey dokey, Judy said.

Rachel stopped in her tracks and looked at Judy.

Judy, have we met before?

No, I don't think so.

There's something about you that seems really familiar.

What part of New York did you say you're from?

I didn't. I'm originally from a little town in upstate New York.

Are your parents still there?

Judy looked down. She hesitated. No, they were killed in a car crash when I was eight.

Rachel fell back and grabbed onto the counter behind her. The blood drained from her face for a moment, and she felt a little dizzy. She tried to collect herself. She took a deep breath and exhaled.

I'm so sorry, Judy. May I ask you what their names were?

Judy thought this was a strange question. How could Rachel from New Hampshire possibly have known her parents from upstate New York fifteen or so years ago?

Rachel realized what she was asking Judy.

I know this must sound like a strange question.

Judy's manners overrode her confusion.

Marilyn and Bruce.

Rachel's face went white as a ghost again. Her hand flew up over her mouth.

What is it? Judy asked. She wasn't sure what to do. Are you okay?

Was your dad a salesman?

How did you know that, Rachel?

Oh my God. Judy, come sit down with me at the table.

The two of them sat at the kitchen table. Judy could hear everyone else in the dining room kidding around and laughing, and she wished she was in there as well.

Rachel leaned forward and took Judy's hands in hers.

Judy, I'm Rachel.

Judy looked at her. Maybe she's very drunk, Judy thought.

Okay. Judy said.

I used to date your father.

Okay?

Judy wasn't really following this.

I dated him while he was married to your mother.

Judy was speechless.

I actually became pregnant while I was dating Bruce. What I'm trying to say is that Meg is your half-sister. You two have the same father.

Judy stared at Rachel. She wished she had had something a little stronger to drink than water.

Umm, what Rachel?

I know this a a lot to process. I had no idea until you mentioned the car accident. You look a lot like your father.

Would you excuse me? May I use your restroom?

Of course. Down the hall on your left.

Judy got up and walked down the hall.

She locked the bathroom door and sat down on the fancy little chair in the corner.

Meg is my sister. Meg is my sister. Rachel was dating my father while my mom and I were home alone. Meg is my sister.

She was having a very hard time processing.

There was a knock on the door.

Judy?

It was Steve.

You okay?

Judy got up and unlocked the door.

What's wrong? Are you ill?

Judy pulled Steve into the bathroom and gave him a play by play of what had just happened in the kitchen.

Now Steve dropped down onto the fancy little chair in the corner.

Judy put the lid of the toilet seat down and sat there.

They both just stared at the floor for a few minutes.

Then Steve spoke.

So, Meg is my step sister, and you and Meg are half-sisters, and my step mother dated your father, and you and I are dating.

Steve burst into hysterical laughter.

Judy looked up at him. She could not believe he was laughing.

This was not a laughing matter.

Stop, Steve. This is not funny.

But Steve couldn't stop.

Judy just stared at him.

Rachel then knocked on the door.

Everything okay in there?

Judy got up again and unlocked the door.

Rachel came in to find Steve bent over, holding his stomach because he was laughing so hard.

Judy looked at Rachel.

I just told him.

Steve, are you okay?

This made Steve laugh even harder. Tears were running down his cheeks.

At least this time it's you crying and not me, Judy stated.

This threw Steve into another bout of laughter.

After a few minutes, Steve finally calmed down, and the three of them came out of the bathroom.

Judy was in a state of shock.

Rachel decided to take charge of the situation. She asked everyone to please sit down at the dining room table.

Before we have dessert, there is something that has come to my attention that I feel we should all talk about.

Meg looked at Steve, who was still recovering from his laugh attack.

What is it mom? Meg asked.

Well....

Rachel told everyone what she had told Judy just a few minutes ago.

There was total silence. Nobody was looking at anybody else. It was awkward, to say the least.

So, Judy and I are really sisters? We have the same father? But he died in a car accident? Meg asked.

Yes, said Rachel, very straight faced.

Shit, that's heavy, Meg reacted.

Steve started laughing again.

He tried to apologize but could barely speak.

What the hell is so funny about this? Meg asked.

Steve just waved his hand at her as if to say, ignore me.

Well, Judy, Rachel said. Welcome to the family.

With this, everyone but Charles burst into laughter. The whole situation seemed so absurd!

I don't get it, said Charles.

This caused even more laughter, and it was then that Meg decided to break up with Charles. She realized that he totally didn't get her, and she couldn't be with a guy who didn't get her. She would tell him at the end of the night.

Once everyone calmed down, Rachel brought out the pies, ice cream, and whipped cream.

They all ate as if nothing had happened.

As the afternoon became the evening, the situation began to feel more comfortable for everyone. Meg started calling Judy sis, and at one point, Steve said, wait a minute; Judy's not my sister, right?

Everyone but Matt looked at him as if they were doing the math in their heads. Matt looked at him as if he had lost his mind.

No, Steve, Matthew jumped in. You're safe.

Oh, thank God, Steve said.

36

Christmas

The next few weeks flew by. Steve's business was growing, as was his love for Judy. They were really good together. When he was with her, the world felt right, and Judy believed she had found a soul mate in Steve. They had a lot of similar interests and were willing to try the things that were different for one or the other.

They also became comfortable hanging out with Matthew and Rachel. The four of them would sometimes go out for dinner or to a show. This grown up version of Steve was happy and felt complete.

A couple of weeks before Christmas, Steve went over to his parents' house. Hey mom, dad, you home?

In the den son, he heard his dad call back.

Steve sat down in the recliner and told his parents he needed to talk to them. They were sitting on the couch holding hands and watching what his dad called "one of your mom's sappy movies".

Matthew picked up the remote and clicked off the tv.

What's up, honey? Rachel asked.

You guys like Judy, right?

Yeah, they answered enthusiastically in unison.

I do too.

Okay... They looked at each other.

I want to propose to her.

Rachel leapt up.

Oh Steve! That's wonderful! She ran over to the recliner and gave Steve a very big, tight squeeze.

Easy mom, you're gonna break my ribs.

Matthew then stood up and shook Steve's hand and pulled him in for a hug.

I'm not sure if you're asking, but you have our blessing.

It only seems fitting that you, Rachel's stepson would marry the daughter of her lover and half-sister of your step sister.

That was well said Matt, Rachel said playfully.

Thank you very much, Matt said.

But seriously, we are very happy for you. When are you thinking?

Christmas.

Oh, very nice, Rachel said. Did you pick out a ring?

Steve pulled the ring out of his pocket. It was a one carat heart cut with baguettes.

Oh, Steve, it's really beautiful! How exciting!

Now listen. Judy has no idea, so can you keep the secret?

Does Meg know? Rachel asked.

No, said Steve, and let's keep it that way. I know that she thinks she's good at keeping secrets, but she would definitely blab.

Got it, said Matthew. Mum's the word.

The next few days were a little bit hectic as people prepared for the upcoming holiday's events and gatherings. And the snowstorm that hit about a week before Christmas created a nice holiday energy in the air. It had been the first of the season and although it dropped about eight inches of snow, it was a gentle storm, and the snow was powdery. In the small downtown, stores stayed open late, hoping to make some last-minute sales, and the town piped holiday music from the little park, giving the whole place a really festive feel.

Judy and Steve were spending much more time together taking walks, going to movies, ice skating, practicing martial arts, or just sitting together on the couch with a fire burning in the stone fireplace in Judy's cottage and looking out the back glass doors at the snow covered woods leading off to nowhere in particular. Judy continued to put out birdseed every morning, so the two of them, well, let's include Chloe some of the time, would sit and watch the variety of birds that came to eat. Their colors were particularly brilliant against the backdrop of the white snow.

Steve and particularly Judy learned early on in their relationship that although they loved being together, it was essential to also give themselves alone time. Judy had learned that because she was definitely and introvert, she needed recharge time on a daily basis or else she would go into somewhat of a meltdown mode. She explained that to Steve at the beginning of their romantic relationship, and although he wasn't always happy about it, he honored her need to be alone, and he always managed to find things that either needed to be done or that he had been putting off and rediscovered he enjoyed doing.

The studio was doing really well too. The student number had doubled since Steve opened close to a year and a half ago, and Meg presented Steve with a great idea to promote the business during the holidays.

Knock, knock.

Hey, Meg, what's up?

Steve, I have an idea that may benefit the studio.

Come in and tell me.

What do you think about gift certificates? Maybe buy five classes, get one free, or a gift card entitling a person to one, two, three classes...I don't know, something like that?

Meg, I think that's a great idea.

Meg smiled. She loved getting her brother's approval.

I already designed a gift certificate on the computer, and I don't think it would cost too much to make up a few and see how it goes.

Go for it, Steve said. And, we'll put an ad in the paper – maybe something like, "Want a new twist on your New Year's Resolution that will give you balance, focus, and strength? Try Tai Chi at Half Moon Studio."

I like it, Meg said. I'll work on other ways to promote starting tomorrow.

Have a good night, Meg. See you tomorrow.

Night, Steve.

Once Meg left, Steve called Judy to see what she was up to.

Hi, Steve, how was your day?

Really good. What are you up to?

Just reading with Chloe on my lap.

Do you feel like getting some dinner?

Sure. Where'd you have in mind?

How about taking a drive to the Japanese place?

Ohhh, yeah, that sounds really good. It's been a while.

Okay. I'm gonna head home and freshen up. I'll pick you up at seven?

I'll be ready.

They hung up, and Judy looked at the clock. It was a little after five, so she had time. She told Alexa to set the alarm for 6:30, and then picked her book back up and continued to read. She was reading *The Art of Racing in the Rain* by Garth Stein, and she couldn't put it down. He was one of her very favorite authors, and she was always happy to find well written novels to escape into.

At six-thirty, the alarm went off, jarring Judy. She put her book down, and Chloe jumped off her with a little unhappy neow sound.

Sorry, baby, I have to get ready. Steve's picking me up for dinner.

Chloe didn't really care. She looked at Judy as if to say, well at least you could give me a snack for disrupting my nap.

Okay, Chlo, that seems fair.

Judy went into the kitchen and grabbed a couple of snacks.
All was then right again in Chloe's world.
Judy went into her bedroom and changed into a pretty sweater and some leggings. She dug her Uggs out from under the bed, combed her hair and brushed her teeth. She put on some blush and a lip gloss. She checked herself out in her bathroom mirror and was satisfied. She came back into the living room and got her coat from the closet.
All set, baby, she said to Chloe. I'll see you in a couple of hours.
Just then, Steve pulled up. Judy threw her coat on and went out the front to meet him.
She jumped into the car.
Hi, Steve, she said with a big smile.
Hi, Judy. You sure moved fast.
Well, I just realized how hungry I am. I hope you brought a lot of money because I plan on eating tonight.
Steve laughed. Oh boy!
They drove to the Japanese restaurant, parked, and went inside. It was nice and warm and beautifully done.
They chose a booth toward the back and settled in. With menus in hand, they discussed their options.
You wanna share a few things, Judy?
Sure. Can we get edamame?
Okay. And how about a few pieces of smoked salmon sushi?
Oh yeah, that sounds good.
You wanna share the shrimp tempura entrée?
Good idea.
They ordered the food along with two beers and began chatting.
So, Steve said. Meg came up with a great idea to promote the studio.
Tell me.
Gift certificates.
Ohh, that is good.
She also suggested a special like buy five classes, get one free. She thought it might encourage people to use these as holiday

gifts.

Yeah, I could see that.

And, I told her I would put an ad in the paper encouraging people to try a new New Year's Resolution.

Very clever, Judy praised Steve.

Thank you.

He smiled.

Their edamame arrived, and they both dug right in. They were past the relationship phase of feeling shy eating in front of each other.

As they enjoyed the edamame and sushi, Steve gazed at Judy.

She is so cute. I can't wait to ask her to marry me. I want to spend the rest of my life with Miss Judy Tanner.

Judy looked at Steve and smiled.

She thought, I really like him. He is good for me. He makes me feel good about myself. How lucky am I?

They ate their tempura and made small talk.

Then Judy asked, so what does your family do at Christmas?

It's similar to Thanksgiving. We gather at my parents' house on Christmas morning, have a huge breakfast, and open presents. Sometimes, some of their cousins and kids come over later in the day; it depends on who's doing what. What about you?

It's usually just another day for me.

Well, not this year, missy. This year, you're gonna have Christmas Taylor style.

I'm looking forward to it.

The next day, Judy taught her class and then told Steve she had to run.

I've got shopping to do now that I am spending Christmas with the Taylor family.

Okay, Steve chuckled, but don't go too nuts.

Nuts is my middle name, Judy said. I'll call you later.

Steve was sitting at his desk trying to figure out exactly when and how he would propose. He thought maybe Christmas Eve.

He would invite Judy over to his place and make a nice dinner. Then, maybe just before dessert, he would pop the question. Yeah, that seemed like a good plan.

Judy headed to the mall. She wasn't usually a mall shopper, but she needed to be in a place where there were a lot of stores and choices all together. She walked and browsed and tried to figure out good gifts for the Taylors. After about four hours, she went to the food court to have a hot chocolate with whipped cream on top and sit down for a while. She sipped and people watched.

There are all kinds of people, she thought. She tried to create stories for some of the people at the food court. She loved making up a whole tale about a person. True or not, it was entertaining.

After about thirty minutes, she continued her shopping. By the end of the day, she felt like she had pretty much accomplished her mission, and so she headed home. Chloe was very happy to see her. She had been alone the entire day, and she didn't like that.

Hi, baby. How's things?

Chloe immediately jumped up onto Judy's lap, turned around a couple of times, and settled in.

Hmm, Chlo, I was going to wrap the presents I bought, but okay, we'll sit for a little bit.

Judy sat staring out the back. She missed her walks, but between the strange goings on and the cold weather-

Her thought was interrupted by movement. Judy jumped up, knocking Chloe off. Chloe landed on her feet and ran out of the room.

Judy ran to the glass sliding doors.

What to do? Oh the hell with it.

She grabbed her coat and opened the door. She headed down the path toward the movement. She decided, maybe stupidly, to confront head on. Enough was enough. This guy was trespassing and disrupting her life, and she was done with it. She wanted her woods back, and she wanted her peace back.

Just up ahead of her, she saw somebody.

Hey, she yelled. The guy turned and looked at her.

Stop, she yelled.

He ran.

She ran.

Damn, she thought, this guy is fast!

Hey, she yelled, although she was pretty out of breath by now.

The guy disappeared.

Judy let out a sigh.

She headed back to the house feeling defeated.

Once inside, she heard her phone ringing.

Hello?

Hey, kiddo.

Hi, Steve.

What's doin?

Welll...

Wellll what? Judy?

Okay. I chased the woods man.

Judy!

I know; it was stupid, but I saw him while I was sitting on the couch, and I just thought, enough is enough.

So, what happened?

I caught up with him in the clearing and yelled hey to him, and he took off.

Yup, that's what he did with me. So, please don't try that again, k?

Okay. I promise.

Thank you.

So, how was the rest of your day?

They talked for a while and made plans for the end of the week.

Sweet dreams, Steve.

Sweet dreams, Judy.

That Friday, Steve and Judy got together at her house for dinner. They were both in a pretty playful mood.

Judy?

Yes?

How about I make a Christmas Eve dinner tomorrow night?

That sounds nice. What are you gonna make?

Well, that's a surprise.

Okay, I'm prepared to be surprised.

After dinner, they snuggled together on the couch for a while. Close to ten, Steve told her he had to go home and go to sleep. He was worn out by the week.

So, I'll see you tomorrow at about six?

It's a date.

Steve kissed Judy.

Night, night, Steve. Sweet dreams.

They will be because I'm gonna dream about you.

Ohhh, that's so sweet. Judy smiled a forced smile, but inside, she was smiling for real.

The next day, Judy went through her usual routine and then finished wrapping gifts for Christmas at the Taylors'.

By that afternoon, she decided to do a second meditation, just to center herself for her big Christmas day. It had been a really long time since she had participated in a traditional family style Christmas event, and despite the fact that she already loved Steve's family, it was still a social interaction she wasn't used to. She sat and went inward, straight to her meadow. The sun was shining, as it always is, and the birds were chirping. She loved the continuity. She breathed and chanted her mantra: yeeeees, yeeees, yesssss. She began to feel very relaxed and comfortable in her space. Then, there was a breeze like the last time, but this time, she sensed a female energy.

Mom? Kay?

It's Olivia, honey. Change only comes when we are ready for it. Judy felt the breeze again and then didn't sense the other energy.

She opened her eyes and grabbed her pad. She always kept her pad near her when she meditated because sometimes, she was so caught up in the process, that she forgot details.

She jotted down the fact that a breeze blows whenever there is a message, and she wrote the name Olivia? She then wrote what she heard: Change comes only when we are ready for it. Huh?!

She thought but didn't ponder it for too long.

By then, it was five o'clock, so she took a quick shower and dressed for her dinner at Steve's. She was excited about the gift she had found for him. It was a Buddha statue with a really great energy. She thought it would be perfect in the studio. She had put a giant bow on it and would present it to him the next day at the Christmas gathering.

Chloe, I'll see you later.

Judy headed out and drove over to Steve's. Parking was a little limited, so she parked down the block and walked over to his condo. She rang the bell a couple of times.

Okay, okay. Keep your pants on.

Hi, Steve. What an interesting expression.

Hi, Judy, I don't know why I said it. Come in.

Steve took Judy's coat and threw it on his bed.

Would you like something to drink?

Ummm, maybe a beer?

Coming right up.

Do you need help with dinner?

Nope. It's almost ready. Make yourself comfortable in the living room.

Judy sat down on the couch and looked around. She noticed that Steve had straightened up the space.

The apartment looks good, Steve.

Yeah, I figured it was time to clean up a little.

Steve handed Judy her beer.

Thanks.

Welcome. Hey, you wanna hear some music?

Sure.

How about Mumford and Sons?

Oh, I like them. Man, I haven't listened to them in a long time.

Alexa, play Mumford and Sons radio on Pandora.

Getting your Mumford and Sons radio on Pandora, replied Alexa.

The first song began, and Judy immediately started singing.

I love this one, she said.

I'm glad, Steve chuckled. You're not a very good singer, are you?

Steve! Judy exclaimed.

Well, I'm keepin it real.

Whatever, she said. I like to sing.

Then sing away.

A couple of songs later, Steve found himself singing too.

Judy jumped up with the beer in her hand and bopped around the living room.

Come, Steve, dance with me.

Steve joined Judy. They laughed and sang and danced.

Then Steve said, I gotta get the dinner.

Feels good to let loose, doesn't it?

Yeah, it kinda does. Okay, dinner is served.

Steve kept the music on but much lower, and the two of them sat down at his little kitchen table.

Steve, this looks wonderful.

I'm hoping you like it. It's tuna steak with baked potato and broccoli with melted Vermont extra sharp cheddar.

They ate and chatted about nothing in particular.

You know, you're a really good cook. How did you learn to cook?

Actually, Rachel taught me. I was happy that my dad married her, but I was almost a teenager and truthfully, was kind of a pain. Rachel tried her best to develop a relationship with me, and we were okay, but not super close.

She tried to get me to do different hobbies with her but nothing stuck until we started cooking together. I really enjoyed it, and it made us much closer. And, the other benefit was that it always made an impression on the girls I dated.

Judy laughed. I could see that. It's certainly making an impression on me. I only hope you're not secretly cooking for others.

Not to worry. I only have spatula for you.

Ohhh, that's corny.

Once they finished eating, Steve cleared the plates. He wouldn't let Judy help, which was hard for her.

Are you sure I can't do something?

What you can do is sit there and let me serve you. I made a chocolate mousse with whipped cream.

Oh boy! This is going to be good.

Steve put the two dishes of mousse on the table and lit a candle.

That's pretty, Judy said. What scent is it?

Balsam.

I love balsam! How did you know that?

Just then, Steve got off his chair and went down on his knee.

What are you do; Oh my God!!

She put her hands up to her mouth.

Steve took her left hand and looked her in the eye.

Judy, I have fallen head over heels in love with you, and I want to spend the rest of my days, good and bad with you by my side. I will be the best partner that I can be to you. I will love you, care for you, and support you. Judy, will you marry me?

Well, by this time, Judy was of course sobbing. She took a couple of breaths and got down on her knee as well so that they were somewhat eye to eye.

Steve, she blubbered. I love you so much. I would be honored to be your partner.

Steve actually teared up a little bit. He took out the ring box and opened it to offer the ring to Judy.

Judy took in an extremely deep breath.

It's so beautiful!

Steve placed the ring on Judy's finger and held her tightly.

I do love you, he whispered in her ear.

They continued to embrace, then kiss, then, for the first time in their relationship, made love right there on the kitchen floor. They laid there for a while, basking in their new life together.

Suddenly, Steve jumped up.

The mousse, he yelled. I forgot about the mousse.

Judy got up and dressed.

Well, let's eat it now, she said.

They devoured the mousse with whipped cream, laughed, and made love again, this time in Steve's bed, shooting each other with whipped cream and licking it off. It was wonderful!

Judy, will you stay?

Judy took a minute to think about Chloe.

I fed her and cleaned her box, so she should be fine.

Yes, Steve, I would like that.

They snuggled and talked and made love well into the early hours of the morning, then fell asleep.

At about eight o'clock, Judy shot up.

What time is it? She asked in a panic.

Alexa, Steve said sleepily. Time?

The time is now eight eleven.

Steve, I have to go home, feed Chloe, and get ready for Christmas with the Taylors.

Okay, Steve said still a little sleepy. How about I'll take a quick shower, grab a coffee, and pick you up in an hour? That way, we can drive to my parents' together and get there by ten.

Okay.

Judy got dressed. She was focused on getting home, and almost forgot that she had gotten engaged to this wonderful and sexy man.

She went over to the bed and leaned over Steve who tried to pull her back into the bed.

Steve!! I have to go.

She kissed him passionately, told him she loved him and would see him soon.

She left the condo and raced home.

Steve lay in bed for a while. Did he really just propose? Did she really just say yes? Was he really ready to be a married man?

Finally, he got up, took a shower, and dressed for Christmas. He washed the dishes from the night before, grabbed his keys, and left. He stopped at the local café on his way to Judy's, not really expecting them to be open, but they were.

Hey, Dennis, Steve said. Happy holidays, man. I didn't think you'd be open.

Hey, Steve. I'm closing early but wanted people to have a chance to get a bite or grab something last minute. You got here just in time.

Well then, how about an espresso with two shots and give me those six blueberry muffins to go.

While Steve sat at the counter, he watched Dennis. He liked Dennis. He was a hard working small business man like Steve. But Dennis' days were much longer. He opened at five am seven days a week and often stayed open till three and sometimes four in the afternoon. He always looked tired, but he always wore a smile.

Here ya go, Steve. The coffee's on me. Merry Christmas.

Steve threw a twenty on the counter.

Keep the change, man. Merry Christmas. Give my best to the family.

Thanks man, you too.

Steve left feeling very much in the holiday spirit. He headed over to Judy's.

My fiancée he said out loud while driving. He practiced introducing her. Hello, Mom. I'd like you to meet my fiancée. Hello, Meg, have you met my fiancée?

Steve pulled into Judy's driveway and got out of the car. He went to her door with coffee and muffins in hand and then realized he hadn't brought her a coffee. He panicked, but it was too late. Judy opened the door.

Good morning, my husband to be, she said with a particularly bright smile. Please come in.

Steve entered and began apologizing.

For what? Judy asked.

I forgot to bring you a coffee. I'm such a knucklehead.

Hey, remember that you're my knucklehead now, so don't be so hard on yourself. Anyway, I don't drink coffee.

You don't?

Nope. Have you ever seen me drink a cup of coffee?

Come to think of it, no. Maybe I knew that on a subconscious level.

That must be it.

Steve then checked Judy's hand.

My lady, that is quite a nice ring ya got there.

Oh, she said. You like it? My boyfriend just proposed to me.

And, I guess from the looks of it, you said yes.

I most certainly did. I am now officially off the market, so don't get any funny ideas, sir.

Well, his gain is all of the other guys' loss.

They laughed together.

I love how playful you are, Steve.

You know, I never really was before, but you bring it out in me.

Well, please try not to lose it. It's a great quality.

Deal. Are you ready to head over to the Taylors'?

Yes. Can you help me put the gifts in the car?

Sure.

Judy pointed to the couch.

Judy, you went a little nuts.

Well, I'm excited to have people to buy gifts for. This is new for me.

Okay, I'll give you a pass this year, but when we're married, I'm gonna pull the reigns in.

When we're married, Judy repeated with a chuckle. That sounds so weird.

I know, Steve said. I think I need you to pinch me.

Judy stopped mid step. She froze.

Steve didn't notice right away because he was gathering up the gifts. When he turned around with arms full, Judy looked like a statue.

Judy? Then louder, Judy!!

She shook her head and looked at him.

You ok?

She blinked a couple of times.

Yes, fine.

You don't look fine. You were frozen like a statue.

She heard the words in her head: Change comes only when we are ready for it.

This must be what Olivia meant, Judy mouthed to herself.

Whadja say, hon? Are you sure you're okay?

No, I'm good. Come on, let's go. I don't wanna be late.

While in the car, Judy made a mental note to explain to Steve when they had a quiet moment. She also felt it might be time to see a therapist. She was clearly still having some loss issues. She decided she would call Dr. Savoy in the morning and ask her if she could recommend someone in the area.

They arrived at the house a little after ten. There was a dusting of snow on the ground, and the smell of fireplaces burning all around the neighborhood.

Judy got out of the car and inhaled the cold air.

I love the smell of burning wood. It's so comforting.

Well, stop sniffing and help me with this ton of gifts you bought.

Judy grabbed some of the packages and together she and Steve headed to the house.

Before they could ring the bell, Rachel was standing in the doorway.

Soooo? she asked excitedly.

Judy held out her left hand.

Oh, oh, oh

Okay, mom. Get out of the way and let us in. My arms are breaking and it's cold out here.

Sorry, sorry, come in, come in. Meg and your dad are in the den.

They all walked in, took off coats, and put the presents under the tree.

Oh, Steve said, I picked up some blueberry muffins from Dennis.

Is he open? Rachel asked.

He was. Just for the morning. He sends his love.

Dennis and Rachel had gone to school together. That was something Rachel loved about the town. Almost everyone knew everyone, and for the most part, they looked out for each other.

Go in and join Meg and your dad. I'm just getting breakfast ready.

Oh, can I help you with that? Judy asked.

Thank you, Judy, but first you have an announcement to make. Go.

Judy and Steve walked into the den.

Merry Christmas, Matthew cried.

Hey, guys, Meg said. Merry, merry.

Hi you too, Steve said, holding Judy's hand.

So, we have something to tell you.

Steve clapped his hands together, and Meg looked confused.

What's going on? she asked.

Steve looked specifically at Meg.

Well, my baby sister, you're looking at an engaged couple.

Meg's eyes grew large, and she looked at both of them.

Get outta here! For reals?

For reals, Steve said.

She ran over to them and grabbed Judy's hand. She then grabbed Judy and wrapped her arms around her.

Oh, Judy. I'm so happy for you. Wow! This has been quite a few weeks.

Judy laughed. That's for sure.

Matthew then came over and hugged both of them.

We are so happy for you two.

After hugs and kisses, Judy said, I'm gonna help your mom with breakfast.

Meg piped in. Oh sure, make me look bad.

Come on, Meg, Judy said. We'll help together.

Breakfast was a huge one, consisting of every breakfast food under the sun. They all ate and chatted happily until no one could eat another bite.

Let's do presents, said Rachel. We'll clean up after.

In the living room they sat down near the tree. We have a tradition, Matthew explained to Judy. Each of us chooses one gift to give to someone. You can't choose a gift that is for you or from you. This begins the gift opening.

So, they all went to the tree and picked up a gift to hand to each other. They handed their gifts to each other and all at once, ripped off the wrapping.

They then continued with the gift giving. Judy was a little bit embarrassed because she realized how many gifts she had gotten for everyone.

She looked at Steve. I think I did go a little crazy.

Steve laughed.

But you picked out some really good stuff.

Yeah, Meg agreed. Thank, you Judy. I love everything.

So, Matthew said. It's now time to watch either *Miracle on 34th Street* or *It's a Wonderful Life.*

Meg, I think it's your turn to choose.

It's a Wonderful Life, Meg said.

She looked at Judy. It's my favorite.

I don't think I've ever seen it, Judy said.

What? They responded in unison. Well, you're in for a treat.

Rachel went into the kitchen to heat up the apple cider, and the rest went into the den to set up the dvd.

Okay, Matthew said. Everyone get comfortable.

They watched and drank cider, and Rachel, Meg, and Judy

cried.

Oh, typical women, Matthew said.

Shut up, Matt. I know I saw some tears running down your cheeks.

Allergies, he joked.

Okay, Rachel said. We'll go with that.

It was mid afternoon when they finished the movie.

So, Judy, Rachel explained. The last tradition is going out for Chinese food.

Really? Judy said. I never would have guessed that. Are they even open?

Oh yes, said Matthew, and you need a reservation because three quarters of the town goes.

Did you make one, dad? Steve asked.

Steve, do you doubt your old man?

I'm not going to respond to that.

We have a reservation for five at four-thirty. It's two-thirty now. Who's up for a game of Monopoly?

I'm going to clean up the kitchen, Rachel said.

Oh, I can help you, Judy offered.

Judy, it's no biggie. Why don't you play Monopoly? That will make four.

Are you sure?

Positive. I enjoy the quiet time in the kitchen to gather my thoughts.

Oh, I get that.

Judy went into the den and sat down.

Hey, Meg, where's Charles today? Matthew asked.

Oh, it didn't work out. He just didn't get me.

I'm sorry, Meg, Judy said.

No biggie. There's plenty of fish in the sea, right Steve?

Right, Meg. And I'm sure you're gonna catch yourself a whopper.

Everybody laughed.

Okay, Matthew said. Four for Monopoly. Be right back.

He left the den and suddenly, there was Christmas music playing from an invisible speaker.

Okay, now we're ready.

The game was fun. Judy had to admit that she had never played it before, but she promised to try and be a fast learner.

You've never played Monopoly? Steve asked with surprise.

Never.

Good, Meg said. That gives me an advantage.

Meg, Steve scolded.

It's okay, Judy said. Bring it, Meg. Let's just see.

You're on.

They played for well over an hour, and Meg in fact did win.

You sure are competitive, Meg, Matthew said.

Good game, Meg said. I challenge any one of you anytime.

Judy, Steve said, we are going to practice all next year so that we can kick Meg's butt.

I'm in, Judy said.

Hey! Meg pouted.

All's fair in love and war, Steve said with a big grin.

Rachel came in.

You guys ready for some Chinese?

Oh yes, Steve said.

Judy laughed.

You have a bottomless pit.

Yes, I do, so you better learn how to fill it up baby!

Oh, get a room, you guys, Meg teased.

37

A New Year

The next couple of weeks were light and easy. Steve and Judy saw each other every day at work and most evenings socially. They celebrated New Year's Eve with Steve's family and pretty much the entire town. Each year, the town did their own version of watching the ball drop; of course, it was on a much smaller scale, but a good time was always had by all. Everyone gathered at the school gymnasium for a pot luck. Then there was a barn dance, and finally the more intrepid would head over to the Village Square for the countdown to midnight.

Toy horns were blown and confetti flew everywhere. It was corny, to say the least, but in a sweet way.

Steve and Judy participated from start to finish and decided it could be one of their new traditions as a couple.

Judy liked the way her life was going and looked forward to a future with Steve. A few nights a week, Steve stayed at Judy's, and occasionally, Judy stayed at Steve's. She didn't like to leave Chloe alone, and Steve got that.

One day, early into January, a couple came into the studio with their son. He was fifteen, and it soon became apparent that there were some issues. Steve was there alone – it was an extremely quiet day, so he had told Meg to go have some fun.

Hi, folks, can I help you?

Yes, we saw an ad in the paper about buying five classes and getting one free and thought this might be a good activity for our son, Brian.

Steve looked at Brian who was looking at the floor. Something about him seemed familiar. He was tall for fifteen and a little heavy.

Brian's a little shy, and so we're hoping that Tai Chi will help to bring him out of his shell, Brian's dad explained.

He spends much of his time walking around, mostly in the woods, but the weather has become prohibitive, so we are trying to find an indoor activity that will burn up some of his energy, Brian's mom added.

That's it, Steve thought. This is the guy from the woods that Judy and I keep seeing.

Okay, well, let me just grab an application, and we can get started.

Steve handed Brian paperwork, but he didn't take it, so his mom grabbed it and told Steve she would fill it out.

Brian continued to look at the floor.

While his mom and dad were putting down all necessary information, Steve tried to talk to Brian.

So, Brian, you like to walk in the woods, huh?

Nothing.

I like the woods too. They're so peaceful. Do you like to watch the birds?

Still nothing.

Brian's dad came over. I think I should explain. Brian is on the spectrum. He is verbal, but very shy. We would actually be interested in private classes, at least to start with. I don't think that Brian would initially do well in a group setting.

Oh, I see, said Steve.

Brian's mom then came over and handed Steve the paperwork. Steve's suspicions were confirmed. Their home address was on the other side of Judy's woods. This definitely was the guy they had seen, and he wasn't harmful.

This is such a relief, Steve thought.

So, did you have a day and time in mind for Brian?

Well, he goes to a special school that lets out at 2:30 each day, so anytime 3:00 or later would work.

Okay, let me check my schedule and see what I can do. I have your number here on the paperwork. I'll give you a call tomorrow, if that's okay?

They discussed the fee, and Steve said he would apply the fifth class as a free one.

It was nice meeting you. I'll see you real soon, Brian.

With that, Brian looked up at Steve for a brief moment and said, k.

Brian's mom smiled at Steve, and as they walked out, Steve heard her say, that was very good, Brian.

Wow, Steve thought. That's tough.

It was Saturday, and the studio was closed on Sundays, so Steve finished some paperwork and ran home to get some things. He and Judy were spending the weekend together, and he couldn't wait to tell her what had happened at the studio.

When he got to Judy's cottage, she was on the couch under a blanket, book in hand, and cat on her lap. Steve had a key, so Judy could keep the front door locked and not have to get up whenever he came over.

Hi, babe, he said when he walked in.

Hi, Steve.

How's the reading going?

Great. I'm almost done with the book.

Steve grabbed a beer from the fridge and lifted Judy's feet up and placed them on his lap.

She reached out for the bottle and took a sip, handing it back before Steve had time to process what she was doing.

Thanks, Steve. I've been trapped on the couch for the past two hours and was getting thirsty.

She smiled.

Well, it's a good thing I came along when I did. Otherwise, I might have found you dead from dehydration.

So, my man, tell me what's new.

It's funny you should ask, my woman. I've solved the mystery of the woods man.

Judy sat completely upright, disturbing Chloe who jumped off the couch.

No, she said her eyes as big as moons and a look of anticipation on her face.

Yes, I did, Steve bragged.

Do tell.

Steve told Judy what had happened at the studio.

Interesting, she said. How about that?

Now, I have a question for you, Steve said.

Yes? Judy asked hesitantly.

How would you feel about working with Brian? I was thinking maybe Thursdays before your evening class.

Oh, I don't know, Steve. I don't have any experience working with people with special needs.

Would you give it a try? I think you would be great with him.

Let me think about it. When do I need to let you know?

I told his parents I would call them tomorrow.

Okay. I'm going to sleep on it.

So, where do you want to eat tonight?

The rest of the night went by uneventfully. After dinner, Judy and Steve picked a movie and snuggled together on the couch until Judy had trouble keeping her eyes open.

I have to go to bed, Steve.

Let's go.

They got ready for bed and curled up under the covers.

I love you, Steve.

I love you too. Sleep well.

Sweet dreams.

Judy was out in about thirty seconds. She slept through till around seven the next morning.

When she woke up, Steve was still sound asleep, so she decided to take advantage of the quiet time and do some meditating to figure out what to do about this special class.

She sat in her meditation spot, and to her surprise, Chloe climbed right into her lap.

Hi, baby. Hmm, is this a sign?

Judy closed her eyes and followed her breathing.

Yees, yees, yees, she repeated. She stayed open to an answer.

As she sat, Chloe began kneading her legs. It felt very nice.

She's never done this before, Judy thought while in a semi-meditative state. I'm going to take this as a positive sign. Perhaps the comfort I'm feeling from Chloe is something I can pass on to Brian.

Judy came completely out of her meditation and went into the kitchen to make some coffee for Steve.

About ten minutes later, Steve appeared. I smell coffee, he said.

They sat together at the kitchen table, Steve with his coffee, and Judy with her tea.

So, Steve, I meditated on your proposal this morning, and I think I would like to try to work with Brian.

Oh, that's great, hon. I'll give his parents a call this afternoon.

So, Judy said. Are you making breakfast? I'm starving.

Steve laughed. Aye aye captain.

38

Struggles

Steve contacted Brian's parents and arranged for Brian to begin working with Judy Thursdays at four-thirty. On Monday, Judy taught her class and then went to see Steve.

Hey, babe.

Hey, Steve. I'm going to head out to the library and look for some information on Autism so that I can be prepared for Brian.

Okay. I'll see you tonight?

Yeah. How about I make dinner?

I never say no to a home cooked meal, Steve said happily.

Judy gave Steve a quick peck and left.

She had always loved the library. Even as a little girl, the library was like a sanctuary. Now, as an adult, whenever she went to a library, she immediately thought of Kay. She and Kay loved books, and they would spend hours wandering through the stacks. But today, she couldn't wander. She was on a mission.

Excuse me, she said to the librarian. Where would I find books on Autism?

The librarian pointed to a row that was headed Special Needs.

Thank you.

The librarian nodded.

Judy went to the row and scanned. She was reading the topics out loud. Alzheimer's, Autism; here we go. She took the first book, sat down on the floor in the row, and started to read. She skimmed through, put the book back and looked for another. She was hoping to find a book that specifically suggested how to relate to someone on the spectrum. As she searched, she found a little book, more like a pamphlet even, entitled, "You and Your Child: How to live with a Person on the Spectrum". Judy took it and sat back down.

Now this is pretty useful, she said out loud. The pamphlet, which was produced by Autism Speaks, offered a number of tips that Judy found to be really helpful. There was also a website. Okay, she said. She took out her phone and took pictures of the pages she wanted to hold on to and headed out.

Judy drove to Whole Foods. Inside, she grabbed a basket and walked the aisles.

What should I make? Oh, maybe a pasta casserole. She picked up some gluten free penne, organic tomato sauce, ricotta cheese, and some greens for a salad.

Okay, now dessert. Hmmmm. Maybe just ice cream.

She checked out and drove home.

Hi, my Chloe, I'm home. Chloe slightly raised her head from her napping position on the couch. She had placed herself in her usual spot, precisely where the sun was shining in, and so wasn't moving for anything.

You look like you're getting pretty toasty, Chlo.

Judy smiled. She loved Chloe so much. For quite a while, it had just been the two of them, and Chloe remained a special friend. Now that Steve was in the picture, Chloe had two people to love, and that was fine with her. She really liked Steve, and frankly, sometimes Judy was a little bit jealous of their relationship because Chloe occasionally chose Steve's lap or Steve's side of the bed.

Judy went into the den and sat down near Chloe. She searched the web for some more info regarding Autism, found a really good site, and was fascinated by what she read:

Helpful Tips to Use when working with People with Autism -

Listen when they say "enough" or "no more." Autistic people are easily overwhelmed with sensory information. They're not trying to be rude. They're trying their best to be comfortable in the world.

Using break cards - A break card is simply a card that says something like "I need a break." Especially helpful for non-verbal children, the card provides another way to communicate that they need to get away from someone or from an activity that is stressing them out.

Pay attention to their "stim" cues. Physically, autistic people engage in self-stimulating behavior (often called "stimming"). These behaviors (such as flapping hands, rocking, twirling, or repeatedly playing with the same objects) calm them down, make them feel good, and help them feel balanced. Don't let stimming worry you. Treat it like a natural behavior and continue doing whatever you were doing. Alert a parent if the stim seems self-injurious.

Try sitting next to them. Not every autistic child prefers close physical proximity, but some do.

Give them their space. Not every autistic child prefers close physical proximity, and most will enjoy having space to themselves.

Compliment them often.

Talk to them like a friend.

Interpret wandering as communication.

Judy made a bunch of notes and actually created some very specific lesson plans. She realized that the plans may have to be thrown out the window, but she felt better having a structure to go in with. She decided to take it really slowly with Brian. She wanted to explore boundaries and abilities with him. They would do some very basic beginner exercises and then increase little by little.

Judy checked the time. It was already five o'clock.

Okay, Judy said. Time to start dinner.

She couldn't remember if Steve said when he'd be home, so she gave him a call.

Hi, hon, Steve said.

Hey, Steve. Did you say when you'd be over?

No, I don't think I did, but I'll be leaving here in about fifteen minutes. I should be at your house by five-thirty.

Sounds good. I'll see you soon.

Judy got out her big pot, filled it with water and put it on the stove to boil. She then put the sauce in a smaller pot and put that on a low flame. She added some olive oil, oregano, and fresh basil. She took out her baking dish and turned on the oven.

She washed the greens and threw in some carrots and cucumbers. She broke up some goat cheese and mixed some olive oil and vinegar with some more of the basil.

Okay, do I have any bread? Yes.

She cut the bread up into triangles to be toasted.

This will be good dipped in olive oil and basil, she said to herself.

The water was finally boiling. Judy poured the penne in and stirred the sauce.

Hey, hey.

Hi, Steve.

Something smells good.

I'm making a pasta casserole.

Well, that's something new.

Yeah. I'm just full of surprises.

Steve hugged Judy. I'm happy to be here with you.

And I'm happy you're here.

How much time till dinner?

Probably about thirty minutes, why?

Come, let's sit and talk.
Uh oh, Judy said.
No, nothing bad.
They went over to the couch.
Hi, Chloe. How are you, baby?
Chloe stretched, yawned, and jumped onto Steve's lap.
What am I, Chloe? Chopped liver?
Chloe was purring so loudly that she started to drool all over Steve's pants.
Oh my God. Are you serious right now?
Steve looked at Judy.
If I didn't know better, I would think that you're jealous of your cat.
What are you talking about? You're crazy, Judy responded.
But she knew Steve was right.
Get a grip girl, she thought to herself. Where is this insecurity coming from? You love Chloe and Chloe loves you. That doesn't mean she can't love others, and of course Steve loves you too.
She got up to drain the penne and stir the sauce. She poured the penne, ricotta cheese, and sauce into the baking dish and put it in the oven.
Okay, this needs about fifteen or twenty minutes to bake.
Come and sit back down next to me. Steve patted the couch cushion next to him.
Judy sat down next to Steve and Chloe. She patted Chloe who gave her smily eyes while continuing to knead and purr and drool.
Judy had to chuckle. Chloe was so happy!

So, Steve started again. I was thinking today that I am spending more and more nights here with you. It feels really natural, don't you think?
Judy was looking at Steve and listening. She nodded.
What was he getting at?
So, maybe I should just move in.

Judy stared at him.

This is big, she thought. Am I ready to share my space full time? How would that work?

How would that work? she asked. I've never lived with anyone before since Kay and college, and those were very different situations from this one.

Well, I would sell my condo, downsize my stuff, and move the rest in here.

Huh, Judy said.

Too much too soon? Steve asked.

Hmmm. Let me process this. We've only been engaged for a few weeks, and I do love you; I just need to wrap my head around having you here full time.

I see, Steve said.

No, please don't misinterpret. Just give me time to process.

Judy got up to check the casserole.

Maybe it was a bad idea, Steve said, a little bit defensively.

No, Steve, I don't think so. It makes sense. The thing is that you have been living with this idea for what?

About a week or so.

Yeah.

So, you're a week ahead of me. I think you know by now that it takes me a little bit of time to absorb change. I'm not great with rushed change. It throws me. I'm a creature of habit and routine. It's what has helped keep me sane through all of the losses I've had in my life. Please be patient with me.

Steve realized that Judy wasn't rejecting him.

It's just that I love you so much and am so excited about you and me being an us. I almost can't wait to have a life with you.

You do have a life with me, and I feel the same. I guess I'm just more naturally cautious.

I get that.

Steve kissed Judy.

Take your time and let me know what you think.

It's a plan.

Judy pulled the casserole out of the oven.

Oh, Judy, that looks fantastic!

She set the table and told Steve to sit.

You wanna a beer?

Yes, sounds good.

She handed Steve a beer then set the two salads on the table along with the toasty bread and olive oil dip.

Hey, this is great.

We'll start with this while the casserole cools a little bit.

Judy grabbed a beer for herself and joined Steve at the table.

Oh, Steve said in between bites of salad and bread. How'd you do at the library?

Oh, yeah. I found some really helpful tips. I spent some of the afternoon creating lesson plans. I'm prepared to make changes as needed but wanted to have a structure in place at least to start off with.

Sounds good, Judy. I know you already have a college degree in Sociology, but I think you would make a natural teacher. Have you ever thought about getting a Master's in Education?

Judy looked at Steve. She hadn't truly thought about what she might do professionally. She had been comfortable, maybe for too long, due to the monies she had gotten. She knew she would have to do something at some point, but never went further than that thought.

You okay? Steve asked.

Huh? Yeah. I just never thought about it. I've been living off my inheritances and the little bit I've been making at the studio. I know I have to think about getting a better paying job eventually so that I have a little cushion and am able to support myself...It's just that your words kind of hit me in the face.

I'm sorry. I didn't mean to upset you, but I see so much potential. I'm not sure you realize how amazing you are.

With that, Judy got up. She took Steve's plate off the table and scooped a heaping helping of casserole onto it. She placed it down in front of him. She picked up her plate and repeated. Once back at the table, she said, careful; it might still be pretty hot.

Steve took a bite.

Oh, Judy, this is excellent! I think I have a new favorite.

Get outta here, she said.

No, I'm serious.

She smiled.

So, Steve, I do think it's a good idea for you to move in. It will save you some money, right?

That's true, but that's not why.

I know. Actually, you could even rent it out, right? That way, you wouldn't be giving it up.

You mean, in case this doesn't work out?

Judy didn't answer.

Judy, are we making a mistake here? Maybe we shouldn't have jumped into an engagement.

Steve, I don't think this is a mistake. Are things always going to be peaches and cream? No. We are two independent, strong people. We are not always going to agree, but what I love about us is that we can talk things out. I feel like you're in my corner, and I hope you feel the same. Yes, there will be tough conversations. Can you handle that?

I do believe I can, Judy Tanner.

Good. Then it's settled. Sell your condo and move in here. And, I do need to seriously think about my professional future. Just probably not tonight.

They finished eating, and Judy cleared the table.

So, you want some ice cream?

What flavor?

She opened the freezer.

Umm, I have vanilla, chocolate, and mocha chip.

Ohh, mocha chip for sure.

A man after my own heart. Two mocha chips coming up.

Steve watched Judy as she prepared the ice cream.

She is extraordinary, he said in his head.

She placed the bowls down on the table.

Here you go.

Thanks, hon.

They gobbled up the ice cream.

Hey, you want to watch a movie?

That sounds good.

They snuggled up together on the couch and clicked the clicker.

Judy felt like an old married couple.

Steve?

Yeah?

Let's not get boring and predictable as a couple, okay? Let's keep our life interesting.

I guess that's what people mean when they say that relationships take work. It's easy to fall into a lazy routine. I'll try to keep us interesting.

I will too.

They kissed and watched tv for a while.

Thursday arrived quickly, and Judy was a bit nervous to meet Brian and work with him.

She got to the studio at three forty-five. Steve was just finishing up with a small advanced class.

She snuck in and watched. She was still learning Tai Chi from Steve, as well as defensive martial arts, but she was craving some more advanced forms. She liked to watch Steve in action. His form was spot on, and it gave her an appreciation for his technique and talent.

When the class broke up, Steve noticed Judy watching.

Hey, there.

Hey.

You're early.

Yeah. I wanted to be in the space before Brian arrives.

I know you're gonna be great.

Hope so.

Steve gave Judy a kiss and headed toward his office.

I've got some calls to make. I'll see you at home.

Judy bowed and entered the space. She breathed and did some warm up.

She stretched and went through the twenty-four a couple of times. She was feeling very focused and relaxed. She then reviewed the notes she had made. She checked the clock and heard Meg greet someone.

Hi, may I help you?

Yes, this is my son, Brian. He has a lesson at four-thirty.

Judy came out into the waiting area.

Hi, I'm Judy. Brian and I will be working together.

Judy shook Brian's mom's hand. She then faced Brian, who was again looking down at the floor.

He's pretty excited about this, right Brian?

Nothing.

Brian, I'm Judy. I'm excited to work with you. Would you like to come into the dojo, and we'll get to know each other?

Brian didn't answer but did follow Judy in.

I'll be right here Brian, his mom said as he walked away.

Judy reminded herself to speak slowly and not overwhelm.

So, Brian, this is where we will be working together. If you have any questions, please just ask, and if you need me to stop or help you, just let me know. I think we are going to be great friends.

Judy worked on getting Brian to communicate a little bit. They did some very basic warm up exercises while Judy asked Brian a couple of questions. At one point, Brian did nod, but for most of the time, he kept his head down. Judy was undaunted. She was prepared and carried on with the lesson.

Then, Brian stopped doing the warm up and sat in the middle of the floor rocking.

Okay, Judy thought. It seems like he's feeling a little bit overwhelmed. Judy sat down next to him and talked about times she felt like things were too much and how she helped herself feel better by taking deep breaths. She spoke very quietly and naturally, as if she were sharing with a girlfriend.

After about ten minutes, Brian stopped rocking and looked at Judy.

Breathing?

Mhmm, she said. Do you want to try it?

Brian nodded.

Okay, first inhale like this.

She took a big breath in.

Then, breathe out.

She blew her breath out.

Brian copied.

And, she said. You can even make a sound when you breathe out. That's really helpful.

She inhaled and then let out her breath while making a sort of humming sound.

Brian did the same.

That's really great, Brian. Good job. How do you feel? Feels good, right?

Brian did it again and again and again.

Really good.

Judy smiled.

Okay, our time is up for today. I had a really good time. Did you?

Yes, Brian said.

Do you want to do this again next week?

Yes, Brian said.

Okay. I will see you next Thursday. It was very nice to meet you, Brian. I hope you have a happy week.

The two got up and went into the waiting room. Brian's mom stood up.

Hi, honey, she said. How did it go?

Brian looked down but said, good.

His mom smiled.

Good.

She then looked at Judy. I guess we'll see you next week.

Sure thing. Bye, Brian.

Judy waved. She turned to look at Meg.

What's the deal? Meg asked.

Judy explained about Brian.

Ohh, that's cool.

Yeah, Judy said.

Steve came out of his office.

So?

It went really well. Brian is going to come back next Thursday.

I knew you'd be great.

Okay, guys, Judy said, I'm going to run to the restroom and then get ready for my next class.

39
Siblings

The weeks ran into months; a routine was established. Judy was at the studio just about everyday. She and Steve were getting to know each other better, learning to compromise and talking about a future together.

One Tuesday, in late spring, Judy had just finished her class and came out to the waiting area.
Hey, Meg.
Hi.
What's up? You seem down.
Nothin.
Meg?
Nothin.
Okay. Come on, spill. What's goin on?
Meg didn't even look up.
What are you doing after work? Judy asked her.

Judy realized that between adding classes, Steve moving in, and just life, Meg had gotten left out in the cold. And, after all, they were sisters, so Judy needed to step up.

No plans, Meg said droopily.
Okay, it's set then. Let's go out; my treat, anywhere you want.
We'll have a girl's night out. It's been too long.
That's okay, Judy. I don't need your pity.

What pity? I want to spend some time with my sis, eating good food and having a couple of drinks.

Welll, okay, she said in a blah manner.

Okay.

Judy tried to sound peppy.

I'll pick you up at six here. See you later.

She went in to kiss her fiancée goodbye and let him know that she and Meg were going out.

Oh, good. She hasn't been herself lately, and I haven't been any help.

Not to worry, Judy said. I got this.

Judy headed home to do a few chores. It was a beautiful day, so she and Chloe went for a woods walk. She was thrilled that the winter had passed and that she had her woods back now that she knew who the presumably "scary man" in the woods was. Actually, Brian was doing really well in her class. He had made progress, was more talkative, and even smiled occasionally. Judy believed that with continual work and positive, safe reinforcement, Brian had potential that they all just might see at some point.

Okay, Chlo, come on. Let's roll.

They headed out, both feeling the energy of the warm air and sun on their bodies.

Oh, Chlo, isn't this great?

Chloe let out a big meow and darted away from Judy. She climbed a little ways up a tree and then jumped off and ran some more.

Spring is a great season, Judy sound out loud.

They walked and walked and came to the clearing.

I have to sit for a while Chloe, Judy yelled out.

She sat down on the grass with her hands behind her for support and looked up at the sky. She took in a very deep breath and exhaled. The sun shone down on her face and felt like love itself stroking her.

This is good.

Chloe came over and climbed into her lap.

Hi, baby. Doesn't the sun feel good?

Just then, Judy noticed movement off in the woods beyond the clearing.

She yelled out.

Brian?

The movement stopped.

Is that you, Brian? It's me, Judy, your Tai Chi teacher.

Brian peeked out from behind a tree.

You wanna join me? I'm feeling the sunshine on my face.

Brian came out from behind the tree.

Come on. It feels really good. Try it.

He cautiously walked over to Judy with his head down.

Hi, Brian.

He continued to look down at the ground.

Brian, this is my cat, Chloe.

Chloe was looking at Brian, a little unsure. Her tail was moving back and forth to release her slight anxiety.

Brian looked at Chloe.

She's your cat?

Yes, Judy said. Come and sit down next me.

Brian sat down awkwardly.

Now watch what I do.

Judy stroked Chloe along her head.

You try. Pick up your hand.

Brian did.

Now touch Chloe's head very gently.

Brian began petting Chloe.

That's great, Brian. She loves that.

Chloe was purring.

Brian let out a little giggle.

You're a natural with her. Do you have any pets at home?

No. Brian shook his head back and forth vehemently.

Hmmm, Judy had a thought. Maybe the studio should get a fish tank. They are pretty therapeutic and would provide some element of animal energy. She would suggest it to Steve.

Judy and Brian and Chloe sat for quite a while petting Chloe and feeling the sun.

Finally, after about an hour, Judy told Brian she needed to get back home.

It was really nice sitting here with you. I'll see you at Tai Chi class on Thursday, okay?

Brian shook his head up and down enthusiastically.

Okay, he said.

They both stood up.

Bye bye, Brian. Get home safe.

She and Chloe headed back toward her house. Judy turned to make sure Brian was heading across the clearing back to his house. When she looked, all she saw was some tree branches moving.

Man, that boy really is quick! she thought.

Back at the cottage, she and Chloe had some water, and Judy got changed to go out with Meg.

Okay, Chlo. I'll be back in a bit.

Judy grabbed a sweater and headed out. She drove over to the studio and went in.

Hi, Meg, you ready?

I don't know, Judy. I don't feel like going out.

Come on, Meg. Do it for me.

Meg looked at her. This was not the bubbly Meg that Judy had come to know.

K?

Alright, Meg said hesitantly.

Steve, Judy called. We're out. See you later.

Steve was on the phone and waved a hand at them.

The girls got in Judy's Prius and headed out.

Where are we going? Meg asked.

I made a reservation at the Copper Door.

Meg looked at Judy.

I remember how much you love that place.

Meg sort of smile/smirked and then burst into tears.

Oh, Meg. What's going on?

Judy was trying to drive and be a therapist – not an easy feat.

Meg completely opened up.

My mom and dad are so happy. You and Steve are getting married. I'm going on twenty-seven, and I can't even maintain a relationship for more than five minutes. I'm so alone. I work at my brother's studio, moved back into my parent's house, and have no partner. I'm such a failure.

Meg was crying hard now. Judy pulled over to the side of the road.

Get out, she told Meg.

What?

Get out.

Meg looked at her in disbelief and got out of the car.

Judy got out and walked around to Meg. She wrapped her arms around her and hugged her hard. She whispered to her.

You are a beautiful, vivacious, intelligent, loving woman, and you are my sister. We all get lost sometimes, Meg. We all face challenges and tough times. But know this – we will always be sisters, and you have me by your side, in your corner. I am right here.

Meg hugged Judy back, and they both cried for a few minutes.

Okay, Judy said, as she wiped her cheeks. Let's go eat a great meal. I believe there's a seafood pasta with your name on it at the Copper Door.

They got back in the car and drove to the restaurant holding hands.

At the restaurant, they were seated and ordered two beers.

A toast to sisterhood.

They clinked glasses and laughed.

Oh, Judy. Thank you. I was sinking fast and didn't know how to come back up.

Hey, that's what sisters are for.

Their dinners arrived, and they dug in.

Oh my God! Meg said. I almost forgot how good this is.

They chatted and laughed and talked about the wedding.

At a lull, Judy looked up at Meg.

Meg, she said excitedly. I just had a mind-blowing idea.

Okay?

I think you and I need to go to India.

What? What's in your food? Are you out of your mind?

No, I'm serious. When I was in India the second time, I was so deeply lost and depressed. Olivia was there for me and the experience was like nothing I can describe. I think it's your time now. Come on. What do you think?

Meg quietly finished her seafood pasta.

Meg?

She put her fork down and looked at Judy.

Judy, you're my sister, and I trust you with my life. Let's do it.

Good, Judy said emphatically. I'll make arrangements.

But you'll be with me, right?

Hell yes!

They shared a chocolate lava dessert, paid the bill and headed home.

Judy dropped Meg off at Matthew and Rachel's.

I'll see you tomorrow, sis. She leaned over and kissed Meg on the cheek.

Thank you, Judy.

Meg had tears in her eyes.

Welcome.

Judy smiled.

When she got home, Steve was in bed reading.

Hi, hon.

Oh, hey. How was dinner?

Fantastic! Meg and I are going to India.

Steve put his book down.

Come again?

Judy chuckled. I know that's not something you hear every day. Thing is, Meg has been really struggling for the past few weeks, and I think this is what she needs.

Can we at least talk about this?

Steve and Judy talked everything out, and Steve couldn't argue that this would be good for Meg. They worked out how the studio would be covered, and since Steve had moved into the cottage, he would take care of Chloe.

Judy called Olivia the next day.

Hi, my love. You are coming to India?

How did you, never mind. Judy realized that Olivia knows everything.

If it's okay, I'd like to bring my half-sister, Meg. She is having a hard time right now, and I really believe that some work at the Ashram is what she needs.

Your intuition and compassion are on target. I've already conferred with Swami Ravi Baba Singh, and he has a spot for both of you.

For both of us?

Often, we more easily see the needs of others.

Judy had learned early on not to question Olivia. She was realizing that Olivia was a higher spiritual being than appeared.

So, we will fly out this coming weekend. I will send you the details of the flight. Thank you, Olivia. I feel very connected to you and am looking forward to seeing you. You are a really special person in my life.

Have a wonderful trip, my dear. I will see you when you arrive.

The next few days were hectic, to say the least. Judy and Meg packed, prepared documents, and made plans. The flight would leave on Saturday morning.

Steve had mixed feelings. The ego in him didn't want Judy to go. Her past was a part of her life that he couldn't compete with. He knew about the love affair, and he felt pretty insecure about what might happen when Judy was in India. On the other hand, he loved Judy for helping his sister. He honored Judy's independent spirit and knew that somehow, on some level, this was way bigger than him. It was inevitable, and his trust would play a serious role.

Friday night, Judy and Steve went out for dinner before the trip. Judy and Meg would be gone for three weeks, which seemed like an eternity to Steve.

You know I'm having really mixed feelings about this, Steve said to Judy over salads.

I know.

There's a part of me that doesn't want you to go. I can't control what happens in India.

You can't truly control what happens here.

Yes, but at least we are together.

We are together with me in India too.

You know what I mean.

Steve,

Let me finish. I love you with my heart and my soul, and I know this is the right thing for you and Meg. The selfish part is mad. You're leaving me. But the bigger part loves you for going.

Does that make sense?

Perfect.

Judy smiled at Steve. I love you so much. You know this picture is all completely connected. You are not a separate part of this. We are all elements. And when Meg and I come back in three weeks, let's plan our wedding. Let's actually set a date, k?

K, Steve said. He took Judy's hand and stared into her eyes. My love.

The next morning was a flurry of activity. Judy was taking care of some last-minute details and reminding Steve about things to do. Steve tried to stay out of her way, but also wanted as much Judy time as he could get. He was still conflicted, but he knew this was the right thing.

Judy kissed Chloe goodbye and told her she would see her in a few weeks. She realized that this was the first time they would be apart for so long.

Steve put her luggage in the car and came back into the cottage.

Ya ready?

Yes.

They drove over to Matthew and Rachel's and went inside.

Meg, Steve called out. Come on; we have to go.

Hi, Rachel, hi, Matthew.

Hey, Judes. You ready for this big adventure?

I am. How's Meg doing?

See for yourself.

Meg was standing in the kitchen doorway.

Hey, Meg, you ready?

I think so.

Believe me, you're ready.

Meg smiled.

Steve put Meg's luggage in the car. He came back inside.

Okay, girls, let's hit the road.

Hugs were had all around.

Call us when you arrive, please, Rachel said.

Wow, you totally sound like a mom, Matthew teased.

Mom, I'll see you Monday morning at the studio.

Okay, Steve. Bye, guys, Rachel waved from the front door as they pulled out.

They pulled up at departures, and Steve got their luggage out of the car. Steve and Judy hugged for a long time, kissed and hugged some more. Then Steve hugged Meg. I love you, baby girl.

Me too, Meg said.

Inside the airport, Meg became a little overwhelmed.

Just stay next to me, Meg. You'll be fine once we get on the plane.

They went through security and found their gate. They had about an hour before departure.

Meg, I'm going to get us some stuff to eat on the plane. Any requests?

Meg told Judy what she wanted, and Judy went to get the food.

As she was heading back to the gate, she heard the announcement for their flight.

Meg looked panic stricken.

I'm here. I'm right here.

They packed the food away in their carry on's and got on line.

Judy smiled at Meg. Here we go.

They boarded the plane, buckled in, and took off. Judy took Meg's hand. Meg was gripping the armrests and had her eyes closed.

You're a white knuckler, huh?

Meg looked at Judy.

You're doing great!

They both fell asleep about an hour after takeoff.

Turbulence shook them awake. They took turns standing and stretching and then each went to the restroom.

Once back in their seats, Judy suggested they eat something. They munched on their snacks and sat dreamily.

Judy?

Yeah?

I'm glad you're my sister.

Me too, honey.

Judy pulled out her phone and pulled up Pandora. She handed Meg one of the ear buds. They sang quietly, holding hands and drifting in thought.

Attention, they heard. Please prepare for landing. Place your seat backs in an upright position and secure your tray tables.

Okay, Judy said. We're landing. And so the adventure begins.

Judy?

Yeah?

Tell me about the Ashram again.

Judy described the Ashram and her experiences.

Just stay open to whatever, Meg. This is your opportunity to grow spiritually, and that is a very precious gift. And, I know you are going to love Olivia. Do you remember the greeting?

Meg practiced, bowing in her seat and saying, "Khamaghani". The man in the seat behind her leaned forward.

That's very good, he smiled.

Thank you, Meg responded. She felt comforted by the acknowledgement.

The plane landed, and everyone jumped up. After about twenty minutes, the girls were headed to the carousel to pick up their luggage and get through customs. Meg was looking around, trying to soak in everything. The hustle and bustle was new to the small town girl from New England. She was very glad that Judy was with her to lead her through the airport. She didn't think it was something she could have ever done on her own, but walking with her big sister, she felt kinda of international and sophisticated. These were new feelings for her, and she liked them.

Once through customs, they headed out to find a cab. The sunlight was strong, and it took them a minute to adjust, but once Judy's eyes focused, she saw a sign. She waved a hand in the air.

What are you doing, Judy?

Look. Judy pointed.

Meg looked over and saw the sign that said, Judy and Meg.

What's that?

That's our limo, my dear.

Ohhh, Meg said, very impressed.

The driver came over. He removed his hat and bowed.

Khamaghani, Judy said.

Khamaghani, Meg said.

The driver recognized Judy.

Welcome back home, he said in a very thick accent.

Thank you, Judy said. It's nice to be back home.

The driver loaded their luggage into the limo, and the girls climbed into the back.

They drove for about thirty minutes. Meg was in awe.

This place is sooo beautiful.

Wait till you see the palace.

What palace?

Olivia's palace. Olivia is royalty, and the family lives in a palace.

Get outta here.

Judy chuckled.

The limo pulled up and Judy and Meg saw people standing outside waving.

Judy jumped out and ran to Olivia. Khamaghani, Judy bowed with palms together. They embraced. Then the others greeted her as she greeted them.

Meg was hanging back, feeling unsure.

Meg, Judy waved her over.

I would like to introduce you to my Indian family.

All at once, they all bowed. Khamaghani.

Meg did her best to repeat the greeting.

I'll have to work on that, she said.

With that, everyone laughed, and Meg noticed one guy in the middle of the group who kind of fascinated her.

Shall we go in?

They all entered the palace.

Oh, my, God, Meg said looking around.

Judy laughed.

Oh, it's so nice to be back.

Come to the back. We've prepared a feast.

They all went out to the back where there was a spread of foods, few of which Meg even recognized. She stood staring, unsure how to proceed. She looked around, but Judy was off in a corner talking to some of the girls.

May I assist you?

Meg looked up. It was the guy she had noticed when they arrived.

I am Aarav. I am one of Olivia's younger sons.

She was captivated. She had never seen a man so beautiful. Aarav was nothing like the guys she had dated back home.

Are you hungry? Aarav asked.

Yes, was all Meg could say.

Judy then looked over and noticed that Aarav and Meg were talking. She decided to give Meg some space to find her way. Anyway, she had a lot of people to catch up with.

Aarav pointed out the variety of foods laid out on the banquet table. Meg was half listening, half fantasizing. Aarav handed her a plate.

My suggestion is that you try a little of everything. There is nothing here that isn't wonderful.

He smiled at Meg. She smiled back and realized he probably knew what he was talking about because he was a little chubby. It seemed like he liked to eat.

They sat down together with plates overflowing.

Here, taste this. Aarav held a fork to Meg's mouth.

He was very passionate about the food. It was sweet, Meg thought.

As they ate, Meg began opening up to him. She told him about her small town, and where she went to college. She explained that she majored in business but wasn't sure what she wanted to do. She talked about her brother's Tai Chi studio and about discovering that Judy was her half sister.

Aarav listened intently. It was as if the rest of the world had vanished, and it was just the two of them. It was really very nice.

Aarav then talked about his life growing up in the palace. He had also majored in business and was working with his father.

Meg realized that although there were so many differences, they seemed alike in ways she couldn't really comprehend.

Olivia had noticed that the two of them had connected and walked over.

How's it going over here?

Aarav blushed a little bit.

You have a beautiful home, Meg said.

Thank you, my dear.

I feel so comfortable.

Well, I am very happy to hear that.

Aarav, how are you doing?

Olivia stared at Aarav. He wasn't her youngest son; he fell toward the end of the middle, and he had always been a little different. Where the rest of her children were fit and athletic, Aarav was a bit sluggish. He loved to eat and read. He's always had a depth to him, but never truly fit in with his classmates. Always a bit of a loner, she thought. In some ways, he was a very old soul; he showed maturity. But socially, he tended to withdraw.

That's why she was so surprised when he instantly connected with Meg.

Aarav?

I'm fine, mother. I'm just helping Meg get comfortable.

Well, that's very kind of you. I'll leave you to it.

Olivia walked away and thought, I need to meditate on this.

As the hours passed, both Judy and Meg started to feel the jet lag.

Judy found Olivia and apologized. I think we need to sleep.

Of course. We've put Meg's things in the room next to yours. There is an adjoining door in case you need access.

That sounds perfect.

Judy hugged Olivia.

It's really really nice to be back.

I agree, said Olivia. Tomorrow after breakfast, I will take you two to the Ashram.

Okay, said Judy.

She went to get Meg who was lounging by the pool with Aarav.

Hey, you guys. How's it going?

I very much enjoy your sister, Judy.

She's a pip, said Judy.

A pip? asked Aarav.

That's a nice word for pain in the neck, Meg explained.

I see, said Aarav.

Meg, I'm going to bed. The travel has caught up with me.

Okay. Aarav, thank you for helping me today.

It has truly been my pleasure.

Aarav bowed to Meg, so Meg bowed back.

We'll see you in the morning Aarav, Judy told him.

Sleep well, he called after them as they walked into the palace.

Judy, I really like him, Meg said excitedly. There is something about him. I can't put my finger on it. It's almost as if we've known each other forever.

Judy smiled.

Okay, Meg, this is your bedroom.

Wow! Meg said as they entered. You have got to be kidding me. Are we sharing?

No, but I will be right next door. See?

Judy walked over to the adjoining door and opened it.

Come look. Whenever I am here, this is where I stay.

Is this hard for you, Judy? I mean after everything?

You know, I've done a lot of meditating on my life and circumstances, and I am okay, but thank you for asking.

Okay, you have a bathroom in your room. Everything you need should be in there for you, but if something is missing, just let me know. I'll see you in the morning. Breakfast will likely be out in the back like today's meal, and it's usually pretty large, so you won't have any trouble finding something to eat.

Will Aarav be there?

I don't know. I guess it depends on if he goes to work tomorrow and at what time. We'll see. Good night, sis.

Good night, Judy.

Judy closed the adjoining door and sat down on her bed. She heard a peacock call from out in the gardens, and it sent her into a flashback. She remembered her first time to the palace, how beautiful and exciting everything was. She remembered how in love with Vihaan she was and how he had snuck into her room to make love to her.

Okay, girl, come back to present. The memories are nice, but you have work to do. Time to rest.

Judy got out her pajamas, washed up in the bathroom, and climbed into her four-post bed.

Awww, this is such a comfortable bed!

She lay down on the pillow and was asleep within twenty

seconds.

40

Meditative Makeovers

The next morning was a glorious one. Come to think of it, Judy thought, she couldn't remember any of her days in India being anything less than glorious. She got up, bathed and dressed, and knocked on Meg's door.
Meg? she whispered. Meg?
She knocked a little louder
Meg!
Nothing.
She turned the door knob and opened the door. She peeked in.
Meg?
She went into the bathroom.
Meg?
Huh...
Judy went downstairs to see if Meg was already up and out.
Sure enough, she and Aarav were having breakfast on the terrace.
Good morning, Judy said as she approached.
Good morning, sis.
Good morning, Judy.
Aren't you the early birds!
Well, I didn't want to miss seeing Aarav before he left for work.
Aarav was grinning.
Well, that's nice, Judy said.
She went over to the buffet and got some tea, fruit, and eggs.

Do you mind if I sit with you?

No, please, Aarav said. He stood up.

Oh, that's very gentlemanly, said Meg.

She then looked at Judy.

So, what's on the agenda today?

Right after breakfast, Olivia is going to take us to the Ashram.

Oh, that sounds interesting.

Aarav, are you able to join us?

Before Aarav could answer, Judy jumped in.

I think Aarav has to go to work.

Well, then I guess I'll see you tonight, Meg said to him with a big smile.

Actually, Meg, we will be at the Ashram for the next two and a half to three weeks.

Meg looked at her in disbelief.

Why?

That's the point of the trip.

But I don't want to leave the palace.

Don't worry, Meg. I will be right here when you return.

Aarav lay his hand on Meg's and a shot of electricity blew right through her.

She looked at Judy.

I'm going to pass on the Ashram part.

Judy looked at Meg in a very serious way.

Meg, we flew all this way to be at the Ashram. There isn't a choice. Olivia has set this up with the blessing of Swami Ravi Baba Singh.

Aarav then interjected.

Meg, when the Swami gives a blessing, it is very, very special.

Go. It's what you should do. I will be here.

Well, okay, Meg said unhappily.

They finished breakfast, and Aarav asked Meg to walk him to his car.

Judy stayed behind.

As the two of them walked through the palace to the front, Aarav stopped and turned to face Meg.

Meg, I realize that we just met, but I like you very much.

Oh, I feel the same, Aarav.

I look forward to seeing you when you return from your spiritual journey.

He smiled and then bent in and kissed Meg.

It was like Christmas and the Fourth of July all mixed into one. He stepped away and got into his car leaving Meg standing there frozen.

Judy came up behind her.

Meg, she said.

Meg was shaken out of her state.

What?

Come back in; we need to pack.

They headed upstairs and packed what they would need for the next three weeks. As they prepared, Judy explained what Meg should expect.

They then headed downstairs to find Olivia, who was waiting in the foyer.

We're ready, Judy said.

Well then, let's be off.

The three got into the limo and made the drive to the Ashram.

This is beautiful countryside, Meg said.

Your sister said the same her first trip.

Huh, Meg thought.

As the limo pulled in, Meg looked at Judy.

Judy knew what Meg was thinking

An Ashram is a place for spiritual contemplation. It isn't based on materialism. The lifestyle is a very simple one. Everyone here plays a role. Everyone has a job to do. All is interconnected.

They got out of the limo, and Meg whispered, I think I prefer the palace life.

Judy saw Olivia smile to herself.

Stay focused and present. Do your best to clear your head of past and future.

They walked to the admin-type building. Swami was actually there.

Olivia and Judy placed palms together and bowed. Khamaghani, they said.

Meg followed suit.

The Swami bowed in return.

It is an honor to be back Swami Ravi, Judy said. My sister and I are very grateful.

Swami Ravi bowed again and left the building.

He's not much for words, is he? Meg commented.

Olivia and Judy looked at each other. Judy then bowed to Olivia. Thank you for this opportunity.

Olivia bowed and left.

Meg watched the limo drive away, and all she could think of was Aarav.

Okay, sis, Judy said. Let me show you where we will sleep, and then we'll get our job assignments.

They walked to the sleeping quarters and entered a very plain, very simple room with two cot-like beds, a small dresser, and a lamp.

This is a joke, right?

There is nothing funny about being here. It is an honor that has been given to you, and you need to start showing some gratitude.

Meg looked at Judy.

Judy could see in Meg's eyes that although Judy had described the experience to Meg, she didn't quite understand.

Okay, Judy said, drop your stuff on your bed and let's go get our assignments.

They headed back to admin.

Hi, Judy, welcome back. You guys are both in the kitchen.

Okay, Judy said. Let me show you the kitchen, Meg.

They walked around the property, and Judy explained that

they would have to get up very early for morning meditation. They would then go to the kitchen to prepare breakfast and then have some free time for contemplation.

They would be expected to help prepare all three meals, and the meals are simple vegetarian meals.

Stay open to everything Meg. Stay as present and focused as you can.

The next few weeks were great for both Meg and Judy. As Meg settled in, she became less dependent upon Judy, giving Judy the ability to independently meditate and contemplate. They also grew closer as sisters and friends. Judy watched Meg find her inner self and begin to evolve as a being. It was extraordinary to see the transformation, and Judy was curious to see if Meg's reaction to Aarav would change when they returned to the palace.

Finally, the day came to return to Olivia's. The girls packed up their things and said goodbye to everyone. As the limo pulled up, Swami Ravi came out to the driveway.
Judy and Meg bowed with palms together.
Thank you, Swami Ravi. This visit was very meaningful.
Swami turned and walked away.
As they pulled up to the palace, Judy could see Meg's excitement building.
Huh, she thought.
They got out of the limo and went inside.
Hello, they called out.
They walked through to the back. Olivia was lounging by the pool.
Hi, girls.
Hi, they said. So, would you like to stay for dinner?
Yes, thank you.

That evening, Judy and Meg dressed for dinner.
Meg, you seem like you have ants in your pants. Are you okay?

I'm just very excited to see Aarav.
Judy smiled.
You think you really like him, huh?
I do, Meg said emphatically.
Even though you just met him and only spent a few hours with him?
Yes.
You do tend to jump into relationships.
You're right, Judy. I have done that in the past. But you know what? This is different. I can't explain it. From the minute I got out of the limo on our first day here and saw him standing on the steps of the palace, I knew. Does that sound crazy?
Yes. But love can be crazy, and I'm surely not one to talk. What is it about the Singh men, Meg?
They laughed together.
I don't know. Maybe they have a way of casting a spell on us.
Well, sis, if you really feel this strongly about it, then go for it. Life is a risk. Jump in.
Meg hugged Judy.

They headed down for dinner, Judy behind Meg. She watched her baby sister enter the dining room with elegance and grace. Wow! I think these three weeks have molded her, Judy thought.
They were seated, Judy by Olivia and Meg next to Aarav, at Aarav's request.
Judy watched the dynamics between the two of them. They were really very cute together. Aarav helped Meg with which silverware for which course and whispered silly things in her ear.
At one point, Olivia leaned over to Judy.
Your sister appears to be smitten.
Judy smiled and nodded. She looked at Olivia for insight.
We don't control love. Love controls us, Olivia stated.
She smiled at Judy.
Judy knew exactly what she was referring to.

How long will you stay before going back to the states? Olivia asked.

I told Steve we'd be back in three weeks, but the best laid plans.

Olivia shook her head.

Olivia, I am not really sure what to do about this situation with Meg.

I see, Olivia said.

She tends to be very impulsive, and she jumps into situations using her heart and not her head so much.

Olivia took Judy's hand.

Let it play out, my dear. I have never seen Aarav so happy. Meg has brought out a part of him that has been dormant his entire life. I'll tell you a secret. He called me three times today from work to ask when you both would be returning from the Ashram.

Ahhh, that's sweet, but I don't want Meg to hurt him, nor do I want her to get hurt, especially so far away from home.

When one loves, there is always a risk.

Judy thought, that is true. She nodded.

Your sister is welcome to stay, Judy. There is plenty of room, and my sense is that this is now where she needs to be to continue her growth and evolution.

Judy looked at Olivia. She respected her tremendously and understood that she had the ability to see far beyond many others' ability.

Thank you, Olivia. You are such an important person in my life and have helped and guided me more than you could ever know, or perhaps you already know that.

Judy smiled.

Olivia smiled.

I will have a serious talk with Meg tonight and try to assess what she truly wants to do.

Meanwhile, I do feel that it's time for me to go back and move forward with my life. Could I stay for a couple more days to get myself organized?

I've told you before; this home is yours for as long as you need and whenever you need.

Judy leaned over and kissed Olivia on the cheek.

Olivia closed her eyes and opened them.

Judy felt a rush of loving warmth run through her. She knew theirs was an extremely special bond.

Later that night, she went out to sit in the garden and organize her thoughts. She wondered if Vihaan's purpose was to bring Olivia and her together. If it was, it worked, she said looking up at the heavens. Thank you, Vihaan.

Just then, a shooting star shot through the sky.

Judy felt comforted. We are all connected, she thought out loud.

She got up to find Meg, who was sitting next to Aarav, both of them dipping their feet in the pool.

Hi, you two.

Hi, Judy, Aarav greeted happily.

Aarav, would you mind if I steal Meg for a few minutes?

Oh, not at all.

Meg, let's walk.

I'll be back soon, Aarav.

Aarav bowed to the two girls.

41
Meg's Shift

So, Meg, as you know, our original plan was to stay for about three weeks and then head home. It seems that this may not be your plan, anymore?

Meg looked at Judy.

I would like to stay, she said.

So, what's you long term plan?

I don't know. All I know is that I feel very happy with Aarav, and I think he feels the same way.

Okay, so let's talk this out. I see a tremendous change in you from the three weeks at the Ashram. You've matured and become more centered. Would you agree?

Yes.

So, look deeply in. Is this the impetuous, impulsive Meg who looks for attention from guys to define her own identity, or is this a mature, independent Meg?

Meg looked at Judy for a really long time. She didn't realize how insightful Judy was. She had totally described old Meg.

That wasn't easy to hear, Meg said.

Truth is often painful to acknowledge.

I truthfully have feelings for Aarav. This is different. I am not old Meg. I can see a life with him. I don't want to sound super corny, but I think I've found my soul mate.

Judy pursed her lips.

Okay, she said and let out a deep breath. Let's go talk to Aarav and Olivia.

They went into the palace. Olivia and Aarav were actually talking in the library.

May we join you? Judy asked.

Yes, please come in.

Meg went in and sat by Aarav.

So, Meg and I just had a very honest conversation.

Meg, why don't you tell Olivia and Aarav what you told me?

The spot light was on Meg. She looked at Aarav.

Aarav, I have never felt the way I feel right now. From the first time I saw you, I knew there was a connection. I don't want to lose myself in you, but instead want to be by your side, as a partner. I feel as if I have found my soul mate.

Olivia then addressed Aarav.

Aarav, my son, what are your thoughts?

I have never felt the way I feel. It's as if Meg is actually a part of me that I have just discovered. I could live without this part of me, I have been doing so for all of these years; however, now that I have this part of me, I would really rather not let it go.

Olivia took Aarav's hand and Meg's hand.

Well, then I believe we should see where this relationship goes. Meg, you are welcome to stay here at the palace to explore your feelings for my son. We will revisit this in a few weeks.

I am honored to have this invitation, and would like to contribute, Meg said.

We will discuss this at a later time. For now, I think we should all retire to bed. Good night, my dears.

With that, Olivia went up to her bedroom leaving Judy, Aarav, and Meg in the library.

Meg and Aarav were holding hands and gazing at each other. Judy could see that there was something very deep between them.

Okay, she said. I'm going to go pack and prepare for my flight home. Good night.

They both said good night without breaking their gaze.

Judy went upstairs and thought about how she was going to explain this to Steve, Matthew, and Rachel. She wondered how they would take the news.

The next morning, Judy came downstairs.

I wonder if the two love birds are still sitting like statues in the library.

She chuckled to herself.

She went out onto the terrace. There was another huge breakfast set up.

Oh man, this is going to be hard to give up.

She filled a plate with all kinds of yummy things and walked over to the table. Some of the girls were there talking about their husbands, boyfriends, children. Hi, guys, she said.

Hi, Judy. Are you already leaving?

Yes, I'm afraid so. It's tempting to stay, but I've got to get home. Remember that you are always welcome.

Maybe one day, a couple of the girls replied.

Judy ate and chatted. Occasionally she looked around for Meg and Aarav.

When she finished, she excused herself and went inside to call Steve.

Hello? he said.

Hi, hon.

Oh hey. So, you ever coming home?

Actually, I am. I have a flight for tomorrow.

She gave him the flight information.

Umm,

What?

Meg won't be with me.

Why not?

She has fallen in love.

Oh, come on Judy. You know Meg.

I do know Meg, and this time is different. She and I had a long and serious talk last night, and I have to say, I think this is her path.

I don't know. Has she talked to my parents?

I don't know. I haven't seen her yet this morning.

Steve,

Yeah?

I love you, and I miss you. I can't wait to see you.

Me too, Judes.

Okay, I'm going to go find Meg and pack for my flight.

I'll see you tomorrow.

Bye bye.

Judy hung up and walked around the property. She was sad to leave but it felt right to go back.

As she entered the garden, she saw Aarav and Meg sitting on the bench. Meg was wearing a Saree.

Hey, she called.

Oh, Judy. Aarav and I were just talking.

About?

Aarav is going to take the next week off to show me around India. He is also going to talk to his father about maybe giving me a job in the company, right Aarav?

Yes. I think with Meg's business background, there might be a spot for her.

Wow! Judy replied. So, this is sounding like it could be a long-term type of thing.

We don't know, but maybe...

Judy looked at the two of them.

Love at first sight, she said, half in thought.

Yes, they both giggled.

Okay. Well, Meg, you need to call your parents and let them know that you aren't returning with me.

I talked to them last night.

Really? How did that go?

They understand.

Really?

They told me they want me to be happy, and I told them I have never been more happy.

Meg looked at Aarav and smiled.

Aarav and I are very very happy.

Yes, said Aarav, with the biggest grin on his face Judy had ever seen.

Then I'm happy for both of you.

Thank you, Judy, Meg said.

Okay, then. I'm going to get ready for my flight. See you guys at dinner.

Judy left Meg and Aarav in the garden. She had some mixed feelings, but admittedly wasn't sure which were related to her and which were just concern for Meg. Being in India always stirred up emotions. She decided to find a quiet spot and do some meditating.

Well into the afternoon, Judy was still sitting. The meditation was a good one. She allowed all to be and felt much more centered when she came out of it. She wandered around the grounds for a bit then went up to her room to finish packing and dress for dinner. She still had a little bit of melancholy but worked on staying present.

As she headed downstairs, she ran into Bandhupala.

Hi, Bandhupala.

Hi, Judy.

Bandhupala wasn't living at the palace anymore. Once he married and started having children, he bought a home nearby. He had come to join for dinner.

How are you doing, Judy?

All is well, thank you. How about you?

No complaints. How has your visit been?

It's been enlightening, as usual.

Judy smiled.

I hear that you arrived as two but are going back as one.

Yes, apparently, my sister has fallen in love.

Aarav is a very special guy. You have nothing to worry about.

I will keep an eye on them.

Thank you, Bandhupala. That means a lot to me.

No problem. Shall we sit for dinner?

Almost the entire family joined to say goodbye to their American sister. They drank and ate and told stories well into the night.

Eventually, Judy excused herself, hugged each and every one of her Indian siblings and went up to bed.

The night went quickly, and the peacocks woke her up pretty early. She got out of bed and knocked on Meg's door.

Meg? she whispered. You there?

She peeked into her room. Meg was in her bed.

Meg.

Huh? Judy heard from under the covers.

Wake up.

Meg moaned and stretched.

Come on, I'm leaving soon.

Oh. Meg said, trying to wake up.

Meg, are you sure about this?

Judy, I have never been more sure about anything in my life. I feel like I was lost back home. I functioned, but I had no direction. Here feels so natural to me. It's like this is where I am meant to be.

Okay. I can't argue with that. I love you, sis.

I love you too, Judy. Have a safe flight. I'll call you in a couple of days.

Judy left Meg's room and felt like she was going to cry. She had just discovered that she had a sister and now she was leaving her half way around the world.

Sometimes life doesn't make sense, she said out loud.

She got dressed and brought her luggage downstairs. It was still pretty early, but Olivia was up and sitting on the terrace.

Good morning, my dear.

Hi, Olivia. I was hoping you would be here.

Are you ready for your flight?

Yes, ready but leaving with very mixed emotions.

Your sister is following her path. This is the first time in her life she is not conflicted.

Judy smiled a sad type of smile.

I know this is hard for you. You have experienced so much loss in your life, and this too is a sort of loss. Remember all is as it should be. Your sister will be safe here and well cared for.

I guess that's all one can hope for.

We will see each other again, my love.

Thank you for everything.

They hugged and Judy left. The limo driver drove her to the airport, and she was headed home once again.

The flight was long but easy. Judy slept, and read, and thought about Meg, and thought about her own life.

She landed, got her luggage, and cleared customs. She had been away for almost one month, and it already felt like an eternity.

As she exited the airport, it was dark, and she looked around. She spotted Steve a few feet away. She had forgotten how good looking he was and just then realized how much she missed him. She wanted this relationship to work. It was a good relationship.

Steve, she waved.

Oh, hey, he waved back. They went to each other and embraced.

Oh my God, Judy. I missed you so much.

Me too, Steve. Me too.

Steve collected Judy's luggage, and they headed to the car.

How was your flight?

Good, easy, long.

Are you hungry?

Yeah, I could eat a little.

They stopped at a little late-night café on the way home.

How did Chlo do without me?

Oh, there's no doubt she missed you. She wasn't so sure about being left alone with me, but we made it work.

Judy smiled.

I missed both of you.

How's the studio?

Numbers are increasing, so I am really glad you're back. I have to find a new front desk person.

Has Rachel been helping?

She's been great, but I know she doesn't want to do it full time.

Maybe I could do it when I'm not teaching. If you and I cover when we're not in a class, we could make it work.

Let's talk about it later.

Steve took Judy's hand.

Hi, she smiled.

Hi, he smiled.

42

Life in New England

Judy slept very late the next day. Between the travel and the emotions of leaving India and going back and rejoining Steve, she was wiped out. Steve had expected that that might happen, so he didn't wake her up when he left for the studio.

Chloe was extremely relieved to have her person back. She got into bed and didn't leave Judy's side.

At about 1:00 in the afternoon, Judy roused.

Alexa, time.

It's 1:15 PM.

What? Judy shot up, scaring Chloe.

Oh, sorry, Chlo. How can it be so late? Did Steve go to work?

Chloe looked at her with lovey dovey eyes.

Hi, baby, Judy said.

She stroked her head and kissed her.

I missed you, my girl.

Chloe meowed, and they both got out of bed.

In the kitchen, she found a note from Steve.

Good morning. There are two croissants and fresh oj in the fridge. Dinner at Matt and Rachel's at six. Hopefully, you'll be up by then.

Oh, Steve, you're the best!

She ate and drank and then had some water. She was felling dehydrated from the traveling. She took a shower and unpacked.

I've got some laundry to do.

She made the bed and got her laundry going and then called Steve.

Hi, babe, he said. Did you find my note?

I did, thank you. Very nice.

What time did you come back to life?

Actually, not till 1:00.

Yeah, I figured you would need to crash.

So, my suggestion is to just chill for the rest of the afternoon, and I'll pick you up at 5:30.

That sounds like a plan. Steve?

Yeah?

How are Rachel and Matt?

Ummm, confused.

Okay. See you at 5:30.

They hung up and Judy finished her laundry. She plopped down on the couch and thought about taking a nap.

Why am I so tired? I certainly slept. Oh well.

She snuggled with Chloe and thought about India. She loved being there. What would her life have been like if Vihaan had survived? Would they have actually gotten married? Would she have been happy as a princess living in a palace so far away from the home she knew? She had to admit that the jet setting was very exciting, and of course, she loved Olivia. Well, no use in wondering. It's not what happened, obviously, and her life is right here in New England with Steve. Still, what if?

She looked up at the clock. It was 5:15.

Ohhh, I have to get ready, Chlo.

Judy jumped up off the couch, and Chloe curled up where she had been sitting.

She cleaned up, put on some nice but casual clothes, grabbed the gifts she brought back for Matt and Rachel, and took her jacket off the hook. It was only the very beginning of September, but the nights get chilly.

She watched out the front for Steve. At 5:30, he pulled into the driveway.

Man, that guy is prompt.

Was that something she liked about him, or something a little bit irritating?

She locked the front door and went over to the car.

Hi, babe, he said.

Hi there.

Ready?

Ready.

He leaned over and kissed Judy.

That was nice, she said.

I've really missed you.

Me too, Steve.

They got to Matt and Rachel's a little before 6.

Okay, Steve said. Here we go.

Judy wasn't sure what he meant.

They went inside and called out.

We're here.

In the den, they heard Rachel call back. They walked through to the back of the house.

Hi, Judy said with a big smile.

The smiles weren't returned.

What the hell? Matt yelled.

Rachel stayed quiet.

I'm sorry? Judy responded.

Dad, come on.

We trusted you with Meg. We let you take her across the world expecting that you would both come back.

Whoa, Judy said.

Dad, relax.

Stay out of this, Steve.

Who the hell do you think you are? Some kinda recruiter for India?

Dad, you're not even making sense.

Back the fuck off, Steve.

Okay, let's go, Judy, Steve said.

Judy was stupefied. She looked at Rachel who looked away.

No, Steve, let's work this out. She looked at Matt and Rachel.

Get the fuck outta my house, both of you, Matt screamed.

Steve grabbed Judy's hand and led her out of the house. They walked around the block a couple of times in silence. Judy was trying to process Matt's anger. Finally, on the third time around, Judy started talking.

What the hell, Steve? I didn't know your dad had a temper, and why is he blaming me? I feel like I've been blindsided. Did you know that he was so upset, so angry?

I knew he wasn't happy, but I can't believe he exploded on you like that.

So, how do we go forward? Judy asked.

I don't know, Judy.

Should we go back and try to talk to them?

Don't know.

They were now on the fourth time around.

Here's the thing, Steve. We can't just keep walking around the block, and frankly, I'm getting hungry.

Steve burst into laughter.

I know laughter is your way of dealing with stress, Steve, but...

This made Steve laugh harder.

Okay, Judy said with a sigh. We'll keep walking.

After the sixth time around the block, Steve got a hold of himself.

Okay, he said. Let's go back; try again to talk to them.

They walked back over to the house and went in.

We're back, Steve called.

There was silence.

Hello? Are you home?

They walked through to the den. Matt and Rachel were sitting in the dark.

Mom? Dad? We've come back to talk this out with you. Could we try to talk about this? Could I turn a light on?

He didn't wait for an answer but went over to the light switch and flipped it up.

Judy looked at Matt and Rachel. They were both crying.

Hey, you guys, Judy said as she sat in the chair near the couch.

I'm sorry. I certainly didn't plot to take Meg away from you.

There was silence.

Steve sat down on the arm of the chair that Judy was in. He subconsciously wanted to protect her, just in case Matthew lost it again.

So, clearly you're blaming me for the fact that your daughter chose to stay in India.

Let me first say that I would never, not in a million years, leave your daughter, my sister, by the way, in any sort of a situation that I felt would put her in danger. With that said, she and I spoke at length, and believe me, I tried to talk her out of this decision. The thing is, she is in love.

Oh please, Matt said.

Matt, I love you, but please don't interrupt. Just listen to what I have to say. You aren't the only one who doesn't have Meg.

So, as I was saying, the Meg who left just about four weeks ago is not the Meg I left in India yesterday. Meg has blossomed. She left here a bit of an immature, insecure child, and guess what, the trip worked. She fell in love, but most importantly, she evolved. She and I spent three intensive weeks at the Ashram, and once Meg found her way, there was no stopping her. It was like she was always meant to be. I want to show you something.

Judy pulled out her phone and pulled up a photo. It was Meg and Aarav sitting in the garden holding hands, and Meg was wearing a saree.

Judy handed the phone to Matt.

You tell me what you see.

Matt and Rachel looked at the photo. Rachel started to cry.

My little girl, she said.

I don't know, Matt said.

Believe me, and I swear this on my mother's grave, if I felt that at any time then, now, or going forward, Meg needed to come back home, I would be the first person on the plane. And

I can promise you that Olivia would never ever let anything bad happen to Meg. It may sound hokey, but Olivia is an extremely evolved being who knows and sees way beyond our abilities. If you would like to, I would be happy to call her and let you speak to her.

Rachel and Matt looked at each other.

Why don't we eat? Rachel suggested.

They all got up and went into the dining room. Rachel brought the dinner in and placed it on the table.

Would anyone like a drink?

Oh, definitely, Steve said. A beer please.

Rachel brought him a beer and sat down.

They ate in relative silence. It was awkward, to say the least.

This is delicious Rachel, Judy said. Maybe you could send me the recipe?

Sure, Rachel said.

So, mom, Steve started. I haven't had a chance to thank you for helping out at the studio. I appreciate your doing that.

Sure, Rachel said again.

The rest of the dinner was quiet and uncomfortable. As soon as they were done eating, Judy offered to help Rachel clean up.

No, said Rachel.

Let's go home, Judes.

They grabbed their things and left without another word.

In the car, Judy turned to Steve.

What do we do here? I don't know how to handle this.

Let's just give them some time. They need some time.

They got to the cottage and went in.

I'm going to bed, Steve.

I'll be in in a bit.

Steve sat in the living room trying to figure everything out.

He decided to call Meg.

Hello?

Hey, baby sister.

Steve?

Yeah.

Hiiii.

Hi. How are you doing over there in India?

I'm great. Wait. Is Judy okay? Is that why you're calling?

No, no. Judy's great. She just went to bed. You know, she's tired after the traveling.

Yeah, I bet. It's a very long trip.

So, Judy told me about you and Aarav.

Yes. Steve, he's so wonderful. We are wonderful. He's kind, and smart, and generous, and sweet, and a real gentleman. He works for his father and is going to get me a job at the company as well. And Steve, I'm living in a palace. Oh, and I learned how to meditate at an Ashram. It's all so amazing! I'm in love, Steve. I'm in for real love, and I am so happy!

That's great, Meg. I'm glad that everything is good.

Steve started to get choked up.

Steve, you okay?

Yeah, I'm good. I miss you, Meg. This was all very unexpected. Tell me about it. But Steve, it's good. It's right. I have work to do on myself, but Aarav and I are going to work on ourselves as individuals and as a couple. It's really good to talk to you, Steve. Give my love to everyone there. I'll call you in a few days.

Steve heard a click and put his phone down.

He went into the bedroom.

Hey, hon, you asleep?

Almost, Judy said sleepily.

I just spoke to Meg.

You did?

Yeah. You're right. She's okay. In fact she's more than okay. She's really doing great.

Come to bed, Steve.

Steve climbed into bed and started to cry. Judy held him close and rubbed his back. He cried and cried until he was heaving. He finally fell asleep in her arms.

The next morning, the doorbell rang. Steve jumped up and

tried to shake off his exhaustion. He opened the door, and his parents were standing there.

May we come in?

What are you doing here? What time is it?

We couldn't sleep and talked all night about this situation. We'd really like to come in, if it's okay.

By then, Judy had gotten up and had joined Steve at the door.

Of course, she said. Please come in. I'll make some coffee.

We brought a danish. Matt handed the danish to Steve.

Steve, why don't you cut up the danish and put it on the table, Judy suggested.

Once the coffee was ready, the four of them sat down.

Matthew looked at Judy.

Judy, I owe you an apology; we, owe you an apology. As you probably assessed, I was freaked out. Rachel was so upset, and I felt completely helpless. We are both sorry for ripping into you. Neither of us slept last night. We feel awful. We're still upset about the whole situation, but it wasn't fair to take it out on you. Can you accept our apology?

Apology accepted.

Judy walked over and hugged both of them.

Actually, mom, dad, I called Meg last night.

Judy looked at Steve.

You did? they asked.

I did. And, she is really happy. She is probably going to start working for Aarav's dad's company, and she and Aarav are doing well. Frankly, hearing her tell me helped.

Rachel started crying.

My baby, she cried.

Matt took Rachel's hand.

Rach, let's call her. Let's call her right now. We'll ask her to come home. We'll tell her we love her and that she needs to come home to her family.

Dad, Dad...

Matt put his hand up to Steve.

Dad, listen. You're not thinking rationally. Please just think about what you are going to say to her. Maybe just listen to her.

Matt glared at Steve.

He's right Matt, Rachel said.

They all looked at her. The thing is, it's Meg's life, her decision. She has got to find her own way. Am I at all happy about it? No, but if we try to force her to come back through guilt or pity, she will resent us. Do we have a right to tell her what her path is? Do we, Matt?

Matt stared at Rachel. He loved her so much. He thought about when they had met. No one could have separated them. They were so much in love, and it didn't take him long to realize it. Maybe Rach is right. Who are they to decide how Meg should live her life? Boy, did he miss her. He missed her quirky silly personality, her boppy energy, and her child like attitude.

Let's call her, he said.

Judy went and got her phone. She dialed.

She heard a sleepy, hello?

Hey, girl, it's Judy. I'm sorry it's so late, but we are all here, and Matt and Rachel would really like to talk to you, k?

Judy put the phone on speaker and handed it to Rachel.

Meg?

Hi, Mom.

Oh, Meg, we miss you so much.

I know, Mom, but I'm really happy.

Hey, Meg, Matt spoke into the speaker.

Hi, Dad. It's good to hear your voices. Listen, I'm doing really well. I'm sorry I didn't come back with Judy, but this is where I need to be right now. It's good. Listen, I am going to go back to sleep. I love you both. I'll call you soon. Bye.

Matt handed Judy her phone. They all just looked at each other. That was that. They didn't have to be happy about it, but Meg had made up her mind.

Okay then, Matt said. We are going to let you guys get ready for your day. Let's talk later.

Rachel and Matt headed home, and Steve and Judy got dressed for work.

Is your head in the game? Steve asked. Do you feel ready to go back to teaching?

Yes, I'm good.

Okay. I'll see you at the studio.

Steve gave Judy a quick kiss and was out the door.

Judy collapsed on the couch. Boy, what a homecoming!

Chloe jumped up on her and settled onto her lap. She purred and kneaded.

That's nice, baby.

They sat for a few minutes and then Judy went to take a shower and try to get her head into the day ahead.

She got to the studio and taught her beginner class. It was great to see her students again and to begin a routine in her life. After class, Judy stayed at the front desk to cover the calls and help Steve with paperwork. She enjoyed working with Steve, being invested in their future.

43
A Christmas Visit

The weeks passed and the leaves changed color and fell. The temperature began to drop, and Judy got out her winter wear. She had never been a big holiday celebrator and felt a little bit of winter blues.

Just after Thanksgiving, Judy got a call from Meg. Apparently, she was feeling a bit blue herself and asked Aarav if they could go to New England for Christmas. As a Hindu, Aarav didn't celebrate Christmas in a religious sense, but his family recognized the holiday as a celebration of peace, and he was very curious to experience a true winter Christmas. They spoke to Olivia who gave her blessing and arranged the flight for them. Meg called Judy.

Hey, Meg, how are you? It's been a while.

I'm doing great, and I have very exciting news.

What?

Aarav and I are coming for Christmas.

Oh Meg, that's great! Give me the details.

They chatted a bit more and hung up. Judy was at the studio. She could hardly wait for Steve to finish his class so she could tell him. While she was waiting, she called Rachel.

Hi, Judy, what's up?

I just hung up with Meg. She and Aarav are coming for Christmas.

Really? Rachel sounded teary.

Are you okay, Rachel?

Yes, just a little down. This is really good news, Judy. Really good news.

I'm sure Meg'll call you to tell you.

Yes.

Oh, the studio phone is ringing. I'll call you later, k?

K.

A few minutes later, Steve's class broke up, and Steve came into the waiting room.

Good class today, guys. See you next week.

Thanks, Steve, they said.

Hey, my fiancée.

Steve, I just talked to Meg.

Oh yeah? She ok?

Yes, and she and Aarav are coming for Christmas.

Judy was beaming.

Oh, honey, that's great. How long are they going to stay?

You know, I didn't even ask. I did call your mom though to let her know.

How did she react?

She sounded happy.

Good. Listen, there's not much going on here for the next few hours. Do you want to head out? I can handle the studio.

You sure?

Yeah, take the rest of the afternoon.

You don't have to ask me twice, Judy said.

Hey, and let's go out tonight. How about the Copper Door?

Ohhhh, that sounds nice.

The next few weeks got colder, and slowly, the holiday spirit increased. The town decorated as it always did, and Judy started to perk up a bit. Her sister was coming home, and that was the best gift she could imagine.

The day before Christmas Eve, she and Steve and Matt and Rachel drove to the airport to pick up Meg and Aarav. They were all so excited; they could barely speak. As a joke, Judy made a big sign that said Meg and Aarav. She also found a limo driver cap at a second hand store and would put it on in the airport. They parked the car and walked over to the terminal. The flight was on time and due to land in the next ten minutes or so. They knew they would have at least a thirty-minute wait, so they went to one of the cafes and had some hot chocolate. They were all in a happy mood. The anticipation of seeing Meg felt so wonderful. As the clock ticked, they got as close as they could to where all of the passengers come out. Judy put her cap on and held up her sign. She was so excited, she thought she might pee herself. As the passengers walked out, the four of them craned their necks to see Meg and Aarav.

There, Matt pointed. There they are.

They were holding hands and had a sky hop behind them with their luggage. Rachel cried out.

Meg! Meg!

Meg sped up her pace, dodging in between the other passengers, dragging Aarav along. Aarav was doing his best to keep up.

Meg wrapped her arms around Rachel.

Mom, it's so good to see you. They hugged and rocked.

Aarav came up behind her.

Hi, Judy.

Hi, Aarav. Aarav, I'd like you to meet Matt. Matt this is Aarav. They shook hands.

And this is Steve.

I've heard a lot about you, Steve. It's a pleasure to finally meet you.

Then, Rachel and Meg separated.

Mom, this is Aarav.

Aarav held out his hand.

I am so happy to meet you.

Rachel hugged Aarav.

Welcome to New Hampshire.

Thank you. I'm happy to be here.

They all walked to the car and piled in. Steve drove to Matt and Rachel's.

Steve had closed the studio for the week so that they could spend as much time as possible with Meg and Aarav.

We'll see you guys tomorrow. We're so glad you're here.

Everyone hugged.

Good night.

After Steve and Judy left, Matt showed Aarav and Meg to their rooms.

Let me know if you need anything Aarav, Matt said.

Thank you, sir.

Night, Dad.

The next day was Christmas Eve. Meg and Aarav came down to breakfast at about eleven.

Matt and Rachel were sitting in the kitchen.

Good morning. Can I make you guys some breakfast? How about scrambled eggs with hash browns?

Meg looked at Aarav who then spoke. That sounds delicious.

Okay, please have a seat. Do you want some coffee?

Yes, please, they both answered in unison.

How did you sleep? Matt asked.

Really well, Meg answered.

So, Matt said. Today is Christmas Eve, so I thought we would drive around a little bit, show Aarav around and then go to the Village Square.

Oh, that's right, Meg said. There are always a bunch of festivities in the Village Square on Christmas Eve.

That sounds nice, said Aarav.

We'll ask Steve and Judy to join us.

And I've made a reservation at the Copper Door for dinner tonight.

Matt looked at Aarav.

That's Meg's favorite restaurant.

Meg and Aarav finished breakfast and went up to shower and dress.

At about 1:00, the four of them got in the car to drive around parts of New Hampshire.
It had snowed a little bit the night before, so everything was covered in white. It wasn't the first time Aarav had seen snow. His family had been skiing in the Alps many times, but somehow, this was different. This was provincial and sweet, very small town.
Everything is so beautiful, Aarav said. So, different from India.
Have you seen snow before? Rachel asked.
Yes, many times. My family often skis in the Alps, but this is different. Very quiet and sweet.
Meg smiled at him.
Aarav took her hand.
At about 4:00, they drove back to the town and parked near the Village Square. There was music and vendors, entertainers, and hot drinks. They met Steve and Judy.
Hi. How was your drive?
New Hampshire is beautiful, Aarav said.
They walked around for about an hour and a half feeling the spirit of the holiday.
Okay, Matt said. Who's hungry?
They all were.
We'll follow you guys, Steve said.
When they arrived at the Copper Door, they were shown to a table by the fireplace.
What a beautiful restaurant, Aarav said, looking around the room.
And wait till you taste the food, Meg told him.
They ate and talked and had a great time.
After dessert, they all went back to Matt and Rachel's and had some wine and hot apple cider.
So, Meg explained to Aarav. Tomorrow we get up and have a huge breakfast. Then we go in by the tree and open gifts. The

family tradition is to then watch a Christmas movie and play some games, and then we all go out for Chinese food.

Really? Aarav said.

Hey, Judy exclaimed. That was my reaction last year.

They all laughed. Steve and Judy then wished everyone a good night and headed home.

We'll see you guys tomorrow, Judy said. She hugged and kissed these people she had come to love so very much.

Christmas morning, Steve and Judy returned to Matt and Rachel's at about 11:00. They had had their own little gift opening at the cottage first. They also began talking about wedding dates but didn't come to any decisions.

Merry Christmas, Steve yelled as they walked into the house. Ho ho ho!

Hey, kids, we're in here. Did you eat?

We nibbled, but we definitely saved our appetites.

Good. Then come and sit down. Eat, eat, and then, it's presents time.

They finished eating and went into the living room. They gathered around the tree.

Before they began, Aarav asked if he could say something.

They all looked at each other.

Sure, Matt said.

They all sat down.

What are you doing Aarav? Meg asked.

Aarav knelt down next to Meg. He took her hand.

Meg, I love you. I want to spend the rest of my life with you. In front of your family, the ones who love you, would you marry me?

Meg stared at Aarav in disbelief. She had absolutely no idea that he was planning to ask her. He presented her with a magnificent ring.

Yes, Aarav, yes.

Tears ran down Meg's cheeks, and Rachel and Judy both had

their hands over their mouths.

Meg and Aarav embraced.

The room was silent. Everyone was in shock.

Judy finally broke the quiet.

Congratulations! She said emphatically.

She began to clap. The others followed suit.

Well, it looks like we have two engaged daughters, Rach. Maybe I should take a second job.

He smiled and everyone broke into laughter.

Judy came over to Meg.

Let's see.

Meg showed the ring to everyone.

Congratulations, my man, Steve said to Aarav. Welcome to the family.

Thank you. That has a nice ring to it. I think I like being a member of an American family.

Okay, Matt said. Let's carry on.

The day was a good one. Gifts were opened, and Judy chose *A Miracle on 34th Street*, which even made Aarav tear up towards the end.

Rachel then went into the kitchen to clean up while the others played Monopoly.

I have to warn you, Aarav. Steve was smiling. Meg is a very competitive game player. This may make or break the relationship.

They all smiled.

I believe I can hold my own, he said.

44

Weddings

The winter was long, cold, snowy, and mostly dreary, so when spring finally arrived, moods brightened along with the weather. Spring brought with it a true sense of renewal. All things felt possible, and Judy could attest to the fact that just being able to take her woods walks again was a great regenerator. She and Steve were doing well and had chosen to get married the next year, probably in early summer, but they hadn't quite pinned down a date.

Judy was full time at the studio, either teaching or covering the front and doing promotion. She and Steve made a great team. Class sizes were expanding, and enrollment was increasing. The studio was turning a decent profit, and they talked about maybe looking for a third part time teacher to pick up the slack.

Judy was becoming very popular with special needs students. She had developed a reputation and was seeing some truly wonderful results with her techniques. She even talked more about going back to school part time for special education.

There were, however, a couple of downsides to their success. They didn't have as much time to practice martial arts or their Tai Chi forms together, but they did their best to squeeze quick sessions in now and then.

More importantly, Judy was feeling a bit crowded. As much as she loved Steve, she was finding it challenging to work with him and live with him. Her personal space was cramped, and it was beginning to wear on her.

Judy spoke to Meg about twice a month. She was doing really well in India. She had gone back to the Ashram for some maintenance meditations, leaving Aarav for a week here and there. She was also working at Aarav's father's company, in a different department than Aarav, and enjoyed it. She had brought some suggestions to her future father in law, and after some research and consideration, he decided to implement them, which increased his profit margin a little bit. This pleased him, which in turn pleased Aarav, which made Meg super happy. She was fitting easily and naturally into the culture and lifestyle. She got along with all of her Indian siblings in law. It was as if she were meant to be there all along.

So, sis, have you chosen a wedding date?
That's a little bit tricky, Meg said. Aarav's family is so large, and the coordination is tough, but we're working on it. How about you?
We're talking about next year, but no definitive date yet.
Judy!
Meg yelled int the phone.
I just had the best idea!
Uh oh.
Judy took a deep breath.
No, hear me out. We should have a double wedding right here at the palace.
Ohhh, I don't know, Meg. That's complicated.
No, listen. The place is big enough for all of us, and I think Olivia would be thrilled.
You think Olivia wants to see her almost daughter in law marry another man? Come on, Meg. Even though we're talking about Olivia, that's a lot to ask of her and Vihaan's entire family, don't you think?
Well, maybe you're right, but it would be so grand and beauti-

ful.

I don't disagree with that, but...

No, I hear you. Anyway, I have to get going. I love you, Judy. We'll talk soon.

I love you too, Meg.

Judy hung up and felt a mixture of emotion come over her as she thought about the conversation.

It would be cool to get married in India. How exotic and amazing, but there's more people involved than just Meg and me, and there's definitely some tough history.

Meanwhile, Meg couldn't drop her idea. That night, she presented it to Aarav. She figured she'd start with him because he would be honest about the whole scenario, including the memory of his brother.

Hmmm, he said as they sat out in the garden. That's a nice idea Meg, but I don't know. Do you really want to share your special day with your sister and brother in that way? Don't you want your wedding day to be just about you?

Boy, she thought. He knows me pretty well.

The thing is Aarav, the old Meg would absolutely have said yes, but since I've been here, meditating and soaking in this wonderful culture, I've gained an appreciation for the fact that it's not always just about me one hundred percent of the time. The universe is singular but widespread. We are individuals with individual needs, but in truth, we are one being, and this understanding has given me an awareness of a greater love. In that sense, I think it would be wonderful to share the most important day of my life with my sister and brother on the most important day of their lives.

You make a strong argument.

Thank you, Aarav. But, one of my concerns is how your family would feel, you know.

Are you referring to Vihaan?

Yes.

Vihaan is missed every day and remains closely in my heart and my family's. It's certainly a delicate situation, but it has been many years since his passing.

Would you like to present this to my mother?

I don't know.

Let's both think about this for a while.

Yeah, that's a good idea.

They snuggled for a while before going in to bed.

As Meg lay in bed, she thought about how fortunate she was to have met Aarav.

He's so supportive, intelligent, and loving. I don't know if I deserve such a wonderful man.

She decided to do some meditation before going to sleep. She didn't want to fall asleep with so much negativity and insecurity surrounding her.

Back in New Hampshire, Judy also found Meg's idea to be sticking more than she wanted to admit. A few days after their conversation, Steve found Judy staring into space.

You okay, babe?

Huh?

You okay? You look lost.

Oh, yeah, no I'm good.

Yeah, that wasn't really convincing. What's on your mind?

Well, a few days ago, I talked to Meg.

Okay?

And, she had an idea that we both agreed was crazy and inappropriate, but I can't get it out of my head.

Tell me.

She thought it would be really wonderful to have a double wedding in India.

Steve stared at Judy.

Huh, he said.

Right? But, still, I don't know.

Okay, let's talk it out. There are a lot of elements to consider here.

Like?

Well, this is our special day. Do we want to share it with Meg and Aarav?

Okay, Judy nodded.

And, if this were okay with Aarav's family, we all have to then go to India and deal with wedding preparations in a foreign country.

Okay. But we will still be going to India for Meg's wedding, so the travel part is kind of irrelevant.

Fair enough, Steve nodded. There are definitely pros and cons. I guess the question is, depending on Aarav's family's feelings about this, are there more pros or more cons? And, I'm mixed as well. On the one hand, it would be cool to share a wedding date with my sister. However, I'd be marrying you in Vihaan's home. Let me sit with this.

Okay, Judy said. I will too.

A week later, Aarav and Meg were driving home from work.

Meg?

Yeah?

I've been doing a lot of thinking about what we talked about a week or so ago.

I know, I know. It was a crazy, impulsive idea. I'm sorry I brought it up.

Well, I was actually going to say that I think it's a nice idea. It will bring the families together and connect all of us in a bigger way.

Ohhh, really?

Yes. So, I think we should check with Steve and Judy and then if they agree, we will see how my mom feels about it.

Hmm.

Hmm?

Hmm. I have to reprocess. I had convinced myself that it wasn't a good idea. You've thrown me for a loop.

The following Sunday, Steve and Judy were taking a woods walk with Chloe. They strolled along through the woods in no hurry and with no particular direction. When they got to the clearing, Steve said, come and sit down next to me.

They sat feeling the sun on their faces, listening to the birds, and watching Chloe dart about.

So, Judes, I have been thinking a lot about the wedding.

And?

And, I am still mixed about it, but I think it would be kind of special to have everyone together and get married along with our sister.

Wow! When you put it that way, it sounds a little weird.

Yeah, but that's part of the reason why I think I like the idea. There isn't anything typical about our families, and so why not embrace all of it?

Okay then. I'll reach out to Meg and see what she and Aarav think.

That evening, Judy called Meg.

Hi, baby girl. How are things in beautiful India?

Things are good, really good. How are things in New Hampshire?

Also doing well. So, Steve and I talked about the wedding...

Oh, Aarav and I also had a conversation.

And what are you guys thinking?

We would really love it if we could all get married together.

Steve and I agree.

Really??? Oh Judy, this is really exciting!

Well, the next big step is to talk about it with Olivia.

Aarav said he would do that if you and Steve agreed.

And, we also need to all have a very serious conversation with Matt and Rachel.

Yes. I will let Aarav know that you guys like the idea, and I'll let you know what happens.

Okay, Meg. Love you.

Love you too, Judy. Say hey to Steve and Mom and Dad.

Will do.

Judy spent the next few days on pins and needles. The entire situation was very exciting but also carried some stress, and she felt a bit out of control because the decision ultimately wasn't up to her.

Either way, she thought to herself, you are going to marry Steve, and that's what really counts. Allow it to be what it will be. Let go.

She meditated and took a lot of deep breaths and was grateful for the distraction of her classes.

In India, Meg told Aarav about her conversation with Judy.

Okay then, Aarav said. I will speak to my mother.

Should I be with you?

Yes, I think you should.

Should we get Judy and Steve on the phone?

Let's you and I speak with her first and see where it goes.

So, that evening, after dinner, Aarav asked his mother if he and Meg could speak with her.

Of course, my children.

They went out into the garden and sat on benches facing each other.

Mother, as you know, Meg and I have been discussing our upcoming wedding. As is tradition, we will have our wedding here at the palace.

Of course, my love. Have you thought about a date?

We have a question to ask you first.

Yes, what is it?

We think it would be nice if Steve and Judy were married here at the same time. We would all like to get married together here at the palace. What do you think?

Olivia looked at them for a long time.

At one point, Aarav started to talk, but Olivia raised a hand signaling that he should remain quiet. She continued to stare.

Meg whispered to Aarav. Is she alright?

Aarav, whispered back, just sit quietly.

He watched his mother as she sat across from them. It was as if she went into a trance like state. After what felt like an eternity, she took a deep breath and began to speak.

Aarav, Meg, you bring an interesting suggestion which causes me some heartache but also joy. I will always carry sorrow in my heart for the loss of your brother, Judy's fiancée, but the love I feel for both of you as well as for Judy is deep and true. So, after consulting, I feel that this dual ceremony will create a bond between the two families that comes from love, commitment, and joy as its glue. This will make us all one family, and that is a precious gift.

Aarav placed his palms together and bowed to his mother.

Thank you, Mother.

Meg followed suit.

Thank you, Olivia.

It is my great pleasure, Olivia said with a little bow to both of them. Now we must discuss a date.

They agreed that the middle of September would be a good time because it's the end of Monsoon season; the weather is usually very nice.

I will speak to your father about the details.

With that, Olivia got up and went into the palace leaving Aarav and Meg in the garden.

Well, I guess we have a plan. In approximately four months from now, you will be Mrs. Meg Singh.

Mrs. Meg Singh. I love that.

Me too.

I will call Judy tomorrow and tell her.

First thing the next morning, Meg phoned Judy.

Hi, Meg.

Hi, Judy. So, Aarav and I met with Olivia to talk about the weddings. She went into a kind of trance, and when she came out of it, she said she thought it would be a nice way to connect the families and thinks the middle of September is a perfect time to have the ceremonies.

This year?

Yes, Judy.

In just four months?

Yes.

That's so soon.

Well, talk to Steve and let me know. Remember that the ceremony will be a typical and traditional ceremony with outfits and henna and the music and dancing. I think it will be quite a great event.

I'll call you in a few days, sis.

They hung up and Judy wasn't feeling as excited as she thought she should be. She was actually feeling more overwhelmed, out of control.

She sat down n her bed.

Maybe this was a bad idea. Do I want to just go along for the ride, or do I want to control my wedding, make the decisions, have it be about me rather than about the family, the day, the universal event? I think I want it all. Ahhhhhh! I don't know what to do, Chloe. Tell me what to do.

Chloe looked up at her. She yawned, licked her lips, licked her paw, and washed her face. She went back to sleep.

Thanks a lot. You're a big help.

Judy sat in satsang and listened to her breathing.

In and out she said in her head. In and out. Yeees. In and out. Ahhhh!

She was stuck. She couldn't focus, and at that point didn't even know what she wanted in terms of a wedding. She was conflicted and upset. Steve walked in.

Hi.

Ahhhh!

Okay, he said. What's going on?

He had never seen Judy in such a state.

Ahhhh! she said again.

Steve walked over to where she was sitting on the bed and sat down next to her.

Judy? Look at me.

She turned and looked Steve in the eyes. She started to cry.

Steve wrapped around her and held her.

Let it out, baby. Let it out.

After ten minutes or so, Judy stopped, took a really deep breath, and began to talk.

I love you, she said. I love you soooo much. I love Meg. I love Aarav and Olivia and my entire Indian family.

Okay.

But I'm not exactly sure I want to get married there in four months.

Hold on, wait. Did you say four months?

Oh, yeah, I haven't had a chance to update you.

Please do.

Well, I spoke to Meg who spoke to Olivia. She loves the idea of a double wedding and wants to have it in mid-September at the palace.

Wow!

Yeah.

Steve stared into space.

So you can see why I'm pretty conflicted. It's so soon, and it would be completely planned out for us. I always saw myself making the arrangements and decisions. But I don't want to disappoint Olivia or Meg.

Judy, look. This is our wedding. Don't give your desires away.

Judy looked at Steve. That was it. She was feeling like she was on the outside looking in and was more of an object than a participant.

I love you, Steve said, and we certainly don't have the money to have an extravagant wedding. Did you even want a big wedding?

No, Judy said. I've always seen myself as a simple kind of person. I had some wedding ideas, but nothing super grand.

Okay, good, because I don't want that either. So, we agree that our wedding will be small and simple.

Yes, we can agree on that.

Okay, so hear me out. What if we get married in India, you know, do the large-scale extravagant wedding and big party with Meg and your Indian family and then next year, we have a small ceremony here in New Hampshire. That way, you get to plan your wedding – choose the flowers, music, venue, etc. It's sort of the best of both, and hopefully, Meg and Aarav will be able to come.

Steve! I think that's a great idea! Yes. I love it! And, I love you! You're a genius! You've totally solved the dilemma.

Okay then. Happy to help. What's for dinner?

I made a vegetarian fried rice. I just need to heat it up.

The next morning, Judy called Meg.

Hey, sis.

Hey, Judes. So, have you thought about the weddings?

I have.

And?

And, we're in. We'll come to India in September and all get married.

That's fab! I think this is going to be really great!

Meg, have you mentioned any of this to Matt or Rachel?

No, I thought you might.

Judy took a deep breath.

Okay. I'll talk to them today. Let's talk in a few days.

Sounds good. Alavida.

Bye, sis.

Hmmmm. Judy prepared herself for what she thought might be a tough conversation. She picked up the phone and called Rachel.

Hey, Judy. Everything okay?

Yes, fine. I'm sorry I'm calling so early.

What's up?

Are you and Matt free tonight?

Umm, hold on, let me check.

Judy heard the phone clunk on the counter and then a muffled conversation.

Matt, you have any plans for tonight?

Nope.

Rachel picked the phone back up.

Judy?

Hi, still here.

No, we're free tonight, why?

Do you think we could all get together for dinner, maybe around 7:00?

I don't see why not. Where do you want to go?

Oh, anywhere is fine. Let's decide a bit later.

Okay, honey. We'll see you later.

Judy got herself together and went to work. She waited till Steve had a break between classes and told him that she asked his mom and dad to go out to dinner so that they could tell them about the plans.

Okay, Steve said. Where?

Do you have a preference?

How about Japanese food?

Steve and Judy picked up Matt and Rachel a little after 7:00.

We thought we'd go to the Japanese Restaurant, if that's okay.

Oh, that sounds good, said Rachel. We haven't been there in, Steve when did we eat there?

I don't know, it's been at least six months.

Oh yeah, it was for what's his name's birthday party.

Howard.

Yeah, Howard.

It was a beautiful late spring New England evening, so they decided to sit outside.

After everyone ordered sake and meals, Judy started the conversation.

So, Steve and I wanted to catch you up on the latest with wedding plans.

There was silence.

Meg and I have been talking quite a bit, and the other night, Meg called with an interesting proposal.

More silence.

Anyway, she thought it would be really special if we had a

double wedding in India at the palace.

Matt and Rachel looked at each other.

But, Judy, honey, don't you want to have your wedding be a special day for you and Steve without sharing it?

So, Steve and I talked it out because, yes, I was very conflicted. Steve actually came up with a perfect solution.

Steve did? Really?

Hey, Dad, you don't have to sound so surprised. I do have good ideas now and then.

You know what I mean.

Steve, why don't you tell your parents your idea?

No, please, Judy. You're doing fine. Continue.

Steve and I agreed that we really just want a small and simple wedding, nothing extravagant. So, we will get married in India.

Because that's small and simple? Matt interjected sarcastically.

No, wait, hear me out, Judy said. We will then have a small New England wedding next year. This way, we can do the whole big total family celebration and the traditional wedding. What do you think?

Rachel and Matt looked at each other.

Finally, Rachel turned back to Judy and Steve.

We think that if you and Steve and Meg are happy, we're happy, right Matt?

Rachel stared intensely at Matt.

Yeah, right, he said with little enthusiasm.

The food arrived, and they all took a little from each other's.

Man, this is so good, Steve said.

So Matt, Rachel said. I guess we're going to India.

Matt was quiet, but Judy decided he probably needed to process. This was a lot to hear.

Judy, how is Meg doing? We haven't spoken to her in a while.

She's great. She loves her job, and she loves the whole lifestyle. She told me that it's as if she were meant to live in India all along.

Life is so funny, Matt said.

They all looked at him.

What do you mean, hon?

I don't know. Did you ever, in a million years, think that we would be sitting here, talking about going to India for a double wedding of your daughter and your daughter's half sister with my son?

No, I can't say that I have ever thought that.

They all smiled.

That's what makes life so cool, I guess, Judy said. We never know where the path is going.

About a week later, Judy called Olivia. She wanted to make sure that Olivia was truly okay with the double wedding.

Hi, my love, how are things in the states?

Things are going really well. How are you, Olivia?

I am well. So, will you and Steve be coming to marry with Meg and Aarav?

That's why I'm calling. We would very much like to have a double wedding in India, but I wanted to talk about it with you. Are you comfortable with this?

As I told Aarav and Meg, there is some sadness, but I feel that this will unite and connect all of us, and that is a wonderful thing.

I agree. Olivia, I love Steve, and I miss Vihaan. Is it okay to have feelings for two men?

I think it's perfectly okay. Our hearts have an infinite capacity to love, and you are fortunate to have not one but two loves.

You always make me feel better.

I'm glad. Let's talk soon.

Thank you, Olivia.

Judy hung up feeling at peace with the direction of her life. She looked up at the ceiling, a symbolic heaven.

I miss you Vihaan, and I will always love you.

She went into the bedroom and took out the engagement ring that Vihaan had given her. It was extraordinary! As she held it in her hand, staring at it, she thought, that part of my life seems like a dream. Vihaan, you were an amazing being. I miss you.

She put the ring back in it's box and tucked it away. She had never told Steve she had it. She didn't want him to feel like he couldn't compete.

Over the next couple of months, arrangements were made through phone calls and emails. Flights were planned, and Meg kept Judy in the loop by sharing every step of the process. By mid-August, Judy began to feel excited about this journey. She would marry the man she loved and be able to share that with her half-sister and Indian family.

I am very fortunate, she said one day to Chloe. Yes, I've had a lot of loss, but I have also had a tremendous amount of love. Chloe meowed at her.

Meanwhile, Steve was busy getting ready to close the studio for a couple of weeks. Many of the students sent their congratulations, gifts, and well wishes. It was beginning to feel very real, and he was a bit nervous about the whole thing. This would be a big trip to a country he knew little about, and the country of Judy's fiancée before him, but he trusted her, and she assured him that there was nothing awkward about it.

Suitcases were brought out and packing ensued. Judy helped Steve because he really wasn't sure what to pack. She reminded him that the palace would have all of his needs, including the traditional wedding outfit.

On the day of the flight, Judy brought Chloe over to one of her student's homes. She had offered to take care of Chloe, which was a great relief to Judy and Steve. They trusted her implicitly.

At eleven, a car picked up Matt and Rachel and then went over to get Steve and Judy. Luggage was loaded, and they were off to the airport.

Here we go, Steve said, sounding a little bit unsure.

Stay in the moment, Judy said. All is as it should be.

Thank you, Swami Judy, Matt said sarcastically.

Judy just smiled. She realized that each of them would have their own experience and ways of dealing with the fear that is often generated when facing the unknown.

They checked bags, passed through security, and headed to the gate. The flight was showing about a thirty-minute delay, something about weather, so they settled in with some magazines and waited.

An hour or so later, they heard the announcement for boarding.

Okay, Judy jumped up. That's us. You ready?

As we can be, Steve said.

They boarded and sat, and Judy realized that she wasn't breathing. She took some deep breaths and tried to let go of the desire to have everyone enjoy themselves.

Half way there, Steve took Judy's hand.

Do you love me?

Judy looked at him. This wasn't a Steve that she was familiar with.

Of course, I do. Why? What's going on Steve?

I guess I'm feeling inadequate. You had a whole big royal life, and I know there is a part of you that mourns that and maybe even wishes you could still have it.

Steve, I am not going to deny that I loved Vihaan, and I love my Indian family, and by the way, I think you are going to end up loving them also. But, I'm here with you, right now, and I have committed my life to you by saying yes to your proposal. We're good together. You are my best friend, lover, and soon to be husband, and I am extremely grateful for that. I understand that this is all a bit intimidating. I am with you. I am by your side, and that is where I chose to be.

Steve looked at her with tears in his eyes.

Judy smiled at him and kissed him on the cheek.

I'm going to shut my eyes for a while, she said.

She drifted off and dreamt of Vihaan. He was floating off in the distance as she was walking across a courtyard which felt like someplace in India.

Vihaan, she called out. She reached out her hand to touch him. He reached out his hand and looked at her. There was a brilliant white light surrounding him, and he looked so peaceful.

I love you, Vihaan, Judy said.

He spoke no words, and yet she felt he was communicating. He seemed to be so close, but when Judy reached for him, there was a great distance.

Vihaan, I can't reach you. Come closer.

Instead, he drifted away from her, still gazing at her with a gentle smile.

Vihaan, she cried.

He floated away.

Please!

Follow your path, Judy. Judy heard a woman's voice. You must honor your course. It is not your time.

Olivia?

Listen to your heart.

I'm confused.

Listen to your heart. The answers are clear.

Judy shot awake which woke Steve up.

You okay? he asked, looking at her with some concern.

Huh? Oh, yes. I'm fine.

She sat back and closed her eyes again. As she drifted back into sleep, she saw herself gliding through the sky. There was no discomfort, only a peaceful bliss. All was perfect.

What seemed like seconds must have been much longer. She was jarred awake by the captain's announcement.

We will be landing in thirty minutes. Please put you seat backs up and return your tray tables to their upright position.

She turned to look at Steve. He was fast asleep. She decided to let him sleep for a few more minutes.

Judy thought to herself. What's the meaning of missing

Vihaan so much? Maybe just the fact that Steve and I were talking about him and India?

This does feel right, marrying Steve. We have a good life together. He is loving and supportive. He's a good guy.

But, was she trying to convince herself?

The plane touched down, and Steve woke up with a quiet snore.

Hi, hon, Judy said.

Are we there?

We just landed.

Steve stretched in his seat.

That wasn't such a bad flight he said. But I'm starving!

Yeah, flying does that to me too. I'm sure there will be something offered once we get to the palace.

Ohh, you think the palace will have refreshments? Steve said jokingly.

Ha ha. Funny man. Just wait.

Once out of the airport, they were greeted by a driver. He took their luggage and held the car door for them.

Khamaghani, Judy said to him. He bowed in return.

It's funny to see this part of you, Steve said.

And it feels very natural, she said.

In the limo, Judy asked Matt and Rachel how they did with the flight.

Yeah, fine. We mostly slept.

About twenty-five minutes later, they pulled up to the palace.

It was night, so the palace was lit up.

Oh my God! Rachel exclaimed.

It's beautiful, isn't it? Judy asked.

Are you freakin kidding me? Steve said.

Judy looked at Matt. His mouth had dropped open, but nothing came out.

As they pulled up to the front door, Judy jumped out.

She ran up to Olivia and embraced her.

I've missed you so much.

The others got out of the car, and Meg wrapped her arms around her mom, Matt, and then her brother.

Is this really happening? she cried. I'm soo glad you're all here. I've missed you.

Olivia invited everyone to come inside and relax.

Introductions were made in the library, and food was brought from the kitchen.

Wow! Steve said. I could get used to this, he whispered to Judy.

Judy chuckled.

They all munched and chatted for a while, and then Olivia asked Meg to show them where they would be sleeping.

Your luggage has been brought to your rooms, Meg said. Please follow me.

Meg showed everyone where they would be sleeping. Judy of course, was in the same room she had been in in the past, but this time, Steve would be staying with her.

Good nights were said, and everyone settled in for the evening.

The next morning, Judy and Steve slept in for a little bit and then Judy said she was going to head downstairs to meditate for a while.

Look for me in the garden, and we'll have breakfast together.

Steve took his time. He fell back to sleep and then finally got up and showered and dressed. He really couldn't get over the opulence that surrounded him. He left the room and went in search of Meg and his parents. Everyone was downstairs out on the terrace having breakfast.

Good morning Steve, Matt greeted him cheerily.

Wow, Dad. You're in a good mood.

I feel like a king.

I'm glad, Olivia said as she entered the terrace to join them. Did everyone sleep well?

Never better, said Matt.

Meg chuckled. You sure are happy, Dad.

Who wouldn't be? Look at this place.

They all laughed.

I am very happy that you are feeling so satisfied, said Olivia.

Thank you so much for your hospitality, Rachel said.

It is my honor and pleasure. So, today, I thought you might want to sight see a bit?

Oh, yes, Meg jumped in. Let's. She smiled at Aarav.

Meg, I'm going to go into work for a bit, and I will join everyone at dinner.

Oh, Aarav, do you have to?

I'm afraid so. I have a very big project I need to finish. He leaned over and kissed Meg.

See you later, she said.

Please enjoy your day, he said to the group.

So, Steve said. I'm going to go find Judy. She said she would be in the garden.

Just then, they heard a very loud screaming noise.

Matt jumped. What the heck?

Oh, that's just the peacocks, Dad. They live on the property.

Wow! I've never in my life heard anything like that!

They're harmless, Meg assured him.

Okay, I'm going to go find Judy, and I'll be back in a few minutes.

Judy had been meditating in the garden for the past hour or so. She was seeking closure after the two dreams she had had during the flight. As she traveled into her meadow, she remained consciously open to whatever messages she needed to receive. She sat amongst the flowers and insects breathing in and breathing out. Ohm, ohm, yeees, yeees. Am I doing the right thing? She sat quietly, listening to the rhythm of her natural breathing pattern.

She looked across the meadow and saw a form.

Vihaan?

The form was still but had a light emanating from it. For some reason, she didn't get up and approach it; she just sat staring at it. The form then came closer. Judy sat still. As the form got closer, she could see that it was somewhat female looking. She had a flowing gown on, and light surrounded her.

Welcome, Judy said. I am humbled by your presence.

As the figure came within a couple of feet of Judy, she noticed that she was floating above the ground.

Are you an angel?

The figure didn't speak but conveyed to Judy that she was her guardian angel. She also conveyed that there was no right or wrong, good or bad, and that Judy should follow her heart.

What if my heart is telling me different things?

They are all connected. Follow your heart.

She then drifted up and vanished.

Judy called out, wait, please wait. She began to cry.

Judy?

Judy thought the voice was someone in her meditation.

Vihaan?

Judy?

She opened her eyes to see Steve standing over her.

Oh, she said.

Are you okay?

Hi.

Judy stood up.

You seemed upset.

I was pretty deep in meditation. Sometimes, it can bring up some tough stuff. I'm okay.

Steve looked at her. He sensed her unease but decided not to push. You wanna get some breakfast? Everyone is on the terrace.

They walked over to the group.

Good morning, everyone.

Some of Vihaan's sisters had joined them.

Good morning, Judy. Welcome back.

Thank you. I've missed you guys.

She looked around. Where's Bandhupala?

His wife is ill, but he might stop by later.

Oh, is there anything I can do for her?

No, but it's nice of you to offer.

She and Steve sat down and had breakfast. Judy introduced Matt, Rachel, and Steve to everyone, and the conversation flowed. At one point, Matt leaned over to Judy and thanked her.

What for, Matt?

This place is fabulous! I haven't felt this relaxed and happy in a long time.

Yeah, it tends to have that effect on people.

Just then, Olivia entered.

Judy put her palms together and bowed. Khamaghani.

Olivia gave her a little bow.

How is everyone this morning?

All good, Steve said as he bit into a toasted piece of naan. This bread is fantastic!

That's naan, Judy explained.

Well, call it whatever you want; I'm calling it delicious!

Everyone smiled and giggled.

So, Olivia continued. This afternoon, after sightseeing, we will have a fitting. I've asked the family's taylor to come and take measurements for the outfits. Please let me know when you are ready to go sightseeing. Meg, will you be the guide this morning?

Yes, Olivia. I am going to show them around the area.

Very well. Lunch will be served at 1:00. Will that give you enough time?

Let's see, it's almost 10:00. I think that's perfect.

Judy, would you mind joining me this morning? I hope that's okay?

Olivia looked at Matt, Rachel, and Steve.

Oh, that's fine, Rachel responded. Matt, let's go freshen up and we'll meet Meg and Steve out front in a couple of minutes. Olivia, thank you again for your hospitality.

Olivia bowed to Rachel. It is my most humble pleasure.

Matt and Rachel headed upstairs, and Steve gave Judy a kiss. See you later, babe.

Have fun, Judy waved as Steve and Meg went through the palace to the limo waiting out front.

Man, this is some lifestyle, baby sis. I get why you love it here.

Meg smiled. It was so much more than the wealth, but she didn't feel like getting into it with Steve.

A few minutes later, Matt and Rachel joined Steve and Meg out front, and soon they were off to sight see.

Meanwhile, Judy joined Olivia.

I believe you had quite a meditation this morning, my dear.

Judy wasn't surprised by Olivia's abilities anymore. Yes, my guardian angel came to me and told me to listen to my heart.

I sense some conflict.

Honestly, I miss Vihaan so much.

Tears started forming.

It's not that I wish I were dead, but I am having trouble letting go. I guess I haven't had proper closure, even after all these years.

Your heart is torn, and in this circumstance, you cannot completely love. You are here, and Vihaan has left the earth and is following his path. The key is to allow him that. By reaching out and trying to hold onto him, you are hindering his growth.

Wow! I didn't realize that I had that kind of influence. I would never want to hold him back.

This is why your guardian angel came to you. Vihaan has appeared to you, correct?

Yes, a couple of times.

This was his way of saying goodbye. You must let him go, for his sake and yours. By releasing him, you will free yourself to move on completely, and you will allow Vihaan to move forward.

Judy began to sob.

Feel your feelings completely, my child. Stay with them. Hold nothing back or in. Allow everything to come up and then send it out into the universe. You are loved and supported. The feelings cannot control you unless you allow them to. Bid them farewell.

Judy sat feeling emotions that she had buried long ago. She realized then that the grief and feelings of loss went deeper than Vihaan. This was the pain she had pushed down as a child when she lost her parents, then Kay, then Maddie. She saw a pattern of grief that was repetitive. She was having an awakening. By letting all of the years of pain and anguish go, she was allowing herself to literally reincarnate without first dying. She now knew that this process would free her. There was a new Judy emerging as she said farewell to all of the old.

She spent much of the day alone deep back in the garden where she knew no one would interrupt her process. She was actively releasing and meditating like she had never done before, and the transformation was awe inspiring. She felt light and had gained an insight and awareness that was truly staggering. She noticed smells in the air and saw the tiniest of beings around her. Her hearing was heightened, and she thought she noticed people nearby, but wasn't sure they were actually real.

As the daylight faded, Olivia approached.

My, love. Would you join us for dinner?

Yes, I would like that.

As they walked to the palace, Olivia touched Judy's hair.

You are a very special person, Judy. You have the sight and intuition. I saw it when I first met you. At that time, you were very undeveloped, but you have made wonderful progress in your evolution to nirvana.

Thank you, Olivia. I feel as though today was particularly beneficial.

They entered the dining room. Everyone was seated at the very long table.

Steve jumped up out of his chair.

Judy, are you okay? I was worried. You look different.

Let's sit and eat, Steve. We'll talk later.

Dinner was served, and the conversation flowed between the New Englanders and the hosts. The mood was light and happy. Matt and Rachel talked about where they had gone and what they had seen.

I've gained an entirely new appreciation for Indian culture, Matt said. The people we met today were all really amazing and fascinating.

Oh, Judy, Rachel then said. You missed your fitting.

Judy looked at Olivia.

Olivia gave her a smile.

After dinner, Judy asked Steve to take a walk. The evening was particularly beautiful. The stars were blinking brightly, and the moon was almost full. The air was fragrant, like a bouquet of flowers, and the tree frogs and crickets were chirping desperately in an attempt to attract a mate.

I missed you today, Judy. What did you do all day?

I actually meditated.

All day?

Yes, and I gained a tremendous amount of insight. Steve, I love you.

And?

There is something drawing me here.

When you say here, do you mean where we're standing or here in the bigger sense?

I mean India. I can't explain it, but it feels like where I need to be.

So, what are you saying?

I'm not sure, but I think I may go back to the Ashram.

And, what about our wedding?

Judy looked at Steve. How could she break his heart? What was she doing? Was this really what she wanted? Could she see herself as Steve's wife? Could she see the two of them living in New Hampshire, running the studio? Maybe there was an Ashram there that she could get involved with? But that didn't feel like where she was supposed to be. Was it because she was here? Perhaps out of sight, out of mind?

Judy?

Judy could see that Steve was becoming upset, and she got it. She wasn't sure what she was saying, doing, thinking.

Steve, I think I need a couple of days to figure things out. I'm going to go to the Ashram for a few days and work out my stuff. I can only hope that you understand. I didn't anticipate this, but I feel I really need to do this.

What could Steve say? He was very confused, but he would never want Judy to be anyone or do anything she didn't want to.

Okay, he said, somewhat exasperated. Do what you have to do.

I'm sorry, Steve. I dragged you half way around the world and am now having some kind of a spiritual crisis. I'll see you in three days.

Judy kissed Steve and walked back to the palace to make arrangements. As she entered, Olivia was there.

All is as it should be, my love. Go and find yourself.

Judy didn't even stop to say goodbye to anyone else. She walked straight through the palace and out into the front where the limo sat waiting. It all felt so natural, almost like a dream.

The driver dropped her at the Ashram. It was quite dark and pretty quiet because of the hour.

My third time, she thought. I like the number three. Three times a charm.

She walked into the admin building and took a step back when she noticed Swami Ravi sitting in a chair.

Judy immediately placed her palms together and bowed. Khamaghani Swami Ravi.

Khamaghani, Judy, Swami Ravi replied. I was expecting you. Please sit here next to me.

Judy walked over near Swami Ravi and sat down.

Judy, you have made exceptional spiritual progress. You are disciplined and insightful. Your humility and commitment are exceeded only by your intuition and compassion.

Judy was frankly kind of blown away. She had never actually had a conversation with Swami Ravi beyond greetings.

Thank you, Swami Ravi. This means so much to me.

I invite you to stay here at the Ashram, to be a mentor to those seekers who will come and go.

Judy didn't know what to say. Was this a test? This offer was completely unexpected.

Swami Ravi, I am so honored by your offer, but I am not sure that is my path. I am supposed to get married next week and go back home to the states.

Swami Ravi looked at Judy and listened. She couldn't tell what he was thinking and assumed he already knew that.

Follow your heart. You already know the answer.

Swami Ravi got up and walked out of the building.

Judy sat for a long time. She felt like she wanted to stay but wondered if her desire was stimulated by denial. The life here was a life she found very comfortable. She loved the simplicity and lack of drama and complication. She loved communing with others who were seeking spiritual guidance, eating simple meals, and meditating. There were few decisions to make and no outside world issues to deal with.

She stood up, left the admin building, and found an empty room. She lay down in the bed and slept. Some stirring woke her up at about four-thirty. She was a little tired but also felt rejuvenated. She got up, bathed, and went to sit morning satsang. She chanted in the main meditation room and as she looked around, she noticed there were many people. She realized it was Saturday, a day when more tend to worship.

She sat for a long time. She found it easy to go inward and realized she was going in deeper than ever before. She chanted and asked for guidance. She was conflicted, although didn't feel the angst normally associated with conflict. It was as if she were witnessing herself in a story of being conflicted rather than identifying with the conflict.

She liked this new level she had attained. Her insight was keen, and her compassion for the world around her was great, but she also saw the world in a different light. She had begun to see truth and the understanding that truth lies within, not without. The challenge was to live in truth while existing on the earth. The outside world seemed so insignificant to her. Of course, because she remained in a body, she had to take care of that body. Her body needed rest, food, water, and hygiene, but otherwise, she had no interest in participating in the outside world.

On day two at the Ahsram, Judy was in a walking meditation along a river and came across a homeless crippled man sitting on the bank. She bowed to him, and he held out a tin cup.
Rupees?
She stopped and looked at him. This poor man, she thought. What a hard life.
I'm sorry, she said. I have no rupees.
But you have those who love you and need you, the man said.
Judy stared at him.
Excuse me?
Go back to your family. You need them, and they need you. Do not seek to live a life alone, in solitude. Your instinct is to abandon those who love you before they abandon you due to your past. You cannot live a full life when you are guided by the fear of loss. All that you need, you have. Live each moment in the moment. Your gift is presence, and you know that.

Tears formed in Judy's eyes. She realized this man in his crippled old body was a spiritual teacher who had come to help her on her journey. She knelt down by the river. She took the man's cup and dipped it into the water. Here, sir, please drink some water. He took the cup. She then cupped her hands and scooped up water which she gently allowed to run over the man's cracked and blackened feet. She massaged them with the water as he sat sipping from his tin cup.

You are very kind, he said. Now go, fulfill your destiny.

Judy stood up and placed her palms together. She bowed to this man. Khamaghani.

She turned and walked back to the Ashram. She hoped to find Swami Ravi, but he wasn't on property. She borrowed the admin office phone and called Olivia.

Are you ready to return, my dear?

Yes, Olivia. I am.

Judy sat out in the driveway leading to the Ashram. She realized that her mind was clear, and her heart was open. She felt a strong love for Steve and knew that this was the right decision.

As the limo pulled up, Steve jumped out.

Steve, what are you doing here?

I asked Olivia if I could be taken to the Ashram to talk you into coming back. I don't want to lose you.

Oh, Steve, you haven't lost me. I lost myself for a bit, but I'm right here. I was actually waiting for the car to bring me back to the palace.

You were?

Yes. Olivia didn't tell you?

No. I asked her if I could be taken to the Ashram, and she said yes; there is a car waiting.

Well, all is as it should be, Judy said. She smiled and embraced Steve.

Come on, Steve, let's go get married.

They arrived back at the palace to find a lot of commotion. Tents were being erected and decorations placed up all around the property.

Looks like a wedding is going to happen here.

Actually, Steve said, two.

He smiled at Judy, and her heart melted. How could she have doubted?

I guess, she said, partly out loud, we get there when we get there. We're only ready when we're ready.

They walked into the palace and found many people gathered. Judy explained to Steve that an Indian wedding can go on for many days.

The ceremony itself would take place on Tuesday, just three days away. There was a lot to do before then.

The days sped by, and outfits were finished, menus set, performers prepared.

The evening before, Meg and Judy were tattooed with henna. Their sisters explained the tradition of Mehndi Rasam (Henna Function). On the night before the wedding, henna is applied on the hands and feet of the brides.

Steve and Judy woke up on Tuesday morning. It was an absolutely gorgeous day. They sat facing each other, and Steve took Judy's hands. First of all, I love your tattoos.

Judy laughed.

Then Steve became serious. Judy, are you sure you want to marry me?

I am, Judy said with a grin. I am.

With that, they washed up and went downstairs for breakfast. Meg and Aarav were out in the garden looking at the decorations.

Good morning all, Judy said.

So, Judy, Rachel said. This is it. Everything okay?

Couldn't be better.

They ate and then Judy kissed Steve. I'll see you at the altar, she said.

She and Meg and Rachel disappeared to get dressed and made up. There was hair, henna, and flowers. The dresses were absolutely gorgeous. Meg had chosen a red and gold headpiece and dress that flared out at the bottom.

It's like it was tailor made for you, Meg. You look beautiful, Judy said.

Judy's dress was a soft green color covered in pearls and small emeralds. Her headdress was sheer and accented with pearls and emeralds. Steve would be wearing a white traditional Indian wedding outfit – a long tapered jacket with straight pants.

Rachel came in to see if she could help.

Oh, my girls. She started to cry. I have never seen anything so beautiful.

Mom, stop crying, Meg told her. Your make up will run.

Meg grabbed a tissue and dabbed her mom's cheek. She smiled at her.

I love you, Mom.

Rachel took a deep breath. I'm going to go get seated. I'll see you both downstairs.

As the girls finished getting ready, they could hear that the ceremony had already begun. The various steps had been explained to them the day before so that they would know what to expect.

In the morning, they all participated in a number of prayers:

Ganesh Puja - done on the wedding day, in the morning. The family of the brides and grooms pray separately to Lord Ganesh whose divine grace dispels all evils and promotes a successful and peaceful completion of the ceremony.

Grah Shanti (Worshipping the nine planets) - The families pray to the nine planets of the solar system. Ancient Indian studies show that various celestial bodies have an influence on the destiny of every individual. During this praying ceremony the Gods associated with these planets are asked to infuse courage, peace of mind, and inner strength to the brides and grooms to help them endure life's sufferings.

Then, Baarat- both Aarav and Steve rode up to the wedding venue on a horse, accompanied by family members, relatives, friends and other guests.

Next is Parch (Welcoming) - The baaratis are welcomed by the brides' family and relatives (Matt and Rachel) with garlands and aarti, with the sounds of shehnais. Shehnai is considered auspicious at weddings by Hindus. The brides' mother escorts the bride grooms to the mandap. The father of the brides then washes the right foot of the bridegrooms with milk and honey.

Arrival of the Brides - The brides are escorted to the mandap by their maternal uncle, female cousins and friends.

Kanyadaan (Entrusting of the Daughters) - The brides and grooms exchange flower garlands. Then the consent of the parents is obtained for the wedding to proceed. The brides' parents give their daughters to the grooms by putting the brides' right hand into the grooms' right hand while reciting sacred verses. The grooms holds the brides' hand and they all take vows to love, cherish, and protect each other throughout life.

Ganthbandhan (tying the knot) - The priest tells the grooms' elder family member to tie the wedding knot, which symbolizes the permanent union between the brides and grooms as husband and wife.

Agni Puja (evocation of the holy fire) - The priest sets up a small fire in a kund (copper bowl). Fire is the mouth of Vishnu and symbolizes the illumination of mind, knowledge, and happiness. The remainder of the ceremony is conducted around the fire.

Aashrivaad (blessings) – Finally, the priest blesses the brides and grooms. Rose petals and rice are given to the guests to shower the brides and grooms with blessings. The married couples also get blessings from the elders of both families.

The reception went well into the evening. Both Judy and Meg did their best to be the perfect brides. They greeted all of the guests and thanked them for coming. There was dancing and eating for hours.

At one point, Judy noticed Swami Ravi in the background. She bowed and he bowed in return. She considered it a true honor that he had attended.

The next day, ceremonies and parties continued on but began

winding down by that evening.

Finally, all relatives and friends had gone back home, just leaving Matt and Rachel, Steve and Judy, Aarav and Meg, and the immediate Indian family at the palace.

At breakfast the following day, Matt and Rachel told Olivia they couldn't thank her enough for her extreme hospitality. They'd never experienced something so wonderful as these past days and would be forever grateful.

You are always welcome here, Olivia told them. This home is your home. We are all family now.

And you are welcome in our humble home.

Olivia bowed in gratitude.

The rest of the day, everyone just hung around recuperating from the grandest party they had ever experienced. Steve and Judy napped, and Aarav and Meg sat out in the garden talking about future living arrangements.

Olivia came to them and handed them keys.

There is a cottage on the other side of the garden. Your father and I invite you to live there. This way, you have your own space but aren't too far away from us. We hope you will consider this offer. Aarav looked at Meg, and Meg looked at Aarav. They could see in each other's faces that this was a tremendous and welcome gift.

Meg then turned to Olivia.

We humbly and gratefully accept this very generous offer. They both bowed to Olivia who looked very pleased.

Three days later, Matt, Rachel, Steve, and Judy packed to head back to New Hampshire. This was a bittersweet experience. There was a part of Judy that wanted so badly to stay, but she knew in her heart, at least at this time, she needed to go back.

Tears were shed, hugs all around. Meg and Aarav promised to visit at least once a year, and that comforted their New England family.

The Indian family gathered at the front of the palace and waved goodbye as the four headed to the airport.

They traveled home with no issue and settled back into a life of routine.

45
Life Resumes

The familiar was comforting. A married Judy and Steve resumed running the studio and growing the business. However, because they worked together and lived together, they tried really hard not to annoy each other, sometimes, unsuccessfully. They had only been back for a few months, but tensions were on the rise. Judy had always been very independent by necessity, and the abundance of shared time was starting to wear thin. Although the routine comforted her, and she loved her cottage, they both found themselves sniping at each other. Their relationship was becoming strained, and neither understood the depth of the problem. Instead of planning a small New England wedding, they found themselves planning separate vacations.

One day in early May, Steve came home. Judy had left work early to do some personal stuff.
I'm home.
Silence.
Judy, I said I'm home.
I can see that, Steve.
Okay, Steve said. Let's talk this out. What's going on?
I don't know what you mean. She did but was in the mood to be difficult.
I think you do.

Okay, Steve. The thing is that I feel like we never have alone time or space.

We have alone time every night.

No, I mean from each other. Aren't you feeling crowded?

I love you, Judy. I love spending time with you.

So, it's not too much for you?

Is it too much for you?

Please don't answer my question with a question.

Steve put his hands up. Okay. Sorry. Is it too much for me? No, it's not.

Well, I guess it is for me.

So what's your solution?

Judy waited to respond because she was in such a bitchy mood, and she didn't want to be unnecessarily nasty.

Well, Steve, I'm not sure.

Judy, you know that I love you, and I will support any needs you have. Do you want to see a therapist?

This infuriated Judy. She was feeling confused and vulnerable but totally took offense to Steve's implication that she needed therapy.

I don't need a therapist, Steve, she said in a hard tone.

Okay, sorry. I'm just trying to help.

Judy grabbed her jacket and keys.

I need some air.

She brushed past Steve and got in her car and drove. She had no destination, but she needed to drive, to see the road, and go somewhere. She ended up in Maine and finally pulled over to sit for a while. She wandered around the small town in the soon to be darkness. Not much was open.

Small towns, she thought. They all shut down so early.

She realized a little bit of the old city Judy was rearing its head. She also realized that it was probably her need to be independent and anonymous. She had done so much work but knew instinctively that she wasn't done.

She strolled and sat and strolled some more. She came to a small diner like place and went in. She sat down at the counter and looked around. There were a few people there, but they didn't look like family types that had somewhere to go.

What can I get ya darlin?

Judy looked up. The waitress was a little bit plump, and had her hair pulled back in a bun. She had a net over her entire head.

Oh, Judy said. I think I need a minute.

Take your time. I will tell ya we're out of the pot roast, and I don't recommend the sea bass.

Good to know, Judy said half out loud and half to herself. As she perused the menu, she thought about her life.

Okay, she said. May I have a grilled cheese on rye and some really crisp fries?

Something to drink?

Ginger Ale? No straw.

Comin right up, sugar.

While she waited, she tried to figure out where so much anger was coming from. After the few days at the Ashram, she was okay with the way her life was heading, so what happened in just a few months to create so much resentment?

The waitress placed her ginger ale in front of her. No straw, she said.

Judy sipped and thought.

Her grilled cheese and fries appeared.

She took a bite.

Wow! she said out loud. That's a really good grilled cheese!

The guys in the booth behind her looked up from their stupors.

Yeah, the waitress said. The cook uses two kinds of cheese.

Judy sat, starting to relax, enjoying her grilled cheese and fries.

After about twenty minutes, the waitress asked her if she could get her anything else.

Do you have chocolate pudding?

We do. Would you like whipped cream?

Yes.

Okey dokey.

After clearing Judy's plates, she placed a glass dish filled with pudding in front of her and then shot a huge amount of whipped cream on top of it.

Some days we have to just endure, she said as she handed Judy a spoon. Enjoy, honey. You look like you could use some good.

The words echoed in Judy's head as she dove into the pudding with whipped cream.

I have nothing to complain about, she thought. I have a loving husband, a great home, a wonderful cat, and a job I love. What is wrong with me? Why am I so angry, depressed, bothered?

She continued to eat her pudding.

The two men, who looked like old fishermen nursing hangovers, got up and said goodnight to the waitress. As they walked past Judy, she heard one of them say, an empty life ain't worth livin.

Huh, she thought. Is my life empty? It doesn't seem empty.

She finished her pudding, paid the bill, and thanked the waitress.

You take care now, sugar. I have a feeling you're gonna be just fine.

Judy walked out wondering what she meant.

There are lessons all around me. So, what am I missing?

She walked back to her car and drove home. It was pretty late when she got in. Steve was in bed asleep, so she quietly got undressed, brushed her teeth and climbed in next to him.

You okay?

I'm okay. Let's talk in the morning.

Within thirty seconds, Steve was snoring.

Judy smiled.

Sunday morning was gorgeous. There wasn't a cloud in the sky, and the temperature was a comfortable seventy-four.

Judy was already up when Steve came into the kitchen.

Morning.

Morning.

You sleep okay?

Yeah, you?

Once I knew you were okay, I did.

I'm sorry I took off like that, Steve. I don't honestly know what's bothering me, but I have been feeling so angry and resentful.

Steve sighed. Maybe I'm not enough for you.

Judy looked at him. She really did love him, but maybe he was right.

Oh, Steve.

You know, we've had a couple of inquiries from Tai Chi instructors. They look pretty qualified, and there's one in particular that I like a lot.

So?

So, maybe you should go back to India.

Are you trying to get rid of me?

No, I'm trying to support your happiness, and frankly, it doesn't feel like it's being here with me right now.

Judy was speechless. She stared at Steve.

Actually, Judy, I'm thinking about stayin with my parents for a bit. Give you some space to decide what you want to do.

Wow! she thought. Am I being selfish here? Whatever is wrong with me is disrupting Steve's entire life.

Have you got anything to say?

She had a lot to say, but she couldn't get any of it out.

Okay, in that case, I'm gonna go pack my suitcase.

Judy watched Steve go into the bedroom. She sat at the table, frozen.

Steve came out with a suitcase and a duffel.

You know where you can find me if you need me.

He leaned in to kiss her and then changed his mind. Judy heard the front door slam and saw Chloe lift her head up to check out the noise.

She sat for quite a while. She wished a fairy Godmother would float in and tell her what to do. She was at a loss. She couldn't shake her ennui. She had no idea what was happening to her. She didn't even feel like meditating. Her funk had taken over. She felt grief welling up inside but couldn't cry.

Is this depression? Judy asked no one.

After about an hour, she called Olivia.

Judy, the answer is within. She heard a click.

Well, that went well, she thought. The answer is within.

Judy took a very deep breath and went into the bedroom to lie down. Maybe inspiration would come. She stared up at the ceiling and breathed in and breathed out. At some point, Chloe joined her. She curled up next to Judy and purred herself to sleep.

Boy, you have the life, Judy said. But, she thought, do I want that life? Do I want to go back to living here alone with my cat? Do I want to be a non-participant in the world? Do I want to be completely alone? Do I want to stay married to Steve?

She drifted into a fitful sleep. She dreamt and tossed and dreamt some more. She woke and realized something had to change. She couldn't continue like this. She turned over and cradled Chloe.

Baby, I think I have to go back to India. She held Chloe for a long time and then got up and called Steve.

Hey.

Hey, she said. Steve, I think I need to go back.

Uh huh. What about us, Judy?

I'm not sure. I'm hoping I'll find answers in India.

You sure you're not just running away?

Judy felt defensive but took a beat.

I'm sure.

Then do what you have to do.

I'll call you when I get there. Steve, will you take care of Chloe?

Of course, I will. You think I would leave her to starve to death? I'm not a monster. I love her, and I would never abandon her.

Judy felt like she should be reading between the lines, but

she didn't have the strength to analyze Steve's meaning. She called the airline and booked a ticket for that afternoon.
She packed some things, kissed Chloe, and left to wait for the Uber.
She was so conflicted, but she knew she had to go.

46

Rediscovery

As she waited to board, Judy thought about what Steve had said. Was she running? If she was, from what? Why was she so unhappy? She'd done so much grief work. Why now was there anger?

The flight felt particularly long. Judy was just so out of sorts.

It was pretty late when she came out of the airport expecting the limo to be waiting, but no one had come to pick her up.

Okay, she thought. You wanted your independence back, so be independent. She took a taxi to a nearby hotel and crashed for the night. She would call Olivia in the morning, but for now, she would sleep.

The next morning, she dressed and went out to find a place for breakfast. I have certainly been spoiled. She looked around at the town. Man, I never noticed the poverty before. There were very skinny cows roaming the streets and scantily dressed people, begging for scraps. She saw mothers and children and old men all with their hands out.

How can this be? she wondered. How have I been so sheltered from this? What is my role? This is awful. She entered a market and bought some fruit. She brought it over to the mother and child and handed it to them. She then gave the rest to the old man. As she walked away, she heard him say, what is good? What is bad?

She turned to look, but he was gone.

What does that mean? Isn't it obvious? Good is good, and bad is bad, she responded out loud to no one.

She wandered around for a while and then went back to the hotel to call Olivia.

Welcome home, Judy.

Thank you, Olivia. Ummm, would it be okay if I came to the palace?

This is always your home. You are always welcome.

K.

Judy collected her luggage and caught a taxi. She gave the driver the address and headed "home".

At the palace, she got out and grabbed her luggage. There was no one to greet her. She realized how spoiled she had been. She was feeling very depressed and confused about everything. She actually felt as though she was hitting bottom.

As she entered the palace, she was greeted by one of the servants. He bowed.

Oh, Miss Judy, welcome.

Thank you, Judy replied. Is anyone at home?

Oh yes. You will find Miss Olivia in the garden.

Judy dropped her luggage and headed to the garden. She was desperate for guidance.

She saw Olivia sitting with her back to the palace.

Olivia? Judy approached.

Come sit. Olivia patted the bench without turning around.

Judy sat down next to her.

She was watching the peacocks.

This is mating season. They are magnificent, aren't they?

They are, Judy agreed.

They sat quietly for a few minutes.

Olivia, I am struggling.

Yes.

I need guidance. My life as I know it has fallen apart. I am carrying so much anger and confusion.

My child, we all have ups and downs. The point is to see them as they are, as lessons, gifts to help us grow and evolve. In the end, the truth is the constant. The rest is simply a story.

I am so lost.

This is story. When you sit satsang, do you not see the truth?

Honestly, I haven't meditated in weeks.

Your ego is creating resistance to truth. You must push through that. Sit in meditation, Judy. Be courageous and sit in truth.

Olivia got up and walked away, leaving Judy in the garden with the peacocks strutting all around.

They really are beautiful, she said to herself.

She got off the bench and sat on the ground. She listened to her breath and chanted to herself. There was a lot of darkness and resistance. She allowed it, greeted it, welcomed it, accepted it. Eventually, she was able to go deeper. She sat for the next few hours just breathing. She didn't visualize; she just breathed.

After about two hours, she began to feel centered. She had a sense of peace and calm that she hadn't felt for so long.

As day turned into night, she came out of her meditation and headed to the palace. She realized that Meg didn't even know she was there. She also remembered that she told Steve she would call him.

She went up to her bedroom and dialed.

Yeah.

Hi, Steve.

Yeah.

I'm in India. I'm at the palace.

K.

So, I'll talk to you in a few days.

She heard a click. She felt awful about hurting Steve. He didn't deserve this, but she needed to get herself straight. It wasn't like she planned to ruin his life.

She lay down in the bed and fell into a deep sleep.

The next morning, Olivia came to Judy's room. She suggested she spend some time at the Ashram. There is need there, she said.

Judy packed some things and headed out. She still hadn't seen Meg, but if Olivia is telling her to go, she must go.

The Ashram was quiet. She entered the admin building and was greeted by a new face. Hi, she said. I'm Judy.

Hi, Judy. I'm Joe. Will you be staying?

Yes.

Okay, let me show you to your room.

Judy followed Joe to the rooms.

Thanks, she said.

Your assignment is outreach.

Outreach?

Yes.

What's outreach?

There is a group of us who go out each day and care for the homeless. We bring food and bandages. We clean them and care for them the best we can.

Huh. I didn't know that. I thought those at the Ashram never leave the Ashram.

We are a special group that goes out. Swami Ravi specifically assigned you to this task.

Well, I am honored and humbled to do this work.

I'll see you at dinner.

Thank you, Joe.

Joe bowed and left Judy. Something felt different. She had always come to the Ashram with humility but also from great privilege. Now, it felt like there was no special treatment. She was one amongst many.

Okay, she said to herself. I will serve.

She headed over to the meditation room and sat for the rest of the day, chanting and breathing. It felt good to be back at the Ashram and to dedicate herself to the service of others.

At dinner, she sat with a couple of other people and chatted about nothing much. They seemed to be passing through on their own personal journeys, and Judy wasn't really relating.

She went to bed immediately after dinner, skipping evening prayer.

The next day, she got up and went to chant. The room was full, and the energy felt right. She finished chanting and then went to breakfast. She looked around for Joe. He wasn't anywhere.

After breakfast, she went to admin to join the group that would go out to feed and care for the homeless, but no one was there. She checked the driveway and still found no one.

That's strange, she thought. Well, I'll go on my own. She packed a bag of food and cloths and began walking. She walked for about an hour without seeing anyone. So, she sat down to rest for a while. As she was sitting, a woman came walking down the road with a very long staff.

She watched her moving along slowly.

Would you like something to eat? Judy asked as the woman approached.

Yes, said the woman. She stopped and sat next to Judy.

Judy took out some naan and fruit and offered it to her.

Would you like me to wash your feet? They must be tired.

Yes, said the woman.

Judy got down on her hands and knees and gently washed the woman's feet.

I hope that feels better, Judy said.

Yes, said the woman.

The woman then got up and continued on her way.

Judy walked some more, not sure where she should go.

By midafternoon, it was pretty hot, and she was pretty worn out, so she turned around and headed back. She got to the Ashram by dinner time.

Again, she looked for Joe.

She asked one of the people cooking and serving if they had seen Joe.

I don't know Joe.

Judy ate dinner alone and went to bed, again skipping evening prayer.

She got up in the morning, went to chant and into breakfast. She was feeling very unconnected to everything. She decided to call Olivia.

Hi, Judy.

Hi, Olivia. Olivia, I am still very lost. I am really struggling and need help.

My dear, continue on your path.

But I don't know what my path is.

Continue on.

Olivia hung up.

Judy was feeling very disheartened. She felt as though she had left the earth and was on a strange planet where she didn't know the language or the culture. She was very alone and a little bit scared.

Okay, I will continue to meditate and try to help those who need.

She packed a bag with food and cloths and went looking for people in need. After a while, she sat again to rest. A teenager came up to her. Do you need food? the kid asked.

No.

Would you like me to wash your feet?

No, Judy said. I am out here to help those in need.

Oh, I thought you needed help.

The teenager walked away.

Why would he think that? Do I look like I'm poor? Homeless?

Judy headed back to the Ashram. She was walking very slowly, feeling very despondent.

I have no direction, she thought, no purpose. I'm honestly not sure I want to go on.

These thoughts scared her. She had had tough times before, but she never thought about taking her own life.

Just then, a young boy approached. He was hobbling because as he got closer, Judy realized he only had one leg.

Are you hungry? Judy asked him

Oh yes, the boy said with a smile.

Judy sat down, and the boy joined her.

Judy took out some bread and fruit and offered it to him.

Mmmm, he said. This is delicious. Won't you eat with me? He smiled and offered her some of the food she had just given him.

Judy was perplexed.

Clearly, you need the food more than I and yet, you are offering to share it with me.

The boy continued to smile. For each to have some is far better than one having all. Your company is as nourishing as the food you've given me, and I am grateful and happy to share this with you.

Judy then asked, do you have a home?

The earth is my home.

It seems you have nothing, Judy said.

I have truth, said the boy. And so my life is complete.

It is not the acquisitions that matter, but the love in our heart. We are one in spirit. We can give and we can take, and to care for others is to ultimately care for ourselves.

The boy grinned. Judy noticed he had teeth missing.

I will be on my way. He bowed and hobbled away.

That boy has absolutely nothing, and yet, he is filled with love and light.

She was so moved by this enlightened boy. He was a teacher. Crippled and homeless, and hungry, and yet at peace.

What became abundantly clear was that Judy had screwed up.

What have I done? kept running through her thoughts.

She knew life would never be the same again, but hold on, was that so bad? she thought out loud.

I'm not a little girl anymore.

Although frankly, I have spent the last weeks feeling like a frightened and almost desperate child.

The protective bubble that Judy had spent so much imagined time in had burst wide open, and there was really nothing to do but keep moving in a forward direction.

Okay, it's true my life as I've known it is gone, but I am ready to redefine myself.

I am a strong, intelligent, independent woman. I make no apologies for my actions and need no one's forgiveness.

As these last words floated through the air, the past few days' "new" Judy thought about "old" Judy.

Life is such an odd thing. When I think about my childhood, I feel as though I am watching a movie about someone else. I guess this is a type of reincarnation. We are always changing, constantly redefining ourselves. Although we live one life, it is made up of many, many different experiences and events, each a teachable moment if we remain open.

Judy also realized that it's not about her. She is no thing. She was having an epiphany.

It doesn't matter what I do, what matters is my perception. There will always be need, pain, loss in the outer world. There is also joy and love. That is the balance. The truth is in peace. Whatever, is. Even the worst conditions cannot control one's internal peace. We assume that something is bad when there is loss, but perhaps that leads to awareness and even awakening. Perhaps there truly is no bad or good but just our judgement. Life is what life is, but we always have a choice as to our perception of it. To end judgment is to realize truth. Acceptance is forgiveness.

She walked back to the Ashram. Swami Ravi was there.
Swami Ravi, Judy bowed.
You have seen, he said.
I have, said Judy.
You must now rejoin the world.
He turned and walked away.

Judy packed her bag and called a cab. She had no expectation and although recognized the beauty and comfort in the material, she had found what really mattered. She arrived at the palace with a sense of freedom. She had unburdened herself from her self-imposed chains of confusion, anger, and judgment.

She would go back home and see what could be done about her relationship with Steve but first, she wanted to spend some time with Meg.

She walked through the palace and into the garden to Meg and Aarav's. Judy called out. Hey, Meg.

Meg opened the door. Judy? Why didn't you tell me you were coming? When did you get here?

Let's go in, and I'll tell you my story.

Judy and Meg visited for the next two days and then Judy got on a plane and flew home.

She walked in to the cottage pretty late and found Steve asleep in the bed.

Steve, she whispered.

Huh? he said in a semi-conscious state. It's me; I'm home.

Steve sat up and started to get out of bed. I'll move to the couch, he said.

No, stay. I can sleep on the couch.

Judy left Steve in the bedroom and grabbed a blanket. Chloe jumped off the bed and joined Judy on the couch.

Hi, baby. I really missed you.

Chloe jumped onto Judy and snuggled in. The two of them were asleep within minutes.

The next morning, Steve came out to find Chloe and Judy asleep on the couch.

Judy?

Judy opened her eyes.

Hi.

I'm gonna go back to my parents' house since your back.

Steve. Judy sat up and Chloe leapt off.

Yeah?

Can we talk?

Yeah, okay.

Would you sit down here?

Steve hesitated but pushed the blanket out of the way and sat down next to Judy.

So, we have a lot to talk about.

Steve didn't respond.

Judy could tell that he was so hurt.

I want to start by apologizing to you. Steve, it was never my plan or intention to hurt you. I just got so lost and couldn't see a way out.

Anyway, I would like to try and mend our marriage if you would.

Steve looked at her. He was a broken man.

Oh, Steve, I really am so sorry.

He began to cry.

Ohhh, was all Judy said. She reached over to him and held him.

Let's try to fix us, k? We'll find a couples' therapist to help us come back to each other.

Steve was still crying but shook his head yes.

They sat together for quite a while in silence.

Then Judy whispered, I love you, Steve.

47

Mending

Spring became summer, and with it, mending. Steve and Judy found a therapist who was right on in her perception of and understanding of them as individuals as well as them as a couple, and Judy liked that she had some training in eastern ways.

Their communication with each other began to improve, and they both worked on themselves as individuals.

Judy continued meditating and evolving and stayed in touch with Olivia. She realized that it didn't matter what she did in her life as much as how she felt about it. She was determined to give her all to whatever task lay before her, and with that came the peace. She had learned that acceptance was forgiveness and with that realization, she was able to let go of anger. She was learning to allow without control. She was becoming free.

Meg and Aarav made annual trips to New Hampshire, and in the following years, with two children in tow – a prince to be and a princess who was already portraying the role at the age of four. The time with them was precious, as was time spent with Matt and Rachel.

Judy went back to the local college and got a certificate in working with people with special needs. She ultimately became the local expert people sought out for advice and help on working with people on the spectrum and with physical challenges.

She and Steve continued to grow the studio and found their balance with each other. They learned to respect each other's space and would take mini alone vacations. Steve was also meditating more, and together, they went on meditation retreats all around New England.

Judy had found herself and the peace she had sought for all those years. She recognized her loss and allowed herself to feel the sadness, but she saw her life as a story which she realized she could affect with her choices. She remained ever the witness and allowed her story to unfold.

It was there the whole time, she thought. Through the losses and sadness, through the loves and successes, through the travel expeditions and spiritual journeys. The story changes, but the peace was there. I only needed to recognize it. She thought of the poem that Kay had shared with her all those years ago.

It's entitled, *Where Family Lives.* It was written by Alice Wills, Kay told her.

Where family lives, I am there.

As you are, we are.

From the start

within my heart

Remains thee

Remember we

Where family lives.

Judy thought of Kay. She was holding her close when she shared the poem with her so long ago.

Do you know what it means?

Judy could hear Kay's voice.

I do now, Kay.

It means that no matter where the people you love are, they are as near to you as you are near to them, so even if you can't see them, they are close because they are in our memories and our heart.

55819631R00241

Made in the USA
Middletown, DE
18 July 2019